Lucid Nightmares

Sam Knight

Print Edition 2016
Knight Writing Press
KnightWritingPress@gmail.com

Front Cover Art and Design by Lance Card

Cover Design and Book Design by Knight Writing Press

Author Bio Photo by Lauren Lang

First Print Publication January 2017

ISBN-10: 1-62869-021-6
ISBN-13: 978-1-62869-021-7

DEDICATION

To everyone who has seen the thing that
makes the bump in the night.

You are not alone.

Er…

That didn't sound the way I meant it…

ACKNOWLEDGMENTS

This book would not be in your hands without the support and effort of many people. From the people who helped start it out at the very beginning; Mary Brown, Phyllis Parrington, and Susan Egaas, through the people who carried it through its growing pains; Tony and Renee Allen, and Kris Kellough, and up to all of my family and friends who kept it alive and brought it out into the world.

Apologies to Editors Keith J. Olexa and Vivian Caethe. You did your best to rein me in, and I thank you both.

Thanks to fellow authors L.J. Hachmeister and J.A. Campbell for helping smooth the edges of a serious edit. Any rough places are my fault not theirs.

Special thank you to Christopher Salas, without whom I would have never joined the writing community in Colorado, and this book would never have escaped purgatory.

To Anna Page who shared her family's stories and legends with me.

To my Mother and Grandfather who instilled a love of reading in me at a very early age.

And to my wife and children who supported me (literally and figuratively) and helped me to do something I really wanted to do.

Thank you all.

PROLOGUE

The boy hid under the old writing desk, knees clamped tight to his chest, knuckles white with strain. His breath came short and quick as his pulse pounded in his ears. Searching the darkness, he found nothing, and his eyes reflected only his fear.

The noises in the kitchen had stopped, but he knew the danger was not over.

The four old witches, one of whom he'd been told was his grandmother, had summoned a demon from Hell. He knew it was a demon from Hell because he had seen it. More than that, he had felt—even *tasted*—the creature's sooty, vile presence.

One of the old women sobbed in the darkness, but he couldn't bring himself to go to her. What could a little boy do against a demon?

Finally, her crying faded away.

Ashamed for not going to help, fear still prevented him from giving up his hiding place. He squeezed his eyes shut and tried not to sob out loud.

The nightmare had started out resembling a séance but quickly turned into a horror movie. The demon had coalesced on the kitchen table in front of the women, and he had been mesmerized by the evil exuding from it. He had *felt* the creature searching for something and, when it looked at him, it was like greasy fingers leaving slimy snail-trails on his soul, slithering away from him, flowing back into the materializing form of the demon, becoming the putrid smelling vapors dissipating into the air around it.

Still panting with fear, he looked out from his hiding place into the dark room, wishing he was anywhere but here.

He wasn't sure what had happened. The old women had spoken only in Spanish, unless they were talking to him.

Silently mouthing a Hail Mary, he crossed himself. He had never paid attention to the words before, but now that he needed the prayer to work, he found himself thinking about them as he prayed.

Hail Mary, full of grace, the lord is with thee; blessed art thou among women and blessed is the fruit of thy womb, Jesus. Holy Mary, Mother of God, pray for us now, and at the hour of our death, Amen.

The prayer made him feel a little better. Not a lot, but helped.

The words didn't seem appropriate, but the more he muttered them, the more fitting they became.

He was going to die.

The demon was going to find him.

He knew from the oily touch against his soul that the demon wanted nothing more than it wanted him. The demon would come back for him.

Muttering the prayer again, and again, just as he had heard his mother do when she was upset, he said the words so fast he wasn't sure what he was saying anymore, but it helped. It seemed to clear away the nasty coating the foul smell of the demon had left in his mouth, but not the filmy feeling on his skin.

After a time, his breathing came easier, although it still caught occasionally. He began seeing again, instead of endlessly searching the darkness with his eyes.

Releasing his grip on his knees, he flexed his fingers to ease the pain. His legs had lost feeling.

Soundlessly as he could, he crawled out from under the desk, listening for the demon's clicking hooves on the kitchen tile. When he was able to stretch out, he sat on the floor, wincing as needle pains pricked at the bottom of his feet and up and down both legs.

He kept his eyes transfixed on the doorway, watching for the demon. The guttering candlelight from the kitchen was dimmer now. Some of the candles must have gone out. Knowing the evil that lie beyond, Victor felt he was peeking through a flickering doorway into Hell.

There was nothing from the old woman who had been sobbing.

He wondered if any of the four old women were still alive. At the instant the demon had appeared one had fainted, or maybe even died, he wasn't sure which.

Involuntarily glancing around the drawing room, he checked for lurking shadows, remembering how the tiny demon had lashed out with an unnaturally long arm, striking down a second old woman.

Her plump, grandmotherly form had flown across the room. The sound of her limp body hitting the wall and dropping to the floor stuck in his mind, as if it had been the only sound made.

The demon itself made no noise other than the dull thud of its gnarled hand striking the old woman.

That woman was probably dead. He could see her form in his peripheral vision as he began crawling into the kitchen, but he refused to look at her.

His legs felt better, but fear still prevented him from standing upright. Shivers of weakness caused his hands to tremble and his knees to shake as he crawled across the cold tile kitchen floor, toward the door he had seen the third old woman run through.

Avoiding spilled wax and sputtering flames, he thought about how the demon had scattered the candles, leaping after a fleeing third woman. With tiny vestigial bat-wings flapping futilely on its back, it had hit the floor hard with small, split hooves clicking on the slick tiles as it scrabbled for purchase. The creature stood upright, less than two feet tall with a face shaped between dog and a horse; long, with eyes on the sides of its head. Its backward-bending, horse-like legs gave it great strength for leaping once its hooves found purchase in the grout between the tiles.

The boy wondered at how something so small could be so strong, and he feared he may have glimpsed fangs under the curling snarl of its lips. Thankfully, he had been in the far corner of the room, away from the demon when it bounded from the table.

The last old lady had jumped up and grabbed something long and silvery from a shelf before determinedly chasing after the demon and the fleeing woman. This final woman, the one he had been told to call *Abulea*, was the one he thought he had heard sobbing. She was his great-grandmother, but he really didn't know her at all.

When the paralyzing terror had finally lost out to the instinct to survive, he had run into the study and folded himself under the desk. Muffled noises had come from beyond the far door but he had not dared imagine what was happening on the other side of those walls. There had been two or three more thumps, followed by an oppressive silence, and then the quiet sobbing had begun.

The entire incident had seemed to take place with an unnatural quiet, as though the world had been covered with cotton.

Now, still on his hands and knees, he reached the threshold of the door the demon had raced through. His mouth was dry and sticky as he peered around the edge of the doorframe. Dim candlelight flickered from behind him, pretending to reveal what lie ahead in the darkness. His heart stuttered at a movement until he recognized his own shadow wavering in the weak candlelight.

After a moment his eyes adjusted enough to discern two forms; one in the middle of the room and the other against the far wall. He was sure these were the women, and that they would be dead, but the

3

vacillating light cast the illusion of movement over everything, making it hard to tell for sure.

The air held the same taste of dank, rotten garbage that had exuded from the demon. The boy wondered if the smell meant the demon was still here or if it had permeated the room the same way it had filled his own senses and covered his skin. He hoped it was just leftover stink.

Crawling toward the shadowy forms, his palm landed on something cold and hard. He fumbled with it in the dark. It glinted with the cold silvery reflection of metal. He drew a sharp breath of pain when he discovered the object to be some sort of knife. He brought his stabbed finger to his mouth and tasted the buttery flavor of his own blood.

The cut stung, but not enough to worry about right now.

He turned the knife over in his hands. It was awkwardly shaped and hard to clutch as a weapon, but he was comforted by it nonetheless. He turned his newfound weapon over and pointed the blade out of the bottom of his palm as he had heard the older kids say was the proper way to wield a knife. It was uncomfortable to hold while crawling. Gripping it while moving ground his knuckles into the hard floor, and he worried about stabbing himself in the knee, but he also worried holding it wrong would make it useless.

This knife must have been what he had seen his great-grandmother grab on her way out of the kitchen. If it was, she hadn't made it very far into this room with it.

Holding his breath, he listened for noises. He could hear one of the women breathing lightly, maybe wetly, as if she were congested.

The woman closest to him was his great-grandmother. The candlelight was dim and the colors were washed out, but her red-checkered apron was discernable. He continued toward her, pausing his own breathing often so he could listen.

When he reached his great-grandmother, he put his hand to her face. Her breath was shallow and slight, but it was there. He didn't see anything wrong with her, other than she wasn't moving, but she was very old and he had seen how hard the demon had hit the other woman.

The moist breathing sound was still there, and it wasn't from his great-grandmother. Maybe the other woman was still alive. He decided not to check on her. He would go for help instead. What did he know about helping someone who had been attacked by a demon? He wasn't even sure he could find his way back to his aunt's house, where the rest of his family was, but he could get a neighbor or someone to help.

He resumed crawling toward the front door. He knew it was there, somewhere in the dark. The old women had closed all the doors and windows to keep out the prying eyes of gossiping neighbors. The only other way out of the house was through the back door into the courtyard, but the courtyard had eight-foot walls, and the gate was padlocked. The front door was the only way out.

He sensed movement and froze.

Searching through the misleading flickers of the candlelight for the source of the movement, he thought it had come from the other old woman. Maybe she was waking up. Maybe he should check on her after all. If she was waking up, she could help the others. Besides she was only a few feet away.

He switched the knife to his other hand and pivoted on one knee to face the old woman.

Staring hard at the dim lump of her form, he tried to make out details. She lie on her side with her back toward him. It looked like she had moved her hand to her face.

Holding his breath, he inched closer, putting every effort into being silent; the horror of the demon still strong in his memory. The wet breathing sound was louder now, but it sounded wrong, like someone softly blowing bubbles with a straw.

Another movement.

He froze. He had seen the movement this time. It looked like the woman was scratching her chin, but her arm hadn't moved.

He raised his head higher to see.

It didn't look right.

His pulse quickened. He moved backward, away from the old woman, in a reverse crawl. The knife in his hand scraped the floor.

At the sound, the demon's head popped up from behind the woman's form.

The boy froze as the demon's beady eyes locked onto his.

Its black eyes reminded him of a mouse's: protruding, hard, shiny, and completely inhuman. The flickering candlelight reflected in them like the burning pits of Hell. Gruesomely shaped, the head was a mix of rat, horse, and dog. Barred teeth and fangs glinted orange in the darkness. The boy had no doubts the dark, wet stain around the demon's muzzle was blood.

There was no time to escape. The boy lurched into a standing position as the demon leapt for him. Reflexively, the boy threw his hands up to protect his face and swat away the attack of the cat-sized creature.

The demon hit him as hard as a full-grown man, propelling him backward over a chair and onto a coffee table. He felt things breaking. He wasn't sure if it was the chair, the table, or his own bones. The weight of the demon on his chest was like a bag of cement. Its fetid smell of rotting eggs and burnt hair suffocated him as much as the burden on his chest. A gnarled hand raked the side of his face, cutting deep gashes under his eye. Wiry legs kicked sharp hooves into his abdomen and thighs.

The boy gasped, unable to cry out. He squeezed his eyes shut in a grimace as fierce as the demon's and waited for the end to come.

The attack lessened and the weight slowly lifted. The pain began fading into dull throbs. He wondered at the strange sensation of death. He had been told dying was painless, but he had expected the pain to stop suddenly, not fade away.

He took a breath and was rewarded with a stabbing pain in his side. Convulsing, he rolled up and clutched his side, causing even more pain. Gasping in pain and for air, he fought to breathe without breathing. The pain was worse than ever as he clutched at his side involuntarily.

Realizing he was not dead, and fearful of the demon, he fumbled about in the broken pieces of wood and glass from the coffee table, forcing himself up. Looking for where the next attack would come from, he clutched the knife tightly. It was slick in his grip and coated with something. Blood, maybe. Maybe his. He hurt in too many places to know how badly he was bleeding.

He held the knife up, ready for another attack, nearly passing out from the pain of moving. There was no sign of the demon anywhere.

Blood flowed into his eyes and obscured his vision. He could feel hot, wet liquids on his shirt and legs.

There was movement behind him.

He wheeled, wiping blood from his eyes and holding the knife up, but he tripped and fell back, sprawling into the pile of glass and wooden shards.

A light clicked on, and suddenly the room was too bright to see anything.

Shielding his eyes, he tried to hold the dagger ready, but the pain in his side, and his position on the ground, prevented it.

"It's okay," spoke a hoarse, thickly accented voice.

He searched through the blinding glare for the voice, waving the knife out into the air, trying to turn to protect himself.

"It's okay," the voice repeated. "It's gone now."

Spotting a figure leaning heavily against the doorframe, hand still on the light switch, he recognized the old lady the demon had sent flying against the wall.

He looked to the knife in his trembling hand and saw it was covered with something slick and black, like tar colored pond scum. Dropping the weapon, he closed his eyes and lay his head back into the broken glass.

He thought that maybe he would like to faint now.

Instead, he allowed himself to drift off slowly, mentally keeping time with the pain throbbing in his leg, ribs, and face. He almost smiled as he imagined they were a like the big bass drums he had seen in a parade once, beating so low you felt them vibrating in your chest as much as you heard them. He was comforted by the sound and feel of the drums as he heard the woman say he was okay.

It wasn't okay.

He didn't think it would ever be okay again, but just for right now, the drums were very nice.

ONE

Dreams were no longer an escape for Jack. The arguments with Julie weighed heavily on his mind and he awoke several times to reassure himself she was still sleeping next to him. The sight of the back of her head, silken black hair pulled back into a ponytail, calmed him and he closed his eyes again.

She hadn't been there last night. Most of it, anyway.

Julie cancelled her plans with Jack to spend the night at the bar with Sandy. Sandy, who had just broken up with Michael, needed comforting. Or so Julie claimed.

The truth was, ever since the miscarriage, things had been tense between them. The emotional rollercoaster had taken its toll on both of them and strained their relationship.

Feeling petty, Jack tried to go back to sleep, but every time he closed his eyes he had visions of Julie leaning into some strange guy on a barstool.

He reached up and tiredly scratched his own mussed brown hair. His arms felt too long, with his hands too far away and not quite part of his body. He couldn't remember ever being so tired before.

Hearing him stirring, Bear stood up from the dog bed and came nose to nose in greeting. Jack scratched the curly black hair on top of the dog's head and murmured a few soothing words. Bear went back to his bed, turning in a circle twice before lying down.

Jack drifted back to sleep but woke so many times he began to dream he was awake wanting to sleep. He thought about getting up and going to watch television, but he was too tired to move.

Startling, he opened his eyes, surprised to find the room had a reddish glow. Normally streetlight filtered in, but nothing like this. The room appeared as though the bedside lamp had been turned on with a red light bulb in it.

The hair on the nape of his neck prickled. Something was in his bedroom.

His heart began pounding as he listened for what had awakened him. Bear's nose whistled as the dog gently snored on the floor next to the head of the bed. Julie was softly breathing next to him. Other than that, and the thumping of his own heart, there was nothing. No distant traffic, no refrigerator hum, nothing.

Jack's ears rang in the unnatural stillness of the room.

Trying to sit up, he found he couldn't. He was paralyzed. His heart rate increased; something he wouldn't have thought possible. Terrified, he rolled his eyes wildly to see around the room, trying to see anything, trying just to move any part of his body.

Except for the reddish hue, the room appeared normal.

He struggled to move, his whole body far away and numb. He tried to kick, tried to sit up or rock back and forth, or yell. None of it worked.

Closing his eyes, Jack tried to bring his breathing under control. Try to relax, he told himself. Just go back to sleep. Try to take deep breaths. It'll be okay.

Bear whimpered and Jack's heart nearly burst. He tried to look over at the dog, but his eyes froze on the entrance to the bedroom.

There was someone there.

A bulky shape filled the doorway; a giant man in a long trench coat.

Jack's breathing became ragged with terror. Immobilized, he stared at the shadowy silhouette. A lump of terror in his throat reduced his breathing to quick wheezing gulps. Wanting to believe the intruder was a man, a burglar of some sort, Jack knew it was something much, much worse.

Bear whimpered again, softly and far away, but Jack couldn't tear his eyes away from the embodied darkness, couldn't move.

The figure remained, unmoving, backlit despite the horrible crimson light in the room. None of its features, if it had any, were discernable. Jack's mind couldn't grasp what it was looking at. The image refused to resolve itself, giving only a blurred impression like a photograph of something in motion.

Jack blinked.

It was gone. The room was dark, the doorway clear, and the red light replaced by the soft amber glow from the streetlights.

Jack's breathing and heart rate were normal, but they began rapidly speeding up again as he recalled his terror. His eyes burned and reflexively squeezed shut as tears flowed to lubricate them.

He had been staring at nothing for a long time. How long? He remembered feeling panic; a fear that his brain had been paralyzed too.

He rubbed his eyes and was relieved his body worked again. Sitting up, his muscles moved jerkily, awkwardly, as if he wasn't familiar with using his body anymore.

Looking around, everything was normal. The dim orange glow from the streetlight was more than enough to see both Julie and Bear sleeping peacefully.

Finally, his heart rate leveling out, Jack took deep breaths to calm himself.

Exhausted, his body began falling asleep even as his mind tried to race around the horror he had experienced. He needed to pee, but he was too tired. Slowly sinking back down into his pillow, he nervously pulled the blankets up to his nose and dozed off while considering putting his head under the blanket.

TWO

Morning sunlight beamed through the bedroom window with a physical pressure on Jack's face, waking him readily as a hand on his cheek. He lay with his eyes closed, wondering what time it was until remembered it was Saturday.

Eventually the warmth of the sun became too much. He opened his eyes to sunbeams streaming through the blinds in dusty rays, each containing galaxies of silently spinning motes. For a moment he enjoyed the peace—until he recalled his nightmare.

Sitting up, he inhaled sharply in panic, looking wildly about the room.

The sun was soothing company, banishing any shadows from the room. Just a dream, he told himself, waiting for the panic to pass.

When it did, he stood and stretched his six-foot plus frame, allowing his fingers to brush the ceiling. Shuffling toward the bathroom, he wondered where Julie was. The open window in the bathroom quickly satisfied his curiosity when Julie's voice floated up from the back yard.

"You stay out of those flowers, Bear, or I'll start keeping you in a kennel!" She was admonishing the dog for damage done the previous week.

He went back into the bedroom, pulled on a pair of jeans and a t-shirt, and then headed outside to stand on the deck. He could see Julie on her hands and knees in the far corner of the yard where the sunlight had just started to hit.

Dressed in old sweats and working at the weeds with a hand shovel, she was beautiful in the sunlit corner of the yard. Her sweat pants pulled tight across her form, accentuating her figure, and her straight black ponytail swung like a pendulum, keeping time with her movements.

"Good morning, Honey," he called.

"Hm," Julie said over her shoulder. "I didn't expect to see you up for a while yet."

"Really? I thought you opened the blinds so that I would get up."

"No, I just thought the room needed more light. I figured you'd sleep until noon."

Jack smiled grimly and tried not to be irritated. This was the start of yet another petty argument and he knew it. Stifling the comment he wanted to make, he asked "How come you're up so early?" Normally Julie was the one who slept until noon on the weekend.

"I couldn't sleep. I tossed and turned all night, so I finally just got up."

"Yeah, me too." Jack stepped off the deck and walked across the grass toward Julie. The dewy grass was cold on his feet and made his toes ache but felt fresh and invigorating. "What do you have planned for the day?"

"Look, Jack." Julie stabbed the ground with her hand shovel. "I really didn't sleep well last night and I'm cranky, so let's not get into it right now, okay? I told Sandy that I would take her out to the mall today to take her mind off Michael."

Jack threw his hands up in an involuntary defensive response. This was not the conversation he had just initiated. This was the one she had been rehearsing in her head for the past twenty minutes. He had already lost an argument he hadn't been aware they were going to have. He turned and headed back toward the house.

"You don't need to act like that," called Julie. "All I said was I don't want to have an argument right now."

"That's fine. I'm going to go take a shower, okay?"

He didn't wait for her response.

Julie's knees were wet. The morning had dew soaked through her sweat pants and the damp was starting to come through the cotton gloves she wore too, but she couldn't bring herself to quit re-planting bulbs and go back in the house yet. She needed to be out of the house, to be outside in the open space. The sun was warm enough to allow her to ignore the cold spots and she was grateful for the good weather, knowing winter was coming soon.

She stopped and pulled the back of her sweats up and her t-shirt down, re-covering her lower back. A sunburn there and her wardrobe would be severely restricted for a week. That didn't go well with a job that required her to wear hose and a skirt.

Grabbing another handful of bulbs, she began sticking them in the ground at random. After Bear dug them up, she didn't have any idea what they were anymore. She was irritated at the dog for having destroyed her soon-to-be flower garden, but she was grateful for something to distract her. She didn't feel like talking to Jack right now and anything she did in the house would put them in the same room eventually.

She didn't mean to be so bitchy, it was just that everything Jack did irritated her lately; in fact, just the sound of his voice had grated on her nerves this morning. She regretted snapping at him already. After messing up last night's plans, she had hoped to make up for it today, but now that probably wasn't going to happen either.

I'm just tired, she decided. She hadn't slept well in ages. She had been having nightmares she couldn't remember when she woke up, and some she didn't want to. Sighing heavily, she arched her back and stretched.

It was hard to admit it to herself but she had been glad when Sandy had called last night. She had been dreading spending the evening at home with Jack. She kept trying to tell herself everything was fine, but something wasn't. She just couldn't put her finger on exactly *what* was wrong.

THREE

Saturday evening found Jack at the bar without Julie. His thoughts were on her as he gazed across the top of the pitcher of beer at Victor Ramirez, who was taking a deep drink from a plastic eight-ounce beer mug.

Vic, as he preferred to be called, put the mug down empty and licked the foam off his thick black mustache. His dark eyes danced with pleasure as he smiled at Jack. Three parallel scars under his left eye stretched into crescents, their stark whiteness deeply contrasting with his swarthy complexion and the inkiness of his eyes and hair. Vic picked up the pitcher from the center of the wobbly bar table and refilled his mug, then topped off Jack's.

"I, for one, am glad that your plans for the weekend fell through, *amigo*." Vic grinned at Jack as he put the pitcher down. "It has been way too long since we pondered the mysteries of life through the clarity created by the use of many *cervezas*. I was beginning to wonder if you still went out of the house or if you were officially an old man now." Vic's voice was deep and rich, full of beguiling Hispanic accent.

Jack smiled at his friend's use of the accent. Vic used it only sporadically and his English was no more accented than Jack's, who suspected that if he had tried harder in high school his own Spanish might have been better than Vic's.

"I think it's official. I *am* old. I just don't feel like going out anymore." Jack tiredly rubbed one eye and picked up his beer mug.

"You seemed ready to get out to a bar tonight. I think maybe it's just the noisy places you don't like."

"Could be." Jack nodded. "I definitely needed to get out of that house because I sure am enjoying the sight of your ugly mug."

Vic picked up his scratched plastic beer mug and looked at it with feigned surprise.

"I thought it was all right. I've been sucking face with it!"

Jack and Vic both laughed and toasted each other.

"I'll have to remember to tell Anita you were sucking face at the bar," said Jack, referring to Vic's wife.

Vic's smile became lopsided as he shook his head with mock sorrow. "She already knows how fond I am of the pretty *chicas*." He sighed deeply. "And that they have no interest in me!"

The scratched mug went to Vic's lips again before he confronted Jack. "So, what's going on? You ready to talk about it yet?"

Jack shrugged, a little embarrassed his friend had so quickly noticed there were ulterior motives for getting together.

"Is it you and Julie?"

Looking away, Jack nodded. "I don't know what's going on. We just…bicker. All the time. And she hates being in the house. Ever since my sister told her the dog was barking at ghosts."

"Bear?"

"Yeah. Remember that thing he does when he walks around the house growling for no reason?"

Vic nodded. "I remember you mentioning it."

"My sister told her it was probably a ghost. Julie's been freaked ever since."

"Was it?" Vic asked.

"What?"

"A ghost."

Jack scowled. "You don't believe that crap, do you?" he asked incredulously.

Vic shrugged.

"Like what?" Jack eyed him curiously.

Vic hesitated for a moment, and then answered with another shrug. "I believe that my great-grandmother saved my life with an egg under my bed when I was little."

"What the hell are you talking about?" Jack laughed.

Vic leaned forward and took on a hushed tone of voice, dark eyes glittering brightly in the dimly lit bar as he thickened his Hispanic accent for proper story telling. His bushy moustache danced on his lip like a living creature, emphasizing the story with its undulations.

"When I was little, only about four years old, I got sick. Really sick. I remember I would dream while I was awake. Sometimes when I was talking to my mother, I would feel far away and couldn't hear her, and other times I would think that someone was there when no one was.

"Finally, my great-grandmother came into my room and told me it was an evil spirit that was making me sick. Then she took an egg, touched it to my forehead and then my stomach, and then to the right and left sides of my chest." Vic made a motion like a Catholic crossing himself before prayer. "Then she wrapped it in a towel and put it under my bed. She told me to be very careful not to touch it.

"The next day I was better. When she came and got the egg, she asked me if I wanted to see what had been making me sick. She took me outside and broke the egg open into a bowl so I could see. The egg was thick, like it had been half boiled, but it was nasty black stuff and it stank horribly. She told me that was what had made me sick and that she would get rid of it so no one else would ever get sick from it again."

Jack awkwardly met Vic's stern expression for a moment before commenting.

"That's quite a story."

"You don't believe me."

"I didn't say that."

"You didn't have to."

"What'd she do with the egg?"

"We buried it. She said it was important to bury it in the deep shade of a tree, were it couldn't be touched by sunlight."

"I thought sunlight was supposed to banish evil things."

Vic shrugged. "That's what I remember. She told me it was caused by the *Ojo*, the evil eye."

"The 'Oh-ho,'?" Jack raised his eyebrows. "So was your grandmother a witch?"

Vic hesitated for a moment before answering. "Kind of. She was a *curandera*."

"Seriously? A witch?" Jack was awed. Vic was calmly talking about modern day witches in his family like something out of a midnight movie on a free cable channel.

"Well, technically a *bruja* is a witch. A *curandera* is more like…a healer."

"A 'brewha'?"

Vic nodded.

"Did she ever do anything else?" Jack's interest was piqued.

Vic frowned and his eyes seemed distant.

Jack leaned in. "What?"

"When I was about ten years old my father took us all back to Mexico to meet our family and … I don't know. That's not something I like to talk about." Vic's accent was gone now, and he his lips had tightened. The three linear scars under his eye turned a light pink color.

Jack, worried he had upset his friend, took a deep breath and tried to sound casual. "I don't really think our house is haunted, I just had a dream I saw a ghost. Julie's talked about it so much I was bound to have a dream sooner or later. It was just weird because I never used to have nightmares."

"Did you dream you saw it, or did you really see it?" Vic took a sip of beer, his eyes on Jack's.

"What do you mean?"

"Sometimes you know, I mean really *know* something, but then later convince yourself it was a dream or your imagination, even though you *know* it was real. You know what I mean?"

"Not really, no," Jack answered, but even as he said it, he thought of how real, how *evil*, the thing in his room had been, and he did understand.

"Tell me about your dream." Vic topped off both of their mugs and waved to the waitress for a refill on the pitcher.

Jack felt foolish but started describing the apparition.

Vic interrupted. "That's not what I mean. Tell me the whole dream, from start to finish."

Jack thought about it for a moment, surprised to find the events of the dream were still so clear in his mind. He decided to humor Vic, and he did feel like he needed to get it off his chest, so he related the tale in as much detail as he could. When he finished, Vic continued to stare at him thoughtfully.

"So you did see something," Vic finally said.

"It was just a dream."

"I hear your mouth saying that. I see the rest of you telling me that you know you weren't dreaming."

Trying to cover his growing unease, Jack rolled his eyes and smirked.

Vic ignored it. "I understand. The time I spent in *Mexico* when I was a kid was the scariest thing that ever happened to me."

Jack leaned back in his seat, putting distance himself and the disquieting countenance Vic had donned.

"So I had a realistic nightmare. So what?"

"So I just wanted you to know you're not alone. I've seen things too. Things I told myself were only terrible dreams. But even after years of telling myself 'it was just a dream', part of me, deep down inside, still knows it was all real. I just wanted you to know…that it's okay."

The waitress arrived with a full pitcher of beer and set it down on the table between the two men. She smiled pleasantly as they dug out money to pay for it. By the time she left, the mood had broken. Jack and Vic seemed to have arrived at an unspoken agreement that they had reached uncomfortable territory and it was time to move on. They lost themselves in the game on the big screen television and passed the rest of the evening with a light banter that got friendlier as the beer went down.

FOUR

Jack woke up with a splitting headache, grateful he and Vic hadn't driven. He didn't even remember the cab ride until he saw the wad of dollar bills and the pile of loose change he had emptied out of his pocket onto the nightstand. Stumbling into the kitchen, he fumbled with a bottle of ibuprofen and a glass of water.

He noticed the little red light blinking on the answering machine through the bottom of his water glass while looking cross-eyed down his nose. Reaching over, he tapped the button to hear the message. He hadn't heard the phone ring. Hell, it could have been there last night when he got home, he wouldn't have known.

The machine beeped and a tinny sounding voice echoed out of it.

"Jack? This is Julie. I just didn't want you to worry. I'm staying the night with Sandy. I think I've had too much to drink to drive home, and I'm just going to stay here for the night." The machine beeped again and fell silent.

Jack stood still as his addled brain slowly absorbed the message. His imagination began to run wild. He wanted desperately to trust Julie, but couldn't stop himself from believing the worst.

He played the message again. Julie didn't sound the least bit drunk. He listened a third time and decided she was at a residential party, based on the sounds of only a few people in the background and the music being at a low level.

Jack dropped his glass into the sink recklessly, as if daring it to break. He hadn't even noticed Julie wasn't home. He had been too drunk. He wondered where she was. She wasn't at Sandy's house that was for sure.

He didn't believe for a minute that Sandy and Michael would be having a party two days after they split up, and he was sure Michael was the kind of man to kick Sandy out, not the kind to let her have the house. So either Julie had lied about the breakup two days ago when she stayed out at the bar all night, or she was lying about where she was now. Either way she was lying.

Jack held his throbbing head between his hands and cursed. A sick feeling ached in his gut. It had finally happened. It was sooner than he had expected, but he had lost Julie to someone else.

A door slammed shut. Jack bolted upright from the couch, his heart pounding. It was dark except for the blue glow from the television screen. It took him a moment to realize where he was. A dark figure stood halfway up the stairs, in the entryway landing between the two floors.

"Sorry if I startled you. The door slipped."

It was Julie's voice. Jack felt muscles in his neck and back relax as he became fully conscious of his surroundings. He had fallen asleep watching football. His head throbbed once, just to remind him of his antics the night before.

"Are you all right?" he asked cautiously, looking up at her. He wasn't sure what to say. She hadn't called all day and was just now coming home. Was their relationship over?

"Fine." Julie's response was curt as she walked up the half flight of stairs and disappeared from his sight.

Well, that went well, he thought sarcastically. Shutting off the television and taking a deep breath to brace himself, he went up the stairs in the dark.

Julie was in the bathroom. He had no idea what to say to her. If he asked where she had been all day, she would get angry. If he asked about last night, she would get angry. If he ignored it she would find some way to turn that against him too.

He reached to the headboard and turned on the small reading lamp before undressing and climbing into bed. Bear came over and put his cold nose up to Jack's, telling him goodnight, and then went to the dog bed in the corner.

Jack lay quietly listening to clicking sounds of Julie moving various items in the medicine cabinet. If he confronted her, she would become argumentative and perhaps use his mistrust of her as an excuse to leave. If he ignored the whole situation, it would only get worse, if not in reality, then in his own mind. What other options were there? He could wait for her to bring up the subject, but that was too much like ignoring the situation. Although he wasn't cold, he pulled the covers up to his neck and stared at the shadows on the ceiling.

When Julie finally came into the room, he found himself talking to her before he realized he was going to speak. "Julie?"

"Hmm?" she responded absentmindedly.

"I want you to know that I love you." He was about to say more, but Julie rolled her eyes toward heaven as if to ask God what she had done to deserve this.

"Look, Jack," she said impatiently, "I really don't want to get into it right now."

"I have something to say and I want you to hear it." Jack was surprised at the calmness of his voice. He didn't feel calm. Lying in bed with the sheets pulled up to his chin, he felt like a child waiting to be reprimanded.

Julie ignored him and turned off the lamp, as if hoping it would make Jack turn off too.

"I want you to know that all I want—all I really, really want—is for you to be happy. And if that means that you have to leave me, I won't stop you. I'll even help you, if I can."

"God! Jack! Can we just do this later please? We both have to work tomorrow and it's late." Julie's voice was loud and angry in the dark room and it reverberated in the walls for a long time. After what seemed like hours, Jack finished the speech he had outlined in his head.

"I meant what I said. I love you, I always will, and I only want you to be happy. If you want a divorce, I'll give you one. No fights, no haggling. But if this isn't what's been bothering you for the past few months, then please tell me how to fix it. I will do anything you want me to, but you have to tell me what it is, because I sure as hell don't know." His voice finally caught in his throat and he shut up. He felt hot wetness around his eyes, and he wiped them off on the sheet he had been clutching so tightly in his fingers.

"What I want is to go to sleep." Julie's voice was cold and quiet. He had never imagined she could sound like that.

Julie sat in her car and watched the eastern horizon as it slowly turned from black to gray. The sun wouldn't be up for another fifteen minutes. Not that it would make much difference today. It had rained during her entire drive to work. Judging by the size of the water puddles reflecting the pinkish-amber glow of the streetlights, it had been raining most of the night. Although she thought she hadn't slept all night, she hadn't noticed the rain until she left the house this morning.

Her night had been long and dark enough without waking up to a day that promised more of the same. Between the problems with Jack that wouldn't stop bouncing around in her head and the vague, upsetting dreams waking her when she did finally fall asleep, she was sure she wasn't getting more than two or three hours a night, and last night had been worse than most.

Jack's words bothered her deeply and she regretted her callus response. She had thought about what he had said all night, and the worst part was he was right. She had been thinking about leaving him, she just hadn't known she was thinking about it, like some half-formed idea of something you do without thinking so you won't chicken out.

She had spent the weekend with Sandy so she wouldn't have to see him and had even pretended to be too drunk to drive home so she could stay with Sandy at her parent's house, how low is that?

Pretty low, she thought. She had lied to Sandy, and to Jack, and she had been lying to herself, too, telling herself she wanted to have fun, to do things, and that she wanted to see Sandy, who needed someone to talk to after her breakup with Michael. The truth was she hadn't wanted to go home and see Jack.

Why didn't she want to be with Jack? Her mind went blank. *There has to be a reason,* she told herself. *You do love him. Remember?*

She thought about things he had done that had really touched her; how hard he tried to cheer her up when she was scared about having a baby, how he tried not to let her see him crying after the miscarriage, how choked up he was when he proposed, and the tears in his eyes when he said "I do".

There were wonderful memories of Jack, but they were far off and distant, as though she had seen them in a movie instead of living them. Fighting off tears, she watched the brightest patch of dark clouds where the sun had risen in stealth. She resolved to make things better with Jack.

Whatever the problem is it's with me, not him. He is a wonderful husband, and I am lucky to have him.

FIVE

Monday morning was dark, damp and depressing. Julie was gone by the time Jack got up at 6 a.m. He felt better physically but worse emotionally than he had the day before. He had tossed and turned all night, but if he'd had any nightmares, he couldn't remember them.

He entered the cubical farm that was his workplace through the back door. It was quiet and dark in the back of the offices, so he turned on the lights as he came through. He had stopped using the front door when he realized Heidi Clark, the overbearing, aging, Gestapo-like office manager, was up there every morning not to help with early incoming calls but to note the arrival times and attire of everyone.

He rounded the corner of his cubical and was surprised to find Heidi sitting in his chair looking up at him. He did a stutter-step, trying not to trip. He had been on autopilot and probably would have sat on her lap if his eyes had been closed.

"Whoops! Sorry! You surprised me!" He smiled as energetically as he could. It was very important to keep up appearances of positive attitudes in this office—especially around spy-like office managers. He met her cool gray eyes with as much warmth as he could muster toward her stovepipe body and stainless steel Brillo-pad hair.

"I am glad you're here early, Mr. Hooper." Her voice was nothing like the Cold War Soviet image she projected. Soft and southern, the dulcet tones belonged with a woman a third her age. "The fewer people there are to overhear this conversation the better." She didn't clip words or carry menacing overtones, but her voice gave Jack a chill anyway. Her prior record spoke for itself. Everyone he knew of who had been fired, or asked to resign, since she had come to this office had done so as a direct result of her involvement.

"Certainly, Ms. Clark." Jack's professional voice took over smoothly. "Should we move to your office, or perhaps one of the conference rooms?"

"No. It won't take that long." She remained calmly seated in Jack's chair, leaving him standing uncomfortably in the entrance of his own cubical. He suspected this was some sort of psychological ploy on her part. It was effective. She had shown she could move in and take over his territory any time she wanted.

"It was brought to my attention that you took a call out of rotation Friday night."

"What?"

"Your shift ended a five o'clock on Friday, which means that your rotation ended. You took a call at 5:10, from the incoming new sales phone line, which you should have transferred to the night shift's rotation."

"I did no such thing!" Jack was incredulous. He had given up almost an hour of his time for a phone call that came right before five o'clock. If he hadn't taken the call, he would have been bumped to bottom of the call rotation.

"Don't raise your voice to me Mr. Hooper. The computers don't lie. You could not have helped but notice the mistake when the phones weren't transferred to the night shift's rotation at five, and you exploited the situation. Because of this incident, and your low projected sales for the month, I am placing you on 30 days probation."

Jack bit his tongue. If he so much as sneezed on the phone in front of a supervisor for the next 30 days, they would fire him.

"Ms. Clark—" Jack spoke when he could hold his tone again, but Heidi Clark was not interested in speaking to him anymore. She held up a hand to stop him in mid-sentence.

"I'm disappointed in you, Jack. I thought you were different." She walked away from him briskly and sharply. It was not hard for him to imagine her wearing a grey uniform and marching as she disappeared around the corner with an air of self-important superiority.

Dropping down hard into the office chair, he wondered that it wasn't frosty cold from Heidi Clark having sat in it. He buried his face into his hands, rubbed his eyes, and scratched at something bothering him on his cheek. A stubble of whiskers under his right ear he had missed while shaving. *Great,* he thought, *one more thing to be irritated by all day.*

He turned on his computer and stared at the screen while he waited for it to boot up. Anger began to make his ears burn. He knew that phone call had come in before five because he had been clockwatching for his date with Julie. The date she had skipped out on to go to the bar with Sandy.

His mouth tightened. He wondered if Julie had already been out with some other guy while he had been sitting here actually excited to spend time with her. This sucked. He had taken that call before five. He *knew* it!

He thought of Vic telling him "…*sometimes you know, I mean really* **know**…"

When the computer was ready, Jack pulled up his call log. He knew what he would see. It would say he had taken a call at 4:50, that's what he would see. Then he would go give Heidi Clark a lesson in doing her homework!

When the page started scrolling, Jack's mouth went slack and his eyebrows furrowed. The computer showed he had taken the call at ten minutes after five.

"Shit…" Jack smacked the escape key with his thumb and the screen vanished as the computer exited to the desktop program.

That's not possible, he thought, looking up at the clock on the wall, then down at his watch. They were a lot less than ten minutes apart. He pulled up the computer's internal clock. It was dead on with the wall clock.

Well that leaves two possibilities, decided Jack, *either someone hacked into the computer log and changed it, or I'm losing my mind.*

He thought about how upset Julie had been with him lately and his weird nightmare the other night. Maybe he had been so distracted thinking about his problems with Julie and getting ready to go out that he had misread the clock.

Well, he thought, *Vic was almost right.* Sometimes you *just* knew because sometimes the inside of your mind was the only place it ever existed.

"You okay?" The voice startled Jack and he jerked in his chair. Charlie laughed a little, but apologized. "I didn't mean to scare you."

Jack looked up at his cube farm neighbor. Charlie's sharp features and long nose often gave Jack the impression of a rat face, not that he would ever say so.

Perceptively, Charlie realized something was bothering Jack. "Missed a call, huh?"

"Worse."

Charlie frowned and furrowed his eyebrows in thought. "Stanley wants to be your new best friend?"

Jack smiled and shook his head. Stanley was the equivalent of the schoolyard bully in the office place. "No. I'm on probation."

"Sales aren't in for the month yet—Shit. Heidi nailed you for something, huh?"

Jack just nodded back in response.

"Wanna talk about it?"

29

"Nah. It's stupid." Jack didn't really understand it so there was no point in trying to explain it.

"Good morning, gentlemen." Trish smiled as she walked up with an armload of mail. They both returned the greeting as the young blonde office assistant handed Charlie a piece of mail.

She graced Jack with big blue eyes that had surely pierced many a man's heart, then she stuck out her ruby red bottom lip and gave Jack a coy smile that would have cost him money at a bar. "Wassa maddaw? Did widdle Jackie get in twouble?"

"Man! This office has no secrets!" Jack groaned at looked at the ceiling tiles.

Trish made a show of digging through the mail and then making a pouting face. "Nothing for you again, Jack. Aren't you making any sales?"

"Nope. No one seems to need anything."

Trish nodded at him in an all-knowing fashion, as if he had finally admitted something she had known all along. "Well," her voice returned to normal and she stopped teasing, "you're not the only one. This is all the mail we got this weekend." She raised her armload to show him. Usually she carried around a box full. "Stanley is the only one doing any good." She clucked her tongue and whispered conspiratorially. "Who'd of thunk it?"

A black look crossed Charlie's face and he turned away.

"Well! You boys better pick it up soon!" She admonished cheerily and patted Charlie on the shoulder as she sauntered off to finish her rounds.

Charlie watched her go with a lingering gaze before shrugging and looking back to Jack while blowing a silent whistle. "Someday I'm going to find out if that is an act or not."

"Of course it is," Jack assured him. "People think it's cute so she does it so they will think she's cute."

Charlie wistfully turned back the way Trish had gone and sighed. "It's working."

"What was with that dirty look when Trish mentioned Stanley? Did he try to bully you into giving him a client again?"

Charlie shook his head. "No. He managed to steal one away."

"What?"

"He offered to only take a two percent commission so they switched over to him."

"Besides being unethical and immoral, how can he afford to get by on a two percent commission?"

Charlie shrugged. "I tried complaining about it, but nobody gives a shit as long as the company makes its sales."

"Big account?"

"The biggest I had."

"Sorry, man."

"Well, since we're both at the bottom of the rotation now, which I'm assuming you are since you're on probation, let's do lunch. I wanna check out that Japanese place where they cut up your credit card on the table right in front of you. You remember that commercial? I heard they just opened one of those around here somewhere."

SIX

Jack got home from work earlier than usual. Traffic was light and there had been no reason for him to stay past five. He had considered leaving early, but he knew a certain someone was watching to see if he did. He tried all day to shake the melancholy haunting him but hadn't been able to. Other than a pleasant lunch with Charlie, the day had passed slower than any he could remember, and even the thought of going home weighed down his spirits.

He smiled weakly as he walked in the house and spotted a bouncing black shape through the sliding glass backdoor. It was good to come home to someone who was always happy to see you. He went to the back door and let Bear charge into the house. The dog ran past him, into the kitchen and back, down the stairs and back, and then circled the living room three times.

Jack shook his head and waited as the dog did its best to break Jack's sour mood. Finally, he gave in to the dog's rambunctiousness and half-heartedly scooped his hand out in a mock attempt to catch Bear as the dog raced by again. Bear swiveled on his front paws to face Jack and then stomped playfully, daring Jack to catch him. Jack hunched over and swung his arms in front of him, ape-like. The dog's reaction was immediate. Bear stomped twice more and let out a joyous bark of contest before charging Jack, dodging his arms and legs, and bounding back outside into the yard. Jack followed, watching the dog tear at the grass in playful challenge.

Why can't I be like that? he wondered. *Why can't I just be excited about something?* He faked a lighthearted holler and ran off the deck to chase after the dog, trying to force himself to have fun.

Julie pulled up the driveway and parked in the garage. As soon as she killed the engine in her car, she heard Jack shouting and Bear barking.

What was wrong? Burglar? Was Jack hurt?

She raced up to the house and fumbled with the keys in the garage door, cursing. Distant memories of forgotten nightmares raced frantically through her mind. She finally got the door open and stormed into the house, leaving her keys dangling in the lock. Tripping in high-heels, she all but tumbled through the house and followed the sounds to the open back door, scared to death something horrible was happening.

The sight of Jack playing with the dog in the grass brought an instant sense of relief and she leaned against the doorframe as the adrenaline surge faded, leaving her weak in the knees. She watched her husband playing with the dog, momentarily thinking themselves a boy and a puppy, and she smiled, just for a moment.

Damn him! she thought suddenly. *He has no right scaring me like that! Bastard!* Her relief boiled away from the heat of the anger suddenly crawling over her. It was irrational, she knew, but lately, he just pissed her off. She felt the turbulent fury raging up in her and hastily left the back door, heading to the bedroom.

She had left early this morning to go think this crap through, and she thought she had. *Damn it!* She had talked to herself calmly and rationally in the car for almost an hour in the parking lot this morning; the rain had been very conducive to calm thinking. She didn't understand why she felt like this. Jack hadn't done anything wrong.

Now she was just pissed at Jack. Maybe it was some kind of hormonal thing, like PMS. Early menopause? She knew it was most likely a backlash effect from her miscarriage, but knowing didn't change anything.

She could still hear Jack playing with Bear out in the back yard. It sounded like Jack had finally tired out and was playing fetch, making the dog do all the work. As she listened, she made a decision and decided to act on it right then, before she could change her mind.

"Jack!" she called out the back door. "Jack!"

"Yeah?" He stopped mid-throw, obviously surprised she was home.

"Meet me in the car. We're going to dinner!" She turned on her heel and didn't wait for his reply. She scooped her purse up off the end table. She didn't remember putting it there, but when she didn't hear the jingle of her keys come from it, she remembered they were still in the door.

Two minutes later Julie was waiting in the driver's seat of her mud spotted little Prius with the silent electric motor running. She had already pulled out into the street, hoping maybe she could get Jack out of the neighborhood before he pissed her off again.

Jack came out of the house through the garage. He started toward her car, but then ducked, startled, as she hit the remote control for the garage door and started it moving down on him. She smiled in spite of her intense need to hurry up and leave. She had finally given him a dose of his own medicine with a prank he liked to use on her.

He had to run and hunch over to clear the closing garage door. As his head popped back up, he flashed the smile that had melted her heart. He jogged the rest of the way and opened the door quickly.

He smiled wryly. "Going my way, beautiful?"

"Just get in the car, Jack." *I will not get pissed*, she told herself. *I will not get pissed. I will not get pissed.*

Jack's smile faltered, but he got in and shut the door. Julie goosed the gas pedal and the tires let out a small but satisfying squeal as she raced up the street. Jack fumbled with the seat belt then finally sat still. Julie noticed he was careful not to look at her.

I will not get pissed. I will not get pissed. God! What kind of mantra is that?

Julie slowly relaxed as they drove. She got better the farther she got away from the house. She had noticed the same thing last week, when she'd been surprised to discover she was looking forward to going to work. It had held true when she had gone out with Sandy, too.

She glanced over at Jack. He was sitting quietly trying not to rock the boat, and they both knew it. He smiled sheepishly at her and she turned back to the road.

She didn't feel good enough to say anything yet, but was surprised at how quickly the tension was flowing away, even with Jack here. She hit the highway and opened up the throttle. Speed felt good. The cool evening air on her face felt good.

"I love you, Jack."

Jack's smile was weak and faltering as he hesitantly turned to look at her. "Are you all right?"

"I don't know. I'm not ready to talk yet. Let's just go have dinner, okay?"

"Okay."

SEVEN

Vic was glad to see Jack come into his restaurant. He was even more pleased Julie was with him. After the conversation Saturday night, he had been worried Julie was leaving Jack. Her presence here forestalled that fear and Vic wrote off the conversation to the ramblings of alcohol.

Jack probably didn't even remember that part of the conversation. After Vic had mentioned the *Ojo*, Jack seemed to have taken it upon himself to make sure any patrons visiting the bar the next day would have a freshly tapped keg of beer. Vic smiled at the memory of Jack holding the twenty-dollar bill up to his nose in a drunken effort to recognize it before passing it to the taxi driver. It had been a good night for reaffirming friendships.

Tonight Vic was frolicking between his normal position as Head Cook and the position of Host. His daughter, Rachel, who usually played Hostess, had received a last minute invitation to a party with a boy she had been swooning over for the last two months, and, being a Monday, business was slower so it wasn't too much of a strain for him. He liked to make a habit of coming out of the kitchen at least every other hour to meet with patrons anyway. It was good business sense to recognize and appreciate regular customers, and Vic enjoyed the socialization.

He greeted Jack and Julie with a feigned ignorance of their identities.

"Good evening, and welcome to *Nuestra Cocina*, where you're *apetito* is our *gana*." His slogan was a play on words lost to most people, declaring his appetite to be for the fulfilling of their appetite. It was still lost on Jack, even though it had been explained to him. That was okay. Vic wasn't sure it made a whole lot of sense either, but it sounded pretty good and it had been his son's idea. Besides, people came in for the good food, not the snappy slogan.

"Hey Vic," said Julie with a mock sultry voice. "I hope your chili is as hot as you are tonight."

Vic smiled wide, his rich black moustache spreading wide across his face without the slightest hint of thinning. "My chili and I will always burn hot in the deepest pits in hell for our hot thoughts of you, *mi chica caliente.*"

Julie smiled back, but not quite as wide. "You'd better be careful, saying stuff like that where Anita can hear you. You might end up with worse than a few fingernail scars on your cheek this time. Rawr!"

Vic's smile stayed wide across his face, but the scars under his eye turned pink, as if they knew they had been mentioned. Early in their friendship, Julie had made up a ribald history for the scars carried by the ever-flirtatious Vic. It had culminated with him being put in his place by the vicious talons of a spurned lover. It was the standard sort of tease between Julie and Vic since the night he and Jack had met her.

Vic had been happy to see his friend Jack, the perpetual loner, finally open up toward someone and have some fun. It didn't hurt to have that someone be young, beautiful, and intelligent. It also didn't hurt she hadn't taken any offense to Vic's own sultry teasing.

"Tonight, I have reserved the best table in the house for you, my friends. I have used up all of my favors with the owners of this fine establishment to ensure that you will have the finest dining experience of your lives."

"I thought we had that experience last time we were here," quipped Jack. "How could you possibly top that?"

"Ah!" exclaimed Vic. "That is the secret of the experience. How indeed? You shall see!"

He picked up two menus from the shelf under the Host's stand and led them toward a booth in the far back corner of the restaurant where the atmosphere was heavy with aroma of cheeses and sauces from the kitchen and sunlight filtered through wooden blinds, casting bars of light across everything.

Julie slid her way around the circular booth seat so she could see back out into the restaurant. Jack slid in from the other direction, but stopped before coming too close to Julie. Vic pretended not to notice.

"Do you want to see menus this evening?" Vic asked, already knowing what the answer would be.

"I'll just have the usual." Jack was already pulling his silverware from the rolled napkin.

"Me, too," came Julie's reply.

"Ahh… My poor, poor friends, I hate to be the one to tell you this, but we are all out of 'the usual' here tonight. I recommend that you look over the menu." Vic's smile trembled with effort not to expand beyond the reaches of his cheeks. He opened up the menus and handed one to each of them, watching with delight as Julie reacted first. Jack took considerably longer but he was the first to vocalize.

"What is this all about?" he asked with a large hint of incredulity in his voice. Julie's eyes mirrored Jack's confusion, but hers showed a large amount of excitement too.

White teeth gleamed under his wriggling moustache as Vic tried to talk around his foot-long smile. "We are just making sure that our favorite customers realize just how much they are appreciated."

The menus were normal on the outside, but the inside had big bold letters proclaiming the dinner courses to be served in honor of Jack and Julie's first anniversary.

Vic's wife, Anita, came out of the kitchen carrying a giant margarita in each hand. Tall for a Hispanic woman, she still carried the extra weight traditionally required of a master cook. In her late forties, her appearance was timeless as large curls of perfect black hair ringed her round brown face.

"Oh, Vic! You already showed them the menus!" Her voice was warm and motherly, yet stern and reprimanding at the same time. She sat the large hourglass shaped margaritas down in front of Jack and Julie before reaching over and slapping Vic lightly on the arm. "I told you I wanted to see their faces!"

Vic's smile turned sheepish as he cringed away from a second mock blow. "They were ready to order!"

A singsong verse came floating from the kitchen, followed by Vic and Anita's son John. Singing off key and out of tune, his Spanish version of Happy Birthday was vaguely recognizable, with 'birthday' replaced by '*aniversario.*'

John's pubescent voice cracked a little, but he made up for it with enthusiasm as he danced out of the kitchen carrying a cake at the end of one outstretched arm like a waiter's tray. He slid the cake smoothly onto the center of the table between the margaritas. It was white with blue trim and lettering proclaiming Jack and Julie's names with a large white and blue candle shaped like a number one flickering in the middle.

"Johnny! Dessert is supposed to be served last!" Anita slapped at John exactly the same way she had at Vic earlier.

John was quicker than Vic and nimbly stepped out of reach before the blow landed. His youthful form was just beginning to show the shape of the man emerging from the boy, but his smile was all a little boy's mischievousness. "Ma! The cake is frozen and has to thaw out! I just thought everyone would want to see it before anything melted!"

Anita made a snorting sound and muttered.

She turned conspiratorially toward Julie. "I swear, never give that man of yours an inch, or you'll lose control!" She shook a finger a Jack, admonishing him for future crimes.

Julie laughed and smiled at Anita. "Anita, it's not our anniversary!"

"Oh!" Vic jumped into the conversation. "But it is! It was exactly one year ago today, give or take a month, that you and Jack met. And since it is common knowledge that neither of you have previously allowed a relationship to last for a whole year without moving Heaven and Earth to end it, we decided that it was a cause for special celebration! Besides, we couldn't be sure that you would stop in for your wedding anniversary," he added with a conspiratorial wink.

Anita beamed proudly at her husband, as if he had at least gotten that part of the plan right.

"Tonight, dinner is on us!" John piped in. "So…pig out!"

Anita pursed her lips as she swiped at John and missed again. "You two are terrible. It's too bad Rachel isn't here. She would have shown some respect! Get out of here!" Shooing Vic and John away, she turned back to Julie and Jack. "Dinner is on us tonight, so you two sit back and relax, and let us do the cooking."

Vic kept an eye on them all night, making sure dinner was wonderful. Anita kept bringing different foods, John kept taking them away to make room for more when they were only half-finished. Vic brought margaritas until Julie begged for mercy.

He and Anita took turns sitting down and talking with their special guests until they finally gave in and turned the restaurant over to their employees and joined them at the table. Finally, after Jack and Julie claimed they could stand no more, Vic drove them home in their car and Anita followed to take Vic back.

EIGHT

Jack was hung over again. He dragged himself into work, barely making it on time. He wasn't used to being hung over this many times in one week, but it had been for a good cause. He and Julie hadn't managed to talk at all, but the time they had spent together was priceless. As he entered the office, he was feeling a good amount of hope they could work out their problems and found he was genuinely smiling, in spite of the throbbing behind his eyes.

A hand slapped him hard in the middle of the back. He jumped as much as from surprise as the shockwave throb the blow sent through his head. He winced as the slap faded, leaving a stinging sensation as it went. It hurt, but mostly he grimaced because the hand stayed in the middle of his back. He didn't turn his head to look, he knew who it was.

"How's it hangin' Jackie-boy?" The voice was thick and stupid sounding, like a stereotypical drunken college football player at a frat party.

"Hey, Stanley. How are you today?" Jack's voice automatically slipped into his professional tone.

Jack considered himself lucky he didn't run into Stanley more than once or twice a week. Stanley was an egocentric, narcissistic, idiot jock—except he was smart, or at least he had managed to convince most everyone else in the office he was. Jack had his own personal theory that it was just an act Stanley had perfected. He hadn't liked Stanley even before Charlie had mentioned a couple of intimidation sessions Stanley had forced on him.

"Doin' just fine, Jackie-boy, just fine." His thick fingers painfully massaged at Jack's shoulders in a gesture that couldn't be interpreted as friendly by anyone who had received it. "I noticed you don't look too good this morning. Come to think of it, you didn't look too good yesterday, either. You doin' all right? I heard you were havin' problems." He hesitated for a moment, but not long enough for Jack to respond. "If you need someone to talk to, you know where I am." He turned and walked away without giving Jack a chance to respond.

Jack watched him go. Something was up. Stanley was never that talkative with Jack. With other people, but not with Jack. Stanley seemed to sense Jack didn't care for him and usually minimized contact, just as Jack did. Not to mention that when Stanley did talk, it was almost always about himself or a girl he had been with. Jack walked away, unease growing in his gut.

"What's up?" Charlie peeked around the cubical wall and smiled. Jack just shook his head exasperatedly.

"Something else happen?" Charlie's voice was a whisper to keep the conversation private.

"Someone big and dumb stopped by to say 'hi' and offer condolences."

"I thought that son of a bitch had a smug look on his face! But, you know, it's hard to tell. He always looks smug."

The sound of shoes scuffing on the carpet sent Charlie back into his cubicle with the rasp of his chair's wheels across the plastic carpet protector.

"Shame on you boys! Gossiping like a couple of old women over here." Trish walked up swaying her hips like a model on a runway and dropped a letter on Charlie's desk. "If I didn't know any better, I'd think you two thought you were better than everyone else in the office." She leaned up against the wall opposite Jack and Charlie's cubicles so she could see into both spaces at the same time.

"So what's going on today?" she asked. "You pushing your luck to the max, or what?" she eyed Jack.

"I'm a little hung over."

"Yeah, I knew that. I could smell you when you walked in here this morning." She winked at Charlie and Jack heard him snicker. She pushed off the wall and stood up straight. "At least you don't look like you slept in *those* clothes." She watched him over her shoulder as she walked off.

"Nothing gets by in this office, does it?" Jack muttered.

Jack got home an hour after Julie and found her already in bed with a wet towel draped across her face. Bear, lying on the floor next to her side of the bed and looking forlorn, thumped his tail quietly in greeting.

"Hi, honey." He started to ask if she was okay, but was cut short.

"Just leave me alone. I don't feel well and I don't feel like dealing with any of your shit right now." Her voice was muffled under the damp towel and she made no physical movement to acknowledge his presence. Jack withdrew from the room angrily, knowing that somehow he had lost another argument he hadn't even participated in.

After a very short evening of skulking around the house trying to be very quiet so as not to raise Julie's ire, he gave up on doing anything and decided to go to bed. He started to head for the bedroom, but then had a mental picture of Julie snapping at him for shaking the bed when he got in. He thought about it for a moment before deciding he didn't feel like putting up with her either.

His head hurt too. He had just as little sleep the night before as she did, and he wasn't allowed to get all pissy like she was. *It's a woman's prerogative to be pissy,* he had heard her say once. He had thought she was kidding at the time, but she sure had been exercising that prerogative to an extreme lately.

"Screw this," he mumbled to himself. The night was too short to spend half of it trying not to move and wake up the wicked witch of the pissy prerogative. He turned around and headed downstairs to the spare bedroom, stopping at the hall closet to pull out an extra comforter.

Julie awoke with the damp towel cold on her face and neck, the warmth of the water having long since faded. She slid her hand slowly over to the other side of the bed to check for Jack, as she always did when she woke up in the night. This time, her questing hand found nothing. She felt a small panic rise in her as she double-checked and confirmed he wasn't there. She pulled the towel off her face and looked around the room. A knot began to form in her stomach.

Julie hated this feeling of fear, but couldn't do anything about it. She had been having nightmares about ghosts ever since Jack's sister had suggested the house was haunted, and although it was childish, she couldn't prevent herself from waking up in a cold sweat, afraid of the dark and of being alone. Julie had tried to talk Jack to about it when Bear's barking and acting strange in the house had frightened her, but he had just laughed.

She was glad Jack wasn't afraid. Having his strong confidence to lean on made it easier to tolerate her own fear. She regretted being

43

snippy earlier. It was strange how thoroughly daylight angers were melted away by midnight fears.

The house was silent and she couldn't hear the television or a radio, so she wasn't sure where he could be. Getting up to look for him, her body rippled with goose bumps that flowed over her in a wave even though the house was warm.

Bear opened a sleepy eye toward her, and she thought about calling him to come with her. Deciding she would probably have a heart attack if he started his growling-barking thing, she left him curled up on the dog bed and snuck out of the bedroom like a thief afraid of waking anyone who might be home.

Stealthily working her way across the living room, she had no problems seeing. The house was dark, but streetlight filtered through the windows. She faltered at the top of the stairs, hesitant to go down into the gloomy darkness below.

The fear was irrational, she kept telling herself, but that didn't make it go away. Sometimes, when she was in the basement, she had the feeling of being watched. She never felt this way before she started having the dreams about ghosts. She didn't have the sixth sense some people claimed let them know when someone was staring at them. The only times she had thought someone was staring at her, it was because she had seen them doing it.

Working up her courage, she cautiously moved down the stairs, sidestepping and keeping her back to the wall. *I've seen* way *too many horror movies*, she chided herself as she moved into the den.

Jack wasn't here. She'd had been hoping he'd fallen asleep on the couch again.

Her feeling of dread was reaching an intolerable level. The only two places left in the house were the laundry room and the spare bedroom, and those were the places she hated the most. There was no rational reason for it, but she had problems going into them in broad daylight, let alone at night. Sure Jack wouldn't be in the dark laundry room, she nervously went to peek into the spare bedroom instead.

When she finally made out Jack's form lying in the spare bed, relief flowed over her, soothing the goose bumps prickling up and down her body. She gazed at his form, watching him sleep blissfully and unafraid.

Anger mixed into her fear and relief. She knew, rationally, he hadn't slept down here to scare her, but it still pissed her off.

Jack sat up straight from a dead sleep, heart pounding. His head swam as he put his hand up to block the blinding light and tried to clear the sleep from his mind. Disoriented, nothing around him seemed right. He lost his balance and fell over onto his outstretched arm.

"Why are you sleeping down here?" Julie's angry voice reverberated through the room.

Jack fought for consciousness and used the sound of Julie's voice to focus on her face. When he finally found her angry visage, he wished he hadn't.

"Wha...?" He managed to moan.

Julie struck a classic pose with her hands on her hips balled into fists. Her long white night shirt caught up unintentionally on one side, revealing her thigh.

"We may be having some problems, *Mister Hooper*, but we are not sleeping in separate beds. *Ever*! Do you understand me?" The tone of her voice was a strange mixture of harsh and loving at the same time.

"What time is it?" he finally managed to mumble, although his eyes were still screwed shut against the light.

"Time for you to get your butt up to bed instead of sleeping down here by yourself, that's what time it is."

Jack tossed the comforter off and sat up wobbly. He managed to make out the clock on the shelf by the desk and was surprised it was only 10:30. He stood, swaying, and tried to look at Julie through squinty eyes.

"Don't you give me that look, *Mister*. You're the one who came down here to sleep."

"But—" He didn't get a chance to give his side of the argument.

"Don't you 'but' me, either. You get your 'but' up to *our* bed, and *maybe* this just might not come up tomorrow and start another fight." She turned on her heel and headed back upstairs.

Jack stood stupidly in his boxer shorts for the better part of a minute trying to wake up enough to grasp any hidden meanings in Julie's words. He scratched his head, realized he had bed-head, and decided he needed to go back to bed.

Stumbling up the stairs he nearly tripped over Bear, who had gotten up to see why everyone else was up. Julie was already in bed with the lamp on the headboard set to dim so he could find his way. He flipped the covers back on his side of the bed and dropped in heavily, shaking the bed. He felt guilty as soon as he had done it, although Julie didn't say a word. He reached up, turned off the lamp, and waited for his eyes to adjust to the dim light coming through the window from the streetlight.

NINE

Jack jerked awake for the second time. He lay still waiting to detect what had woken him. Bear whined pathetically from his corner, chasing something in his dreams, and Jack realized that was what he had heard. He closed his eyes and felt the tide of sleep wash over him again. Just as the undertow caught him, Bear whined again, pulling him back to the surface of consciousness, but not up into attentiveness.

"Bear…" he moaned tiredly.

The dog whimpered quietly.

"Bear, wake up," Jack said it louder. The dog went silent and Jack started drifting away again.

Bear yelped, and Jack sat up on his elbow, looking at the sleeping dog in the dim light. "Bear! Wake up!" he called in a loud voice. "Bear! It's just a dream, wake up!"

The dog's ears perked up and he opened his eyes sleepily. Bear stretched his legs out sideways looking at briefly at Jack, before his eyes rolled back up into sleep again.

Jack dropped exhaustedly back onto his pillow, wondering what dogs dreamed of that made them do that in their sleep. He began to get prickles on the nape of his neck as he wondered if dogs had nightmares. Maybe Bear was having the same kind of scarlet nightmare he'd had. He ignored the tingling of fear as best as he could, which wasn't hard tired as he was, and he pulled the sheets up to his chin and drifted off toward sleep once again.

Bear whined.

Jack sat up angrily in his sleep, dreams mixing with reality and his sleepy mind berated the ghost in his nightmares. "Damn it! Leave the dog alone!" he muttered angrily, defying the ghost he'd imagined to be bothering the dog. The sound of his voice stopped the whining again, and he dropped back onto his pillow with vague thoughts of having defended Bear. "Pick on someone your own size!"

It did.

Pain lanced though Jack's brain. A white-hot shaft of agony speared through his head behind his eyes. His heart thudded furiously. His breath came in quick shudders. Fear and pain enveloped him.

It was the ghost. He *knew* it.

He tried to get up, but his consciousness swirled around him. He fell back onto the bed and lost sense of his body.

Left by the piercing pain that had lanced through his head, a scarlet ball of fire burned in his brain. He could see it. He knew the fireball was in his brain, but even as he looked inward at it, he was spinning in an endless void, an eternal blackness that centered around him and the fiery ball of pain.

It ripped his thoughts away from his mind and incinerated them, as a sun might wrench atmosphere from a planet that had drifted too close. Somewhere, barely felt, hardly noticed anymore, the ghost that had started the fire laughed at him.

Jack wanted to scream, to cry, to do *anything* that might affect the unendurable pain, but his struggles were lost in the void between his own thoughts.

Fight…, he thought. But it was so hard to think. His thoughts were miles, light years, apart, reduced to wisps of vapor he couldn't concentrate on, couldn't even find…

Only the pain was real. It was the only thing left.

He was losing. He knew he was losing a battle, but he couldn't seem to even think about it.

Fight! A voice came from very far away, almost gone. *Fight!* The voice distantly cried out. *Fight! Damn it! Fight!* From far away, almost offhandedly, he noticed the voice was his own. A thought he had managed to almost catch.

Yes, he thought, *yes that was my voice. I should have fought…*

He felt the growing peace of someone who knew they had died. As he began drifting off into a pillowy nothingness, the pain snagged at his attention again momentarily, as it was the only thing left. Then it, too, started drifting farther away.

Somehow, unable to think, he knew he only had enough time for one last thought, and it needed to be a good one. Then it was too late. He had waited too long for that last thought and now he wouldn't get it.

Please, God. Please help me. He heard his own detached voice cry out through the nothingness.

The pain returned, exploding and trying to engulf his consciousness once more. He convulsed and could almost felt his body again. It was impossibly distant, but his left fist was clenched tight, quivering against his thigh spasmodically, a momentary beacon back to existence before he lost his body again.

Back in the void, alone with the flames of pain looming behind his eyes, he could see their scarlet glow just as clearly as he could feel the pain.

But things were different now. He could sense himself again. His body was here, a part of him, and he could see exactly where in his brain the agony was. His thoughts were becoming more cohesive and a sense of strength and power of will flowed into him. He could fight!

Thank you, God. Thank you. A part of him cried out with a joyous gratitude, elated for a second chance.

He concentrated on the pain and found it to be a forge, smelting agony out of raw nothingness then hammering and pounding it into pure torture. The pain increased as he focused directly on it, growing more intense as he fought his way closer. Part of his mind tried to recoil as he mentally twisted and turned toward it, but the only other choice was to go back into the emptiness.

FIGHT! He ordered his mind to pull together. He had to fight.

But how could he fight it? It was in the middle of his brain.

His formless being circled around the fire in his mind, floating in the nothingness around it, finding the size of it, seeing how bright its pain burned, testing how strong it was.

It's a fire, smother it, he thought.

Just get rid of it! another part of his mind cried in desperate terror, still writhing in pain and agony. That part that now believed, without reservation, he was being attacked by a supernatural entity.

If it could create pain from nothingness, then he could create from nothingness, too.

He imagined giant curved metal plates flying in from the empty infinity around him, coming together, slamming into a spherical shape around the hot pain. More and more they came, faster, as he gained confidence, slamming into place with imaginary echoes of ringing metal. He covered the sphere with a second layer and then a third just to be sure.

Then he examined the dull throb of pain thrumming out from the encased affliction like earth tremors.

Mentally, he felt oddly numb. What should he do now? He stared at the encapsulated pain for a long time. Finally, he turned back to his original source of help.

Please, God. I don't know what this thing is. Please help me again. Please take it. Please.

He imagined the sphere, and the pain it contained, rising up. And slowly, painfully, it began to float upward, up toward the inside of his skull, to his forehead. He imagined it passing out of his head and felt it depart his body, leaving an empty pain in a hollow behind his eyes. He almost thought he could see it floating in front of his face, oddly small now in the dim light of the bedroom. He imagined God taking it for him and he thought he could just make it out, rising up to, and then through, the ceiling and then on up into the heavens.

He lost sight of it as exhaustion overcame him and he fell into a dreamless darkness where he huddled around a throbbing ache in an empty hole behind his eyes.

TEN

What did the doctor say?" Julie asked as she dropped her keys into her purse and kicked off her heels. Jack could hear Bear dancing on his back legs, excited Julie was home.

"They said I don't have an aneurysm and it's probably a migraine headache. But they're going to test me for susceptibility to seizures tomorrow morning. Oh, and I'm not allowed to go to sleep tonight," Jack answered over his shoulder as he stirred the meat-helper he was cooking for dinner. Julie hated the stuff, but he was cooking so he knew she wouldn't say anything about it until later.

She picked up her shoes and dropped her purse on the end table on her way to the bedroom. "Does that mean I have to wake you up every hour to make sure you're still alive?" Her voice muffled as she went around the corner of the hallway.

"No. It means I have to stay awake for 24 hours before I take the test tomorrow." He raised his voice so she would be able to hear him. When she came back, he filled her in on his day at the emergency room as he finished setting the table and dishing out the food.

He hadn't mentioned the ghost to the doctor out of fear she would hold him for a psychological evaluation. Nor did he mention the nightmares to Julie, afraid she would get spooked again. He wondered if he should. What if they weren't just nightmares?

When it had been happening, he'd been pretty damned sure it was real.

But the normalcy of the kitchen around them, the smell of dinner, the conversation, all made it hard for him to believe it could have been anything but a bad dream. He put it out of his mind and continued chatting with Julie.

He felt as though he was babbling, but he was enjoying the fact they were having an honest to God conversation instead of arguing. Their conversation involved a lot of eye contact, and he found himself mesmerized by her deep green eyes. It had been a long time since they had gazed into one another's eyes. He hadn't realized how much he missed that.

The conversation continued to flow smoothly and soon he could tell they both felt as though a great tension had eased. Somehow, Jack wasn't quite sure when, they found a quiet reaffirmation of their love in each other's hesitant eyes.

The only rough part was when Julie kicked Jack out of bed and sent him downstairs so he wouldn't fall asleep.

Jack was bleary-eyed and sick of infomercials. He glanced over at Bear lying on the dog bed in the corner and staring off into the spare bedroom. The dog had been staring into that room for the better part of an hour now as he stayed up to keep Jack company.

The glowing green numbers of the clock on the DVD player showed it was a little after midnight. Jack wasn't sure he could make it until his appointment at nine without falling asleep. He decided to ask Julie if she could drive him. Already shaky and jerky from lack of sleep, who knew what six more hours would do to him.

He muted the sound on the television with the remote control and got up to go dig through DVD's for something better to watch.

The way the eerie blue glow of the television had lit up the downstairs had given him the creeps earlier, and now he had every light on. The odd quiet, with the television muted, brought the feeling back. Goose bumps crawled up his arms and he rubbed them to shake off the mood.

He put a disc in the player and sat back down to watch it. He was just about to turn the volume back up when he noticed Bear's ears perk up and the dog began growling low and quiet, almost inaudibly.

Julie had yelled at Bear for months to get him to stop barking and growling in the house, but Bear had only toned it down instead. The dog had a habit of barking for no apparent reason, which would have been fine if he was outside, but he only did it in the house. The fact that Jack's sister had suggested Bear didn't like the ghost hadn't made Julie feel any better about it.

Bear had continued to growl and bark in the house until Julie became jumpy and skittish when it happened, eventually confronting Jack as to whether or not he thought it could be a ghost. He had laughed and hurt her feelings.

He still felt bad about that.

Now, as he watched the quietly growling dog, Jack could see the hair on Bear's back rise and bush out. Bear was still looking into the spare bedroom, but instead of staring straight in, the dog had adjusted his gaze to look higher, as if expecting to see someone walk out of the room.

Jack's goose bumps came back and shaking them off didn't work this time.

Bear's gaze narrowed and his eyes seemed to focus on something. Ears laid back, his head turned slowly as his eyes tracked across the room, his growl deepening. Bear's eyes never blinked as they followed something Jack couldn't see from the doorway of the spare room, across the living room, and finally to the bottom of the stairs. As he stared at the bottom of the stairwell, Bear's growl lightened until Jack could no longer hear it.

Suddenly Bear remembered Jack was in the room and looked over at him. The dog's tongue lolled out of the side of his mouth in a friendly pant and his tail started wagging. Getting up excitedly, he ran over to Jack, putting his nose on the couch next to Jack's hand.

Jack stared at Bear for a moment, hoping the creepy feeling would subside. It didn't. He reached out and scratched Bear's ears, feeling foolish for being frightened.

He patted the couch with his hand and Bear jumped up onto the cushion next to him. Wrapping his arms around the dog, Jack buried his face in its fur and took a deep breath, relishing in the reality of the dog's scent. After a few moments, he finally felt his tension begin to release.

He smiled at Bear and rubbed the dog's head vigorously. "Yeah, you're a good boy. Yes you are. I don't know what the hell that was all about, but you're a good boy."

The dog happily turned his nose upward to get his neck scratched as Jack wondered about ghosts and nightmares.

"Good Morning. Anything good on?" Julie leaned over the railing to see downstairs where Jack was still watching television. Her silk robe was falling open and would have been very provocative, had she not been wearing a knee-length T-shirt underneath.

"Define good," Jack answered wearily. "I have learned that MacGyver's first name is Angus, that bats are not blind, and that we could both get into shape with a convenient stored-under-the-bed home gym for only $39.95 a month for six years. I also watched the *Jungle Book* so many times I know all of Baloo's lines."

"Well, as long as you're learning." Julie flashed him a sly smile.

He stared at her for a long moment. He was so tired he was seeing weird blurs of light around her, as if she were in a flashback sequence in a television soap opera. He blinked his eyes a couple of times to clear them but it didn't work.

"How did you sleep? Did I make too much noise?" Jack's voice was softer now, responding to the tenderness he felt toward her.

"I slept better last night than I have for a long time—and not because you weren't there." She pointed an accusing finger at him to forestall any smart remarks. He raised his hands in mock surrender and smiled back at her.

"Hey, can you take me to the appointment? I'm not sure I'm in any condition to drive."

Actually, I am sure I'm not in any condition to drive, he thought as he watched Bear pad down the stairs shrouded in another blurry cloud of light.

"Yeah, I kind of figured. I already called and left a message saying I would be late."

"You know, you could take the whole day off." Jack eyed her and wriggled his eyebrows wolfishly.

"Why? So I could hang out here all day after you pass out?" Her tone of voice was as teasing as his facial expression had been. "I'm going to go take a shower. Let me know when you're ready to go."

Jack rested on the examination table, unable to remember the last time he had been awake for over twenty-four hours. He'd never been one to pull all-nighters, not even in his college partying days, and his mind was fuzzy and starting to play tricks with him. The blurry glow he had seen around Julie earlier had spread to everything he looked at.

The technician was in the corner of the room, fussing with some kind of machine with the same kind of graph paper chart lie detector tests had in the movies. She had just finished sticking little white electrode things all over his head with glue that reminded him of honey.

When he commented on the sticky substance, she explained how grateful he should be to have hair short enough it would wash out easily. He realized she was probably going to be the one who took the things off too, so he decided be nice to her, lest she take large chunks of skin off with them.

Turning his head to the side, he watched her fiddle with the equipment. She was a middle-aged woman, with richly dark skin, who exuded energy from her oversized frame. Jack had found himself comfortable in her presence almost instantly.

He blinked his eyes trying to clear them. She was surrounded by a diffuse greenish-colored haze he attributed to her green scrubs, but the colors of the haze and her uniform were different.

Sighing heavily, he reached up and rubbed his eyes for the umpteenth time. It still didn't improve the blurs in his tired vision.

Once the equipment was ready, the test consisted of little more than listening to clicks and beeps in a set of headphones, and Jack had problems not dozing off. Finally, the she told him to go ahead and take a little nap and he complied almost instantly.

Jack awoke slowly as the technician's voice permeated through the fog of his mind quietly, as if she was used to gently waking sleepers.

"Are you awake now, Mr. Hooper?"

Jack scrunched his eyes shut hard for a moment before opening them to the bright world again. "Yeah," he replied breathily. "I'm awake."

"Good. I'm going to take these off you now, and I didn't want to startle you when I did." As she spoke, she pulled off a sensor near his left temple. She was careful, and other than the hair it pulled, she made it hurt less than a bandage.

"Do you normally deal with people who have migraines?" Jack asked.

"I normally deal with everyone who needs an EEG." She smiled at him gently.

"What I mean is, I have some questions, and I already know what the doctors say, and I would like to hear the opinion of someone who isn't…" Jack looked lost for a moment while he searched for the right word. "Someone who isn't… *restrained* by their professional reputation."

The assistant raised a dark eyebrow into a high arch as she eyed Jack warily. "What does *that* mean?"

"I mean I don't want a textbook answer. Look…" Jack sat up and met her skeptical brown eyes with his own. "What I want is to know if this is normal." Leaving out any reference to a ghostly assailant, he explained about his dream and the pain that was still there even now. She politely listened with a neutral expression on her face.

"See," he finally concluded, "I know that the doctor says this is normal, because it is within the realm of possibilities, but I've never heard of anything like it. Have you?" Jack watched her intently as she mulled over his question. The greenish haze around her seemed to flicker with her thoughts. "And that's another thing. Ever since this morning, I keep seeing weird… auras around everything. You look like you have a greenish glow around you right now. Is that normal? Am I just that tired? God!"

He rolled his eyes up toward Heaven to emphasize the statement.

"I really am that tired." He nodded to her in an absentminded way then put his palms to his eyes again and held them there, trying to force them to not be so tired. "I'm sorry. I shouldn't be bothering you. I know you're not the doctor, I know you're not allowed to give diagnosis, and I know I'm so tired I'm stupid right now. I'm sorry." He dropped his hands from his face.

She met his eyes for a quiet moment before answering. "It's okay. I get a lot of tired people in here." She reached for another of the white things pasted to his head. "When you get home hold a warm wet washcloth on each of these for a minute, it will help get the goop off."

When she finished pulling them off, she wiped off most of the sticky stuff herself, but Jack was still grateful for the advice. They didn't say anything else to each other, and Jack was trying to think of a way to apologize, but he had already done that. Best to leave with a minimum of fuss he decided.

When she said she was done, he carefully slid off the bed, making sure his feet would hold him, and quickly headed for the door.

"Mr. Hooper." The assistant called out behind him and he stopped and faced her. "The office will notify your doctor of the results, probably tomorrow."

"Thank you." He smiled at her and started to turn away when her voice called again, quietly this time.

"Mr. Hooper."

"Yes?" He turned only partially toward her this time.

"Green is what I see when I search for my true self. If you see violet when you search for yourself, then we are seeing the same thing. I've never seen violet before."

Her eyes were so piercing he was afraid to answer.

"Get some sleep, Mr. Hooper."

ELEVEN

Jack stared at his reflection in the bathroom mirror. He *looked* normal. He stared deeply into his own eyes and turned his head from side to side, trying to get different angles. It was the same no matter how he turned. His reflection *was* normal.

He glanced down at himself again warily. His actual body, unlike his reflection, was shrouded in a purplish colored haze.

Nervously, his eyes flicked between his body and the mirror, unable to comprehend the odd glow around his body that didn't reflect in the mirror.

Ever since the conversation at the doctor's office, he had been horrified to see himself surrounded by a violet haze. He had remained silent as Julie took him home, not wanting to panic or seem crazy, but he couldn't help but notice the purple glow all around his own body.

No one else seemed to notice. No one else looked purple to him either. Everyone else looked like the lab technician had; they had soft blurs of color around them, not a bright purple glow!

He managed to keep his cool until Julie had dropped him off at home, but now he thought he might be going insane. Was it the power of suggestion? Just because the lab technician had said she saw violet was he seeing it, too?

It was a strange shimmering thing, like the pools of color floating across a soap bubble, but its edges were indefinite. It just faded away around a foot away from his body. He watched as various hues of violet, purple, and blue flowed and mixed with a life of their own, increasing in speed as he became more distressed.

Seeing himself like this gave him a sickly feeling in his stomach, like when he had wrecked his car when he was sixteen. He knew something was wrong with him now.

He turned on the cold water in the sink and began splashing handfuls of water on his face. Closing the stopper on the drain, he let the sink fill with cold water, being careful to keep his eyes closed and not to look down at himself again. When the sink filled with cold water, he shut the faucet off, held his breath, and stuck his face into the water.

The shocking cold was comforting. He used to do this when he would get bad fevers, or sometimes when he was hung over. It probably wasn't good for him, but it felt good. After much too short of a time, he had to pull his face out for air.

Rivulets of water tickled as they ran from his hair down off the end of his nose. The cold left a stinging sensation on his cheeks. Holding his head over the water in the sink until the water stopped dripping, he took a breath and put his face back in again.

This time he got his head in far enough his forehead bumped the bottom and water covered his ears, plunging him into a peaceful quiet punctuated by the sound of his own heartbeat. He felt a part of himself start to relax even as his heart pounded and his lungs strained for oxygen.

Bear came in to see what he was doing just as he came up for air again.

Jack stared as he noticed the dog was surrounded by colors too. A soft golden haze with pinkish swirls encompassed him as he sat looking up at Jack.

What did this mean? Jack turned back to his own hands and the violet colors he found there. Had he suddenly become psychic? Could he suddenly see auras? He didn't even believe in auras. They were just like tarot cards and palm readers; a bunch of crap made up by people who take advantage of other people's gullibility—weren't they?

His head swam and he had a wave of something like nausea, but not. He was too exhausted. His body was shutting down on him. He patted Bear's head and plodded his way to bed.

Bemusedly, Jack turned in a circle, taking in the living room. It all looked hazy now. Everything had some kind of fuzzy light around it; from the plants and furniture, to Bear sleeping in front of the sliding glass doors. Some things, mostly Bear and the plants, were much brighter and consisted of more colors, but everything glowed.

He drifted over to Julie's five-foot tall slender-leafed palm plant in the corner and looked closely at the leaves. He could make out the 'real' green of each leaf inside of its swirling orange-green aura.

Moving to examine Bear's sleeping form, he concentrated on the colors in the air around the dog. They were the same as before. Pink and gold…swirls? Clouds? No. They were swirling, mixing in and out, and around, and through each other, not quite blending but not really separate either. They were the colors of... faithful? Truthful?

No, that wasn't quite right. Jack couldn't find a word for it, but somehow those colors made him feel safe.

The furniture all had glows too, but much fainter, with less swirling movement going on. They were... white? No, it was more like an off-white color. More... neutral.

That's what color they were, he decided as he wandered over to the couch; neutral. Yes, he felt good about that.

Looking back at the plant, he knew what color it was now. It was plant color. *I wonder why I never noticed that before,* he mused, deciding it must have been too obvious, something he hadn't ever taken the time to notice before.

As he got closer to the couch, he could make out faint outlines in its aura, outlines like shadows of people sitting on the couch. He moved even closer, intent on the nearest one. It was... Julie?

Yes, he was sure now. The shadow was definitely Julie and she was talking. Talking to... Sandy. Telling Sandy how much his sister's ghost story had spooked her.

He couldn't actually make out any words, yet somehow knew what she was saying and whom she was saying it to. He waited and watched, but that was all she did, over and over again, like a record skipping. But it was only there when he tried to see it.

He moved to the other shadow on the couch and saw it was Sandy. She was upset? Embarrassed? She was hissing at Michael. She was mad at him for bringing drugs with him to the party.

Jack remembered this now. This was where Julie and Sandy had been sitting during Julie's birthday party. Sandy had gotten upset about something Michael had done, but Jack hadn't ever known what.

This was too weird!

He reached out to see if he could touch the shadows, but his own violet shrouded hands passed right through them.

Although...

He came closer and tried to touch the shadow again. His own aura reacted to the shadow, as though making an effort to avoid contact with it. He tried again and found he could easily force his aura into the space the shadow occupied, but he could actually feel it resisting the contact.

He studied his hands in wonder. What did the violet color mean? Why did...?

His thought stopped as he watched his hands quickly fade away into nothingness... *I'm dreaming.*

Jack sat up in bed. The afternoon sun lit room, and he was still too tired to focus his eyes properly. Moaning softly, he dropped back onto the pillow and slept again.

Julie was talking to a young blonde woman Jack didn't recognize. It was hard to hear what they were saying, as if they were far away, although he was close enough to touch them. He had to concentrate to understand them.

"I don't know," Julie was saying, "Jack just gets on my nerves or something, I guess. There really isn't anything *wrong* with him."

"Is that what the doctor said?" the blonde-haired woman asked with a smirk on her round face.

"You know what I mean." Julie rolled her eyes. "But no, except for one more test result, he's fine as far as their concerned. I don't know. When I'm here, I feel like... like... I know that he's wonderful, but once I get home and start talking to him—I'm sure that he's doing this kind of stuff just to piss me off."

"Maybe you need a vacation," suggested the blonde.

"No. This is the only place I feel sane."

"That's why you need a vacation."

Jack was confused.

He was in Julie's office. How did he get here? He had been at home.

At the thought, the world swirled away again.

Jack found himself walking through the living room looking at the diffuse colors outlining everything again. Bear was still asleep in the sunbeam streaming through the glass doors. Everything just as it had been before.

Am I dreaming this time? He looked down at his hand. Normal— except his skin was blue. No aura this time, just blue skin.

Yep. I'm dreaming.

He waited, expecting to wake up. When it didn't happen, he mentally shrugged and began walking aimlessly through the house. It was hard to see around the edges of his vision, like a dream sequence on an old television show, but he was able to focus in on anything he wanted to.

Drifting back toward Bear, Jack reached out to pet him. The dog rolled onto its back, showing his belly for petting, but didn't wake up. Jack petted him for a moment, thinking it odd the fur felt perfectly normal.

He decided to go downstairs and instantly found himself standing in the middle of the downstairs living room. The sudden change of scene didn't surprise him; after all, this was a dream. He slowly turned in a circle. Everything appeared just as it did in real life.

Do I always have dreams like this? Why don't I remember them when I wake up?

Something on the shelf caught his attention and instantly he was there holding it. It was a tiny wooden penguin, very poorly carved and hardly recognizable as a penguin. He felt a pang in his heart.

In Junior High School, a girl had given this to him. She had made it in woodshop. He knew she was flirting with him. He hadn't been attracted to her, but he had been too embarrassed to turn it down, so he had kept it. She had been killed in a car accident not long after.

She was the first friend he had ever lost, and it hurt all the more that he hadn't been a good friend in return. He had kept the little wooden penguin. Except...

The penguin was gone. It vanished shortly after Julie moved in.

He felt another pang of guilt. He had secretly accused Julie of getting rid of it for some jealousy reason, although she claimed to have no idea what had happened to it.

Then Jack was standing in the backyard, on the deck. The sunshine was bright, but not warm. The penguin was no longer in his hand. He looked down at the deck and somehow he *knew* the penguin was under it.

How did he know that? *This is silly!* he berated himself. Then he remembered this was a dream. *Strange how you can forget you're dreaming,* he thought.

Now that he realized it was a dream again, everything became sharper. He could see every blade of grass on the lawn. He let his eyes wander up into the sky and remembered the flying dreams he'd had as a child.

Well, he decided, *it's my dream, after all.* He jumped up into the air and soared over the houses.

TWELVE

Standing in the basement living room, Jack eyed the empty place on the shelf where the penguin had once sat.

Unable to shake the otherworldliness of the dreams, he wondered if he should go look under the deck and see if it was there. Part of him insisted it was, as sure as if he had already crawled under the deck and seen it.

But why would it be there?

The sun had set and darkness was engulfing the backyard. The curiosity would have to wait until tomorrow.

He plopped himself down on the couch and reached for the remote control to the television.

Idly wondering where Julie was, he decided she would eventually contact him. It was becoming typical of her not to let him know what she was doing. She probably went back out to the bar with Sandy again, looking for someone who didn't 'get on her nerves'.

Wait a minute… that had been a dream.

He was in enough trouble with her already; there was no way he could get away with holding one of his dreams over her head.

The television remote wasn't working. He got up to go turn on the television by hand, but stopped halfway to the set.

The room was bathed in the blue light normally cast by the television, which was definitely off. Where was the light coming from?

A faint sound caught his attention and he cocked his head, listening. Someone was crying. A child. The cries were small and far away, but they gave him the chills, and he shuddered involuntarily.

He noticed a reddish glow from the spare bedroom and realized that was where the crying came from.

A sense of dread and fear descended upon him, but he forced himself to move toward the bedroom. His legs moved jerkily, as if they were afraid of the room and didn't want to go there.

He peeked through the doorway, searching for the source of the red glow. It was like a cloud slowly seeping into the house from the window and suffusing into the room. A horrible, evil, red cloud. It flickered where it met the blue light, making small white and silver sparks as it consumed the blue.

The blue light filling the rooms emanated from the closet.

Jack's heart began to thud in his chest. He *knew* the red glow was consuming the blue light, feeding off it, destroying it.

With horror, he watched it swirl with the colors of scarlet, crimson, red, and ...blood. It steadily devoured the blue light, working its way toward the closet.

He wanted to run, to hide, get as far away as he could, but he felt a deep need to know where the blue light was coming from. Unable to fight the compulsion, he clumsily forced himself farther into the room.

The closet doors were closed, but the light came through as though they were transparent. In the center of the blue light, he could discern the outline of its source—a shadow, like the ones he had seen on the couch, but much stronger. The shadow was the source of the glow and he could tell she was a little girl, not more than eight or nine.

Rocking herself and crying, she wanted her mother but was too afraid to call out. She just kept rocking and sobbing, and the red glow crept closer and closer.

Jack felt his throat constricting. He had to help her. He had to do something. His chest heaving with fear, he tried to move, but couldn't. He couldn't even look away as the red glow flowed into the closet and caressed the little shadow.

It was bad. What he was looking at was bad. It was evil. Hate. Destruction.

Malevolence emanated from it as it slowly drank up the blue light, feeding off the life force of the little girl, lapping at it leisurely, as if she were only an appetizer.

And she was. It would be coming for him next. He was the main course.

The red fog began to spread across the room toward him.

He tried to run, but he couldn't move. It didn't matter. It would find him. He couldn't escape. Resignation began setting in. He was going to die.

The crying grew weaker. The little girl was being consumed and her blue light was all but gone.

That was why it was coming for him next.

Everything was hopeless. He couldn't help the little girl, he couldn't help himself, he couldn't even move. He was going to die. The evil was going to devour his life force.

"No," he finally was able to murmur. The sound escaping his lips gave him more strength and he was able to say it again, with more force. "No."

He managed to shake his head with more force as he said it again and again. "No. No. No! NO!"

"NO!" Jack yelled and sat up in bed. Covered in a cold sweat, he could still hear the echo of his own voice. Bear came running into the room and jumped up onto the bed without waiting for permission. The dog licked at his face while Jack tried to clear away the fog obscuring his consciousness.

"Okay. Okay!" Jack threw up his hands to block the dog's tongue. Bear deftly snaked his head around Jack's arms and scored more licks as Jack fell backward and rolled over to bury his face in the pillow.

Although it spared his face, it left his ears exposed and Bear attacked them like they were covered with barbeque sauce. Jack rolled again and found the dog sitting on his chest panting gleefully.

"Now you're in for it!" he growled as he tried to catch the dog in a headlock. The two of them tumbled off the bed and landed on the floor with a resounding thump. Jack let out a startled "Oomph" and Bear backed off just long enough to make sure he was okay and then launched another tongue attack.

After wrestling with Bear, Jack's fear and tension had faded, but, as he stood in front of the bathroom mirror and brushed his teeth, he looked himself in the eyes and was worried about his sanity. There was no violet glow around him now. Had there ever been? Was that part of the weird dreams too?

He had never had dreams like those before. They were so... real. His memories of them were as clear as any he had, in fact clearer than most. He couldn't remember any details about driving to the doctor's office with Julie this very morning, only that they had done it. He couldn't remember most of the day in the emergency room yesterday, only that it was long, boring, and full of florescent lighting. But his memory of standing in the middle of his living room, with everything around him glowing with its own light, was so vivid that he was sure he could pick out which leaf he had been examining on the palm plant.

Worst of all, the sobbing from a little girl he couldn't help still echoed in his ears.

Scratching at his mussed up hair, his fingers came away with goopy adhesive left over from the EEG test. He went back and checked his pillowcase. There were yellowish smears on the fabric.

He took the pillowcase off and plodded toward the laundry room. Halfway down the stairs, a sense of unease came over him. The memory of the red glow swallowing up the room was still fresh in his mind.

Finding himself holding his breath, he realized he was straining for the slightest hint of a child crying in agony. But there was only silence.

Forcing himself down the stairs, his confidence increased as he went farther without any sign of a glow. He tossed the pillowcase into the clothes hamper and pulled a clean one out of the closet, stopping to grab an armload of clean clothes to take back upstairs.

The entire time he was downstairs, he couldn't bring himself to look into the spare bedroom.

As he put away clothes, he began to get angry. *What's wrong with me?* He wondered.

He had done his best to ignore and discount the nightmares, but they were growing steadily worse. Maybe he had freaked himself out with a few nightmares and the fear had been self-perpetuating into new nightmares.

Jack almost sighed with relief as he realized there was a rational explanation. He felt a tension leave his shoulders, he wasn't insane. He was just having nightmares.

As if on cue, his head throbbed a hollow pain in that same empty place he had gone to sees the doctor about. Nightmares didn't explain the pain he still had.

Was it possible just *dreaming* he had been attacked had created a real pain? The more he thought about it, the more he realized people laid many claims to the ability of the mind over the body. Fakirs fire-walked and laid on beds of nails, Yogis folded themselves into airtight boxes and hibernated for days, and glass eaters, and sword swallowers, and who knew what else. It was on television all the time.

It seemed so obvious now.

Somehow, he had let his own mind affect him the wrong way, and it was making him jump at shadows.

He felt better. He knew what was wrong. Now all he needed was to know how to fix it.

THIRTEEN

Julie came home to find Jack staring at the computer. She tried to engage him in conversation, but he was too distracted to pay attention to her. When she asked if the doctor's office had called with the test results, he just grunted "no" at her. She tried talking to him about what he was doing, but that didn't work either. He was on the Internet, and she saw something on the screen about dreams, but when she had asked what he was doing, he had gotten weird.

At least Bear was happy to see her, having met her at the door with the usual amount of unbridled enthusiasm.

Fine, she decided. He could spend all night making love to the computer if he wanted. At least he wouldn't be doing other things to irritate her. She had made more than enough of an effort to talk to him. Whatever was wrong now wasn't her fault.

She went into the kitchen to find something to eat. Disappointed Jack hadn't made any dinner or had leftovers from lunch, she went for the old standby, baby carrots and ranch dressing, while she rummaged for something more substantial. She gave up in disgust and decided to go down to the storage area in the laundry room and get some spaghetti.

The wholesale membership club thing was a great way to get things cheaper, but their small kitchen meant they had to store the excess stuff downstairs.

At the top of the stairs, she hesitated before pushing herself onward. She grew angrier as she went down the stairs. It was Jack's fault she was afraid. If he and his sister hadn't been joking about ghosts, the stupid idea never would have crossed her mind.

Maybe that's why she didn't like being home. And maybe that's why Jack irritated her so much. Maybe he had spooked her so badly with that stupid idea that subconsciously she was always afraid of the house, not just at moments like this when she was directly confronting her fear of non-existent ghosts.

Would that account for why there hadn't been any problems between her and Jack when they had gone out for dinner? Maybe she wasn't really mad at Jack. Maybe she was just stressed out, without knowing why, and with no direction to vent it except toward Jack.

Deep in reflection, she had hardly noticed grabbing the spaghetti package from the pantry and heading back to the stairs. She stopped in the middle of the den. It didn't look so bad. It wasn't so spooky.

I can get over this, she told herself. *There is nothing to be afraid of here. Now if only I could stop having those stupid nightmares. Especially the one with the little girl crying in the spare bedroom.*

Julie shuddered at the thought. It was just so weird, and she hated how it always ended with her fainting when she touched that weird red cloud.

Jack leaned back from the computer screen and stretched his arms up into the air. He could hear Julie doing something in the kitchen as he arched his back and rubbed his eyes. He was surprised he had been on the Internet for over three hours. There was so much information to be had, but so much of it was childish, trying to be cute, or just flat out misleading.

He had skimmed through a dozen websites and had been disappointed at how many of them all plagiarized from the same place. Not that it mattered. After reading three completely different interpretations about how auras looked and what the colors meant, he was pretty sure that either what he had seen had not been 'auras' per se, or whoever had written about them hadn't ever seen them. He had given up pretty quickly on that one.

However, he had been very happy with what he had found out about dreams. At least one website tried to be professional and scientific, rather than the mumbo-jumbo hoopla he found most everywhere else. Based on their information, he had come to the conclusion that what had been happening to him was called a 'lucid dream' and that many people actually found them desirable. According to their literature, he should be able to learn to control the dreams. In fact, they offered numerous helpful hints and even some electronic gadgets that were supposed to induce the dreams.

A month ago, no—a week ago, he would have found the website quaint, at best the hobby of well-educated new age hippies or something, but right now he was grateful for their efforts allowing him a little peace of mind. He wasn't going insane. He was just having problems telling his dreams from reality. He was going to be just fine.

Their information said a 'lucid dream' was one wherein the dreamer had lucidity, or being aware of what was going on in the dream. This was an idea that had never occurred to Jack before. Up until now, his dreams had been kind of like watching a movie filmed from the first person point of view. At least the ones he remembered anyway.

He had always been *involved* in his dreams, doing things and waking up happy or sad or whatever, but these 'lucid dreams' were the first time he could remember thinking to himself during a dream. He had been making conscious choices, instead of the usual way of blindly going through the dream accepting whatever weirdness was happening.

Apparently some people have so many lucid dreams they began to get confused about whether or not they were dreaming. This was an often enough occurrence the website had listed ways to check if you were awake or dreaming, and they seemed to make some sense.

He got up and headed for the kitchen to talk to Julie. He owed her an apology. When she had come home, he had been busy trying, in a very real way, to preserve his sanity.

Jack felt better now, better than he had in a long time, aside from being a little tired from lack of sleep and the strange pain in his brain reminiscent of a pulled tooth's dry socket.

Julie was stirring spaghetti sauce on the range top when Jack came up behind her, put his arms around her waist, and nuzzled her neck. He felt her tense up and stiffen, but he ignored it and whispered gently into her ear.

"I'm sorry." He kissed her earlobe gently. She ignored him. He felt the warmth of her back pressed against his chest and he pulled her close and began slowly swaying back and forth in time to imaginary music, pulling her side to side with him as he went, willing her to dance with him.

"What are you doing?" Her voice was flat.

He kept his voice soft and continued to sway, although she had started actively resisting the motion. "I'm trying to express my love and affection for you, you wondrously loving, gentle, and forgiving wife, you."

She pulled away and twisted to look back over her shoulder at him. "If you're horny, you'd be better off by yourself after ignoring me like that."

Jack gave up and pulled away from her, leaning up against the counter next to the sink. "I'm not horny... although now that you mention it, I really enjoyed last night." He waggled his eyebrows and grinned.

It didn't faze her in the slightest. "I'm glad that you did, and hope that you hold the memory dear, as it will probably be a long time before it happens again."

Jack sighed. "I just wanted to apologize and spend some time with you." When she didn't say anything, he looked over her shoulder at the sauce she was stirring. "Is there enough for two?"

"Hrmmph."

"Look, I really am sorry. I was looking up stuff on the internet because I've been worried about myself, and I didn't feel like the doctors addressed the issues that had me the most worried."

She turned to look at him now, her gaze still level and unreadable, so he continued, hoping he was making progress.

"It's kind of scary, you know?" His voice dropped in volume as his emotions started to show through. "It got even worse today after I got home from the appointment."

With that, Julie finally turned all the way to the side to look at him, one hand still idly stirring the sauce on the stove, all but forgotten. "You had another stroke, or whatever it was?"

Jack had almost forgotten about that, and it had been his whole reason for going to the doctor. A startled laugh found its way out as he realized he had been so worried about being insane he had forgotten there could be a valid medical problem to deal with. Although he now thought it was possible the pain, which throbbed in acknowledgment of being mentioned, was illusory, caused solely by the dreams and left over like an afterimage in the eyes from a flashbulb. It could be only as real as his memory of it.

"You think that this is funny?" Julie's voice showed she was dangerously close to a total meltdown and her patience was gone. She pointed the plastic spatula at his chest, sauce dripping from it like a bloody murder weapon.

"No, I don't!" he said quickly. "Look… I didn't tell you the whole story." Julie's eyes narrowed and he knew he was treading in deep water. "Remember I told you I dreamed about the pain in my head?"

No answer.

"I didn't want to say anything, because it sounds totally stupid, but I think that I've got it figured out now, so I can tell you the whole story, okay?" He learned forward and used his eyes to prod her for an answer this time. "Will you at least let me tell you what happened?"

Reluctantly, Julie broke her silence with a mumble and a nod of the head. The action seemed to remind her she was holding a dripping spatula and she turned around and stuck it in the sauce, then grabbed some paper towels to clean the sauce off the floor.

"Okay," Jack said, glad for the reprieve. "I think it started with that stupid thing my sister said about ghosts, remember?"

Julie froze with her eyes locked on him. "I do *not* need to hear any more ghost stories!" She stood up quickly and turned away from him to throw away the dirty paper towels.

"It was just some stupid nightmares."

"It's not funny, Jack. I mean it."

"Okay." His hands went up in the defensive position again. "Okay. I just wanted to try to explain."

She turned her back on him and stirred the sauce with gusto. Jack chose not to continue the conversation.

Julie lay in bed listening to Jack's soft snoring. She hadn't been able to sleep a wink so far. *Damn him! Just when I think I can deal with this stupid ghost thing, he has to go and bring it up again. The same damned day even!* She was fuming and afraid of ghosts at the same time.

She had no idea which one was worse. Whichever one was fading out at any given moment was quickly and equally replaced by the other. At this particular moment, she was more angry than scared. She decided she preferred the anger. It was a much warmer emotion. It kept her company much better than the fear did.

Unfortunately, it was harder to hold on to than the fear. The fear seemed to perpetuate itself without any help at all, and why not, anything not helping the anger helped fuel the fear. She had to work to keep the anger going. Maybe that was why she liked it better. It gave her something to do.

This time she focused on Jack's snoring to help feed her anger. It wasn't working, as he was only snoring a little, and even that was pretty quiet.

Damn it! she thought, trying to be upset he wasn't snoring enough to help her stay angry.

Finally, she reached over and stuck a finger in his ribs.

"Huh!" Jack sat up straight with a start, looking around wildly, his hair sticking out in odd directions.

"You were snoring again." Julie told him. It was hard to keep a flat tone of voice; she almost burst out laughing at the look on his face.

"Oh…" he breathed and slumped back onto the pillow.

Unbidden, a grin slid across her face in a contorted wave as she fought to suppress it.

Well, she thought, *that didn't work. I'm not angry at all anymore. I'll have to remember to use it next time I'm not scared.*

FOURTEEN

Jack sat in his cubical with his chin on his hands and his elbows on the desk, staring at the computer monitor. He had stopped paying any attention to what was on the screen long time ago, and instead had been playing with the afterimages the white letters left on his retina.

A website had said to see an aura all you had to do was stare at something long enough, preferably in front of a solid background. Obviously, whoever had written the page expected people to be more gullible than he was. It was nothing more than an after image on his retina.

Sitting up, he stretched his back. It had been a long morning. He had absolutely nothing to do, and other than the doctor's office calling to tell him his tests were completely normal, nothing had happened at all.

Charlie hadn't come in today, so he had no one to commiserate with. He hadn't spoken with Heidi Clark, although she had surprised him when she smiled a greeting at him. He had expected a hefty butt chewing. The board in the break room showed his name at the bottom of the rotation again for calling in sick the last two days.

Pleasantly surprised to see he had lost track of time, he decided to take himself out to lunch at a favorite spot. It was a little out of the way, and a little pricey, but the gourmet pizza was wonderful.

He had his hand on the push handle of the back door when he felt a resounding slap on the back. He knew what the words would be before they were spoken.

"How's it hangin', Jackie-boy?"

The 'Jackie-boy' thing he could take, but he hated the surprise slaps on the back. As he turned to glare at Stanley, the testosterone rush that made him want to punch the man in the face faded.

Stanley's voice usually carried all though the office, loud, boisterous, and thick. Jack's mental picture of Stanley was the high-school punk jock he had always hated so much, the one who shut skinny kinds in lockers for no reason at all or put ointment in someone else's jockstrap for a laugh. Looking at him now, Jack was surprised he had forgotten just how big Stanley was.

Easily a football player, more likely a pro wrestler, Stanley was only six foot tall or so, but he had the barrel chest of an ox and the arms and legs to go with it. His suit clung to his body oddly as most men weren't built like that. He wore his hair in a crew cut, squared off on the sides and top. It nicely complemented his square face, which Jack privately thought might be steroid induced. He was darkly tanned for his bodybuilding exhibitions, which he never tired of, yet never did very well in. Of course, the girls never cared whether or not he won, and that, Jack suspected, was the whole point—unless narcissism counted.

Jack changed his mind about directly showing attitude toward Stanley, and smiled instead. "How are you today, Stanley? Sales doing all right?"

A smile flashed across Stanley's perfect set of teeth, contrasting with his bronzed face. "Higher than ever. Looks like you're having problems though. What's this I heard about you trying to sneak an incoming call ten minutes late? I didn't think you did that kind of thing, Jackie-boy. All this time you had me thinking you were damn near a boy scout, and now I hear you're a sneaky bastard." Stanley's grin turned malicious and he waved a thick stubby finger at Jack. "Don't ever let me catch you near my customer files, or I'll give you more than just two days suspension and probation."

Jack returned Stanley's smile but he was sure he could never match the spitefulness it contained. "Don't worry. I don't want any of your clients."

"Maybe, maybe not." Stanley pushed his way past Jack and out the door before he stopped and turned back. "By the way, no hard feelings about the Redimont account, huh? I guess they know the better deal when they see it." Stanley didn't even try to hide his smirk as he turned and walked away.

Jack got a sick feeling in the pit of his stomach. Redimont was Jack's biggest and best customer, if he had lost them somehow…

Jack was in Heidi Clark's office before he even realized he was going to go there. As she looked up from the paperwork on her desk, he realized he had no idea what to say.

"Yes, Jack?" she drawled politely.

"Uh… what happened with Redimont?" He felt stupid as soon as he had asked the question. Not only would she not understand the question until after he explained himself, but she probably had no idea what had happened anyway.

"Oh, that," she answered casually. "I forgot that you weren't here and didn't know." She smiled apologetically. "I have already called them and asked why they wanted to switch sales representatives. They gave the usual song and dance about wanting someone who shows a fresh interest in their needs."

Jack didn't even raise an eyebrow. He knew perfectly well this meant one of the other sales reps had gone around him and offered them a better deal. "I suppose that they requested Stanley by name?" It was more a statement than a question.

"Of course. You want to make sure that you get the person who is willing to take a cut in commission in order to gain your business, now don't you?"

Jack felt angry and empty at the same time. First, he has all these problems with Julie, then he has nightmares that hurt his brain, then he gets in trouble at work, now this. What else could go wrong?

He snapped out at Heidi in a momentary fit of frustration.

"By the way," he said with a sneer in his voice, as he turned to leave at the same time, "I just wanted to thank you for telling the whole office that I was suspended for trying to steal phone calls. It was bad enough being accused, but to have everyone told I did it is just peachy!" He shut the door behind him, just a little too hard, before Heidi had a chance to respond.

Well, that was childish of me, he thought as he headed for lunch.

Aww, screw it. He slammed the back door, too.

Jack didn't go to pizza place for lunch. He didn't eat lunch at all. Instead, he went to an office park a few miles to the south to calm down. It really was a park, about a half-mile long, built around a stream flowing through three different ponds. The whole thing was a courtyard for the office buildings surrounding it.

He often wished he could find a job in one of the offices around the park. How nice it would be to just step right outside of the office and spend your lunch reading a book next to the babbling brook. Maybe eat your lunch under the giant pine tree on the hill above the second pond. Of course, it would be even better in the summertime. Now it was crisp and cool with the threat of a frost in the air.

Sitting on a nice park bench, the kind with comfortably curved seats and backs, Jack faced out toward the second pond. He had brought Julie here on their second date. They had walked along the path in the light of a full moon.

Now, in the diffuse light of the overcast sun, it was not hard to imagine he was again looking at the pond in the moonlight. Silvery with mild ripples from the stream flowing into it over a foot high waterfall, the pond had an almost surrealistic appearance. It had been perfect.

That had been their first kiss. Real kiss, that is. The first little peck on the cheek goodnight from their first date didn't count.

She was a good kisser, and had left him weak in the knees. The thought had crossed his mind that she didn't just kiss; she made love with her lips. He remembered staring at the pond and feeling drunk, although he hadn't had any alcohol.

How long had it been since she had kissed him like that? Probably about as long as it had been since he had taken her somewhere romantic he thought.

Jack realized he had been staring at the pond a long time. Looking at his watch to see how much time he had left, he was startled to see a violet glow around his hand.

Excitement and nervousness rose in his gut. Was it real this time, or was he dreaming? Everywhere, the world had subtly shaded auras. The trees were lightly shrouded in green and orange hues; the grass was the same, but fainter.

Jack wondered if it was because the grass was browning and going dormant for the winter.

The water flowing through the brook had a magical blue glow to it, as though someone had made the stream out of blue neon lights. Looking up into the sky, afraid it would be orange or red like a science fiction movie about another planet, he found it completely normal.

He examined the purple aura around his hands again. What did it mean? He felt like he should know. Somehow he *knew* the water was the right color, and so were the trees, and the grass, and even the sky, but he didn't understand why his color was violet. Was violet the wrong color for him? Just because he knew when things were the 'right' color, did that mean he would know when something was the 'wrong' color?

What color am I?

His watch beeped, indicating he was late going back to work. He looked at the watch out of force of habit. His hand was no longer surrounded by violet. All the trees and the grass and the water were normal.

I was dreaming again, he thought. *I must have dozed off, and started dreaming.*

It was so real.

Of course, that's why the website had those things to test whether or not you're dreaming. It hadn't occurred to him to try one. Angry with himself for not realizing he had been dreaming, he left the bench and headed back to work.

Arriving back at work, Jack found a yellow sticky note on his computer screen asking him to meet with Heidi. Sheepish after losing his temper, he meekly entered her office and quietly took a seat.

Heidi got up and closed the door quietly before returning to her desk. She organized the papers she had been working on, put them aside, and then spoke with a voice so quiet Jack had to lean forward to catch every word.

"I did not tell anyone in the office you were suspended. I did not tell anyone you were placed on probation, and I most certainly did not tell anyone why. The only thing I did was move your name back to the bottom of the call list each day you didn't show up." Her eyes were piercing and cold. "The incident was logged into the personnel files, as per protocol. That is where it ended. I do not spread rumors about my employees, no matter how true or deserved they are, and I would thank you very much not to make any more such accusations."

Jack began apologize, but Heidi wasn't done speaking.

"You have acted in a manner that I would have thought very out of character for you if I had seen it last month. However, I have seen it quite a bit lately, and I am beginning to believe that I have made a mistake in judging your character. I won't bother to ask you for an apology, however, if your malcontent attitude persists, I will be forced to take disciplinary action." She turned away from him and back to her pile of papers. "That is all. You may return to work now."

Jack felt put in his place. He deserved her chastising, and probably more. He stood slowly and began slinking toward the door when a thought occurred to him.

"Ms. Clark?" he ventured carefully.

After a moment, she paused in her paperwork, but did not deem to speak.

"I, uh…" He cleared his throat.

She took over in his hesitation, tired of the routine. "I told you no apologies. Now, go back to work."

"I wasn't…" He stammered before composing himself. "I wasn't going to apologize, although you certainly deserve one. I wanted to ask you a question." He waited but she didn't look up again. "If you didn't tell anyone why I was put on probation, and I didn't tell anyone, then how does Stanley know?"

FIFTEEN

Jack fumed as he left Heidi's office, carefully avoiding the eyes of the other workers. He heard one of them whisper a speculation he must have been fired. He didn't bother to correct her. It irked him that Heidi didn't care Stanley had stolen his best customer *and* knew things he shouldn't.

All right, he admitted to himself, he hadn't exactly been nice and polite, and when he got in trouble, the first thing he had done had been to take two days off which surely hadn't helped matters at all. Nonetheless, he had just offered what he thought was good evidence that Stanley was up to no good. After all, Stanley knew why Jack been in trouble without anyone telling him, right? That meant Stanley was, at the very least, getting into personnel files.

On top of which, Jack knew that call had come in before five, and Stanley knew Jack was in trouble for taking a call after five….

Aw, hell, Heidi is right, he thought, giving up on the idea. There was nowhere near enough reason to suspect Stanley. Not to mention Jack had been in her office to complain about Stanley stealing away a client right before he accused him. That made Jack an unreliable source of what Stanley had and hadn't said.

He rounded the corner and found Charlie had come in for the afternoon. He was talking intently on the phone, while an older woman paced nervously behind him. She had a very bright white aura around her.

Jack shook his head in frustration. It must be something wrong with his eyes or his head, because he wasn't dreaming now. He stopped and checked his watch just to be sure. The hands indicated it was 1:35. He looked at the white intensity surrounding the woman, then back at his watch. It hadn't changed. He tried it a third time. It was still 1:35.

The webpage about lucid dreaming said that if you were dreaming, watches, newspapers, signs, or whatever you could read would keep changing as you read the same thing over again, sometimes even while you were looking at it.

Well, his watch definitely was staying the same, so he must not be dreaming.

He sighed and made his way past Charlie and the gray haired woman. As he moved by, the woman watched him, her eyes pleading, imploring for help as her hands tightly squeezed an old-fashioned style handbag held up in front of her chest. She was obviously distressed. He stopped and turned to her.

"Are you okay?"

"Oh!" She shook her head very agitatedly and waved a hand wildly in frustration at Charlie's turned back. "I really have to go! I'm so late! I just needed to tell Charlie that I put everything in the top of the closet when I had company last month!" She motioned quickly at Charlie, who remained extremely intent on his telephone conversation, and hadn't noticed she was here.

"If you're late, why don't you go ahead and go. I can tell him when he gets off of the phone." Jack smiled at her reassuringly.

"Oh! You are *such* a dear! Would you?" She clapped her hands together excitedly around the handbag as the eagerness spread from her eyes to her whole body. He half expected her to hop up and down in place like a little girl.

"Of course." Jack gave her the most reassuring smile he could muster. "Anything else I can do?"

"Just tell him that I love him!" She grinned delightedly, already hurrying away. Jack grinned at her as she turned back and waved vigorously at him before turning the corner.

He watched after her for a moment, and realized he felt better inside. There was more to life than petty squabbles with co-workers and problems on the job. There was family, and friends, and all the good little things about them. Things like having your mother stop off to see you at work. At least he assumed she was Charlie's mother.

He thought of his own mom, and realized it had been a long time since he had called her. *I should do that tonight,* he decided as he sat down at his desk.

He reached up and pulled down the yellow sticky note telling him to go see Heidi, and turned on his computer. He was considering calling Redimont when he heard Charlie stop talking and hang up the telephone.

He stood up and put his head over the cubical wall.

"Hey, Buddy!" Charlie jumped, but Jack ignored it. "I didn't figure to see you today. I thought you were sick."

Charlie shook his head. Something obviously was bothering him and he didn't look to be in the mood for jovial conversation.

"Anyway," Jack went on after Charlie failed to respond, "there was a lady here for you while you were on the phone, I think it was your mom, but she was in a hurry so she wanted me to tell you that she 'put everything in the top of the closet when she had company last month.' " Jack used his fingers to emphasize quotes as he repeated the message.

Charlie's face went white. His lip trembled just a little as he stared sickly back at Jack.

"Are you okay? You look like your gonna puke." Jack walked around the wall and into Charlie's cubicle. "You sure you're not sick?"

Charlie tried to speak, but he choked. He cleared his throat and tried again. "Who came to see me?"

"I think it was your mom. She said to tell you she loves you." Charlie stared at him blankly. Jack held his hand up in the air. "About this tall, short curly white hair, flowery pink and blue dress, old fashioned handbag. Sound familiar?"

Charlie was shaking like a leaf. "What the fuck, Jack?"

"What?"

"Fuck you." Charlie's voice trailed into a horse whisper as he shakily began gathering up things from his desk and putting them into his briefcase.

One of them caught his eye. It was a funeral announcement, and the woman in the photograph was the same woman he had just seen.

"Hey," Jack's voice went hoarse and the hair on the back of his neck started to rise. "I'm sorry. I didn't know. I was just guessing it was your mom. Maybe it was your aunt or somebody."

"Fuck off!"

Jack felt the hair on his arms continue to prickle as he stepped away to give Charlie space.

Could that really have been Charlie's mother?

Charlie slammed a drawer shut and stormed away. Jack felt sick to his stomach. He didn't want Charlie to leave thinking he had done that on purpose. He started fallowing just in time to see Charlie going out the back door.

He hurried catch up, hoping he could convince Charlie he hadn't been teasing.

He was halfway to the door when Trish stopped him.

"That was really cold, Jack. I can't believe you did that!"

"I didn't! I—"

"I heard you do it!" Her face was as hard as stone as she turned and walked away.

"Nice goin', Jackie-boy!" Jack whirled at the painful slap of Stanley's hand in the middle of his back. "Not only did you piss off the only dweeb in the whole office who liked you," he whispered harshly into Jack's ear, "but you just ruined any chance you had of ever doin' the only really good looking chick in the whole building! Guess there's no point in you signing the sympathy card they're passing around the office, now is there?"

Jack fumed. His eyes burned hate at Stanley, who calmly ignored it.

"I have to admit though," Stanley put a smirk on his face, "*I* thought it was funny!"

Jack fought down the rage, looking over his shoulder at the back door. There was no way he could catch up with Charlie now. He turned back to Stanley and gritted his teeth.

"You're an asshole," he finally blurted out.

"You're a loser."

"At least I don't steal other people's clients!"

Stanley smirk stretched wide. "Are you accusing me of stealing?"

"Why not?" Jack growled, his anger boiling. "I know you've intimidated Charlie into giving you some of his clients. Who else have you done that to? Huh? Why not just steal some while you're at it? Can't do it on your own, might as well take someone else's!"

Stanley's face reddened and he growled as his giant fist reached for Jack. "You little…"

"Bring it on!" Jack tensed.

"THAT IS ENOUGH!"

They both whirled to find Heidi standing rigid with her hands on her hips.

"You two will go to my office immediately. If you cannot do so civilly, I will call Security to escort you out." Her voice left no room for anything other than obedience.

Jack felt his face flush. Most of the office workers were surrounding them, staring with their mouths agape. His shoulders slumped. He would probably get fired now.

He resignedly made his way to her office, followed by Stanley, who took the time to share a few jeering faces and words with a couple of his office buddies.

Dropping into a chair in Heidi's office, Jack found himself looking at a picture of her with her daughter and granddaughter.

She doesn't deserve this, he thought, remembering the warm family feeling he'd had just a few minutes ago.

Had that really been Charlie's mother? Had he dreamed it? Stanley had said there was a sympathy card being passed around for everyone to sign. Had he seen it, subconsciously realized what it was, and incorporated it into one of his lucid dreams?

Heidi walked in and shut the door with a quiet click that somehow filled the room ominously.

"Miss Clark, I can explain everything." Stanley's voice was smooth as silk, just like all the sales representatives. It made Jack grimace.

"Not yet." Heidi sat down. "First, we are all going to sit here quietly for the next five minutes and make sure our tempers are gone."

"But—" Stanley tried again but was interrupted by Heidi's hand in a gesture Jack felt he was getting to know all too well.

They sat in silence and Jack contributed by internally chastising himself while he looked anywhere but at Stanley or Heidi. Don't give her any crap, he reminded himself. She doesn't deserve it.

Besides, this time he had done it to himself. He never should have lost his temper, never should have confronted Stanley. He felt the anger drain out of him and a quiet sense of peace flowed over him as he resigned himself to whatever Heidi decided to do. She probably wasn't going to fire them, or she would have called Security right from the start. Or maybe that was why they were sitting here quietly for five minutes. Maybe she was waiting for them to arrive. He thought that would be justified and settled in to wait for them.

"Well now." Heidi finally put aside her paperwork after ten minutes. "I hope that was long enough."

It had been long enough for Jack. He was sleepy and his mind had wondered off on several tangents. He met her gaze, unsurprised when he saw an aura. He was starting to get used to it.

Heidi was bathed in a light yellow aura with lighter blue swirls drifting through it. Her aura didn't stretch out nearly as far as the one around the person he thought had been Charlie's mom. It wasn't nearly as bright either. Maybe he was getting better.

Stanley's aura was an angry red and an ugly brown. It repulsed Jack, reminding him of nasty, smelly water with junk slowly floating around in it. He turned away so he didn't have to see it anymore.

"Who wants to go first?" Heidi's accent was polite and calm.

"It was my fault," Jack admitted.

"Damn straight!" Stanley blurted out.

Heidi gave a narrow gaze and Stanley sunk back into his chair. She turned back to Jack. "Anything else you want to add?"

Jack shrugged, watching the swirls in her aura circle around lazily.

Finally, she turned her attention back to Stanley. "You said you could explain. Now is your chance."

Stanley looked at Jack crosswise and cleared his throat. "I was just telling Jack how awful that prank he played on poor Charlie was."

Jack started look away when he noticed the swirls in Stanley's aura begin to agitate. As he watched Stanley talk, the browns deepened toward black spots and the reds became… angrier. He watched intently as Stanley gave his own account of their conversation. The colors darkened and sickened each time it was different from Jack's recollection. Suddenly Jack realized what it was. *He's lying!*

"Jack! You already had your chance," Heidi admonished.

Jack sat back up and blinked. He hadn't realized he had spoken aloud. He must have lapsed further into this dream than previously.

Stanley gave him an angelic expression, but his eyes sparked mischievously and his aura pulsed with an angry laughter. It reminded Jack of his dream about the glow in the basement. That must have been some sort of an aura too.

As he made the connection, his dislike for Stanley grew. Stanley's aura was full of bad colors. No, not colors exactly. They were colors, but as he watched them, he began to discern they were more. They were anger, and hate, jealousy and spite, and dishonesty, and insecurity, all rolled up to comprise his entire personality.

Jack almost laughed. He'd always thought Stanley was shallow, but this was horrible.

Stanley must have sensed of Jack's amusement as he stopped talking and glared at him. "What are you staring at?" he demanded.

Jack started to say 'your aura', but decided that wouldn't go over well, so he changed it to "Your lies."

"My lies are just as true as yours."

Jack did laugh now. "That would be true, but I haven't told any yet."

"Says you."

"Gentlemen…," Heidi cautioned.

Jack held his hand up to forestall her for once and maintained eye contact with Stanley. "As long as we're going to tell lies, why don't you tell us a made up story about how you set me up to look like I took a call after five when I didn't?"

That did it. Stanley's aura contracted in on itself and Jack knew he had hit a surprise blow.

"Jack!" Heidi exclaimed in shock.

"I don't know what you are talking about." Lie.

"How did you steal my client?"

"They called me!" Lie.

"How did…"

"JACK!" Heidi interrupted as she and Stanley stood up at the same time.

"I don't have to take this shit!" Stanley shoved Jack in the chest.

The physical contact was all it took. Jack had enough of Stanley's slaps in the back, his picking on Charlie, and his lies. Fire burned in Jack's belly as he stood with a slow, angry determination, looking Stanley in the eyes.

"You sit back down in that chair and shut up." He pointed at the chair, his voice ominously commanding obedience, his stare unwavering and angry. Stanley's aura shrank inward and dimmed as Stanley's eyes widened in surprise and fear. They stared at each other until, confusedly, Stanley sat down gingerly and, most amazingly, kept his mouth shut.

Heidi stared at the two men, hand on her office phone, ready to call Security.

"Now then…" Jack sat back down calmly, trying not to show his anger or his shock that Stanley had actually listened. "I want you to tell Ms. Clark exactly how you got into the computer, and why."

Stanley swallowed hard and began talking haltingly. Hesitating a couple of times, he quickly started talking again at the slightest prompt from Jack.

Nervously, Stanley explained to Heidi that he had taken a job as a night janitor with the company that cleaned the offices in this building. He'd made copies of the keys so he could get access to the computers when no one else was around. A friend of his worked for a competing company and they paid him to provide customer information and help convince them to switch over. He even admitted to bullying Charlie and three other co-workers into giving him clients. When he finished he looked back at Jack nervously, as if seeking approval.

Taken aback, Jack hardly paid attention to what Stanley was saying. How had he made Stanley admit all of this? Why had Stanley confessed? As he watched, Stanley's aura lost luster, becoming more translucent and faint.

Heidi listened to the whole story in quiet awe, eyes flicking between the two men. She swallowed hard and cleared her throat. "Is there anything else you want to tell me, Stanley?"

Stanley looked to Jack, who nodded back, unsure what else to do.

"Well, I helped George Carter slash your tires when you fired him," Stanley picked at his fingers where his hands were folded in his lap. "And I've been stealing office supplies. Not much, just some paper and notebooks. I've been stealing bagels from the café downstairs. I cheated in the last bodybuilding contest—I've been taking steroids. And…"

"That's enough!" Heidi stopped him. "Why did you tell me all of this?" Jack could tell she was watching him out of the corner of her eye as she asked Stanley the question.

"I—I don't know. I just…had to." Stanley seemed confused and his aura had returned to its normal size, but was fainter and more of an orange color than it had been. He slumped in his chair, looking thoroughly beaten. "I'm sorry. I don't know why I did those things. I just did. I knew they were wrong, but I did them anyway."

"Well." There was a long pause as Heidi mulled it all over. Finally, she asked, "What do you think I ought to do about this, Stanley?"

"I don't know," he murmured and put his head in his hands. "I can't undo the things I did."

"No, you can't. And I don't think I could prevent the district manager from firing you either."

Stanley looked up and then away again. "I know."

"But perhaps if you wrote me a detailed report on how you accessed the computer, and who you gave the information to, I might convince him not to press any charges."

"Charges?" His voice cracked.

"You didn't think what you were doing was legal did you?"

"Well, no, but…"

"Unlawful entry into the computer system and release of confidential customer information are Federal offenses. Not to mention industrial espionage. And I'm sure the janitorial service won't be pleased to hear how you used them."

Stanley looked much smaller and weaker than a man of his bulk should have.

"Write me that report, type up your resignation, and I'll see what I can do to prevent them from bringing charges against you." Her voice was strong and stern, yet motherly.

Stanley nodded and quietly got up and left the room.

Heidi and Jack stared at each other for a long time.

"Do you want to tell me how you got him to admit all of that?"

"I don't know." Jack had been wondering the same thing. The best idea he could come up with was that his lucid dreams were overlapping his consciousness, like sleepwalking. Somehow, his unconscious mind, knowing the clues when someone was lying, had shown them to his conscious mind in the form of a dream. It was a stretch, but it was the only explanation he had been able to rationalize so far. Either that or he really was seeing auras. "Maybe he's just a big blowhard and I blew back too hard."

"Uh-huh, and maybe you know something else you're not telling me."

"Like what?"

"Like something else you know he doesn't want you to tell me?"

"You think I've got some kind of leverage on him to make him talk?"

She nodded. "The thought had crossed my mind."

"What could be worse than the crap he just confessed to?" Jack held his hands out.

She searched around the papers on her desk for a moment and finally picked up a pen. "I should call the district manager," she said.

Jack took the hint, got up, and headed for the door.

"By the way, I think you need to work on your attitude and your temper if you're going make it through your probation."

She didn't look up at him.

SIXTEEN

Jack drove home slowly, carefully avoiding the stranded cars spotting the sides of the highway, his thoughts on Stanley and what had happened. The weather finally made good on its promise and started snowing about four o'clock. Unfortunately, the sun had made a strong showing from sometime around two until the time it had started snowing. This made for warm streets that melted the falling snow into water, which quickly froze into black ice as the sun disappeared.

One of the SUV's on the side of the road had a woman inside, gesticulating wildly while yelling at her cell phone. She was stuck good, he decided, looking at the mud up to the axle where she had slid off the road and broken through the frozen layer, down into the mud below.

Jack continued on past slowly, letting his car find traction wherever it could. She, or at least her SUV, would be there until it got cold enough to freeze all the mud she had churned up, or until a tow truck came along. There was no way any normal vehicle was going to pull her out tonight and the tow trucks might not even bother to come looking until enough snow fell for them to get better traction.

The thought to stop and help her crossed his mind, but only briefly. If he stopped now, his little Celica might never get going again. Driving on the ice was a cautious dance, balancing between letting the ice do what it wanted and keeping the car's momentum aimed in the right direction. If you lost the momentum, or tried to force the ice to give up traction, it was all over. Besides, she had a cell phone and appeared to be already yelling at someone to come get her.

Jack drifted forward, wrapped in the quiet cocoon of his car. He never drove in this kind of weather with the radio on. It was full dark now as he concentrated on the road in front of him, trying to ignore the snow coming straight at the windshield like millions of moths seeking the light of his headlights. He was careful to watch the road instead of the snow. The snowflakes were a hypnotic, swirling, galaxy of flakes, and he did his best to keep his eyes on the shiny black pavement that was reluctant to reveal itself in the headlights.

He jerked suddenly, scaring himself, afraid he would jolt the steering wheel and lose control of the car on the ice. Breathing heavy with his heart pounding, he took his foot off the gas and gently began pressing the brakes. His eyes probed the darkness ahead, searching for something he *knew* was there. He didn't know how he knew, and or even *what* it was he knew, but he was sure he *knew*, and he had to deal with it *now*.

Glancing in the rearview mirror, he was relieved there were no headlights behind him. The other cars must still be getting around the ones trying to get back on the road.

Looking back down at the road, his heart leapt into his throat.

A woman stood in the middle of the road waving her arms, trying to warn him off.

Jack pushed the brakes harder, hoping desperately to stop in time. The woman lost her footing on the ice and fell flat on her back across the road. Wrenching the wheels toward the side of the road, he grimaced as the car moved in a slow motion glide covering the distance to the woman on the ground, unable to find enough traction to change the car's direction.

In an eerie silence, the car slid to a stop at a skewed angle, so close to the woman he couldn't see her. But in the headlights he could see why she had been in the road. The dark undercarriage of a van, turned on its side, blocked the middle of the road. The dirty wet buildup on the bottom of the van was indistinguishable from the dirty icy road and the night he had been driving into.

His knees went weak. *That's* what he had known.

Jack sat still in the silence for an eternal second, the snowflakes falling dreamily around him.

The rear-view mirror still showed no lights. Desperately hoping visibility was high enough for people to see his hazard lights, he turned on his bright headlights to illuminate the van and slowly backed up until he could see the woman's form on the road.

His heart was a lump in his throat. She hadn't moved since falling.

Leaving his car running, he got out, walking stiff-legged toward the woman. His ears seemed full of cotton and he was sick to his stomach. She didn't move as he approached.

A horrible gash crossed her forehead, bleeding down her face. Blood pooled next to her head.

Jack swallowed hard and tried not to slip on the ice as he knelt next to her. His hands shook as he reached out to touch her.

His hand stopped a full six inches from her cheek. He didn't need to come any closer; he could see what had happened now. The back of her skull was leaking fluids other than blood. Her aura was dim in the wash of the bright headlights, so dim he couldn't make out a color, but it was different around her head. It was wrong. He could sense it more than he could see it, and with his hands so close to her, he could feel it more than sense it.

From deep inside of him, from a part of himself he didn't recognize, came a response. He put his hands above the top of her head and felt her aura. It was broken, no longer a interconnecting whole, and it was fading fast. He closed his eyes and spread his fingers wide, never touching her. A brief, intense spark of golden-green light flashed between his aura and hers.

Startled, not sure what had happened, Jack pulled his hands away. From the night, the sound of children crying reached his awareness. So deeply entranced in the woman's aura, he had forgotten where he was, and the van next to him. His stomach knotted and he *knew* this wasn't over yet.

Standing up, he shuffled across the icy road to the van as fast as he could without falling. At the front of the van, he noticed a logo of toy blocks and the name of a day care service. His blood ran cold.

He peered in through the broken front windshield, but the spider web shatter pattern prevented him from making out anything in the darkness beyond. Muffled crying came from more than one child in the van as he searched for a way in. On its passenger side, the van's large side door was buried, useless. At the back, he found it had no rear exit, leaving only the driver's door, which was currently acting as the ceiling of the van.

He climbed onto a tire, jumped up, and strained to pull himself onto the uppermost side of the van. Snow and ice made it slick. He looked down at the caved-in door. It wasn't ever going to open again.

Sliding down off the top, he ripped the front of his coat open on the jagged door, and ran back to the broken front windshield. Peering into the front sea until he was sure no one was in it, he kicked at the broken windshield, hoping to make an exit.

The cries inside grew louder.

"It's okay!" he yelled. "I'm coming to get you!" He kicked again, loosening some of the glass from the bottom corner of the van's frame. It all stayed connected, like the flap of a tent. As he pulled, it tore away a third of the way up, coming off like an ice-covered blanket, spreading tiny cubes of glass everywhere. He tossed the sheet aside and bent to put his head in.

"Are you guys still in here?" he called, trying to make his voice sound as calm and friendly as possible to children.

"Yes." A single weak response came out of the darkness.

"Good, 'cause I'm coming in, too." He did his best to not sound scared

He crawled in, awkwardly trying to find a way to stand on the inside of the passenger side door, and hit his head on the steering wheel as he stood up. He couldn't see inside the dark van.

"Are you guys okay?"

"I'm a-scared," came a weak reply that may or may not have been the same voice as before.

"Me, too!" The second voice hiccupped with sobbing.

"Okay, okay. We'll get you out of here," he said in a confident voice.

"I can't see!" Another voice came out of the darkness.

"It's okay, I can't see either."

"Will you turn on the lights?" It was the sobbing voice.

Jack fumbled at the dashboard until the lights came on and the inside of the van lit up. The road outside became visible and Jack hoped it would help other cars see the accident.

Turning, he found three small children fastened into child safety seats, trying hard to hold their heads upright to look at him.

"There! That's better!" he said with the best grin he could muster up. "Are you guys all right? Anyone hurt?" Three wide-eyed faces awkwardly shook sideways back at him. "Okay! Let's get you out of here!"

He stepped over the passenger's seat, straddling it, putting him in reach of the little girl strapped into the single seat. He looked past her to the other two children. An empty three-quarters sized bench seat was between him and them. It would take some effort to get them out.

"Hi, honey. My name is Jack. What's yours?" he said to the girl in front of him. If his voice trembled, she didn't seem to notice.

"Mindy."

"Well Mindy, let's get you out of this seat." He fumbled at the clasps and buckles.

"Like this," Mindy said smartly and punched a bright red button with her thumb. The clasp released and she tumbled out of the seat. Jack caught her and lifted her out gently.

He looked back at the two boys strapped into the back seat and made a hard decision. "I'm going to take Mindy out and then come back for you two, okay?" Though their cheeks were glistening from fresh tears, they both nodded solemnly.

"Okay, Mindy, you have to crawl out carefully, so don't cut yourself. When you get out, stay right there and wait for me, okay?" He couldn't see her face, but could tell she nodded her head. "Okay, let's go."

Mindy duck-walked out, rather than crawl, and Jack did his best to protect her head. He followed, snaking through the glass as quickly as he could. Scooping her up, he quickly headed into his car's headlights. As they rounded the van, the woman on the road moaned and propped herself up.

"Miss Weisling!" Mindy called out and the woman turned her head, dazed.

"Mindy?" She sounded confused.

Mindy kicked her legs at Jack to be let down, but he held on to her. "Hold on, Mindy," he said gently. "Miss Weisling bumped her head and doesn't feel too good yet. Do you understand?" Mindy put a hand to her head and nodded sympathetically. "Good. I need you to help her, okay?" Mindy nodded again and he sat her down. He gripped her hand as they approached the woman.

"Where's Danny and Joey?" Miss Weisling asked, her voice rising as she spoke.

"They're still in the van. Mindy is going to help you while I go get them, all right?" The tone of his voice when he said 'all right' told her she needed to agree, and she nodded her assent.

Jack hooked his arm under Miss Weisling's and steadied her as she got up, slipping on the ice slicked with her own blood. Then he pulled at her and Mindy to get them to the side of the road.

He took off his ripped coat, tossed it on the snow, and motioned for them to sit. "I'd let you sit in my car, but until some more people get here, it's probably safer on the side of the road." Miss Weisling nodded silently as she clutched Mindy to her and brushed large snowflakes out of the girl's hair.

Jack hurried back to the van, skittering on the ice and watching down the road for oncoming lights. There still weren't any. A blessing, he thought as he crawled back into the van.

"All right, who's Danny, and who's Joey?" he asked as he crawled back into the van.

"I'm Joey, and he's Danny," said the boy on the bottom.

"Well, Joey and Danny, I'm Jack. It's very nice to meet you boys." He grunted as he squeezed between seats to get to them. There wasn't enough room to maneuver around the middle bench seat. Kneeling down, he tried to reach the boy on the bottom, but could only get one arm to him. The buckle needed a second hand to resist the button push.

"Okay, Joey. I'm having problems reaching you…" He panted as he tried to reach. "…So I'm going to help Danny first."

He stood up and reached for Danny, who whimpered and tried to pull away.

"He doesn't like strangers," Joey's said.

Jack took a deep breath to keep calm. Cars must be coming anytime now, and this was the worst place to be when they got here.

"Can either of you guys undo your own seat belt, like Mindy did?" He mentally crossed his fingers.

"Mom told me I'm not supposed to do that anymore." Joey sounded worried.

"This time is an exception to the rule, Joey. Your mom told you about exceptions to the rules, didn't she?" Jack squeezed his torso around to look at Joey, who nodded hesitantly.

"Good. We'll let your mom know that I told you to, and Danny, here, he can be your witness that I said to do it, okay?" He glanced up at Danny who didn't seem to like the idea but didn't say anything.

"Okay," Joey answered and pressed the big red button. With a sharp click, he tumbled half out of the sideways turned seat. Jack's hand shot out and caught one sleeve just in time to stop Joey from smacking his head on the floor.

"You're okay," promised Jack. "You're okay. You just need to get your feet under you and stand up." He pulled at Joey's sleeve, trying to help him stand, but Joey seemed to take forever to get his footing.

Please, God, Jack found himself praying silently, *please give us just a little more time.* He was sure it was just a matter of time before a car hit the van in the poor visibility of the snowstorm.

Joey grabbed Jack's arm, pulled himself upright with a grunt of effort, and planted his feet firmly.

"Good boy!" Jack praised him with a quick grin, and then turned to Danny. "Hey, Danny! You know Joey, right? Is it okay with you if Joey unbuckles your seat?" He didn't wait for an answer; instead, bracing himself carefully, he grabbed Joey by the back of the pants and lifted the boy up to Danny's chair. "See if you can get that one, too, would you, Joey?" he asked through clenched teeth as he tried to hold the boy up. If the either of the boys answered, Jack was too busy straining to hear it.

It seemed an eternity until he heard a metallic click and Danny fell, knocking Joey out of Jack's grasp. The boys tumbled into a heap onto the floor and into the shattered glass that had been a passenger window.

"You guys all right?" Jack called as he un-wedged himself and bent down to where they had landed. Danny started to cry and Joey looked scared. "We're outta here!" Jack tried to make it sound exciting. "Come on! Crawl through there! Come on!"

While the boys untangled themselves and began crawling out, Jack felt the time pressure. Every sound made him flinch and each time he expected a car to slam into them. Time was running out.

He began to feel sick to his stomach. He *knew* time was running out.

Fighting down panic, he lifted them over the passenger seat one at a time, setting them in front of the broken windshield. "Okay, now we have to crawl out, so be careful –and no pushing!" He hoped the standard phrase would keep the boys calmer. Doing his best to hold the glass up for the boys, he began to worm himself out. Dropping to his knees, he rolled out and stood up, grabbing a boy under each arm.

His stomach knotted and his eyes went wide as headlights bore down on them, moving impossibly fast. There was no time to get out of the way.

Diving for the median, still holding the boys under his arms, he landed on his face in gravelly snow as the speeding vehicle careened by, spewing slush all over them.

There was a horrible dull smacking sound and Jack rolled over to see the van spinning away to the other side of the road, narrowly missing Mindy and Miss Weisling as it went off the shoulder. The SUV that hit it was also spinning, then its wheels caught traction on something and it flipped, once, twice, and then gently rocked back upright.

Jack could hear both boys crying as he dropped his head back into the icy slush and closed his eyes.

"Thank you, God," he whispered.

SEVENTEEN

Julie glanced at the clock again. Jack was late, and she was worried.

She pointed the remote control at the television and switched channels for the umpteenth time. For the last twenty minutes she had been flipping back and forth between the local channels, hoping for an update on the roads, but all she had seen were teasers touting "more news at ten…"

Chewing her fingers, she looked over at Bear sleeping in his normal place on the dog bed in the corner, glad he wasn't doing the bark-at-nothing thing. She wouldn't have been able to handle it tonight.

As another news blurb ended with "details at ten…," she was forced to accept that none of the stations were going to say more. Disgruntled, she turned off the television.

In the sudden quiet, the whole house was different. It was empty and colder. She shuddered. Glancing at Bear, who had stirred at the sound of the television shutting off, she was relieved to see him wag his tail at her. The dog got up and came over to her, resting his nose on her knee. She stroked his ears absently while she listened to the house noises.

The blower on the furnace gently hummed, making a background noise rarely noticed until it stopped. Something clicked as it rolled around in the dryer, a sound she had loved as a child. The ice machine in the refrigerator popped, startling her until she recognized it.

Out the ground-level window into the front yard, the snow glowed with the amber light from the streetlamp. She liked having the light there. Thanks to the streetlight filtering in around the blinds, the house was never completely dark.

As she watched the large flakes of snow float down, she briefly considered going out to shovel the driveway. She quickly dismissed the idea and considered turning up the heat.

As if to taunt her, the furnace chose that moment to shut off, leaving the house eerily quiet but for the rhythmic tumbling of the dryer. Suddenly feeling very small and alone, she was grateful to have

Bear with her. "Come on, my little Bugaboo. Let's go scrounge up something to eat."

She stood and started up the stairs, Bear following closely behind. Halfway up Bear let loose with a single "Woof!"

Julie nearly fell down.

Terrified, she searched for anything that might have cause the dog to bark.

There was nothing. Only her and Bear.

Bear growled low, still standing behind her on the stairs. He twisted his head around to look back toward the bottom of the stairs.

"Damn it!" she yelled at Bear. "No!" She admonished him with a finger point. "No barking!" Her heart raced as the dog cowered under her wild gaze and she immediately felt bad for screaming at him. Her voice faded to a whisper as she repeated herself. "No barking."

She stopped shaking her finger at the dog and leaned against the wall weakly. She could feel the pressure of her heartbeat all the way out at her fingertips. Shakily, she raised a hand and rubbed her eyes.

Bear growled again and she eyed him from between her fingers. The hair on his neck bushed out and his growl grew loud enough to be a warning.

Julie felt the hair on the back of her own neck rise and her bladder was suddenly too full. "Stop it, Bear," she told the dog hoarsely, but the rumbling in Bear's throat moved closer to a snarl and the dog turned his whole body to face the bottom of the stairs.

Julie began backing up the stairs, eyes searching for anything that could be causing the dog to act like this. The furnace came back on with a low thump of gas igniting and Julie inadvertently let loose a small squeak.

She rubbed her hands up and down her arms, trying to smooth goose bumps, and backed farther up the stairs. Bear held his ground and crouched into an attack stance. Julie began to shake with fear as she thought she could hear the sound of a little girl crying and she became convinced there was something there for Bear to growl at.

They weren't alone.

Jack hit the button on the garage door remote while he was still halfway down the block from home. The snow was deep enough he would need momentum to get up the driveway and into the garage. As he turned into the bottom of the driveway, his car fishtailed and he gunned the motor as he went up the drive and into the garage next to Julie's car.

Stomping on the brake, he stopped just short of where he would normally have parked. He eased the car forward and stopped again. He considered backing out and trying again to make more room between the cars, but a quick glance in the rearview mirror at the drifting snow dissuaded him.

He was glad to be home. It had been a trying experience to give the police a statement about the accident. He had been at a loss when they had asked him about all the blood. He knew it was from Miss Weisling's head, but she showed no sign of injury, other than the blood matted in her hair and on her clothes, and she didn't remember what had happened. Everyone else had been accounted for too, but the paramedics and the police had insisted there must have been someone with a serious injury to leave that much blood and they forced everyone to go over their statements again and again.

Jack pleaded ignorance, as had everyone else, claiming only that he had seen Miss Weisling fall and hit her head, knocking herself momentarily unconscious. Miss Weisling supported his story and little Mindy had told how she had helped carry Miss Weisling out of the middle of the road.

The police hadn't been satisfied with the explanation. Even the woman in the SUV that hit the van had only minor injuries, to the great surprise of everyone who saw the mangled vehicles. Jack continued to maintain his story and, after an hour, they had finally let him go.

Jack wasn't sure what to think about what had happened. He felt as though he had been in a trance from the time he knew there was danger until the police had shown up.

Squeezing out of his car, trying not to bang the door against Julie's car, his efforts rewarded him with fresh slush and mud on his clothes. It didn't matter. He was soaked and covered with mud from lying in the ditch with the boys. He kicked the toes of his shoes against the step in front of the door to the house and tried vainly to get some of the mud off. Giving up, he took off the shoes and left them in the garage as he entered the house.

"Honey, I'm home!" he called out trying to be upbeat. There was no answer. He hadn't expected one. She hadn't answered any of his calls so he figured she had probably gone out the bar with Sandy again. There would probably be another note on the kitchen table. He looked down at his muddy clothes and decided the note could wait.

He stripped his pants off while still standing at the garage door and winced as flakes of semi-dry mud scattered across the floor. Wishing he had taken the pants off in the garage with his shoes, he peeled off his soaked socks and pulled his shirt off over his head without bothering to unbutton it. His legs were blue in spite of having sat in the back of a warm ambulance wrapped in blankets while giving his statement.

Shivering in his underwear, he gathered up the filthy clothing and headed for the laundry room. At the first step, he dropped the clothes, nearly tripping over them, as he tried to accept what he was seeing.

Julie, curled in a ball, at the bottom of the stairs, unmoving.

"Julie!" he cried out, stumbling the rest of the way down the stairs. Landing on his knees next to her huddled form, he called out again and put a hand to her face. Her skin was cool and she didn't respond to his touch. His gut wrenched as he tried to evoke any response from her still body.

"Oh, God, no…" He sobbed as he frantically searched for a pulse. Hands shaking, he tried her wrist and then her neck. The pain in his stomach almost made him vomit, then he thought he saw her chest rise with breath. "Please, please, please…" He repeated the word as he waited to see if her chest moved again.

It did.

He let loose a long ragged breath of his own and began rocking on his knees in excitement. "It's okay. You're going to be all right. You're okay." He touched her face again. She didn't respond as he caressed her cheek and searched for any sign of a wound. He found nothing.

An idea came, as he remembered Miss Weisling. He could fix Julie. Whatever was wrong with her, he could fix it. He had already done it once tonight, why not a second time? Nervously, he licked his lips as he tried to remember what to do. Last time it had been so simple, he had just…

He didn't know. He had just touched some damn glow around the woman's body. There wasn't any glow around Julie. He stared hard at her. He tried looking away. He tried closing his eyes. He tried everything he could think of, but all he could see was his own tears.

The paramedic put his hand in the middle of Jack's bare chest to stop him as he tried to follow the gurney out the front door.

"Sir," the paramedic was polite but firm "you are having a very difficult night, I know. So please allow me to give you what little advice I can in this situation. Although you might think that you want to ride to the hospital in the ambulance with your wife, you *really* do not."

Jack tried to sidestep the man, who expertly repositioned himself in front of Jack again.

"Sir, please reconsider. If you ride in the ambulance, you will arrive at the hospital unprepared. This means that you will be without a way home, without any money to call anyone from the payphone, and without any clothes."

Jack suddenly realized he had been in his underwear the entire time the paramedics had been at the house, and the man blocking his way was really doing him a favor.

"Not to mention that you still have a houseful of police and inspectors," the paramedic continued.

Jack nodded dumbly. The whole night had turned into a blur, and he had almost walked out on it while still in a frenzy. "Thank you," he mumbled.

The paramedic nodded sagely. "I recommend you call a friend or family member for transportation, as you will likely find you are in no condition to drive." With a final nod of affirmation, the paramedic turned and jogged off to catch up to the ambulance before it left.

As the ambulance pulled away, Jack was left standing on the front door step in his underwear, staring at the neighbors across the street who were staring back. Red and blue emergency lights chased each other in circles, reflecting off the snow and windows up and down the street, eerie without the sirens that normally accompanied them.

His head swirled with fears and silent prayers as he watched the ambulance turn the corner slowly on the slick streets. A gust of wind blew snow into Jack's face and he realized he was in danger of frostbite. He staggered awkwardly back into the house, numb feet slipping on the snowy mess left by the feet of the paramedics and police.

The paramedics had grilled Jack hard about Julie's medical history, seemingly not believing him when he told them she was not diabetic, did not use drugs, and had no history of seizures or head trauma. When one of the paramedics asked about pets, Jack had realized he hadn't seen Bear since he got home.

One of the paramedics found Bear in the spare bedroom, unconscious and bloody. At first, they thought someone had attacked the dog, but closer examination showed that the blood, which was scratched into and smeared all over the bottom of the bi-fold closet door, had all come from Bear's front paws.

The unconscious dog set off fears of a gas leak or carbon monoxide poisoning, and the paramedics had quickly moved to call in Public Service. The house had erupted into a pandemonium of frenetic people quickly moving through Jack's daze.

Before taking Julie, the paramedics had assured him she was stable with a strong pulse and regular breathing, but they refused to speculate on the nature of her condition. He overheard one of them talking about various types of comas, but they had also talked about carbon monoxide poisoning, seizures, and a range of other things.

He walked back into the house gingerly, self-consciously picking up the clothing he had dropped earlier and ineffectually trying to use it to cover himself. It had been kicked out of the way by the paramedics, the police, and the inspectors, and was now strewn all across the basement, mixed with the snowy mess made by the boots of all the people who had been through the house.

Embarrassed, he pulled on the muddy pants just as one of the police officers approached him from out of the laundry room, where the inspectors were checking the furnace and the water heater.

"Public Service says there's no gas leak and no evidence of carbon monoxide." The officer informed him professionally. "They'll be out of here in about five minutes."

Jack nodded, not knowing what to say. He'd already given another statement and they had checked out his story about the earlier accident.

For a moment, the officer dropped his cold professional voice and sounded genuinely concerned. "I'm sure she'll be all right. According to dispatch, you're batting a thousand tonight."

For the first time, Jack saw the officer as a person instead of a uniform. "What do you mean?"

"You're a regular hero. You're up to three children, two women, and a dog, all in one night. I can honestly say that's the most I've ever seen by one person."

Jack let loose a small grunt. "I don't feel like a hero. And I didn't save my wife from anything."

"Sure you did. She's going to be just fine because of you. Look." The officer pointed to the dog bed where Bear was watching them with his eyes half lidded. One of the paramedics had given the dog oxygen and another had swabbed and bandaged his raw paws, and Bear had slowly begun responding to the people around him. Now Bear appeared to be merely exhausted.

"See how well he's doing? I'd wager that whatever happened to your wife is the same thing that happened to him. She'll recover just as well as he is. Although, us poor humans take a little longer sometimes, right boy?" He knelt down and scratched Bear on top of the head gently.

Jack hoped the officer was right. He hugged the clothes in his arms closer to himself, suddenly cold. The paramedics had opened all the doors and windows as soon as they were worried about gas.

The officer stood back up with a creak of leather from his thick utility belt and eyed Jack before speaking again. "I know it's not my place, or any of my business, but if I were you, I would get a shower, a shave, and a good looking outfit before I went to the hospital."

Jack laughed. He was barefoot and shirtless, streaked with dried mud, and near blue with chill. He was afraid to imagine what his face looked like. "Yeah," he answered, "I wouldn't want to scare off any of the nurses."

"Actually," said the officer, looking sympathetic, "I was thinking of the media."

"Media?"

"Yeah. Police logs are public record, not to mention they scan our radio frequencies. Someone is going to realize your name came up twice tonight. The local stations have already interviewed a couple officers to get the story of you rescuing those kids for the ten o'clock news." He gave Jack a meaningful look. "You don't strike me as the Jerry Springer type. I'd bet you don't want the attention, but doesn't 'hero's wife tragically stricken while he was saving children' sound like a great human interest story to you?"

Jack's mouth gaped. "They wouldn't..." he started, but the officer interrupted him.

"They would. And if they think of it, they will. You've seen the type of privacy invasion that turns up on TV every night, who do you think those poor people are? They're you, and me, and him," he said pointing to Bear. "Just warning you. It could happen."

The two inspectors and the other police officer came out of the laundry room.

"All done," said the other officer.

"Here." The first police officer handed Jack a card. "On the off chance that something else turns up, give us a call." He gave Jack a reassuring smile and followed the others out the front door, leaving Jack feeling more naked than he had when he had been in his underwear in front of eight people.

Numbly, he wondered whom he should call. Neither Julie's parents nor his own lived within a two-hour drive, and in this weather he was hesitant to panic anyone who might try to drive out tonight, especially since he couldn't give them any answers yet.

Vic didn't live too far away, and he owned a big four-wheel drive truck. As soon as he thought of Vic, Jack knew he was the right person to call.

Jack called and quickly blurted out as much as he could about needing to go to the hospital to see Julie. After a calming reassurance from Vic that he would be over immediately.

Staring at the phone after hanging up, the nauseating knot of grief and pain in his stomach overwhelmed him. He dropped to the floor, put his arms around Bear, and cried.

By the time Vic arrived, Jack had managed to take a shower. He met Vic at the front door in slacks and undershirt, cursing the muddy wet mess his bare feet stood on. Rushing around the house trying to find more clothes, he did his best to explain what had happened.

Listening to Jack's ramblings, Vic sat quietly and petted Bear, who had limped up the stairs to see him.

When they finally got into Vic's truck, Jack found himself grateful for the powerful heater. His house hadn't recovered from being aired out, and his shower had been too short to warm him up.

The ride to the hospital was interminable. Jack couldn't stop picturing Julie's face, slack and pale. Vic's face was pinched in concentration as he steered the truck across icy roads and through the heavy snowfall.

"Thank you," Jack said and immediately regretted it. The words felt inadequate.

"It's what I'm here for," answered Vic without taking his eyes off the road.

"I mean it," added Jack, trying to reinforce his meager show of appreciation. "That guy was right. I'm in no shape to drive. I would have gone a hundred miles an hour and killed myself in this weather."

"Is that a comment on my driving?" Vic smirked.

"No. It's a thanks for being here when I needed you."

Vic met Jack's eyes for a brief moment, before returning to the road. "I know. Don't get all mushy on me. We've got enough problems already, without you making our wives think we're having an affair."

Jack smiled. Vic's playful teasing always made him feel better.

Upon arrival at the hospital, Jack and Vic were informed that there was no change in Julie's condition, but she was stable and in no immediate danger. Jack assumed they had left off the words 'of dying' as they still didn't know what was wrong, so how could they possibly know whether or not she was in danger?

They sat silently next to Julie's bed in a curtained off room in the Emergency Department, watching Julie's slack face for any sign of life, and watching each other for any signs of despondency. It seemed like ages since anyone had come to check on Julie, but Jack understood they were waiting for test results to come in and there were electronic monitors on her to tell them if her situation changed.

His head drooped over Julie's hand, which he held in his own, and he continued to repeat the same silent plea over and over in his mind.

Vic sat quietly in the chair next to Jack trying to be unobtrusive yet supportive.

As Jack stared at the wedding rings on his and Julie's fingers, he realized the purple glow around his hand was back. He blinked his eyes but it was still there.

Vic was sitting in a light orange colored haze, looking like he may have dozed off, but when he looked at Julie's face, she was not suffused with the haze Jack had come to think of as auras.

Her features had only the light colored aura of everything else around her. He reached out, putting his hand to her cheek, feeling for her aura, as he remembered doing with Miss Weisling, but he found nothing, like putting his hands through a hole in the wall he hadn't known was there. It was unsettling and felt wrong.

Panic rose in his chest. Something was wrong. Just as when he had *known* at the accident, he *knew* Julie was…

Jack felt as though he had just woken up, although he was still standing over Julie. He looked around the room quickly and saw everything was normal. There were no auras anywhere. He felt an important piece of knowledge slipping away, just like dreams always did, and try as he might, he couldn't recapture it.

He had known what was wrong with Julie, but now he couldn't remember what it was. An unrealized revelation had slipped away before solidifying enough to be held onto. A terrible sense of loss and frustration built up inside of him and he found himself breathing deep and blowing out, trying to forestall a panic attack.

Vic heard the heavy respirations and woke up. He gently put a hand out onto Jack's shoulder. "You okay?" he asked quietly.

It was just a dream, Jack told himself, just another one of those damn lucid dreams. Well, that proved they were just dreams, didn't it. Supposedly, a lucid dream could be controlled, and he did seem to be able to control what he was doing, but, because his 'sleepwalking' lucid dreams superimposed themselves on top of reality, they could only make him believe so much.

He hadn't really healed that lady at the accident. She was already waking up, and his dream incorporated it. If he could really do something like that, he would have just now done it with Julie.

Silently he cursed himself for being gullible, for having false hope. He wearily turned to Vic. "Yeah," he breathed. "I'm okay. It was just…nothing. It was nothing."

Vic nodded. "Let's go get some coffee. You could use a little perk-me-up. Maybe we can get you a quadruple espresso."

EIGHTEEN

When Vic dropped him off at home at six-thirty in the morning, Jack was exhausted. In the confusion of the night, Bear had been left in the house, so Jack let him out and watched as Bear high-stepped through the snow, walking carefully on his bandaged front paws, looking for a suitable place to go.

After Julie was moved into the intensive care unit, the nurses had urged Jack and Vic to go home and get some sleep. All of the initial tests had come back negative and the best guess had been a coma for unknown reasons.

As he let the dog back in the house, Jack realized he was supposed to be at work in forty-five minutes. He stumbled to the phone and realized he needed to call Julie's job too. He left a message on her supervisor's voice mail and then called to leave a message saying he wouldn't be in. He was surprised when, instead of the answering machine, Heidi Clark answered the phone.

"Uh…" His brain locked up while he tried to shift gears to talk to a person instead of a machine. "This is Jack. I won't be in today," he said bluntly.

"I know," came Heidi's soft Southern reply. "I saw the newspaper. I am so sorry about your wife. Is she going to be okay? Do you know anything yet?"

"Uh…no."

"Look, you do whatever you need to. I'll cover things here for you. Don't worry about the job, okay?"

"Okay."

A knock on the door and Bear's barking stopped Jack from climbing into bed. Stumbling to the door, he was startled to find a news camera in his face when he opened it. Bear wagged his tail violently and kept trying to push his way past Jack and out the door.

"Can I help you?" he asked as politely as he could manage, remembering the heads-up the officer had given him the night before.

He could picture it now: A fifteen-second looping clip of Jack looking like an idiot slob slamming his front door in the newswoman's face. He didn't want to be on the news like that.

"Hello!" An attractive black woman dressed in a violet suit cut to show cleavage stepped out from behind the man brandishing the camera. "I'm with the news, and we were hoping to ask you a few questions about last night."

Jack didn't say anything. He was seeing auras again and he could tell the woman was nervous by the swirls of colors around her. There was something in her aura that reminded him of Stanley's lies, but different.

He noticed the car parked in front of his house where the ambulance had been less than ten hours ago. It was an old beat up boxy gas-guzzler, not what he would have expected a news crew to use. Then he realized how young the girl was; still in college, or maybe even just out of high school, he guessed.

"Who did you say you were with?" he asked.

"The news." Her smile barely faltered. "We were hoping—" Jack cut her off in mid-sentence. The strange things he was seeing in her aura were half-truths. She wasn't exactly lying to him, but she wasn't telling the truth either.

"Is that a specific news company or just news in general? Don't you guys usually have identifying marks on your equipment other than a skull and crossbones?" He pointed at the camera operator, whose camera prominently bore a snowboarding logo.

The woman's smile finally faltered.

A thought occurred to Jack. "You're an independent aren't you?" he asked. "Trying to get a break somewhere so someone will notice you?"

The woman's eyes flashed and the colors in her aura lit up like the 4th of July. He had hit a nerve.

"We were hoping to speak with you about last night. You're being called a hero, you know." Her professional voice wavered slightly as she fought to regain her composure.

"Look, I just got home. I've had a long night, I'm tired, my wife is in the hospital—maybe dying. It's barely seven in the morning, the sun is hardly up and you're knocking on my door asking for an interview. Cut me some slack, huh?"

The woman held steady and met his gaze. The man holding the camera kept it on Jack's face.

"Tell you what," Jack said resignedly, "why don't you turn off the camera for a minute, come inside where it's warm, let me get cleaned up, and then we'll talk."

The woman's face held mostly steady but Jack could see excitement in her aura. "You mean it?" she asked.

"Yeah. On the condition that you do your best not to make me look like the idiot that I am."

She grinned and motioned to the man with the camera. He lowered the camera and revealed a freckled face with a bright red goatee. He wore a black stocking hat with a silver 'X' embroidered into it.

"I want an exclusive," she bartered back, trying to get a dominant look in her eye.

Jack used his leg to push Bear farther back into the house, and waved them in. "Don't worry about your feet, as you can see the guys last night didn't." He gestured to the mud tracked up and down the stairs. "And don't worry about Bear. Unless you dissolve under intense licking, he poses no threat."

He led them into the living room and pointed to the coffee pot on the counter in the kitchen. Looking at the cameraman, he said, "The coffee and filters are in the cabinet above it, help yourself. I'm going to go wash my face."

He returned a few minutes later wearing a clean shirt, his face pink from scrubbing, and his hair combed. His guests were quietly sitting at the dining room table, which by some miracle was clean, sipping steaming cups of coffee. Bear was at their feet, putting his head in their laps, basking in the attention.

"Allow me to introduce myself," he said trying to be civil. "I'm Jack Hooper." He proffered his hand to the woman who took it with a lady-like sideways handshake.

"Myla Jenkins." She smiled warmly. Her dark almond eyes were much softer now. He turned to the cameraman who stuck his hand out quickly.

"David Rowe." He shook hands firmly.

Jack sat down where they had been thoughtful enough to place a third cup of coffee.

"What kind of interview are you looking for?" Jack asked sipping gingerly at his coffee. "Do you want me to be grieving and distraught, or brave and stoic?"

David laughed aloud and Myla's mouth gaped.

"Are you some kind of actor or something?" she asked.

"Nope—just a cynic. I've seen the fake crap on the news." He sipped at his steaming cup, realizing he was so tired he was being cocky.

"I'll drink to that," retorted David with another chuckle.

"I was hoping for an honest interview." Myla cocked her head to the side and raised an eyebrow.

"Honest won't work." Jack held the mug cupped in his hands and close to his face savoring the aroma. "I'm too damned tired and spent. If I act the way I feel right now, people will think I don't care."

"Then how about we try it both ways?" asked Myla.

Jack shook his head slowly. "No, I don't want it to look like we staged an interview if someone buys your tape and you 'accidentally' give them the original." Myla pursed her lips but didn't say anything.

"All right, I'll give you honest," Jack conceded.

The interview was going by faster than Jack could have hoped, and Myla and David seemed to be nice people. David coached him on how to hold his head and where to look, so that he didn't look stiff or strange on camera, then went and got a second camera so they could film both sides of the interview.

While David set up the two cameras, Myla went over her questions in advance so he would have a chance to answer intelligently. They were pretty much what he expected; how did he see the accident, was he scared, tell us about the rescue, how did he find his wife, how did he feel, how does he feel now, how is she, and on and on.

When they started the interview, he was so exhausted he actually forgot he was on camera until Myla sprung a surprise question on him.

"So where did all of the blood come from?" Her eyes twinkled with an inner joy as she caught him off guard with the question.

Jack answered as intelligently as his brain would allow on such short notice. "Huh?"

"The police and the paramedics both reported a large amount of blood at the scene of the accident, and Gloria Weisling herself stated in a telephone interview last night that she had been covered in blood from head to toe." Myla's reporter instincts were in full throws and she attacked without reservation. "If all of the children were trapped in the van, and Gloria Weisling was unconscious, then you would be the only person who would know where all of the blood came from."

Jack tried to sputter an answer, but Myla pressed on, leaning forward with her arms across her stomach to give the camera a good view of her ample cleavage. "Gloria Weisling reported that she remembered having some sort of head injury before passing out. She also states, and the paramedics confirmed this, that she doesn't have so much as a bruise from the accident or from when you saw her fall down and hit her head.

"Mr. Hooper, the police think you might be hiding something. The parents of those children think that you are a Guardian Angel. They are calling you their Guardian 'Snow Angel'. And Gloria Weisling is claiming that you are a miracle healer. What do you say to all of this?" Myla's face was the picture of openness and innocence as she awaited his answer and projected breathless sex appeal toward her camera.

Jack swallowed hard. He was afraid to lie on camera. It might show. He was afraid to tell the truth, because he didn't know what it was. And now he was afraid he was taking too long to answer the accusations.

"Well, as for all the blood, and, yes, there was a lot of it, I can't tell you anything more than I told the police. I thought it was Miss Weisling's, but it is as you said, as far as I know there wasn't a scratch on her or the children. As far as the opinions of the parents go, I just did what I would hope anyone else in my situation would have done. If God chooses Guardian Angels by putting certain people in certain places at certain times, then maybe I am one, but that would be His doing and not mine. And as far as some sort of miracle healing…" he paused to catch his breath.

"I think it was a miracle that everyone survived that terrible situation, let alone with such minor injuries. But if there were any other miracles, well, I think credit needs to be given where credit is due. God was with us all last night." He could tell by the look on Myla's face she was going to pin him down harder if he didn't give her a direct answer.

"If I could perform a miracle healing, don't you think that I would have healed my wife too?" His voice choked and tears came unbidden to his eyes. He wiped them away quickly, trying not to let the rush of emotion and his fatigue show through, but failing miserably.

Myla nodded sympathetically and sat back up, putting away her cleavage for the emotional ending of her interview. "Many people have already sent their prayers out for you and your wife, Jack. Our prayers go with you too. Thank you for taking the time, during this terribly painful ordeal, to speak with us. God bless you."

NINETEEN

Jack slept fitfully. Finally, he felt as though he was getting some rest when someone began incessantly ringing the doorbell, sending Bear into a fit.

Jack got up with blood in his eyes. He held Bear back out of the way and pulled the door open quickly with a snarl on his face and then felt stupid as Vic stepped back in surprise.

"Don't kill the messenger!" Vic cried in mock fear throwing his hands up into the air.

"Is Julie all right?"

Vic cringed, his witticism having had the wrong effect. He lowered his voice somberly. "No, I'm sorry, she's just the same."

"Oh. No, I'm sorry. Come on in." Jack stepped aside and held the door open, which Bear took as an invitation to pounce up on Vic.

"I can't. I have to get to the restaurant," he patted Bear on the head. "I was sent to tell you that your in-laws are at the hospital and that they have been trying to call you for hours. There seems to be something wrong with your phone."

Jack grunted in acknowledgement. "I turned it off. People kept calling to see if I could heal them."

"I suppose that would tend to happen after someone accuses you of being a miracle worker. Anyway, here is Anita's cell phone number." He handed Jack a printed card with the name and slogan of their restaurant. "Call the catering phone number. Anita is at the hospital with your family, and they are waiting for you to call."

"Thanks Vic. I'm sorry that you had to go down there again. I'm sure that you haven't had enough sleep either."

"It's four in the afternoon. I got eight hours, didn't you?"

"Four? Man! I feel like I only slept an hour after those people left."

"What people?"

Jack told him about Myla and David and the interview.

"Oh boy. You think people are calling you now, you just wait until that video hits the news!" Vic shook his head as he spoke. "That's going to peg you forever."

"No! I made sure that I told them I wasn't some sort of faith healer."

"It doesn't matter what you told them! If the press bothers to ask you about it, then that's good enough for most people. Think about it! Every time you see someone interviewed on the news for a crime, your first reaction, almost every time is 'Oh yeah, they're guilty!' Anyone out there who thinks that they need a faith healer will call you now, just to make sure for themselves!"

Jack was stunned. Vic was right. Fear began creeping into the recesses of his gut and he felt nauseated. What if he had healed that woman? What if the world found out about it? His knees went weak and he sat down where he was on the doorstep.

"Are you okay? You don't look good."

Jack held his head in his hands and didn't answer.

"Jack?"

"I need someone to talk to."

"Hey. I'm right here." Vic reached down and put his hand on Jack's shoulder. "You can tell me anything."

"No. I mean I need a psychiatrist. I've gone off the deep end, and I don't need to pull you in with me."

"Try me."

"Okay." Jack stood up. "If the restaurant can wait a little longer, come on in."

He walked back into the house and motioned for Vic to sit at the table while he got coffee.

"It looks like you need a new rug." Vic noted the heavy mud tracked throughout the house.

"I think I need a new house."

Vic laughed, but Jack's face stayed frozen in seriousness.

"This might take a while. We should get any phone calls out of the way first," Jack said in a matter-of-fact voice as he picked up the phone and called Anita's cell phone number. After assuring Anita he was all right and then assuring his in-laws of the same, he passed the phone over to Vic who quietly told Anita she would have to go take care of the restaurant, as he was going to stay and talk with Jack for a while. By the time they got off the phone they had already drank the re-heated coffee and Jack was pouring them each a cup of fresh brew.

"I don't know where to start." Jack cupped his coffee mug in his hands.

Vic smiled a lopsided smile, his bushy black moustache sliding across his face. "Start at the beginning."

"Do you remember when I told you I saw a ghost?"

"You mean when you dreamed you saw a ghost?" Vic smiled warmly.

"I used to mean that, but I'm not so sure anymore."

"What changed your mind?" Vic leaned forward. His eyebrows lowered and crowded together.

"It—it attacked me." He watched Vic closely for any sign of disbelief. Instead, he got a look of surprise.

"It attacked you?"

"Yes. And I think it attacked Julie, too. I think that's why she is in the hospital." Jack's heart was thumping with fear now. He had started telling his secrets, and there was no going back. Before he lost his nerve, he forced out another sentence. "There's more. I think it affected me somehow. I think I'm having psychic visions."

Vic's lips pursed as he watched Jack attentively.

Jack took a deep breath and let out his last secret fear.

"And I think I did heal that woman's injuries. When I first saw her, she fell on the ice and cracked her head open. There was blood everywhere. She should have died." He whispered the last words, looking down at his coffee.

They both sat for a time. Finally, Vic cleared his throat. "Are you sure?"

Jack nodded.

"Then you need some serious help."

Jack's face flushed. "I told you I needed help! I'm losing my mind!"

"Not that kind of help. I know someone. Someone…you should go see."

Jack put his face in his hands again. "You know a shrink?"

"I don't mean a psychiatrist. I mean a friend."

Jack looked up wearily. "What kind of friend?"

"A very old, very wise, friend. I've known her since I was a little boy, and I know she can be trusted to do her best to help you—and Julie."

"I don't understand."

"Remember I told you my grandmother was a witch? Well, Fidelina is too, and if what you are saying is true, she can help you."

"What do you mean 'if' it's true? Vic! I'm losing my damned mind here, and you're encouraging me!"

"When did you stop thinking it was a dream and start thinking that the ghost was real?"

"I still think it was a dream. I just doubt my own sanity now."

"Fine. What has made you doubt your sanity? Tell me what happened."

Jack leaned back into the chair and took a deep breath.

"First I thought the ghost attacked me, but there's no such thing, so I thought it was just some kind of migraine headache I somehow incorporated into a vivid dream." He sat up and leaned forward again. "I researched this. I think it was a lucid dream. I was dreaming, but I was conscious at the same time. They can seem so real, some people can't tell them apart from reality. I think that's what has been happening to me, except somehow, it's happening when I'm awake. It's like I'm sleepwalking, only I'm awake, or something like that. I don't know."

Jack's voice became more animated, trying to convince himself. "I have had maybe a dozen different dreams where I thought I was awake, but I wasn't. I would wake up absolutely convinced it was real, part of me was *positive* that what I saw was real, but it couldn't have been. Then, once, I realized I was dreaming, and I decided to fly, and I did! That proved I was dreaming! Right?"

"Did you ever check on any of the things that you saw?" Vic interrupted.

"Like what?"

"I don't know. What did you see in these dreams that you were '*positive*' was real?"

"They...were just weird. Mostly I would dream that things around me had auras, that I had an aura."

"Many people believe in auras."

Jack shook his head. "Not like this. When was the last time you heard someone talk about the aura of a couch?"

Vic smiled slyly. "Never."

Jack smiled grimly back. "See?"

"But I have heard them talk about the aura of a knife." Vic's eyes twinkled.

Jack waved him off.

"I am serious. And plants and animals, too."

"You're not helping, Vic."

"You're not letting me, Jack. What else did you see in your dreams?"

Jack sighed huffily. "I saw Julie talking to someone at her office. I saw some sort of evil glowing aura in the downstairs...eating...another glowing aura. Hell, Vic, they were stupid. I even woke up convinced that I knew where to find an old memento I accused Julie of throwing away."

"Where was it?"

"I dreamed it was under the patio deck in the back yard."

"Was it there?" Vic waited, but Jack didn't answer. "Did you check to see if it was there?"

"No!"

"Why not?"

Jack's lips twitched, but no sound came out.

"Why not?" Vic pressed him.

"I didn't want to think about it, okay? Maybe I was afraid that it would prove I was going insane!"

"Maybe it would prove that you weren't?" Vic waited for Jack's thoughts to settle.

Finally, Jack glared at Vic. "Fine. Come on. I'll show you. It won't be there, and you'll see, I was just having dreams." He got up and opened the sliding glass door. The dog pushed by him to beat him outside.

"Well?" He turned back at Vic. "Are you coming?"

Vic, still at the table, shook his head. "I've got nothing to learn from what you find, and I personally feel that these little moments of self-actualization are best enjoyed alone."

Jack turned a little redder and stomped out onto the deck, his footfalls echoing under the wood planks.

On his stomach with his arms outstretched as far as he could reach, Jack felt around under the deck . The rocks were gouging into him and it was bitter cold, but he dug his toes into the grass under the snow and inched his body a little farther under the deck. He had seen it, but was refusing to allow his mind to accept it until it was in his hands. He finally got one finger on it and rolled it over toward himself and grabbed it tightly in his fist. He refused to look at it as he inched back out from the crawlspace.

He knew what it was, and he knew it was in his hand, but he still couldn't accept it. When he finally pulled himself out from under the porch, he sat cross-legged in the snow and stared at the little wooden penguin in his hand.

His mind was blank. He was afraid to think, afraid of what answers he might find, afraid of new questions he might ask, and afraid of not only what, but how, he had known all along.

Vic was still at the table as Jack lumbered back into the house, ashen. Jack's knuckles were white in a clenched fist as he sat back down at the table. Carefully, he held his hand out over the table and dropped the small carving out of his fist. It was dirty and had chew marks on it making it look even less like a penguin than it had before, but it was unmistakable.

Jack stared at it intently as he spoke. "I didn't tell anyone that I thought it was there until I told you."

The silence stretched until Jack looked up.

Vic looked pained as he asked, "What did you decide?"

"About what?"

"Were you dreaming, or not?"

Jack's face twitched a little. "I had to have been. That was the same dream that I went flying in."

He searched Vic's eyes for any sign of his own insanity. Finally, he could come up with no more options. "How do I get in touch with your friend?"

Anita paced back and forth between Jack and her husband with a deep sadness in her eyes as they stood in the restaurant's kitchen. "Vic, I thought we had left all of this kind of crap behind us when we moved out here."

"So did I, but they need help." Vic's eyes pleaded with just as much sadness and Anita turned away.

"Jack," Anita turned and pointed a thick finger with a long, green painted fingernail at his nose, "are you sure this was your idea? Vic didn't put any stories or ideas in your head?"

Jack nodded solemnly. "All Vic did was to help me stop lying to myself."

The green-tipped weapon spun to cover her husband, but Anita had run out of words. She lowered her pointer and as voice trembled. "If I ever—" She pursed her lips. "I'll...I'll probably never sleep well again."

"Anita, I swear this had nothing to do with me. I don't know what started it."

She nodded but didn't answer. Finally, she turned her back on them and went back to cooking, tears on her cheeks. Jack noticed she quietly pulled out a rosary and kissed it, quickly looking upward before slipping it back into her blouse.

Vic turned and walked out of the back door of the restaurant, and Jack followed.

"What was that all about?" Jack asked quietly, pulling the door shut behind him.

Vic squinted into the setting sun before answering. The light shone red highlights in his black hair and sparkled gold in his sad eyes.

"I can't go with you, Jack. You're going to have to go see Fidelina by yourself."

"What? I don't even know her! She's going to think I'm some kind of lunatic!"

"No, she won't. I'll call her and tell her you're coming. But even if I didn't, she would know when she saw you. Hell, she might even know already and be waiting for you." Vic turned and put a hand on Jack's shoulder.

"I'm sorry, Jack. You know I will do anything I can for you, but my family always has to come first, as you know yours does. That's what family is." He sighed. "Even though you are family, as far as I am concerned.

"If I go with you, Anita will never believe that I didn't get involved in this, and I will lose my marriage, which would mean my family."

"I still don't understand, Vic. What does Anita think that you did?"

"She doesn't really think that I did anything. It's just… Look, it's a long story, and you're not ready to hear it yet. Trust me on this, and about Fidelina. And I promise I will watch over Julie while you are gone. We all will. I promise."

Jack sat silently next to Julie's still form and held her hand. Her parents were back at the house trying to get some rest. Her mother had offered to stay at the hospital with him, but he had politely refused and told her she needed her rest, too. Her father had been a bit gruff, but not nearly as accusatory as Jack had steeled himself for.

His head drooped and his forehead touched Julie's hand.

What was he going to tell them? What would they think about him abandoning his wife, their daughter, while she lay comatose, to run off like some damned fool to see some sort of Hispanic witch? There was no way he could ever convince them there was even the remotest possibility it might help.

Hell, he couldn't even bring himself to believe it could.

What else was there he could do? Staying here, he could do Julie no good. He lifted his head and wished she would open her eyes and look into his.

As he watched her rhythmic breathing, he forced himself not to think about how he had *known* what was wrong with her all along. Not to think about how he had *known*...that her soul was gone.

TWENTY

The dusty black highway faded into the dark New Mexico night without any delineation to show where it vanished into the void of the night. Jack concentrated on driving the car as hard as he would have in a snowstorm, keeping his eyes on the faded yellow lines down the center. It was warmer than he was used to and the rushing air coming through the open window was not cold enough to keep him fully awake. The glowing clock read 1:11 in the morning.

He smiled to himself. It made him think of Julie. She had always told him it was good luck to see the clock at 1:11. He had suggested 2:22, 3:33 and would be lucky too, with maybe 11:11 the best of all, but she had insisted only 1:11 was lucky.

His smile faded as he remembered the look on her parent's faces as he explained he was going to go see about getting help from a 'specialist' Vic knew. Her parents had tried to object to his going, worried he was just having problems coping with the situation. Jack had put his foot down and insisted he had to try. He felt bad lying to them, but what else could he have said? 'I've gone insane and I'm going to go get help from a witch' would not have gone over well.

Hours later, here he was, proving to himself he had lost his sense of better judgment. Driving down a black highway in the middle of the night, in a different state, looking for help from a *curandera* he had never met.

He shook his head as he argued with himself. He wasn't even sure what a *curandera* was, let alone whether or not he really wanted help from one.

Assuming she could help.

He watched the faded white line on the side of the road to make sure he didn't drive off into the darkness.

Vic had assured him Fidelina was a very good friend and there was no reason to worry. He insisted, at the very least, she would be able to answer Jack's questions.

Something big and black ran across the road in front of the car. Jack hit the brakes hard, swerving wildly. The car skidded as the form disappeared into the night.

Just a cat. His knees went weak as he realized he'd missed it.

He slowly picked up speed, continuing down the highway. He hadn't come close to hitting it so much as it had startled him. In the night, he wouldn't have seen it at all if it hadn't run through the beams of his headlights.

At least I'm awake now, he thought, swiping his hand through his hair.

Driving past a reflective green sign, it left a streaking afterimage in his vision. Only five more miles to the freeway exit he had been told to take. He was closer than he expected. He hadn't even been looking for the sign yet.

Jack glanced into the rear-view mirror. He thought he had seen another black cat running alongside the road. He watched the mirror for a moment but didn't see anything. The night was too dark.

Turning his attention back to the road, he came up on another mile marker. He slowed a little to try to read the number on it and was shocked to spot a black cat with gleaming green eyes sitting under the small sign. The cat languidly turned its head, watching as the car went past.

Jack became a little unnerved. The rear-view mirror again only showed the black of night. He couldn't remember the number on the sign.

Wide-awake now, goosebumps crawled up his spine. He took a deep breath and blew it out slowly. He was overreacting to nothing and stressing out for no reason. The road would be clearly marked and it didn't matter if he didn't know the mile marker.

Relief washed over him as he reached the next marker and there was no sign of a cat anywhere. Only two miles left until he reached his exit. Out of near habit now, he looked in the rear-view mirror again.

Twin green eyes gleamed in the back seat.

"Shit!"

He slammed on the brakes, ducking his head. The tires squealed through the empty night as the car fishtailed to a stop. Jack was out the door so fast he left the car in gear and it coasted off the road toward the ditch.

"Shit!" he yelled again from the middle of the road. He flailed his arms over his head trying to wave off anything that might be near. Frantically looking around, he saw nothing.

The dim red illumination from the car's taillights faded as the car crept farther away.

"Holy shit!" His body was tingling with adrenaline and he shook himself to clear away the excess energy.

Looking around the empty night, he saw nothing but himself and his slowly rolling car, its interior lit by the dome light, which had stayed on when he had failed to close the door. The car reached the far side of the ditch and began making a horrible scraping sound as the angle of the incline drug the bottom of the open door across the ground.

"Aw…shit!"

Jogging after his Celica, he caught the car easily. Jack ran alongside and searched the lit interior long enough to satisfy himself there was nothing inside. Putting his right foot in the car, he hopped twice on his left leg to match momentum, he jumped in and hit to brakes to stop the car.

Staring out into the New Mexico desert, where the headlights shone off into infinite darkness, he cursed again. He cursed whatever it was he had seen, the damage to the car door, and his own cowardice.

Damn it! He could have killed himself, or worse, he could have killed someone else. He had to get a grip on himself.

He leaned his head forward onto the steering wheel and closed his eyes, taking a deep breath to calm himself. Then he backed the car out of the ditch and out onto the freeway.

Driving even more cautiously than before, although he was more alert, he was relieved when he finally spotted the off-ramp. He pulled onto the ramp and stopped at the stop sign, dutifully checking for any cross traffic. Then he nervously checked his mirrors for anything with glowing green eyes.

He sighed and shook his head, feeling both stupid and relieved there was nothing in sight.

After only a few minutes, the car crested a ridge and Jack found himself overlooking a small town. It was larger than he had expected after talking to Vic, and he wondered if Vic's directions would still be good, or if the city had changed too much in the twenty years since Vic moved away.

He considered finding a hotel and waiting until morning, although Vic had insisted Fidelina would be offended if he did not stay with her. The thought vanished as he spotted the street he was looking for.

A dark form, running low to the ground, darted between the houses and his stomach knotted. A quick tingle ran down his spine, but dissipated when the dog ran under a porch light and off into the night.

Grunting in frustration, he hit the steering wheel with the palm of his hand.

This is ridiculous. No, he told himself, *it is way past ridiculous and on into paranoid.* He sped up, hoping he would find sanity at his destination although he knew this whole visit was as far from sanity as he had ever gone.

When he thought he had gone too far, he spotted a house light glittering through a thick copse of trees and blue reflectors marking the sides of a driveway. He stopped at the edge of the driveway, checking the house numbers on the mailbox were the ones he was looking for. Turning the car into the driveway, the headlight beams brushed across a worn looking house, revealing a figure half hidden in the shadows cast by the porch light.

Well, no going back now, he decided as he tried to spot the figure again. The headlights finished skimming across the house and came to rest on a separate garage with an open door. He silenced the motor, turned off the lights, and got out of the car before he lost his nerve.

After the long road trip, the night was quiet without the car noise. The figure moved toward him. Backlit by the porch light, it floated like a shadow.

"You must be Jack. Welcome to my home." Her voice was pleasant and rich with Hispanic accent. As she came closer, he stuck his hand out in greeting. Her slight form nimbly stepped past his hand and gave him a warm motherly hug. She smelled like flour.

Awkwardly, he hugged her back and felt how small and wiry she was.

"You must be Fidelina." He barely tripped over her name.

"Please," she stepped away and pulled him back toward the lighted porch, "call me Lena. Everyone else does. Come into the house, I have hot coffee ready, and you have come a long way."

"I appreciate you staying up to meet me, I know it's late and you must be ready for bed."

As they moved into the light, he could see her weathered and leathery face. The skin on her hands matched the deep brown of her face when she reached out to open the screen door.

"I am an old woman, Jack. I need very little sleep anymore, and when I do, it is usually in the middle of the day or at church." She smiled up at him as they entered the house.

The brightness of her nearly perfect teeth surprised him. Her hair was black as the night they had just come in from, and her blue eyes glittered, almost giving off their own light from the supple folds of her aged face.

"I see you had a traveling companion this evening. I hope it didn't disturb you too badly." Fidelina was looking out the screen door.

Jack turned to see two green eyes flash in the dark and then disappear at the entrance to the driveway. He swallowed and cleared his throat so his voice wouldn't sound shaky. "Is that your cat?" he asked as nonchalantly as he could.

Fidelina clucked her tongue. "You know that wasn't my cat."

Jack felt ashamed, as if she had caught him lying.

"But it is interesting you saw it as a cat. Most people, if they see it at all, see it as a dog. I had a cousin who swore it had been dressed in a top hat with a cane when he saw it."

"What was it then?"

"Just a curious traveler. It likes to visit other travelers who are on…interesting journeys." She turned away from the door.

"Come on," she shooed him toward the 1960's style gold flecked Formica kitchen table. "The coffee is getting cold and my feet are tired."

Jack sat as Fidelina busied herself getting coffee. The décor, fifty years out of date, gave the illusion of shabbiness, but it was homey, clean, and in good condition.

Fidelina sat a steaming mug in front of Jack before seating herself across from him. Taking a delicate sip of the scalding liquid, she caught Jack's gaze.

"I have already talked to Vic, and I understand your apprehension about coming to see me."

Jack was embarrassed and started to try to defend himself, but she waved him off.

"I already know about your wife's condition—and yours. But I want to hear the entire story, from the very first thing you can think of, and I want every detail, no matter how small or unrelated."

Flustered, he hesitated. How was he going to explain himself to this little old lady he didn't even know? Before he could stop himself, he blurted out a question and instantly felt stupid. "Are you a witch?"

Fidelina's face scrunched up as a huge grin spread across it. "I'm sorry, Jack. It has been a long time since I talked to anyone who was…a nonbeliever. I should have made you more comfortable first. To answer your question, yes, I guess I am." Something in Jack's face must have caught her eye. She smiled, more kindly this time, and asked, "What did Vic call me? *Curandera? Bruja?*"

Jack nodded half-heartedly, afraid of offending her.

"There are many words for what I am. Mostly it depends upon where you are from as to what word you would use. That, and what you think I am. You could call me a witch, or a shaman, or a spiritualist. It doesn't change what I am." Her voice was quiet and strong, her accented words clear and concise.

"Vic said there was a difference between types of witches…I mean *brujas* and *curanderas*."

"He would still carry that distinction, even after all these years." She sounded affectionately annoyed. "Vic's grandmother insisted she was a *curandera*, not a *bruja*. Where she grew up, *brujas* were evil, and *curanderas* were good. Where I grew up *curanderas* were herb masters, more like a midwife, and *brujas* were just witches. Both were good. The occasional evil ones of either kind were called *diableras*, women of the devil. In the recent history of the English speaking world, any type of witch was considered evil and in danger of losing her life, so English really has no word for a 'good' witch.

"There is really only one difference between white magic and black magic. White magic is only used to help someone, never for personal gain."

She shifted in her chair while assessing Jack's reaction. "I know you feel silly, and afraid, and confused. I have seen people thrown into the world of the supernatural before. It has just been a long time since I have been around someone from outside of my own culture. The Mexican people are a very superstitious people and they hear things from the day they are born you likely have never heard. They accept and fear these things and when they come to see me they already know who and what I am." She paused and thought for a moment.

"Vic told me you were to be trusted. I assume he told you the same about me. Please trust me long enough to at least find out if I can help you. If you don't trust me, I can do nothing for you."

"I'm sorry. I came out here because I don't know what else to do. I don't know what is wrong with me, or my wife, and I don't feel like I can trust anyone, especially myself. I feel like I might be losing my grip on reality, and then Julie…"

She smiled again, a grandmotherly feeling emanating from her. "Why don't you tell me the whole story, Jack…and I want you to treat it like a scary campfire tale. I want every single detail, and I want it punctuated with every ounce of emotion you felt when it happened."

TWENTY-ONE

Jack woke late in the afternoon and found Fidelina hanging laundry on a line in back of the house. After insisting he eat, she asked if he would drive her into town to run some errands.

They parked near the center of the small town Main Street shops and walked, as Fidelina had multiple places to go.

The first was a candle shop, where an elderly lady behind the counter greeted Fidelina and pulled a bag already filled with an assortment of candles out from behind the counter. Fidelina paid for them without checking the contents and they spent less than a minute in the store. Jack hardly had time to return the greeting of the sales clerk before they were back out on the sunlit sidewalk.

He had to hurry to keep up with the spry older woman as she hurried down the town's main street purposefully, easily weaving around cars and other pedestrians. Finally, stopping in front of a small store, she turned to Jack and said, "I want you to talk to Bernardo. He works in here."

The hand painted sign over the door read *La Peluquería* in florescent pink and blue letters over a black background. The tinted windows were too dark for Jack to see inside, but the faded red and white striped pole and the fanciful caricatured silhouettes painted on the windows indicated a barbershop.

Fidelina opened the door and motioned Jack to enter. It took his eyes a moment to adjust. A row of barber chairs were lined up in front of mirrors covering the entire length of the narrow room.

Opening the door rang a small bell and summoned a young Hispanic man from the back. The man wore black pants with a pink dress shirt. His hair was immaculately slicked back.

"Greetings! How may I help you today, sir?" His accent was much lighter than Lena's and, if Jack had not been self-conscious about being a stranger in a little town, he wouldn't have noticed it.

"I…uh…" Jack was at a loss and half turned back toward the door where Fidelina was just following him in.

"He's with me, Bernardo."

"Ah! Doña Lena! I'm glad to see you! Mama just told me I was overdue to go see you." Bernardo's accent came into full use now that he was talking to Lena, but his accent was of the younger generation, missing much of the crisp pronunciation and inherent politeness found in the older woman's. "She thinks I'll go back to my old ways unless you keep reminding me of what happened."

"I'm glad I could save you the trip, Bernardo. Here you go." She reached into the bag from the candle store and pulled out a large white seven-day candle. Bernardo took it, seeming overly grateful for it, and reached into his pocket and pulled out a twenty-dollar bill, which he handed to Fidelina.

"You remember how to do it?" she asked him very seriously, the money disappearing into the folds of her dress.

"I couldn't forget if I wanted to." He smiled as though at an inside joke.

Fidelina scowled. "I hope you wouldn't want to forget."

His smile vanished and he turned a little pale. "No. I wouldn't want to."

"Good. As long as we are making sure you want to remember things, I want you to remember that night for Jack."

Bernardo looked a little ill, but he puffed out his chest and managed to sound belligerent. "You want me to tell him? Why would I do that?"

Fidelina's grandmotherly smile returned, filling the room with reassuring warmth. Bernardo relaxed visibly, but was still hesitant.

"Jack is a friend of mine, and I am helping him learn about some things he does not yet understand. I was hoping your experience would serve as an example for a lesson I want him to learn." She leaned in toward Bernardo. "That way I can help him—like I helped you."

Bernardo nodded. "Yeah, okay. If you think it will help someone else, too, I'll tell them." He got a nervous look on his face, took a deep breath, sat down in the nearest barber's chair and motioned for them to do the same.

"Five years ago, I was the worst kind of person there is. I had drugs in my veins and murder in my heart. The details don't matter. What is important to understand is that I was on my way to kill someone. Two people, actually.

"I crashed my car out in the desert, a couple of miles from where I was going. Instead of taking God's sign I should stop and go home, I was determined to press on. Ignoring my injuries, I dug my pistol out of the wreckage and continued on my way, using more drugs to ignore the pain. In the haze of my hatred, and the drugs, I pushed on to where I was going.

I'd like to say I was drunk and high and didn't notice the warnings, but I did. The demonic howls of the coyotes, the thunder of distant hooves, the hellish fire in the clouds. But I ignored them. I had murder in my heart and I ignored them until he was upon me."

Bernardo took a deep breath and ran his hand across his forehead, his voice shaking.

"*El Diablo,* tracking the evil in my heart, found me and marked me."

Jack shifted nervously. Bernardo's intensity was growing, as if he were daring Jack to deny his story.

"He ran me over where I stood in the road, trampling me down with his fiery hooves. Even then, my heart was black. I fought to keep going on, not to live, not even to escape him, but to get my revenge on someone else. To kill.

"Satan danced on my soul, claiming it for his own, the evil in my heart such that I hadn't even needed to finish the deed. He marked me as someone who wastes their last breath on an evil intention. I don't know why he didn't kill me. Every day, I struggle to escape his grasp."

Bernardo finished his story with a quivering voice.

"But I don't know if I can."

His hand, holding the white candle Fidelina had given him, was shaking. Jack stared at the large partial U-shaped scarred area on the back of it. He felt the hair on the back of his neck rise.

"I am doing this for Doña Lena, so don't think it means anything to you," he said looking Jack in the eye. "Here is your proof that I have danced with the devil."

Bernardo pulled his shirt off over his head and stood facing them with his arms out to his sides. Dark brown U-shaped marks covered his chest and arms. He turned a slow circle to show he was covered in them. Some were distinct, others faded or overlapping, but two in the center lower back were angry red, as if they had been branded onto his skin only yesterday, as if blood would start welling out of them at any second.

When Bernardo faced forward again, his eyes were hard.

"They don't bleed much anymore, unless I really think about doing something I shouldn't. The ones on my face faded after Doña Lena began helping me. The bald patches on my head are almost gone now.

"It has been five years, three months, and two days since I woke up in a hospital bed—still screaming. The doctors said the scars and broken bones were from when the car ejected me. The police said I was so high on drugs I walked five miles in spite of my injuries.

"The people I had been going to kill called the police when they heard someone screaming. The police report doesn't say they heard demonic laughter and a herd of horses run by…because the cops thought they were high, too."

TWENTY-TWO

Out on the street, Fidelina walked slow and gave Jack a chance to think. "You have questions?" she prodded after a long silence.

Jack nodded. "Do you have answers?"

"As good as you'll get anywhere else, and better than most." She smiled her grin of perfect white teeth at him.

"No. I don't want to ask my stupid little nitpicky questions, you'll think I don't believe."

Fidelina clucked her tongue. "Haven't you ever heard there is no such thing as a stupid question? How are you going to learn if you don't ask? How will you see what is real, if you don't question reality? Ask your questions."

"Okay. Why, if Satan came for Bernardo's soul, is he still alive?"

"Good question!" She smiled again. "Even Bernardo hasn't asked me that! Why do you think?"

"If I knew that, I wouldn't have asked you."

"Yes, yes, yes, but think about it. Why is Bernardo still alive?"

Jack stepped around a faded lamppost as they continued down the street. "The only answer I can come up with is that it didn't happen."

"Then explain the hoof marks all over his body."

"Either the doctors were right, and they are an unusual scarring caused by the car accident, or..."

"Or what?" she pried.

"Or it's psychosomatic. It only happened in his mind, but it was so real to him, it affected his body physically."

"Is that what you think?"

"That's what I think is happening to me. Only maybe his was worse. Maybe it was more real for him."

Fidelina stopped walking and turned to face him. "If you really believed it was all in your head, you wouldn't be here talking to me now."

"Yeah, but—"

"No 'buts'. You and I both know something real is happening to you. Something outside of your own mind has affected you, your wife, and your dog. And it is something you need to understand before you can do anything about it." Her finger waved in front of his nose. "You came here to learn. I am teaching you as a favor to Victor. If you don't pull your head out of your ass and stop wallowing around in fear and self-pity, then you might as well go home and bury your wife now!"

Her eyes had turned hard and cold and she reminded Jack of a real witch for the first time. He took a step back away from her accusing finger. "What do you want me to do? Throw away my sanity? Pretend I'm in a movie where I can ignore reality and do…whatever?" He threw his hands up. "I don't know what to do!"

"Humph!" she snorted. "Then I guess I will have to tell you what to do! For starters, you need to accept everything I tell you is real! Is true! Then *maybe*, you will learn something."

She turned away, and then stopped, looking at him sideways. "If you have to pretend you are in a movie, pretend it is one where the monster gets you if you refuse to believe it exists."

They reached a small park in the center of town, green with grass and elm trees. Mothers watched over small children crawling over a jungle gym and digging in the giant sandbox. Fidelina made her way to an old wooden bench with peeling blue paint and sat down gingerly.

"Now that you have had time to think about it, why is Bernardo still alive?"

Jack sat next to her and took a deep breath. Only one way to play the game, he decided. "The only thing I can figure is, if this is all real, either God stepped in and saved him, Satan thinks he is worth more alive than dead, or he did die but the paramedics pulled him back from the grave."

"Very good! Those are all very good possibilities!"

"So was I right?"

"I don't know."

Jack's eyes narrowed as he regarded Fidelina.

"I didn't say I had all of the answers! Some things just cannot be known! But, if we pay close attention, we can make educated guesses."

"So what is your educated guess?" Jack's voice sounded a little too snide, even to himself.

"Do you remember what Bernardo said? His last thoughts were not of penance, nor even a cry for help. God helps those who help themselves—but only when they ask for it." She winked at him conspiratorially, and he half expected a jab in the ribs. "Since he did not ask for God's help, he most likely did not receive it."

He could tell she was trying to lighten the mood. Grateful for the attempt, he tried to smile back. "So you think it's one of the other possibilities I mentioned?" he asked.

"It is possible, but I don't think Bernardo died or he wouldn't be here. The doctors could have resuscitated him, yes, but I think his spirit was too far gone from the cares of this world to have come back to his body. He didn't care if he lived, he just wanted his revenge."

"But isn't that what spirits always come back for? To right some wrong someone did to them, terrorize their descendants for generations to come, and get revenge?"

Fidelina watched two children chasing each other around the swing set and pursed her lips. "Only the ones that make for good campfire stories and tour bookings at castles. Yes, it happens, but generally, when someone dies their spirit finds such peace in the next world they don't care about revenge anymore. Just love. But that is a different lesson, so on to the third possibility."

"Satan thinks Bernardo is worth more alive?"

Fidelina nodded distantly in a rocking motion that used most of her upper body before turning back to look at Jack again. "Please, don't use his name too much, it attracts his attention. There is a power in names. If he hears his name too much, he thinks there is either a church sermon about him or someone is calling him, either way he comes to hear what is being said. He is very vain and likes to listen in—it goes with the territory."

"Just part of the job, huh?" Jack tried to lighten the mood again.

"Yes, you could say that. To understand him, you must understand his job."

"He's the Great Tempter of Man, right? Bringer of Disease and Pestilence and all that kind of stuff."

"Yes and no. If you study the Bible, and look for his origins, you have to do a lot of looking. There is surprisingly little in there, yet everyone thinks they know who or what he is, and people have many differing opinions.

"He is not called 'Father of Lies' because he creates them, but rather because he told the very first one. Supposedly, he was an angel, or whatever you want to call God's host of heavenly creatures, and, like man, he was given free will. Also like man, he used his free will to go against God's wishes, leading to his being cast out of Heaven."

She shifted her hips on the park bench and dry paint flakes fell off onto the grass underneath. "Ultimately, it is up to us to decide if he was really a serpent, or what he did to get cast out of Heaven. Some people believe he was cast out because he was proud and jealous of God's power and wanted to rule everything himself, others think he was jealous of man and the rule over the Earth given to man by God. I once heard someone believed the fight with God was to allow all souls re-entry into Heaven for an eternal afterlife but God refused, wanting each man to earn it individually."

"If that were true," pondered Jack, "then there would be no reason for him to do evil."

"Hmm. Perhaps. Unless 'evil' is merely a consequence of doing whatever you want without regards to God's will or hurting others. 'Evil' could just be doing what he wants to do."

They sat in silence for a while before Fidelina spoke again. "It doesn't really matter. People have been contemplating his nature and purpose for all of history. I doubt we can figure it out while sitting on a park bench on a warm sunny morning." She smiled at him and the twinkle was back in her eyes.

"Anyway," she continued, "I figure Bernardo was spared for one of three things. One: the evil one revels in his power and, having exerted his power over Bernardo, he has created someone whose entire family and friends group will know and fear him. Forever. That is what power is all about, huh?

"Two: having the gift of free will, and having been created by God originally as a creature of good, it is possible he does little things like this to save the souls of people, like Bernardo and his family, by putting the fear of God, or rather the devil, into them so they will avoid Hell in the future. Who knows? An immortal being with free will, infinite time on his hands, and no one to tell him what to do…" She shrugged. "His thoughts and reasons would be completely incomprehensible to us. He may wax and wane between repenting his own sins and committing new ones out of sheer spite."

Jack nodded as he tried to understand. "So really Sa—ah, *his*, reasons may be even more vague and incomprehensible than God's. I suppose it makes a scary sort of sense. And the third possibility?"

"Ah, the third reason. I think this is the most likely. It may have not been him at all."

Jack was confused. "You mean…," he hesitated to say it after how irritated she had been before, "it was all in his head?"

"No," she said exasperatedly and Jack winced. "I mean it could have been some other demon or devil, there are many of them you know. I don't believe it ever told Bernardo specifically who it was, only that Bernardo would wear Satan's mark."

"Why would another demon have done it?"

"Why? Why not? Some believe that when the devil fell from grace, he took one-third of Heaven's minions with him." Jack raised his eyebrows in surprise and she nodded at him as she continued. "But, not all of Hell's minions came from Heaven. Many have been created since, out of hatred, evil, jealousy, and who knows what else, by both the other minions of Hell and by mankind.

"I can tell you little more, for there is little about the origins of Hell known to any living person, but I can tell you that just as there are more creatures on this Earth, large and small, than both of us together could ever hope to know, so are there many, many, creatures of the spirit worlds, both good and evil. The best you can do is learn to watch and try to recognize. Although not all snakes are poisonous, you know enough to be wary of any you see, and although not all dogs are friendly, you check to see if they will let you pet them when you meet. It is the same way in the world beyond ours. Some creatures are good, some bad, some both or neither. Some are little more than the equivalent of plants.

"It is hard to call a rose evil for its thorns or a Venus Fly Trap good for eating insects; they are merely what they are. You must always keep that in mind. People are just people. It is rare you find one truly evil, or truly good, for that matter. Everything else in nature is the same way. Everything in…supernature is too. Is that a word? Supernature?"

Jack laughed as Fidelina's quizzical look suddenly made her seem years younger and happier, easily throwing away the seriousness of their conversation. "I don't think it's a word, but it probably should be."

"Anyway, if it wasn't…*him*," she nodded her head and gestured downward with her eyes dramatically, "and it was another demon, it is possible it didn't have the strength to kill Bernardo, even in his weakened condition."

Fidelina noticed Jack's 'eyebrows furrow and explained. "Creatures of the netherworlds are generally very weak outside of their own realms, as are we. That's why you don't usually hear of anyone killed by demons, why most people have never seen a ghost, why science can't prove anything…'supernatural' exists."

"But we do hear about those kinds of things."

"Yes, but very rarely. And there is never enough proof to convince the nonbelievers. Instead of imagining the spirit world and our world as separate worlds, picture it is as one. Instead of Hell being a place entirely apart you can get to only by dying, think of it as the ocean. Our world would be more like the land. We can get our bodies to the depths of the ocean rather easily, but to get there without dying requires specialized people who know what they are doing and have the right equipment. Meanwhile, normal people occasionally find the beach and stumble around on it until they get their feet wet, sometimes accidentally getting in over their heads. They rarely find a shark, or even a clam, unless they go looking for one. Sometimes, like a sea turtle, a demon will crawl out onto the land to lay eggs of evil somewhere, but on land they are slow and weak. Just like in the water we are slow and clumsy. Are you following my analogy?"

"Yeah, I think so."

"You can take it further. There is more to the supernatural world than we can know, and it is like the air over the land. The creatures of that world are like birds, masters of the air, but when they touch the ground, they are very venerable and easily chased off. Some of the birds can go into the sea, but not for long. Some of the fish can fly through the air, but only for short distances. Some land creatures can swim, some can fly, but eventually they have to come back to land. In this way, the realms all overlap and intersect with each other, but are all part of the same world. Out of their normal habitat, the creatures are mostly helpless, but that does not mean they are harmless." She held up a warning finger for Jack to take emphasis from.

"If I threw you out of an airplane, you could wave your arms around and scream pretty good, but that's about it. You are helpless. But are you harmless? No. If a bird flying by gets too close and you grab it, you could kill it easily, assuming the grabbing didn't kill it already." She cracked a smile at him. "If you kept calm enough you could learn to control the angle of your decent, and although you would die when you landed, you might well destroy some target you have aimed for."

"Anyway," she waved her hand at the air, "you got the point."

Jack's head spun with the analogy. "Wait," he said. "There was one other thing I wanted to ask about Bernardo."

Fidelina relaxed back onto the bench and waited for Jack to gather his thoughts.

"About Bernardo's…hoof mark…scars." He stumbled over the words as his mouth and brain moved at different speeds.

Fidelina smiled at his hesitancy. "The ones on his back stay red as the incident stays fresh in his mind, that's why they bleed when he thinks of doing things he shouldn't. They are kind of like stigmata. You know stigmata, the bleeding from hands and feet like Christ? But he got the opposite mark for being the opposite of pious."

"No, I kind of guessed that from what he had said, but…why are the scars shaped like horseshoes? Aren't demons supposed to have goat feet? You know? With the split toe thing?"

Fidelina raised her eyebrows in surprise. "Another very good question, Jack. You are most observant. It is all in Bernardo's head. He got scars shaped the way he expected."

"But you said—"

"Yes, yes, yes. I know I told you to throw out the psychosomatic theory, and I meant it. But that doesn't mean the mind has nothing to do with it. If you go walking on the beach in our analogy, you are not going to do it with your body. At least, I hope you don't." She gave a little shudder as if at some thought too horrible to comprehend. "No. If you walk on that beach, or fly through the air, or whatever, you are going to do it with your mind and your soul, not your body. However, your body is a very large part of who you are and what your mind does affects it very much. Bernardo was trampled, mentally or spiritually, in the spirit world and brought the scars back with him and placed them on his body himself. That is why I have been able to get the ones on his face and head to fade. They are not truly of our physical world, they are of his spiritual world, and he expected them to look like horseshoes, not split hooves."

Jack nodded slowly. "What else does the mind affect like that?"

Fidelina pursed her lips. "I don't know if you are ready for that lesson. You are too good of a student, guessing the classes ahead of time." She paused, then stood up off the bench and began walking.

Jack had given up on getting an answer when she finally turned to him and answered. "It affects everything."

TWENTY-THREE

As Jack puzzled over her teachings, Fidelina stopped and nodded to a little girl, no older than two, who was waddling toward her from the sandbox. The child's arms were open wide in anticipation of a hug, although she was still several yards away.

"*Mija!*" A young Hispanic mother hurried to catch up. "*Mija!* Come back here!"

"It's all right, Nora!" Fidelina waved to the racing mother to get her attention. "I have her!"

The woman's face showed a visible relief and she slowed to a walk. Her eyes flicked back and forth from her daughter to Jack, and he realized she hadn't seen Fidelina at first and had been concerned about the strange man her daughter had been rushing toward. The little girl reached Fidelina, who scooped her up in a grandmotherly hug.

"Oh, *Ita!* You know better than to run away from your mama!" Fidelina chided the small child with a gentle voice and was rewarded with an embrace around the neck. The little girl peeked around Fidelina's head at Jack and he waved at her. Shyly, she hid her face in Fidelina's hair. Fidelina chuckled.

"I didn't know you had a shy bone in your body, Carmenita!" She smiled as she pulled the child away from herself and held her out at arm's length to look at her. "Look at you! Pretending to be shy! Who taught you that?"

Carmenita's mother caught up and answered for her daughter as she took her out of Fidelina's hands. "Her Auntie Lupè has been teasing her about her blue eyes and playing peek-a-boo with her."

"Well, that will do it."

The little girl continued to stare at Jack until he looked away and smiled at the mother instead. "You have a very beautiful little girl," he told her.

"Thank you." She smiled demurely and seemed to wait for him to say something more. Finally, with a slightly confused glance toward Fidelina, she broke what was starting to stretch into an awkward silence. "You should hold her," she said sternly and held out the child

Jack. The little girl began squirming and twisted away to avoid being handed to him.

"Uh…" He watched as the girl tried to get away. "That's okay. Thanks anyway." He held up his hand in refusal.

The woman's eyes flicked nervously to Fidelina, who took the little girl and stepped close to Jack. "It's okay, Nora." She smiled at the mother. "Here, Jack, just for a moment," she assured him.

He hesitated again, feeling uneasy as these women insisted he hold the child. "No, thank you. It's quite all right. She really is a beautiful child, but I don't need to hold her."

The girl's mother was visibly agitated now.

"Jack," Fidelina hissed. "You are embarrassing me. Take her."

Stiffly, he reached out and took the girl, who immediately began kicking her legs and trying to get away. Nora was still anxious, but not as much as before he had taken the child.

He smiled weakly as he handed the child back to its mother.

"Yes," Fidelina agreed with his earlier comment as though nothing strange had happened, "Carmenita certainly is a beautiful girl." Then she gave Jack a sharp look. "It's too bad she can't seem to stay clean. Look at that dirt on her forehead. Jack, clean it off, would you?"

The child was nearly immaculate, and there was certainly no dirt on her forehead. Confused, he started to say so when he felt Fidelina's foot kick the side of his.

"That looks like it will be tough to get off, you'd better use some spit." Her voice was a stage whisper as she nudged his foot again. Her expression left no room for him to argue with her.

"I, uh…I don't have any tissues," he mumbled stupidly.

"Use your finger!" she hissed and stood on his foot.

Grimacing, he licked the end of his finger and reached for the unseen dirt on the child's forehead. The mother stepped closer, eager to have him clean the spot. He rubbed a place high on the child's brow as he pretended to clean dirt off. The mother visibly relaxed, and quickly swung the child around to rest her on the hip farthest from Jack.

"Well, Doña Lena, I really must be going." She was obviously in a hurry to get away from Jack. "We will be out to see you soon." She lifted the child up in a meaningful fashion as she spoke.

"I'm sorry, dear." Fidelina finally took her weight off Jack's foot as she stepped forward to pat Nora on the arm. "Come tomorrow," she told Nora. "And don't you worry, it will be okay. Trust me."

The woman, holding her child close, smiled grimly and turned to go without ever looking toward Jack again. The little girl, peeking over her mother's shoulder, finally waved at Jack, who decided it best not to wave back.

Fidelina walked back to the peely-paint bench and sat down. Jack limped slightly as he followed and sat next to her.

"What was that all about?"

"Have you ever heard of the *Ojo* –the evil-eye?" she asked tiredly.

"No. Yeah. Vic mentioned it once. I don't know what it is. Isn't the evil-eye just a dirty look?"

Fidelina shook her head. "That is what it is reduced to in modern slang, but the 'dirty look' is just the beginning. It is a sickness, of sorts, brought on by…envy? Jealousy? I don't know. It is very rare, but it happens, especially to children, often times when someone admires their beauty, charm, or whatever, and then is not allowed, or refuses," she looked sideways at him, "to touch them."

Jack scrunched up his eyebrows as he realized he had done something wrong.

"There are evil spirits in the world, Jack, and they feed on things. They especially like human things, and children are the best and easiest to feed on." She gestured toward the playground sadly.

"I don't expect you to understand. It is not your culture, but when you bring something to everyone's attention, like how beautiful she is, then don't touch the child, it is like you are putting her on a pedestal. You are admiring, you are saying she is too good for me, I should not be allowed to touch her.

"This attracts the evil spirits. They come to see what is so good you won't defile it. What can be so worthy? Then when they come to see, it is a child. A young helpless thing who has lots of new life energy for them to steal away and live off of. You see?"

"I don't get it." He shook his head, remembering Vic's story of his great-grandmother saving his life with an egg.

"When these creatures move in and start feeding off of the children's life force, the children may become very sick and can die. 'Modern medical science' cannot help properly, only make the pain last longer."

"Is this the sickness they cure by passing an egg over the body?"

"Yes!" Fidelina perked up excitedly, seemingly surprised her student knew more than she could have hoped for. "The egg contains an even more helpless life energy. It is small, but the evil spirit can't pass up the opportunity for a quick easy snack, and has to leave the child to get it, then we use a spell to trap it in the egg and kill it."

She smiled at him, as if she were the one who had suddenly gained an understanding of what was being explained. "Come on. I have more shopping to do."

At the end of Main Street they came to a small house with the word *Herbarium* painted across the front window in small and unobtrusive letters. Fidelina turned to Jack and spoke quietly.

"I need to buy some things here and it will draw attention if you do not come in with me but it is important you do not touch *anything*, and if you have any questions, it would be best to save them for later." Without waiting to see if he understood her wishes, she turned and went up to the front door of the house and knocked.

The door opened immediately and an alluring woman answered the door. Her hair was black as night and the whites of her eyes and teeth flashed against her dark auburn skin. She wore a deep necked scarlet dress with a sash pulled tight to accent the difference between her ample chest and waspish waist.

Her eyes locked with Jack's and she struck a seductive pose in the doorway. One hand languidly reached up the doorframe, and she leaned into it, thrusting out her hip, and allowing a perfectly shaped, dark skinned leg to slip out from under the translucent summer dress, exposing it deeply to the thigh. Her voice was silk chocolate as she greeted Fidelina, her sultry gaze never flickering from Jack's soul.

"Fidelina. *Bienvenidos.* I am so glad you brought someone to see me. A new customer, I hope." Her eyes never wavered from Jack's and the slightest hint of an inviting smile played across her deep scarlet lips.

Jack found he could not take his eyes off this woman, this personification of Latin sensuality.

"Mercedes, I would like you meet Jack Hooper. He is a good friend of Victor Ramirez."

At the mention of Vic's name, Mercedes broke eye contact with Jack and made a quick glance at Fidelina. Her smile flickered and her leg disappeared back under the dress as she stood straight again.

Then a wickedly malicious grin broke wide across her face. "Oh." The word came from Mercedes' throat like a soft moan. "And how are Victor and his dear wife, Anita?" She looked to Jack for an answer, but his response was silenced by Fidelina's.

"They are still happily married." Fidelina's voice was not icy, but still managed to carry a tone of finality.

There was a moment of quiet before Mercedes backed into the house and gestured fluidly with a long slender arm, her bright red painted fingernails pointing the way.

"Please, come in, and tell me what you are looking for so that I might better provide it for you." Her demeanor was cooler, more distant and professional, but she still gave Jack an occasional glance, causing something deep inside him to stir alarmingly in reaction to her presence.

Uncomfortable with his body's unnaturally strong desire for this woman, Jack did his best to stay on the opposite side of the room from her, trying not to notice how her mesmerizing figure rolled around the room like waves in a slowly spinning glass of red wine.

He studied the tables and bookcases filled with dried powders and herbs. The scent of rosemary and perfumed candles was heady. Books, candles, crystals, and other various things he thought were perfectly in keeping with a New Age spiritual supply store, were everywhere.

A row of photographs of young Hispanic men in small silver frames caught his eye and he stepped forward to examine them. There were a hundred or so, all young and healthy looking, captured on film in various moments and poses. Had there only been one photograph, he might have thought it Mercedes' son or nephew, but there were so many, and, other than being Hispanic, they had little familial resemblance. Looking closer, he saw each silver frame had a name engraved on it. Juan Alvarez, Miguel Muñoz...there were so many of them, but the one that caught his eye was on the very end.

It had the name Victor Ramirez etched into it. Without the name, Jack would have never recognized the clean-shaven boyish face, even with the three white scars under the left eye.

He was so intent on the photograph, Mercedes startled him when her voice flowed over his shoulder like a soft caress on the cheek.

"Those are my old boyfriends. I think perhaps you recognize one of them, no?" Her voice and accent were beguiling and full of the promise of a midnight rendezvous on a deserted moonlit beach. "Alas, they are old history. I keep them here to demonstrate the power of my love charms." Her voice made subtle hints as she indicated the pendants he had been leaning over while examining the photographs.

"Here let me show them to you." She picked up a tightly wrapped bundle of string, about the size of her thumb, attached to a heavy silver chain. "This is an *uitzilintzin*. Inside of it is a hummingbird. The Aztecs wore them over their hearts to call the love of the one their heart desired. They felt that by binding the wings of the hummingbird, so too would they bind the wings of love. Care to try it?"

She held it up to put it on him and he quickly stepped away. "I already have the love of my heart's desire. Thank you." He felt awkward and stiff legged around this woman and was positive Fidelina's warning not to touch anything had been about Mercedes.

Mercedes stuck out her bottom lip in a pout that would have won an Oscar in the early Twentieth Century. She laid the charm back down and languidly flowed over to a different bookcase. "How about *piedra imán*, the blessed loadstone that attracts money to you?"

Her bosom heaved slowly and her eyes washed over him gently, creating a new kind of hunger, a yearning for power and wealth, a desire to possess. Nervously, he glanced at the little yellow silk tie-drawn bag she held out to him.

Jack flinched as a reddish glow flashed out toward him from the trinket.

He stumbled back, farther from her this time, narrowing his eyes as he felt like he was really seeing her for the first time.

She was not nearly as attractive as he had thought. And she was much, much older than he had thought, too. She had a strange reddish aura in the air around her, following her like smoke, and as he became aware of the shelves behind her, he noticed many of the things she sold had a similar emanation about them.

"I—I'm sorry, but I don't think you have anything I need," he stammered, uncomfortable to be surrounded by so much…evil.

He fought the urge to run out of the house and searched for Fidelina.

She was right behind him and he felt immense relief at the sight of her. He moved nearer to her earthy brown aura.

Fidelina was looking at him in an odd way. His gaze flicked back to Mercedes, who was also staring at him as if in deep concentration. Self-consciously, he looked down at himself and saw the violet glow around himself. Comparatively, his was at least twice as big and bright as either Mercedes' or Fidelina's auras.

Before he could say anything, Mercedes spoke again, but his time her voice was flat and cold. "I think that you are right…Jack. I think there is very little here that you would need."

TWENTY-FOUR

Jack and Fidelina didn't speak on the way back to her home. He wasn't sure what to say after the way she and Mercedes had looked at him. Embarrassed at first, as though they had caught him doing something wrong, the feeling had turned sickly as he realized he could no longer disregard the supernatural things that had happened.

Obviously, they had both seen him manifest a purple colored aura, and been taken aback by it.

Mercedes had been anxious for him to leave after that, and Fidelina, too, had distanced herself.

Tired of the silent treatment, as they pulled into Fidelina's driveway he asked, "Lena, did I do something wrong?"

"What do you think? Do you think I like being used? Huh? Do you think I like being tricked?" Her eyes were granite as she peered into Jack's face.

His pulse quickened. This was not a woman he wanted angry with him. If he had met someone like her before, he would have just thought she was charismatic, but now...he could sense her power. And he was afraid of her.

"What I don't understand," her voice dropped to a near hiss, "is what you want with me. Why are you here?" Her eyes bored into his and he wanted to blink, to look away and hide his face, anything but bear the weight of her gaze.

"I—I told you already. Vic told me—"

"You mean you told Vic!" she spat the words and he flinched. "Don't bother lying to me, I have heard of people like you. What do you want from me?"

Jack was flabbergasted. He sat, petrified. He had no idea what was going on, and even less of an idea what to do about it.

"Pfaw!" Fidelina got out of the car and slammed the door in disgust.

Jack sat alone for a long time, realizing he had somehow worn out his welcome. He got Fidelina's purchases out of the trunk of his car and took them into the house. Fidelina was nowhere to be seen. He sat the bags on the gold-flecked kitchen tabletop and thought about trying to apologize. Finally, he decided it would be better if he just left.

"What are you doing?"

He turned around and almost fell over Fidelina, who was standing only inches from him.

"I, uh, I just brought your things…in," he said gesturing lamely at the table as he tried to regain his composure.

Then his gut constricted. Fidelina held a long, wicked silver dagger in her large knuckled fingers, ready to plunge into his chest.

"Whoa!" He tripped again, backing away from the blade, and fell over one of the kitchen chairs. Panicked, he scrambled to untangle from the chair, dragging himself into the corner of the kitchen, as far away from Fidelina and the knife as possible. His chest heaving, he swallowed hard and waited for her to attack.

Fidelina stood still, a far-away look on her face, watching Jack hide in the corner like a scared child. She lowered the knife and sat it on the table, then seated herself, watching Jack.

Not wanting to do anything that might end his reprieve, Jack stayed right where he was and watched her back.

"What did you think I was going to do to you just now?" she asked.

"I thought you were going to kill me!"

"I was."

"Why?"

"Because," she answered quietly, "I am afraid of you."

Jack almost laughed, why would anyone be afraid of him? Then he remembered Stanley. No flicker of smile reached his face.

"I thought you were manipulating me," Fidelina said. When he didn't say anything, she continued. "And I thought I had to protect myself."

Jack's eyes flicked to the dagger on the table. It was glowing bright enough to be a light source, had it not been an aural glow that did not reflect.

"Ah! Now you see it, don't you?" Fidelina had spotted Jack's eye movement. "It is sad, Jack. That dagger is the reason why I now trust you completely, and why you no longer trust me."

Jack didn't take his eyes off the dagger. There was something about it. It wasn't safe to ignore it. Shaped like a crucifix turned into a dagger with an ornamental handle, the glow of its aura was unlike any Jack had yet seen. Bright and pure, yet it was…evil?

"You remind me of Victor, lying there, tangled in the chair like that. The first time I ever talked to him, he was pointing that very dagger at me and lying in a pile of broken coffee table, all tangled up and looking like you do now. Except he was only eight years old at the time."

She picked up the dagger from the table, laid it on the floor, and gently slid it across the kitchen linoleum to Jack. "Be careful when you pick it up. It affects everyone differently. It is a blessed dagger, and it has the soul of a demon trapped inside of it."

Jack's eyes flicked back and forth between her and the dagger, unsure what he should do.

"Go on." She nodded. "I am giving it to you. I know, *now*, that you won't hurt me. I just have to convince you I am still trustworthy."

Never taking his eyes off Fidelina, Jack untangled himself from the chair, sat it upright, and then sat in it. He was sure she was telling the truth; her aura was solid and without any flickers or dark spots.

He was also sure he did not want to touch the dagger. He could see its aura even when not looking at it, as though he had a third eye, the sole purpose of which was to watch the dagger so he would always know where it was. Hesitant to distract himself from vigilantly watching the dagger, he finally responded to Fidelina.

"I trust you." He phrased his words carefully. "I just don't understand what just happened. Or what happened at Mercedes' store for that matter. But I trust you. You can keep the dagger."

Fidelina raised her eyebrows. "You don't want it?"

"No." Jack's voice was firm.

"How odd," she muttered to herself. Getting up, she retrieved the blade before returning to the table. She laid it on the table and motioned for Jack to bring his chair back over to the rest of the dining set. "Most people can hardly refrain from touching it, yet you are actively repelled by it?" She waited for him to confirm her interpretation, which he did with a slight nod. "Why don't you want to touch it?"

"It's evil." He could hear his normal voice creeping back into the conversation.

"But it is blessed."

"But it is also evil."

"Cannot a thing be both?"

"Obviously, as this *is* both," he told her. "But the evil in it corrupts the good. Irrevocably."

She sat looking back and forth between him and the dagger. "It sounds to me like you have pegged the nature and the curse of

Original Sin. Once your eyes have been opened to the evil, they can never be closed again." She contemplated Jack's countenance while he pondered hers in return. "Tell me, Jack. Can you still see the dagger's aura?"

Jack was shocked to find he couldn't. The fixed beacon that had called his attention to the dagger like a compass needle pointing to North was gone. "No. Not at all."

Fidelina nodded. "But before, when you could, you could see it without even looking at it, couldn't you?" Jack nodded a short curt nod. "I think I am beginning to see the problem here."

"You know what is wrong with Julie?" Jack's voice rose as his heart leaped with hope.

"No. I know what is wrong with *you*. You were chosen by Guadalupe. Jack…you will have many terrible trials ahead of you."

She reached out and patted his hand with sadness in her eyes. "I will do whatever I can to help you."

TWENTY-FIVE

As Fidelina put away the things she had bought, Jack found himself looking at the silver cross-shaped hilt of the blade on top of the table. He could feel the echo of the way it had acted like a beacon in his mind. Fidelina had been right; it did call to him. It made him want to pick it up, which was a very large reason why he did *not* want to pick it up.

An odd-looking thing, the blade was too long and skinny to be a knife, yet not thin enough to be a pick. He kept imagining blood on the blade and caught himself glancing back at the gleaming edge to make sure it was still clean.

He shivered and resolutely turned his back to the dagger.

Moving into Fidelina's family room, he was drawn to a small table in the corner. It was some sort of shrine. Amazed at its simplicity, it struck him as being very holy, in the manner only the humblest of things can be.

In the center of the table was an area covered by a white cloth with a statue of the Virgin Mary. She was standing on a crescent moon with an angel at her feet, and she was shrouded in a midnight blue cloak with stars on it. He stared at her brown skinned face in wonder. How similar to what he had grown up with, yet how very different.

The statue had a large candle on either side of it, and a small votive candle in front of it. At the front of the table, there was a small teacup on one side and an incense burner on the other. They appeared to be well used, yet well cared for, antiques.

"That is Our Lady Guadalupe."

Jack startled and turned to see Fidelina standing behind him.

"You would know her as the Virgin Mary."

"She looks different."

"All people's religions fit their cultures. This is where I work most of my magic." She caught Jack's look of surprise. "I am a witch, after all. What did you expect?"

"I just…uh…other than the knife thing, you've been such a normal person, I kind of forgot you were a witch."

"Hah!" Her eyes twinkled. "I suppose all the normal people you know tell you stories about demons and take you to potion shops!"

Jack felt his cheeks flush. "I mean you're not...you're not a...weirdo."

"Hah!" She laughed then chuckled with genuine mirth. "Mighty high praise coming from someone seeking a witch doctor cure!"

He looked away, embarrassed.

"I shouldn't tease you. Of course I am normal. So are you. Everyone is normal. Except for the occasional weirdo. You're right. I can see why you might have been expecting crystals and opium incense. We can go get some if it will make you feel better."

"No thanks. I feel silly enough already. What kind of magic do you do?"

"I do whatever I need to."

"Like...?"

Fidelina sighed. "I help cure illness, find work, help with wandering spouses, help find true love... Whatever people need of me."

"Does it work?"

Fidelina gave him a frown. "I thought I told you to trust me. They work if Guadalupe wills them to work. I am just a humble servant, asking for help on behalf of those who come seeking it.

"Look, Jack. I know you came here for answers, and I know you feel like I'm stringing you along, but I am doing my best to give you a crash course in dealing with the supernatural world. I have to be careful not to mess it up, or I could be doing you, and Guadalupe, a great disservice."

"I appreciate that but..."

"Jack. Ask yourself this. What have I asked of you? Money? Time? Energy? What am I gaining from this? You see? I am doing this for you. I have nothing to gain here, as far as you know. So trust me."

"As far as I know? What do you have to gain from this?"

She smiled at him. "I knew I shouldn't have said that. I was doing this as a favor for Vic, but now I am doing it as a favor to you, as a colleague, and to Guadalupe, as I am sure she has sent you to me."

"A colleague? What does that mean?"

"It means there is nothing I can do that you can't do a hundred times faster and better."

"What?"

"Go pick up the knife. There are answers in it."

"I don't want to."

"It won't hurt you. You saw me holding it. It's not like it's got poison on it or something. You'll be fine."

"Why do you want me to pick it up so badly?"

"Have you picked up psychic residue off of anything yet?" She saw the confusion on his face. "Has an object told you anything about its owner, or the last person who used it?"

"A couch told me what an argument was about, I guess."

"That is what the knife will do. Go pick it up."

TWENTY-SIX

Jack stared at the sliver crucifix-turned-dagger until he finally steeled himself enough to pick it up. It was cool in his hand and felt calming and protective, not at all like he had expected. He sat down and brought the blade closer to his face, inspecting the detail on the hilt: a simple cross with each arm having a protruding seam down the middle giving it a three-dimensional effect. It was obviously antique and a myriad of tiny scratches had etched into the soft silver over the years.

He turned it over. The reverse side was identical. He wondered what Fidelina had expected to happen when he picked it up. It certainly hadn't answered any of his questions, although he was surprised to find it felt more protective in his hands than it did evil. Like the feeling of protection from a gun in a time of crisis, mixed with the loathing that the gun had killed someone dear: a thing hated, but nonetheless accepted as necessary.

He was about to lay it back on the table when something caught his eye. Deep in the crevasse where the blade came out of the bottom of the cross was a small discoloration. He held it up to get a better look. It looked like old dried blood, except black—much too black.

The world shifted, becoming dreamlike and vague, and Jack became unsure where he was. How did he get here? He noticed his hands were blue. No aura, just blue.

He had seen that before. In the dream telling him where to find the wooden penguin his hands had been blue, but there had been no aura. What did that mean?

He was dreaming again, of course. He glanced down at his watch to see if the numbers stayed steady while he read them, but his watch wasn't on his wrist. Then he remembered he had proven that dream was real by finding the penguin.

He became aware of four old women sitting around a table. They were conducting a séance. He was in a kitchen similar to Fidelina's, but smaller, and the furnishings were very old. The old women were chanting in Spanish. They sounded far away.

Movement caught his attention.

A small boy stood in the corner, watching with eyes big as saucers. He couldn't have been more than eight years old, but it was hard to make out his features. The room was dark except for lit candles around the table. The flickering light cast moving shadows across all of their faces.

Jack tried to move closer to hear better, but he was frozen in place. His hands and feet responded normally, he just couldn't change locations in the room.

Experimenting, he found he could turn in a circle and see all around.

As he turned to look back at the table, a glint of reflected candlelight called his attention to the shelf on the wall. He leaned in closer and saw a knife resting next to a photograph of Jesus. The same knife he had been holding in his hands just before he had found himself here. He wondered what would happen if he looked at it while he was in a dream induced by looking at it.

He reached out to pick it up, but his hand passed through it, touching nothing.

A gasp sounded behind him. He whirled to find the four old women staring at the center of the table in shock. One of them, the youngest in appearance, seemed ill. As he watched her with growing concern, his vision began to change and he could see their auras.

Instantly he recognized Fidelina's aura, as if once you knew someone's aura, you knew it forever. The boy! It was Vic! The aura wasn't the same orange he had seen around Vic before, but he knew it was him just the same. Was this a memory he was seeing? If so, whose was it? How long ago had this happened?

His attention went back to the youngest woman. Possibly in her forties, she was markedly younger than the rest. His eyes flicked to Fidelina who looked nearly the same as she did today. How old was she anyway? Judging from young Vic's appearance, this had to be at least thirty years ago!

Something was familiar about the youngest woman, too.

She swooned. Her aura flickering as a horrible, pulsing mass of putrid red energy reluctantly pulled away from it like a leach from skin.

As the thing floated to the center of the table, Jack could see it sucking at the auras of everyone in the room, like a black hole pulling the gas from five neighboring stars at the same time.

The youngest woman's head dipped again and Jack recognized her face. It was Mercedes. She was old, but recognizable. How could she be older when Vic was younger? Why hadn't he recognized her aura?

Before he could look closer, the disgusting red cloud in the middle of the table wrapped itself in energy stolen from all five auras and began to take form.

Jack's skin crawled, and his stomach churned as a demon appeared on the middle of the table. Somehow, using the strength stolen from the women's auras, it wrapped reality about itself and gave itself flesh. Standing two feet tall, it cocked its equine head to the side. Its beady black eyes protruded and glinted in the candlelight.

Mercedes lost her battle for consciousness and slumped in her chair, falling to the floor.

The hideous creature flexed its ugly little bat wings and deftly swatted Fidelina with a long crooked arm, sending her flying out of her chair and into the wall, where she crumpled into a heap.

Jack tried to run to her, but he couldn't move. He tried calling out, but no sound came from his throat.

The demon, seemingly hearing Jack's soundless call, barred dog-like teeth at him. Its fangs were too long and glistened with sticky saliva.

Jack's distraction was all the time the third and fourth women needed. One jumped out of her chair and into a stance that would have done a commando proud, the other flung herself through the doorway into the darkness of the room beyond.

The demon hesitated then leaped after the fleeing woman, knocking candles off the table. Hopping and jumping awkwardly on horse-like legs, its tiny bat wings flapped futilely as it slipped on the kitchen tiles. It finally found a foothold in the grout and was out of the room in a blur of motion.

Young Victor crawled frantically along the wall, heading into a different room. Jack tried to follow, but still couldn't move.

The last of the women, who appeared to be the oldest of them all, spryly leapt at Jack. He yelled and tried to get out of the way as she slammed her fist through his spectral head and pulled the knife from off the shelf.

Obviously unaware of Jack, she turned and ran after the demon. Jack was pulled along like a kite on a string, unable to stop himself from following. As they entered, he couldn't see anything.

Wait. Yes, he could. He could see auras.

The first old woman was lying on the floor, next to the far wall. Her aura dimmed even as he watched, flickering at her head and neck where there was damage.

He stood behind the old woman who had drug him into the room. She cast a bright earthy toned aura, greens and browns, but the aura didn't reflect off of anything, so it didn't reveal the room. He remembered seeing the auras of the furniture in his house, and tried to do so now, but nothing happened.

Where was the demon? Was there another way out? Could it be behind…?

Just as he turned to look, the demon leaped off the wall and into his face. Even as he threw up his hands, he felt foolish for flinching from the dream a second time.

Then the weight hit him hard.

He fell backward, the demon on his forearms like a cat on a screen door. The two of them slammed into the old woman, knocking her to the floor and sending the knife she was holding clunking to the floor.

Free of the demon, Jack jumped up quickly, surprised and horrified it could touch him. He went into a fighting stance, turning and searching for the next attack.

He found the demon sitting on the middle of the old woman's back, looking confused. Slowly turning its head, the creature sniffed at the air like some kind of freakish rat. The woman was unconscious, her aura showing damage on a hip.

Jack's skin crawled as he realized the demon had no aura. That was why he hadn't seen it in the room.

The demon moved toward the old woman's head, grabbed a handful of hair, and lifted her head back to expose the neck. The woman regained consciousness just in time to see the wicked twinkle in the demons beady black eyes.

Jack realized it was going for her throat.

NO!

He tried to yell but no sound came out. The demon looked at him anyway, regarded him curiously, as though it couldn't tell for sure if he was there. Finally, it seemed to decide Jack didn't matter and lunged for the woman's throat.

Jack was just close enough to try. He kicked, connected, and sent the demon flying against the far wall.

It landed hard, scrabbled into a fighting stance, and curled its lips in a soundless snarl, barring fangs. Swinging its long snout back and forth, oversized clawed hands reflexively clutching at the air, it sniffed at the air again.

Jack couldn't pursue the creature. He could look all around him, just as he had done before, but also as before, he was stuck in one place, unable to move away from the knife.

The demon held its place, eyes searching, nose quivering, and ears twitching, seeking any sign of its adversary. Jack realized it did have an aura, but it was very difficult to see, hidden under the demon's self-created flesh as if the aura was holding the flesh in place from the inside out. The energy swirled, hidden under the physical mass the demon had pulled around itself at the table, but occasional bits leaked out like nasty tendrils of smoke. Not at all like the other auras he had encountered, it reminded him of the dream about the red cloud in the basement.

The thought chilled his bones. Had Julie been attacked by something like this?

The fallen women did look much as Julie had when he had found her, except they still had glowing auras.

They still had souls.

The old woman at his feet was sobbing, and he was pretty sure her hip was broken. He kneeled down and tried to heal her. He could see her aura, sense it, but he couldn't affect it.

The demon warily skulked its way over to where the first old woman lay unconscious and began nosing at the wound in her neck.

Jack struggled futilely. He wanted so badly to go help the old woman, but he just couldn't move. He tried yelling again, but the demon merely peeked an eye over her body, its tongue beginning to probe at the wound.

Jack felt ill. He wondered if it were possible for him to throw up here, wherever here was.

As he watched the demon lap at the woman's blood, he noticed the skin on the demon began to thicken. The places where the aura had been steaming out began to seal up, and the demon grew taller, somehow feeding on her to build and strengthen its physical body.

A movement from the kitchen caught his eye. The boy—Vic.

He watched Vic silently crawl across the kitchen, moving slowly toward the room with Jack and the demon.

Go back! He tried to scream, but couldn't make a sound. Could this really be the past? It must be; Vic was only a boy. He had thought it just a dream, or a memory of some sort, but he had affected it. Was the past set in stone? Could Vic be hurt, or killed? Run Away! He screamed silently at the boy again.

The boy didn't notice. Had the demon? Jack's heart leaped. Had he just brought the boy to the demon's attention by trying to yell? He whipped his head around to look at the demon. Completely ignoring Jack, having deemed him harmless or perhaps not even there, it was becoming more aggressive with the old woman's throat. Jack couldn't stand to look at it.

His stomach lurched as he turned to find the boy already in the room, crawling toward him. He watched in terror as Vic put his hand on the knife and inhale sharply as he cut himself.

Jack looked back to the demon. It hadn't noticed.

Sucking at his finger, the boy clutched the dagger fiercely.

Jack felt himself pulled along with the movement of the knife in the boy's hand.

He silently willed Vic to hurry and leave, but the boy carefully checked to see if the woman with the broken hip was breathing. Seemingly satisfied, the boy began working his way toward the other woman. Jack was pulled along with him.

No, no, no...

Jack was afraid to try to call out again; the demon might look up and see Vic. He wanted the boy to stop, to not go where the disgusting creature was making sucking sounds at the old woman's injured neck. The boy stopped.

Yes! Get away, Jack willed as hard as he could.

The boy began to back up. Then the knife scraped the floor.

The demon's head popped up and it spotted him.

The boy jumped up and the demon leaped at him. Vic reflexively brought the knife up in a silver flash as they met in the air.

The demon impaled itself on the knife as their momentum hurled them both past Jack, then pulled him along as the knife moved.

They landed hard on a coffee table. Glass and wood shards exploded out from underneath them. Vic screamed as the demon raked its claws across his face, leaving three parallel lines of blood under his eye. Its cloven feet kicked repeatedly at the boy's thighs and stomach and the boy grunted with the impacts.

Fear coursed through Jack. Vic was going to die! He had to do something!

Desperately, he grabbed at the demon, but his hands passed right through its leathery hide—right through and into the nasty aura it was trying to protect. The vileness of it covered his hands like warm oil, slipping through his fingers. He tried to grab handfuls and pull it out of the false body.

The monster kicked him in the face with a cloven hoof and his head rocked with the blow, but he held on to its internal substance. Its self-made hide was too strong or too thick; Jack could not pull its essence out of the protective shell. Then he saw there was more than nasty black ichor leaking out around the wound from the dagger.

Wisps of the cloud-like substance of the demon's aura were also leaking out though the wound. Jack slid his ghostly hands sideways around to the wound in its belly and pulled at the slimy red glow that was its innards, squeezing it through the rent flesh.

The demon threw back it head as if to scream, but no sound came out. The physical body was already dissipating into the air. The spiritual body stayed in Jack's hands, coating them like glowing red tar.

At first, he tried to hold on to it, prevent it from reaching the boy, but then he realized it was holding onto him.

It was climbing up his arms, seeping into his skin, becoming part of him. The evil was entering his hands, burning like salt in a wound.

Jack panicked.

This couldn't be happening, it couldn't be! He wasn't here. His body was back at Fidelina's kitchen table, thirty years in the future.

Wake up! he yelled at himself. *Wake up!*

TWENTY-SEVEN

Jack jerked back to the reality of sitting at the kitchen table with the cross hilted knife in his hands. He dropped the knife and it clattered on the table. His hands were still pulsating and glowing red. The demon had somehow attached itself to him!

He yelled in horror, knocking over his chair as he leaped to his feet. How to get rid of it? It was still working its way up his arms. Eating at his aura.

He called out for Fidelina, running back into the living room where he had left her before. She was nowhere in sight. Dread set over him as the demon climbed up to his elbows. His hands had gone numb and he could no longer move his fingers. His heart pounded as he desperately tried to think of anything he could do to rid himself of the demon.

On the verge of freezing with terror, he realized he needed to fight.

This was like before. Like when he had been attacked in his dream. He had to fight to survive. But how?

He looked at his hands, useless to him, encased in the red aura.

His eyes fell on Fidelina's humble altar. The fourteen-inch Guadalupe, so much like the Virgin Mary, yet so different with her azure robe and swarthy skin tone, called to him. He felt overcome with the need to pray for forgiveness. For the way he had been acting lately, for leaving Julie behind while she was so sick, for being a jerk to Heidi, for being spiteful with Stanley, for upsetting Charlie, for so many things.

Remorse set deep and he dropped to his knees in front of the altar.

Never much of a spiritual man, Jack prayed. He prayed for forgiveness for everything, for not having more of an appreciation for life, for idly wasting so much of it on self-indulgences, and for not paying enough attention to God. Not being Catholic, he also prayed for forgiveness if he offended by praying at Guadalupe's altar, but not to her. He prayed for Julie and for her parents. Jack lost sense of himself, and of the demon, while he was praying.

He lost track of time kneeling on the floor in Fidelina's living room.

Finally he ran out of things to pray for and looked up into the face of Guadalupe. "Thank you," he told the little statue, not sure who or what he was talking to. His heart felt lighter than in as long as he could remember. He tried to remember the last time he had gone to church, or even prayed, and could not.

Then he remembered. He had prayed when the ghost had attacked him in his sleep. At the last moment, when he should have died, he had prayed. And God had saved him.

What was it Fidelina had said? 'God helps those who help themselves. But only when they ask for it.'

He looked at his arms. The demon had made no progress while Jack had prayed, but it had not subsided either. As he watched, it resumed creeping up his biceps. He closed his eyes in silent prayer and asked God to help him again.

Nothing happened. The demon continued to advance. His arms were mostly numb now, with a prickling of pain setting in.

His panic returned, drowning out the peace he had felt. God wasn't helping him this time. The demon was nearly at his shoulders. He was losing very quickly.

How could he fight this? How had he fought it before, at home? He tried to calm himself. What had he done before? He had imagined locking the pain of the ghost into a sphere and getting rid of it. Would that work again?

He closed his eyes and imagined the demon. It had already taken both of his arms and was expanding to meet in the middle, where it would get his neck and chest. Would his heart go numb too?

Forcing himself not to think about it, he envisioned massive steel plates flying in from infinity to surround the demon, but the demon was in him. The plates surrounded him as well as the demon. They couldn't isolate it. What to do now? His breathing began to labor as his chest started to succumb.

A new idea occurred to him.

He visualized his own aura growing stronger and brighter, pushing back the demon aura, forcing it to retreat from his chest. Gratefully, he felt his breathing ease up, but he didn't dare stop and give the evil thing a chance to renew itself.

Pushing with his own violet energy, he forced the evil red glow down his arms, back toward his hands. The farther it receded, the more it resisted and the harder it became to move it. He strained, holding his breath, every muscle in his body tense, like he was going to explode from the inside. Finally, it was back to only his hands, but, on the verge of passing out, he couldn't push any harder.

Now he visualized the plates coming in again, this time enclosing his own hands inside the sphere. Thick walled steel plates flew in from the outer reaches of his mind and slammed together with satisfying clanks, one layer deep, two, three. He put a fourth on for good measure and stopped pushing.

The demon was trapped in the sphere. He could sense it trying to get out, but he was sure it was trapped.

The problem was, so were his hands. Still numb from the effect of the demon on them, he had only a vague sense of them, but he could feel the demon slowly eating away at them, pulling energy to sustain itself.

This was nearly as bad as before. The demon was still feeding off his aura, only slower now that it had to wait for his aura to keep spreading down into his hands. He had to be rid of the demon or it would eventually find a way to steal his entire aura.

Would that be the same as taking his soul? Maybe his life force? He wasn't sure, but he knew it was bad.

He couldn't see any other alternative. Sooner or later, if he left his hands in the sphere with the imprisoned demon, the demon would win.

Jack imagined chains, connecting to the walls, ceiling, and floor, coming out to hold the sphere solidly in place. He took a deep breath and, bracing himself, ripped his hands out of the sphere by sheer physical force.

The momentum of the pull sent Jack stumbling across the room backward. He fell down and landed hard on the seat of his pants, jarring his teeth and bruising his tailbone, but he hardly noticed. His eyes were fixed on his hands.

His aura had ripped away from the wrists down. An aching loss resounded through his soul, worse than the first time a girl he had a crush on had laughed in his face, worse than being stood up at the prom, worse than the death of a friend—even worse than Julie lying in the hospital.

He wanted to cry. He ached so badly in his soul. Morose, melancholy, and even suicidal depression subdued him. It was grief, sorrow, and guilt. Longing and loss and every terrible feeling he had ever had all rolled into one horrendous, inescapable moment.

The demon had taken part of him with it, one he could never get back and would always miss. Dimly, part of him was grateful to be alive, thankful to God for helping. He was sure God had provided the idea to trap the demon. Just as sure as he had been when God had given him the strength to fight the ghost in his bedroom so long ago.

Praying a silent thank you, another idea occurred to him. He opened his teary eyes and focused on the severances in his aura at his wrists. The aura just ended. No jagged edge, no fading, just a straight line where it had been removed. His hands felt cold and lifeless, and were nearly unresponsive when he tried to move his fingers. He stared at his violet aura and willed it to grow down his wrists and across his palms.

Slowly, dimly, the glow spread, each finger tingling painfully it rejoined his body in life, but the rest of his aura dimmed, thinning as it spread itself out. When it finally finished, he gasped with exhaustion, his mind numb. The melancholy faded to a tolerable level, no more than the loss of his dog when he was twelve, but his hands were part of him and alive again.

Exhaustion flowed over him and he slumped silently.

TWENTY-EIGHT

Jack felt a tickle on his back and rolled over onto his side. The bed was warm and comfortable, a cozy cloud holding him gently. He sighed with the pleasure of warm safety as he felt Julie's hands begin to massage his tight shoulder muscles and he relaxed even further.

The warmth of her body comforted him as she moved closer and spooned into him, still soothingly working the tensions out of his back. He sighed with pleasure as the feelings of love surrounded him with warmth. Julie moved closer and reached her arms around his chest to hold him tight and he did his best to melt into her. Her hands slid across his skin like silk, softly caressing his chest and arms.

Her warm breath nuzzled his neck and he sighed again as she teasingly nibbled at his ear. It was so good to be back home and safe. Her hands slowly began working their way lower and he felt himself beginning to respond to her affections. She was so warm against his skin, so comforting and soothing.

One hand slid into his underwear and he felt a quick electric thrill shudder up and down his body as she took hold of him. *It has been so long,* he thought as he rolled over to be closer to her. He put his arms around her and pulled her closer to him, burying his face in her hair and breathing deeply of her scent. He had so missed the way she smelled. The scent of perfume tickled his nose and throat enticingly and Julie's mouth worked its way across his neck and cheek seeking his.

Something wasn't right.

Her arm wrapped around his head and pulled him close to her mouth, her tongue probed at his lips teasingly.

Something wasn't right. Some part of him insisted again, not right.

He pulled his face away from the tantalizing tongue and felt her wrap her leg around his hip, pulling him in closer to her body. The heat of her breasts warmed his chest as her hand moved to work him out of his underwear. He sucked in air in pleasure at her touch.

Not right, not right, not right.

Julie pulled his mouth back to hers.

Julie…

Julie was in the hospital! He tried to sit up but found himself entwined in arms and legs. A hand pushed him down flat on his back.

He shook his head to clear the dream. The room was dark, but he was definitely entangled with a woman. This wasn't Julie!

He tried to push the stranger off, but she was much too strong and resisted him easily.

"No," he whispered.

"Yes…," she moaned back in a low growl.

He felt himself go flaccid as his body followed his mind's orders and began to find her uninteresting.

"Yes…" She moaned again into his ear seductively and tried harder to restore his potency, moving gently but firmly closer to him, bringing her hips in to meet with his.

"No!" He almost managed a shout as her mouth covered his. He felt his body reacting again even as his mind began to fear rape. He had heard it could happen to a man, but had never understood how. Even now, his body continued to respond though his mind was filling with fear and anger.

He had to do something; it was only a matter of seconds until she would manage to get him inside of her, and no matter what happened after that he would always feel as though he had been unfaithful to Julie. Closing his eyes, he tried to force his body to stop responding. Imagining himself going limp, he felt it begin to happen. The woman moaned in a manner that expressed her displeasure and yet was a come-on at the same time.

A strong tingling sensation formed around him and the woman sighed happily as his body began to respond to her again. Opening his eyes in surprise, he found himself bathed in a deep red glow. It wasn't exactly an aura, more like pure energy. He was being force fed some sort of energy and his body was responding to it, tingling and reacting everywhere!

Unable to resist the feeling even while the fear and anger boiled in his mind, he unwillingly moaned as a shiver of pleasure crawled across his body. Just imagining himself limp wasn't going to stop this. There was too much energy, too many sensations to ignore.

The glow played across his skin in a familiar way, and he remembered the demon eating away at his aura. Could he do the same? The woman took him in her hands and began trying to move herself into position. His hips involuntarily moved to help her.

Jack grimaced and began to imagine his violet aura absorbing the red glow.

The woman stopped moving, frozen in place. Then she screamed. A high, piercing shrill, needling through his ears, her cry helped him regain control of his body. He focused on the sound pulling himself away from her even as he visualized the red aura slowly turning violet.

She punched hard at his chest, pushing them apart. Painful cries ripped out of her throat. He ignored her and kept his attention on the visualization until he could see his own aura appearing through the haze of red energy surrounding him. He felt himself growing stronger as it ate the red energy.

The woman's aura finally showed through the red glow and he knew it was Mercedes, but the aura was wrong somehow, different from when he had met her.

When the red energy was finally consumed from around his body, he almost stopped but he realized there was more. Looking at the aura of the woman at the edge of the bed, he saw a small red line of energy drawing to him from her.

He was sucking her energy from her like a straw in water.

Horrified, feeling like a cannibal, he almost stopped again, but then he saw the first edge of the red tinge pull away from her aura.

A demon.

Like the one earlier, but different. And somehow he was pulling it out of her aura. It clung to her, invisible claws dragging lacerations through her aura as he pulled it away. Her cries of pain stopped suddenly and she was gone.

Jack was alone in the room with a very small cloud of red energy. Shocked, he looked around, but there was no other sign Mercedes had ever been there. He could feel a small struggle coming from the demon, but knew better than to give it any chance at all. Now that Mercedes' aura no longer mixed with it, he could feel its evil clearly. He continued absorbing the energy into himself until it was gone entirely, leaving him alone in the eerie quiet of the dark room.

He sat in the dark and examined his own aura. The violet hue was steady, and the intensity of the emanation was brighter than ever. He had worried absorbing the evil thing would give it a foothold against his aura, like the demon in the knife had taken advantage of, but he could neither see nor feel any indication it was still with him at all. Except...he felt good. He felt strong, and vibrant...and young!

Fidelina threw open the door and light burst into the room. Jack moved to cover himself and was shocked to find he was fully clothed, except for his shoes. Fidelina saw his shocked expression and nearly blushed.

"You are a big man for such a small woman like me to move about the house. I didn't have enough strength left to undress you. I didn't think you would mind."

Jack shook his head numbly.

"I thought I heard something, so I came to check on you," she continued. "Is everything all right?"

Jack shook his head again. "Mercedes was here."

Fear and anger both played across Fidelina's face as she quickly turned her head to glance around the room. Her eyes fell on the window, the light of the moon just beginning to shine through the gossamer thin curtains. She hurried over to it and searched for something.

"Ay! Those kids! They'll be the death of me yet!" She hissed and turned back to Jack. "Are you all right? Never mind, that is a stupid question. I know you are fine, or you wouldn't be talking to me. Hold on a minute."

She stormed out of the room and returned quickly with some quarters and tape. He watched as she blessed each quarter and then taped two to each pane of glass, one facing in and one facing out. As she finished, Jack could not restrain his question any longer.

"What are those for?"

"These will keep her out, so you don't have to worry about her coming back. I'll go check the other windows and make sure Pepe's kids didn't take any other quarters with them."

Jack got up and followed as she checked the other windows in the house. "How do those keep her out? They're just quarters."

"They won't keep her out physically, she can still walk into this house, but they'll keep out all but the most powerful of spirits, including hers. Have you ever heard of putting a horseshoe over the doorway for good luck, or placing crosses on each wall of a house? It is a similar thing. Many people use expensive silver or amulets, but quarters work just as well."

She caught the confused look on Jack's face as they rounded a corner into a back bedroom. "Remember my analogy of the spirit world? Spirit worlds are like land, or sky, or water? Imagine this builds walls around my house so things have to go around, so they can't just drift through here whenever they want.

"It also keeps things in. That is why I like to use the quarters. See? The face watches both ways when I use two of them. That way I don't worry about something nasty escaping from here if I accidentally let it loose—like that demon you were playing with this afternoon. Although that one was strong enough it might have ignored the quarters. But these are strong enough to keep Mercedes out! They have for years! Until now." She looked a little sheepish. "How did you get rid of her?"

"I, uh, absorbed her energy…demon…thing. What happened anyway? What was she trying to do? You know, other than the sex thing."

Fidelina turned to face him, peering intently into his eyes. "You absorbed her demon? You had better tell me the whole story."

Jack stood awkwardly in the hallway relating the incident as well as he could while keeping it a PG rated story. Fidelina's eyes went wide with surprise and fear, not that Mercedes had been there, or even at what she had been doing, but instead at what Jack had done.

"Put your shoes on," she told him. "We have to go help her."

"What?"

"We don't have time to discuss it. I will explain it to you in the car."

TWENTY-NINE

Jack drove as fast as he dared on roads he didn't know. Fidelina insisted Mercedes was in great danger and needed their help. He wasn't sure he wanted to help, after what she had done to him. Or rather what she had tried to do.

"Mercedes is what some people would call a *diablera*." Fidelina explained. "She would fit most people's idea of what a witch would be, in any culture."

"Then why are we going to help her?"

"Why would you go to help someone who had overdosed on drugs?"

Jack hesitated long enough she answered for him. "I know you wanted to say you wouldn't, but you would, and you know it. You would, because it is the right thing to do. Also, just because someone is addicted to drugs doesn't mean they are evil or bad, they just have problems. I personally think those are serious problems, and I know some of them become evil to support their habits, but they are just people, Jack. Everyone is just another person, just as deserving as you or I, especially when it comes to second chances and helping hands from others."

Jack looked sideways at her. "There are way too many criminals in our society to be that generous. They would be more than happy to take advantage of you a third, fourth, and fifth time."

"I didn't say they deserved to walk all over you. You need to use common sense, but at the same time, you need to know when not to turn a blind eye. Besides, she is a friend."

"So what was she doing in my room? Stopping by to say hello?"

Fidelina smiled the faintest of smiles, but sadness echoed around her eyes. "In a way, yes. In her way. You would be flattered, if you could appreciate how she picks out a victim."

Jack clenched his jaw and kept his eyes resolutely on the road.

"She only picks the absolute most virile of men for her victims, so she must have considered you worthy. Of course, you were pretty impressive in her store today."

"Would you please explain to me what exactly happened in there? I don't understand it."

"I thought you had realized by now. We saw your true aura—after you were strong enough to hide it from us completely."

"I wasn't hiding anything! It just came out of nowhere! It scares the hell out me when it happens!"

"Turn here!" Fidelina pointed, but Jack missed the turn and had to stop and turn around.

Fidelina ignored his driving, watching his face for reactions as she continued explaining. "Most people who are strong enough to hide their aura only succeed in making themselves appear dark to those of us who can see auras. They end up looking like they don't have an aura. Of course, that just makes them stand out in a crowd if you can see auras.

"Mostly, they hide their auras to prevent other people from approaching them. If they can't, or don't hide it, someone with a strong aura will have effects on normal everyday people who can't see auras. People generally have an immediate trust or an instant attraction to people with strong auras and they feel the need to go introduce themselves, try to be friends, ask for help, or even just say hello."

"It happens more than you would guess," she told him. "The best politicians and con men take advantage of their natural appeal to others."

"So, I naturally attracted Mercedes all of a sudden with my bright purple aura?"

"Well…that and we had just seen it replace your plain *caca* brown aura of the all-American over-stressed workaholic."

Jack glanced sideways at her again. He hadn't ever heard those words in a thick Hispanic accent before, and they sounded odd. Not to mention he was surprised to hear a nice little old lady like Fidelina call something shit brown. "So?"

"So, not only did you hide your true aura, you showed another one in its place. I have only heard of someone strong enough to do that once before, but I—Well, I thought it was a just a legend. A story old women like me used to scare off the young girls who thought they wanted to learn *brujeria*." She chuckled quietly to herself.

"I should have known it would turn out to be true. After *La Llorona* and *El Cucuy* turned out to be real, I should have never doubted anything I was taught."

"What are those?"

"Spirits. Monsters of the supernatural world. Your culture would probably call them the 'bogeyman'. Nothing important. Although… Hmm." She pursed her lips. "You might be on to something there, Jack. Let me think about it. Turn here." She pointed to the intersection with Main Street. "Mercedes lives all the way down at the end."

"You never told me what she was going to do."

"Hmm?" Fidelina seemed lost in thought.

"You never finished telling me what Mercedes wanted."

"Oh. She wanted to suck the life energy out of your soul—just like you did to her."

Jack parked the car with a jolt. He looked to Fidelina, but she was already getting out of the rusty Celica. Had he really taken life energy out of Mercedes' soul? Was that why he felt so good? He flexed his chest and arm muscles a little. It did feel good. And he felt stronger.

He also felt a little queasy at the thought of why he felt so good.

He hadn't been trying to do anything like that. He had just wanted to protect himself. He would likely never forget Mercedes' awful scream as she had vanished. Had he sucked out her life like some kind of psychic vampire? He didn't like the thought of killing someone, especially like that.

"Are you coming?" Fidelina called to him from the doorstep and started pounding on the door. He got out and shut the car door, wincing at the peculiar noise it had made ever since he had scraped it on the highway. He jogged up to the door and then felt guilty about the over-abundance of energy he had.

"Is that what she did to Vic? Rape him and suck the energy out of soul?" he asked as he reached her side.

"She tried. Vic managed to stop her, with a little help from his wife, Anita."

"That must be why Anita didn't want him to come with me."

"That, among other things." Fidelina was beginning to look worried. She pounded on the door again. Just as she started to try the door, it opened.

Mercedes stood in the doorway, dressed in baggy jeans and T-shirt and looking disheveled. There were heavy bags under her eyes and she had dirt on her hands, knees and face, but she smiled wide when she saw who it was.

"Oh! Lena! I am so glad you came! Jack! Thank you so much!" The screen door banged behind her as she rushed out and threw her arms around Jack in a bear hug. "How can I ever thank you?"

"Uh…" Jack tried to back away, but then accepted the hug awkwardly as he realized there was nothing supernatural about it. His body had no unwanted reactions toward her. In fact, Mercedes was plain, unattractive, and…old. He gave Fidelina a confused look and was surprised to see tears in her eyes as Mercedes let go of him and threw her arms around Fidelina.

"Oh, Doña Lena, oh, I am so sorry! I have been so awful! How can you ever forgive me?" She leaned down and began sobbing into Fidelina's shoulder, and her words became choked and unrecognizable as she continued trying to apologize.

Fidelina patted her on the back gently and rocked her side to side. Jack watched as the two women cried together, not wanting to interrupt.

Seeing Mercedes in the dim yellow bug light of the front porch, he couldn't understand the desire, the raw lust, he had felt for her at her store, let alone his inability to resist her at Fidelina's house.

When he first laid eyes on her, she had been a Latin sex goddess whose beauty would haunt his dreams for the rest of his life, but now… Now he saw her hair was streaked with dingy gray, not the pure midnight black he remembered, and her sensuously slender fingers actually had large bony knuckles where they desperately clutched to Fidelina's back. Uncomfortably aware he was trying to imagine her body under her clothes, he turned away and looked out into the night.

Finally, the two women broke their embrace, and Mercedes stepped back, wiping her eyes and nose with her sleeve. "I don't have much time, hurry. Come in." She sniffed as she opened the screen door and gestured for them to enter.

As Jack followed Lena through the door, his eyes met Mercedes' and he was shocked to see an open adoration reflected in them. "Thank you so much, Jack. You have saved me. Truly." He was also surprised by the wrinkle lines around her eyes. How had he not noticed them before? How old was she?

He remembered her in the vision with the demon. He had thought she was older when he had seen her there, but she had been so young when he had met her today at the *Herbarium*, and now she was old again. His eyebrows bunched together in thought as he followed the women through the narrow mudroom at the house's entrance and into the living room.

He slowed in wonder as he looked around what appeared to be a 1970's love nest. The smoky, musky scent of incense filled the room. Fake animal furs of all colors and patterns were draped over furniture around the room. Shag carpet, white with islands of pink, covered the floor so thickly it would have been easy to trip in it, and the furniture...

The furniture was oddly erotic. A giant black leather hand-shaped chair filled one corner, while in another was something resembling parallel bars with extra seats, cushions, and footrests all covered in spotted leopard skin. The cherry-red love seat had no back and was the shape of a sensuous mouth. A gas fire place, burning bright and high, sat in the middle of the room open on all four sides with a bear skin rug at one end and a zebra skin at the other.

Jack's mouth was fully agape as he stopped to gawk. The two women moved on into the kitchen, not noticing his halt.

Fluorescent black lights were installed inconspicuously around the room and, here and there, were bead curtains and other things in neon green, red, orange, and yellow, all glowing magnificently in the black light. The largest lava lamp he had ever seen, easily three feet tall, graced the far corner with slowly rising lumps of orange 'lava' right next to an entertainment system with more blue luminescent dials and red LED lights than he could guess functions for.

Jack was engrossed by the dozens of mobiles made up of fluorescent planets, astrological symbols, and other more intricate patterns hanging from the ceiling. Some hung so low they would have to be ducked under, while others would have to be walked around. Mood lights hid behind small palm plants and furniture, casting secluded shadows around the room.

But the most entrancing effect was created by the mirrors.

All four walls, the ceiling, all the shelves, and the entertainment center were made of mirrored surfaces. The upraised centerpiece fireplace was mirrored. The air vent hood for the fireplace was mirrored. A disco ball with hundreds of mirrors on it hung from the ceiling above the lava lamp. Even the backs of all three doors leading out of the room were mirrored.

It was an infinite world with pink and white skies and floors, and fluorescent stars filling the air in between. Jack's mind boggled as he tried to take in the whole scene with its mood lights turned low, fireplace lit, and black lights bringing the mobiles to life, all reflected infinitely, by the mirrored walls.

As he stared off into the distant reflections, he felt a subtle change in his vision and realized he was seeing auras again. There were

175

intense spots around the room. Places where he could pick up dim and transparent shadow-memories, as he had on his own couch at home. He stepped over to a particularly strong one at the lower corner of the raised fireplace pit.

Looking into it, he saw a shadow of Mercedes, as he had first seen her, young and painfully beautiful. As he leaned over and concentrated, it became more real, more solid, almost as if he was actually there. She was nude and sprawled on the floor, her unbelievably beautiful body twisted in pain. Blood ran from her nose and lips and was smeared on the mirrored tiles of the fire pit as another shadow, a nude man held her face pressed to the mirror and screamed at her about how she liked to see her reflection now.

That was the entire memory. Over and over again, Jack saw her perfect face smeared against the mirror, heard the echo of the man yelling, and watched a single tear escape from her crystal blue eye.

He stood up, his heart heavy. How could anyone treat such beauty so badly? Then he remembered her attack on him. Beauty really was only skin deep.

He turned to leave and noticed a memory of her curled up in the palm of the giant black leather hand, like a small kitten. She wore loose gray sweats but shivered as she sobbed. She didn't say anything, but, as if he could read her thoughts, he knew she was unbearably lonely. His heart ached for her sadness.

He tried to leave the room without paying attention to anymore of the shadow-memories, but memories of screams made him turn and look at the parallel bar-couch.

Two different memories vied for his attention. In one, Mercedes screamed with intense and uninhibited pleasure as she vigorously had intercourse with a different man. They were twisted into a position Jack wouldn't have imagined possible, and he wondered at how they did it without hurting themselves, let alone falling off the padded bars.

Embarrassed, he quickly turned away from the memory and just as quickly wished he hadn't. The other memory calling for his attention was taking place right next to the enraptured couple, on the same piece of furniture, with more screams, but these were different.

Mercedes was screaming in pain, screaming for mercy, screaming in despair and agony. A new man was in this memory. He had her wrists and ankles tied to the bars of the odd couch.

Jack winced as he watched the memory. The man burned her with his cigarette and pricked at her with a knife. As before, Jack could read the thoughts behind unspoken words. This man was going to kill her, and he was enjoying the fact she knew it. He wanted her to know it. He wanted her to squirm. It felt best when they squirmed.

Jack recoiled in horror. This man's thoughts were vile. He couldn't stand them, they made him ill, and they repulsed and frightened him. He tried to get away from them, but the only way he could find was to go back to the agony of Mercedes' pain. Unable to remove himself from the shadow-memory, he chose suffering the pain with her rather than experiencing more of the evil of the man's thoughts.

Mercedes' thoughts were different than Jack expected. Although she screamed in pain, the screams of horror were not for what was happening to her, but for what she was about to do.

The shadow-memory man wrapped himself around her, holding the knife in one hand and the cigarette in the other. The man pressed as much of his skin against her as he could, the better to feel her twitch and writhe as he pricked and burned her. Jack could feel the pricks of the knife, as if he were actually in Mercedes' body, and worse, hard as he tried not to, he could feel the man's excitement building as the man felt her skin squirming against his skin, as if Jack was in both of their bodies at the same time.

Jack tried to pull away from the memory, to get away from the pain and the horror. He fought as hard as he could, fearing for his own sanity, feeling the sensations of the body of not only the tortured, but of the tormentor. If he had been in his own body, he would have vomited. He tried again to get out of the shadow-memory, but it held onto him, as if he had a supernatural obligation to watch it through. All he could do was try to ignore the vile thoughts of the evil man as best as he could.

He felt Mercedes' resolve set firm. He could tell she had chosen to live, to fight back, and yet, there was a deep despair, as if she had somehow chosen to die at the same moment. He could sense she had chosen to do something of unspeakable horror, something she couldn't bear to even think about. Something she thought was even worse than what was being done to her. He winced with her, in pain as the cigarette scored again, and shivered with the man, in pleasure as he burned her. Nothing could be worse than what he was experiencing right now.

Mercedes began pulling herself together, steeling herself, and her tormentor laughed out loud at her effort. Then, suddenly, the man went rigid. The point of his knife quivered at the empty air next to her throat, ashes fell unnoticed from his cigarette onto his naked thigh. Jack was finally released from the physical sensations of their bodies and drifted back out to seeing the shadow-memory like an impartial observer.

An unusual aura appeared around the two figures, coming from Mercedes and spreading out over the man. It strengthened as it encompassed the man, and Jack recognized it as a demon. The same demon that had attacked him tonight, the one he had ripped out of Mercedes' aura and absorbed into his own self this very night.

The man's soul screamed in anguish as it was consumed by the demon, and, through contact, by Mercedes as well. The pitiful wail echoed off of Jack's own soul as the man's shadow-memory slowly vanished, leaving only Mercedes' shadow-memory, tied to the bars, crying.

Her tears were not of relief, nor of anger for what the man had done to her, but of a whole-hearted sickening guilt for what she had done to him. He no longer existed. Not in Heaven, not on Earth, and not in Hell. Mercedes wept for what she had done, and Jack wept with her. It was the most awful thing he had ever seen.

He had never suspected a man's very soul could be killed.

Is this what had happened to Julie? Had someone, or something, absorbed her soul? He thought of the red glow eating away at the blue glow in his basement and the little girl crying in the closet. Had he been seeing the little girl's soul being fed on by some horrible demon?

Unlike the abrupt ending of some of the other memories, the rest of this memory slowly faded out. Mercedes cried for what she had done while she remained tied to the bars for a long time, wallowing in grief, guilt, and self-pity. Jack cried with her, not only for what she had done, but for the memory of the little girl in his basement, and for Julie's empty body lying in the hospital.

If there was anything truly evil, any sin sure to prevent entry into Heaven, this was it.

After an unbearably long time, the memory faded out and released Jack. This time, thankfully, he made it out of the room and into the kitchen without being captured by another shadow-memory.

THIRTY

Jack slowly entered the kitchen, still stunned by the visions of the shadow-memories. Fidelina and Mercedes were seated at the kitchen table, pouring over the contents of a dirt-encrusted tin box. A small trail of dirt clods led from the rear exit of the kitchen all the way up to a pile of dirt on the table the box sat on. Jack wondered how long he had been in the grip of the shadow-memories.

"Oh, there you are!" Mercedes looked up with an excited girlish look on her face. "I was wondering where you went."

Jack caught Fidelina's eye. "Was I gone long?"

"No. You were just slow. Why? Is everything all right?"

"I, uh…" He glanced at Mercedes. "I just…was looking."

Mercedes grinned wide. "Quite the room isn't it? It took me a long time to get it how I wanted it." She sighed deeply. "Ah, so many memories. Oh, well." She turned back to the box.

Fidelina noticed Jack's distress and got up from the table and moved over to him. "What happened?"

He shook his head and smiled. "I just saw some of those…visions. What did you call them…psychic residue?"

Mercedes got up quickly. "Oh, I am so sorry, Jack. I should have known you would be so sensitive. Please! Tell me what you saw. I know I can reassure you. I've entertained a wide variety of people in my time, and some of them had very unusual…tastes. I'm sure whatever you saw wasn't as bad as it looked."

"It's all right. Really." Jack did his best to smile reassuringly, but he could tell it came off as a grimace instead.

Mercedes moved over to where Jack still stood just inside the door. "You saw it, didn't you?" Her voice was flat and toneless as she realized he knew her worst secret.

"I don't know what you mean."

"You saw me destroy Antonio's soul."

Fidelina's head whipped around and Jack nodded, unable to meet their eyes.

"I have regretted what I did to him every hour of every day of my life." Mercedes stared at the floor, her voice low. "I didn't mean to do it. I mean, I did mean to do it, but I didn't want to. It was just so…and he…" Her voice broke and the tears began flowing again. Her sobbing made her words unintelligible. "Ay! *Dios mío!*" she cried and ran out the back of the kitchen.

Fidelina hesitated, looked at Jack, and then, with a determined look in her eye, hurried after Mercedes. Jack followed, afraid of finding more shadow-memories if left alone again. He arrived just in time to see Mercedes pull a three-foot statue of Guadalupe out of a closet, clutch it to her chest tightly, and fall to the ground crying. Fidelina was quickly at her side, holding her tightly.

Jack watched awkwardly for a moment with a feeling of déjà vu, and then turned away. The room, which was drab and plain compared to the living room, had a trail of dirt leading to the metal box. It came in from the back door. He followed it and let himself out into the backyard.

The night air was cool, bordering on cold, and his breath puffed away into the cloudless night as he tried to let go of some of the tensions squeezing his body. His eyes adjusting to the dark, he was soon able to make out a hole dug under a large elm tree. Presumably, this was where the box on the table had come from. For a moment, he was fearful of encountering another shadow memory but there was nothing here.

He stood listening to the night, wondering whether he should go back into the house. He didn't want to see the crying woman, but, at the same time, he understood her guilt. He shared her guilt. He was afraid to think about it too much, feeling as though he had been there, had participated, had been responsible.

He looked up at the brightly shining stars. He didn't know much about the night sky, but he tried to find the Big Dipper anyway. He couldn't find it, but almost half of the sky was blotted out by the elm tree. Glad to have a distraction, he walked around the tree searching for a familiar constellation in the sky.

About halfway around the tree, a fluttering motion in the upper branches caught his eye, and he stopped. He stared at the spot where he had seen the movement, but the darkness hid it well. Keeping an eye up in the boughs of the tree, he continued walking around it. A silhouette became visible against the starlit night sky near the top of the tree. An owl.

Jack stopped and stared. He couldn't remember ever actually seeing an owl before. Much larger than he would have expected, it was big enough to carry off a cat. The owl twisted its head to gaze down at him regally. It let out a loud hoot and turned away indignantly, as if annoyed it had been seen.

Jack smiled to himself. It was peaceful to be a kindred spirit of the night, lost in the shadows. He stood motionless watching the great dark shape, afraid if he moved the owl would fly away and break the serene spell of the moment.

A quiet sob caught his attention. He turned, expecting to find Mercedes had followed him into the night, but the door to the house was closed and the yard was empty. Another sobbing sound, louder now, pulled his attention toward a neighbor's house.

He looked out into the night, but couldn't make out much. The houses in the area were spread wide, had no fences separating the properties, and were butted up against a wide, open field. The empty open space added to the darkness of the night.

The crying increased, working its way up toward a pitiful wailing sound. Jack felt an instant kinship in the sorrow and grief reflected in his own heart. He was compelled by the sound of utter despair to go see if he could help. Surely someone must have just died to provoke such lamenting. It echoed the pain he felt in his soul.

He started toward the house the sound was coming from. The owl launched itself from the tree, rattling branches and leaves. It was hard to tell in the darkness, but he thought the owl had glided off in the same direction. He hurried on, following the growing sound of a woman's howling grief.

After a moment, he made out movement. Some sort of fluttering whiteness, barely visible in the gloom of the dark. The crying came from there and he headed toward it. As he got closer, he recognized clothing, hanging out on a line to dry, billowing softly in the slight breeze of the chill night air.

Then he spotted her. A young woman in a long white dress flowing out around her like a cape in the wind. Her face was buried in a child's shirt hanging from the clothesline. Her hands clutched tightly at it as she wailed in misery.

Jack's heart went out to her. She was so distraught, he feared it was over the loss of the child the shirt belonged to. He hesitated to intrude on her sorrow; there was little comfort he could offer a stranger over the loss of a child.

Just as he turned away to respect her privacy, she let out a terrible wail, turned away from the clothes on the line, and ran off into the dark.

His heart stuttered. He was sure she had just made a horrible decision to do something drastic. He hesitated only for a moment before running after her, hoping to catch up in time to stop her.

It was not hard to follow her in the dark. Her billowing white dress was nearly luminescent in the starlight. But she ran amazingly fast, and Jack was hard pressed to keep up. He had another pang of guilt as he realized how good he felt since absorbing the demon's aura. He felt stronger and faster than he had ever felt before, but somehow, he still couldn't catch up with the woman. "Wait!" he called to get her to stop, but she seemed to renew her efforts instead. "Wait!"

He stumbled in the dark, catching his feet on rocks and trying desperately not to turn his ankle in any holes. He lost sight of her as she neared some trees and he slowed with another misstep. His heart raced and his lungs burned, but his body felt so good he thought he could go on like this for hours. If only he knew where she had gone, he would use his newfound endurance to outlast her. It was incredible she could run so fast. He blew a puff of steam into the cold air as he realized he had lost her.

A flash of white movement off to the left caught his eye and he spotted her much further away. She had come out of the trees and was entering a wide-open area. He took a deep breath and started after her again, reveling in the power of his own body. He got no more than five feet when he heard a heart-freezing screech and something hit him in the back.

The shock of impact made his legs gave out and he tumbled forward, somersaulting, and landing hard with his face in the dirt. He heard the screech again and looked up just in time to avoid a diving owl.

Its cry ran chills up his spine and its claws left burning trails where they barely scraped his face. The worst part was he had seen a human face on it.

"Holy shit!" he cried as it looped above to come back for another pass.

He stumbled and tried to keep running after the woman in white, doubly motivated now that some sort of human-faced bird was attacking him. The owl came at him again, this time from head-on, and this time he was positive he saw a human face across its avian features.

"Damn it!" he yelled in terror as it came for another pass at his face. Suddenly, the owl acted stunned, nearly falling out of the air and barely missing his knees as it swooped past.

"Serves you right," he muttered, regaining his balance and turning to chase after the woman again. He had no idea why a creature like this would try to stop him from helping the woman, but it just set his resolve to get to her before anything bad could happen.

"Jack!"

He heard a distant cry come from behind him.

"Jack, Stop!"

He turned and spotted two forms hurrying toward him. He couldn't make them out, but it had to be Fidelina and Mercedes. "I can't wait," he yelled back to them. "I have to help her! I'll come back!"

"No! Don't go!"

He heard the plea but turned to run on anyway.

THIRTY-ONE

Jack took no more than three steps before the owl hit him from behind again. He tripped and fell, one knee hitting a rock and sending a sharp pain through his leg, rendering it numb and useless.

"Damn you!" he yelled at the owl again. This time it not only seemed stunned by the curse, it actually fell out of the air and landed with a soft thump just out of sight.

"Jack! Stop!" He heard Fidelina or Mercedes call out from behind him again, but he was stopped now.

His leg hurt. He searched for the owl, but didn't see any sign of it. He hoped the thing was dead. He turned his head to see if the woman in white was still in sight, hoping maybe Fidelina could get to her in time to stop her from doing anything rash, but saw nothing of her in the inky darkness.

It took the old women a long time to reach him, and when they did, they were in bad shape. It had been a long hard trek for them to chase after him. As Jack watched Mercedes' bent and gasping form puffing steam clouds into the dim light, he knew her to be the old woman he had seen in the memory with Vic as a boy.

"Are you getting older?" he asked her bluntly.

She nodded, her face obscured by her own breath as it puffed out rapidly in small clouds. Fidelina was gasping too, but not as badly as Mercedes.

Fidelina knelt down and put her hands on Jack's knee, took a deep breath and began muttering in Spanish. He felt prickles on his skin as he realized she was muttering a prayer. His knee started to grow hot.

"I can't believe he can't just do that himself," Mercedes gasped.

Fidelina stopped her incantations and stood up. "I told you, he doesn't hide it on purpose. It just comes and goes."

"Well, if I hadn't seen him entranced by *La Llorona* with my own eyes, I never would have believed it. It's a good thing you tripped and fell!" she admonished him.

"Tripped nothing! It was that damned owl with the human face!" he cursed, pointing toward where he had seen it fall. It might have been his imagination, but he thought he heard it squawk in response. The old women exchanged looks and Mercedes hurried toward where he had pointed.

"What happened to the owl?" Fidelina asked him. Her voice was low and serious.

"It kept attacking me! It hit me three or four times!"

"What happened to it?" she demanded.

"I don't know." He shook his head. "It just…fell. Over there somewhere." He pointed at Mercedes' back.

"That owl saved your life, Jack."

"The hell it did! The damned thing was trying to kill me!"

He definitely heard it squeal this time. Mercedes cussed under her breath.

Fidelina jerked back away from him. "You cursed her!" she accused.

"What? I don't know how to curse something!"

"What did you say?" she demanded again, much sterner this time.

"I don't know! Wait. I said 'damn it' or maybe 'damn you', I don't know."

"*Madre de Dios!*" She stood up and ran after Mercedes.

"Aw, shit! What did I do this time?" Jack muttered to himself as he stood up gingerly. Surprised at how much less his knee hurt now, he hobbled after the women.

He caught up with Fidelina at the same time she found Mercedes kneeling next to the sprawled form of the owl. It was spread out in the dirt with wings and legs pointing in all different directions. One wing bent awkwardly, broken, Jack was sure.

"Who is it?" Fidelina asked her as they ran up.

Jack looked back and forth between them with confusion, but they ignored him.

"Rosa," Mercedes answered quietly. "She is going to be okay, but the owl's wing is broken." She pointed a bony finger at Jack. "It's a good thing you weren't turned on! You almost killed her as it was! If you had been using that big purple thing you call an aura, she would probably be burning in Hell right now!"

Jack had the decency to look properly admonished even though he didn't understand what had happened.

"Probably not," Fidelina assured him weakly, "but Mercedes is right. Let's get her back to the house." Fidelina stepped in and gently picked the owl up. The huge bird was an armful for the small woman, and she had problems standing up with it, causing it to flap and squeal.

"Let me." Jack stepped in and took it from her. He was surprised again at its size and marveled at its weight. He hadn't realized birds got this big. The owl made an effort to peck at his face then went still.

"Be careful with her," Mercedes ordered him. He just nodded.

"Do you see that?" Fidelina asked him pointing down and out into the darkness.

Jack turned to look and saw a flicker at the bottom of a deep quarry hole. His heart leapt to his throat. Had the woman in white thrown herself off the edge and into the rocks below? He started to cry out to the others but then realized the flicker was just the rippled reflection of stars on the cold black water at the bottom. As his initial shock began to fade, it occurred to him he would have been dead on the jagged rocks below if it hadn't been for the owl in his arms.

He stared numbly down into deadly trap, wondering how he could possibly have missed it in the dark. Looking back up, straight ahead toward the horizon, he wondered where the woman had gone. He was sure he had seen her running across open ground straight out in front of him—but there was no open ground there, only a gaping pit.

"She is called *La Llorona*," Fidelina's voice came softly from behind him. "The weeping woman. Sometimes she is called the White Woman, or something else, but everyone agrees she is crying over the loss of her children. Some say she killed her children to be with a man who then spurned her. It is warned if you get too close to her, she will mistake you for one of her children and pull you into the water with her."

Jack shivered and the owl in his arms made a soft mewling noise. He didn't think the woman had mistaken him for one of her children, but, glancing down into the water at the bottom of the pit, he wondered if she had intended to pull him in. Then he remembered her crying on the child's shirt on the clothesline.

"Why would 'la yerona' cry over the loss of a child, and then want to kill someone else?"

"Remember when you asked me about spirits that roamed the Earth looking for revenge? Some are doomed to always repeat the same mistake. I don't think *La Llorona* wants to kill anyone, I think she is perhaps cursed to lure them to their deaths."

"How many people has she killed here?" he asked nervously.

"Here?" Fidelina glanced at the quarry then at Mercedes, who silently shrugged. "None here. That I know of."

"She does this in other places too?"

"She does this all over the Hispanic world. Throughout Mexico, women take down their drying clothes before dark, out of fear *La*

Llorona will come and cry on them. It is an omen that a child will die if she cries on its clothes."

"I saw her do that!" he cried. "She was crying on those clothes over there!" He pointed with his chin toward the house with the laundry flapping in the gentle night breeze.

"That is the Gonzales' house," Mercedes whispered to Fidelina. "María and Mario have one little boy, named Hector."

"Ay!" Fidelina exclaimed with an exhausted frustration. "This night is going to have no end! You take Jack and Rosa back to your house and I will go help the Gonzaleses."

Mercedes nodded and beckoned for Jack to follow as Fidelina began carefully picking her path toward the house in the dark.

THIRTY-TWO

What is Fidelina going to do?" Jack asked Mercedes as soon as they started walking.

"She is going to try to break the curse of *La Llorona*. She will try to convince the Gonzaleses the threat is real, then she will perform a cleansing ceremony by burning the boy's clothes that are hanging on the clothesline, and then she will bless the house and the family. It will take some time."

Jack stumbled in the dark with his sore knee and the owl made another mewling noise he equated to a moan. "Sorry, uh...Rosa," he muttered to the owl. "We're almost there."

He glanced at Mercedes, and then quickly put his eyes back to the ground so he wouldn't trip. "Why would this...uh, owl, try to save me like that?"

"This is no ordinary owl," Mercedes answered somberly. "She is...well there are a lot of names for what she is. Around here, the kids call them the *achutè*. Where I grew up, we called them *las chusas*, because they are owls, *lechuzas*, but they are also *brujas*, witches."

Jack nodded to her to let her know he knew what *brujas* were. The owl in his arms seemed to cock its head to listen to what she was saying as they walked.

"Owls have a closer tie to the supernatural world than many other animals, and they are often willing to help carry the spirit, or awareness, of a person with them. Many *brujas* use them to spy on other people. And each other." She gave the owl a sideways accusatory glance and it shifted uncomfortably in Jack's arms.

"But some, like Rosa, try to use this special relationship with the owls to help others. She and a few others have taken turns watching over this quarry for years, protecting children from getting hurt here by frightening them away. They usually stay in the old water tower, where they can be high enough to see anyone coming from a long ways away. That is why the children here call them *achutè*, named after the water tower."

"So what happened to her? Why is she injured?"

"You cursed at her!"

"I've cursed at plenty of things. It never did any good before."

"Rosa is using the Holy power of Our Lady Guadalupe to perform her magic. When you cursed at her, you sent bad and evil thoughts to disrupt this Holiness."

"I guess it's a good thing I didn't use the f-word, huh?"

"It would have been better if you had. That is an empty cuss word, nothing but a vulgarity. What you said—that was an actual curse. If you had been using your...I don't know what to call it, your *other* aura, you might well have been powerful enough to actually banish her to He—" She cut off the word as she realized it might again hurt Rosa.

"If it is such a Holy power, how come it can be used to spy?"

"Oh, it can be used for a lot worse than spying. I only said Rosa was doing it by using the Holy power of Our Lady. It can be done using darker powers also. And, I think, someone like you could probably do it on the strength of their own personal power."

"Hah! I can't even tell when I am going to be able to see auras, let alone do something about it."

"You just need some time and practice. Maybe a little training."

"So Rosa is the owl? Or is she trapped in the owl's body? I don't understand."

"Neither. Her energy, her spirit, is with the owl right now, but she is not trapped."

"Then why doesn't she leave?"

Mercedes gave him a 'someday you'll understand' smile. "The owl is still just an animal. It is just a creature, knowing only that it is in pain. It doesn't understand what is happening to it. Rosa is staying with it to keep it calm so we can help it. It is not the owl's fault it got hurt, it was her fault for using the owl, and she won't abandon it to suffering for helping her."

"You mean it's my fault for hurting it."

They reached the back door of Mercedes' house and she held it open for him to carry the owl through. The owl became nervous going into the house, but was in too much pain to do anything about it. He held it quiet while Mercedes put together a box with some towels for the bird to lie in.

When the owl was comfortably tucked in, Jack sat down at the table and breathed a deep sigh of relief. He felt emotionally exhausted, but guiltily noticed his body still felt great, other than his knee.

Mercedes sat down opposite him and they sat quietly while she tried to catch her breath. She looked old now. Not just a couple of wrinkles, but old enough he wouldn't have recognized her as the same person who answered the door tonight, let alone the woman he had met at the *Herbarium* this afternoon.

"I don't mean to be rude, but…what is happening to you? Why are you getting so old all of a sudden?"

Mercedes laughed quietly. "It's not all of a sudden. I've been old for the last fifty years. It's just that I am no longer staying young." Her eyes twinkled at him as her lips formed a wrinkled and weathered smile. "You did this to me, and I couldn't be happier about it." She reached across the table with a knobby, blue veined hand and patted his hand in a motherly fashion, quite different than she had been this afternoon.

"I don't understand."

Mercedes leaned down to check on Rosa. The owl was quietly watching them. "We'll have to wait for Doña Lena to come back to heal her. I can't do it. I don't have the strength.

"I never did have the strength to heal, or to do much else either. I had a little talent, just enough that Doña Isabella was kind enough to take me in and teach me." Her voice dropped and Jack was afraid she was going to start crying again.

"Doña Isabella was able to teach me to understand and to see, but I was never strong enough to do anything. I couldn't help anyone. I could hardly even bless a candle." She let loose a short sob, but choked it down. "I was mostly content just to be included in *brujería*. It made me feel important to know things other people didn't, it made me feel superior." She sighed.

"Maybe that is why my abilities were so weak. No matter how hard I prayed to Guadalupe, I never got any results I felt I could take responsibility for. I think that was my downfall—in more ways than one.

"I think Guadalupe ignored my prayers because they were self-centered. Even if I was praying for someone else, I still wanted the credit for getting Guadalupe's attention, for bringing about the miracle. I wanted people to know it was me, that I could do it. I betrayed Guadalupe's trust, by doing it for my glory, not Hers." She bowed her head reverently before continuing.

"Then my selfishness led me to searching for other ways to get results. I had entertained the idea of finding ways of power other than Guadalupe for years, but when I started growing old…" Her voice trailed off. She cleared her throat and continued.

"Doña Isabella was old when I first met her, I never found out exactly how old, but I think she was at least eighty. I was twenty-five. By the time I was fifty, I looked my age and then some, but Doña

Isabella still looked the same as the day I met her. Even if she had only been fifty when I met her, she would have been seventy-five by then, but she still looked like a healthy strong fifty year-old. That was a long time ago. You know, back when old people looked old. Not like now, when medicine can keep them healthy and strong for twenty or thirty extra years. She lived another thirty years. My best guess is she was over a hundred and thirty when she died."

She stopped and rubbed at her liver-spotted hands and swollen knuckles. "Even by today's standards, that's pretty impressive, huh?" She turned her eyes back to Jack. "What if I told you that the day before she died, she still looked like a healthy fifty year-old, and had walked five miles to my house to give me this?" She gently patted the metal box. "And to chastise me one last time for my behavior. She knew she was finally going to die, but she didn't tell me."

She shook her head sadly. "I knew it was Guadalupe's power and strength that kept Doña Isabella, Doña Lena, Doña Rosa," she sadly gestured toward the owl, "and the all of the others young and strong. I wanted to be young and strong too! But I wasn't." She choked on her words again and her voice trembled slightly. Jack wasn't sure if it was from emotion or the onset of old age.

"I decided to find another way. I learned to siphon energy from other people to keep myself young. It is easiest during sex -especially from men. They so completely let down their guard during sex that they actually give some of their life energy away. I think perhaps it helps to form a new life if one is being conceived. But when they give that little bit away, it is so easy to take more…" She met his eyes and blushed, her wrinkled face quickly changing color.

"I used that energy to stay young and to give myself more power. I was finally able to do so many of the things I could never do before. And the demon you exorcised from me…I don't even know when it showed up. I was so wrapped up in myself. Then I actually started becoming younger, not just holding off on aging. And beautiful—I was never so beautiful in my life." She had a wistful look in her eyes then sighed heavily.

"By the time I realized there was a demon involved, I couldn't have gotten rid of it if I had wanted. I was already addicted to having it around. It acted like a battery for me. It would help me to preserve the energy I had stolen so it would last longer, and it used its powers to make me younger and more beautiful—the better to attract more men and gain more energy. Of course, it fed on the men too. But now that it's gone, I no longer have an energy reservoir to draw from, and this is the result." She waved her gnarled hands to indicate her aging body.

"My first attempt to gain power was such an awful thing, I should never have even thought about trying again. I ended up hosting a demon that time, too. I think you would call it being possessed, although it is not the same thing."

She leaned over to the owl again, looked into its saucer eyes, and gently reached out and stroked its head. "I am so sorry Doña Rosa. I hope you can forgive me." Jack could have sworn the owl acquiesced. "I almost got her killed. And everyone else, too," she whispered sadly. "If it hadn't been for Victor, I think all four of us would have died the night they finally rid me of that demon."

Jack flinched at the mention of Vic's name. Suddenly he knew exactly which demon had possessed Mercedes the first time, and he realized he knew who Doña Isabella and Doña Rosa were: these women, these *brujas*, were the four old women in the shadow memory of the knife.

THIRTY-THREE

Jack and Mercedes sat at the table and stared at each other. Dried tear tracks scored the old woman's face. The silence between them had grown long and uncomfortable. Even an inquisitive hoot from the owl hadn't been able to break it. Finally, Jack looked back down at the table to avoid the old woman's tired stare. Mercedes began rummaging through the dirty tin box on the table just to have something to do while they waited for Fidelina to come back from the Gonzales' house.

After a few minutes of staring off into space, Jack was pulled back to the present when he heard Mercedes inhale sharply. She was tightly grasping a faded yellow paper with an envelope paper clipped to it. He had seen her pull the paper out of the box and unfold it carefully, but he hadn't been paying attention to her. She eyed him strangely and then eyed the paper again.

Jack decided he just didn't care anymore. He put his face back in his hands to wait for Fidelina. He would take her back to her house tonight, maybe try to get a little sleep, and then he would go home.

Since coming out to get Fidelina's help, he had seen too many strange things to comprehend, or even believe. Unfortunately, not only could he no longer explain things away by calling them dreams, he couldn't even pretend it was all in his mind.

Worst of all, he still wasn't any closer to helping Julie. If anything, he felt further away.

How could he possibly stay sane while talking to an owl, which sometimes seemed to have a human face and attacked you in the dark of the night? He was sure he would never be able to handle the horrible experience of being in two other people's bodies at the same time again without losing his mind. And watching this old woman get older right before his eyes? Who could deal with something like that?

He wished he had never left Julie's side. The scream of that man's soul still echoed in Jack's heart, and the agony of battling not one, but two demons—he wished he had never taken Vic's advice to come down here.

It was no wonder Vic hadn't wanted to talk about any of the things he had seen in Mexico. Now he understood why Vic's wife had been hurt and angry when they had discussed coming to see Fidelina. There was no way Jack ever would have believed either of them if they had warned him what to expect. The story about the *Ojo* Vic had told him was the tamest damned thing he had run into since he got here. What the hell would he see if he stuck around another day? He didn't want to know.

The rapidly aging woman ignored Jack's self-pitying behavior as he sat brooding with his chin in his hands. She leaned over the side of the table, showed the wrinkled and yellowed paper to the owl, and whispered just loud enough Jack could hear, but not loud enough for him to make out what she was saying. When the owl hooted softly in response, he decided he couldn't tolerate any more weirdness and would wait for Fidelina out in the car.

The chair scraped the floor as he stood up to leave. He stumbled slightly, refusing to make eye contact with either the woman or the owl. He hesitated to go back through the living room with its awful shadow-memories, so he headed for the backdoor instead. He was out of the kitchen and halfway to the door out when he heard Mercedes' voice call to him, pleadingly.

"Jack. Please. Before you go, please look at this."

He hesitated. He didn't want to deal with anything else tonight, nor ever again for that matter, but the old woman's voice was pathetic. He could hear an old age quaver in it now. How cold and heartless would he have to be to walk out on someone who was rapidly dying of old age right before his eyes?

"Please, Jack," her voice came drifting out of the kitchen again. He heard the owl give a soft hoot, and he shook his head at the stupidity of thinking an owl was encouraging him. He hated the idea of staying, but he hated the idea of leaving the poor woman alone even more.

He returned to the kitchen, and she held out the yellowed paper in her hand.

"It has been so long now that I have tried not to think about Doña Isabella and how badly I failed and embarrassed her that I had forgotten all about this. This box is filled with her personal belongings she gave me the day before she died. There isn't much. A few trinkets, really, but she knew she was going to die, and she wanted me to have them. I was too involved in myself to realize why she would give me her personal effects at the time.

"After she died, five years ago, I buried everything that reminded me of her out in the back yard. I was tired of feeling guilty every time

I saw them and I had no intention of repenting my evil ways." She made a face of disgust at the thought of how she had been.

"God only knows why she would have wanted me to have them. Maybe she knew one day, if I ever managed to come to my senses, I would find comfort in them." She ran a now gnarled hand lovingly across a tarnished silver picture frame of another old woman. "I'm just glad I didn't throw them away."

Jack recognized the photograph as the old woman he had tried to protect from the demon attack in the shadow-memory of Vic's childhood, the one with the broken hip. It was strange to see the old image, to know a woman, whose living face he had first looked upon this very afternoon, had been dead for five years.

"Maybe she was able to see things clearly enough to know I would need this today." Mercedes' other hand was still outstretched, holding the yellowed piece of paper. Reluctantly, he reached out and took it from her.

He turned the paper over. It was worn, not only with age, but also with use. The many wrinkles in it made it soft and floppy, and he had to use both hands to spread it well enough to see. It was a pencil sketch of a man's face, light and faded with age, but still clear.

"Doña Isabella carried it with her for thirty years. Whenever she met new people she would show it to them and ask if they knew him. She never found anyone who did."

Jack felt the hair on his arms and neck prickle. The sketch was unmistakably a drawing of him. Even with the aged fold lines of the paper running through the face, he couldn't deny it was a near perfect sketch of him. He sat down numbly, staring at a drawing of himself apparently made thirty years earlier. If he hadn't seen Mercedes pull it out of the box himself, he would have called her bluff. But he had, and he knew it had to be genuine.

"For years she had insisted someone else had been there and fought the demon. We all thought Guadalupe had helped Victor to trap the demon in the blessed knife, but Doña Isabella insisted she had actually seen a man there, standing over her, protecting her." Mercedes sighed deeply at her memories. "The longer she spent trying to find out who it had been, the less any of us remembered she had been looking. Or at least, the less I remembered. I was caught up in my own pettiness." She was quiet for a long moment of regret before she looked up again.

"Sometimes, not very often, Guadalupe will allow people to see the way of things yet to come. I suppose that is what this is." She handed him the envelope that had been clipped to the paper, plain and unmarked except for an unbroken dripped wax seal holding it shut.

With a strange mixture of apprehension and curiosity, Jack folded the wax seal and snapped it open. Inside the envelope was a neatly handwritten letter. He gently pulled it out and began reading.

> *Dear Mr. Jack,*
>
> *First, let me apologize if I have gotten your name wrong. It is very difficult to see such things clearly. I have spent much time trying to find you, and I have finally discovered there was a very good reason why I have been unable to do so. You are not yet here. How this is possible, I do not understand. It is but yet another example of the great complexity and wonder of God's creation. Therefore, as I will never be able to speak with you in person, I am leaving this message in care of Mercy with the hope she will be able to give it to you.*
>
> *Our Lady has finally seen fit to call me home, and I must go to Her soon, but first there are details to wrap up.*
>
> *The first is, thank you for saving the lives of my grandson, my friends, and, of course, myself. Although I cannot repay this kindness, please always know it was deeply appreciated.*
>
> *Secondly, as you are reading this letter, you must have gotten it from Mercy, and in order to have done that, you must have saved her a second time. On her behalf, I thank you deeply. She is like a daughter to me and I would please ask you to pass her this message: We all forgive you, especially Antonio, who claims it was the best thing anyone could have done for him.*
>
> *Finally, you, Mr. Jack, as near as I have been able to ascertain, are in a unique situation for modern times. I have spent so much time searching for you in the hope you would be able to teach me how to better use my abilities and to better serve Guadalupe, only to find that you are the one who will need the guidance. You are, and will be, able to do things other people cannot imagine and will not believe. In order to deal with this, you must do what you feel to be right. If you always stay true to that, you will do just fine. I know this seems a cryptic message, but it is the best I can do with the limited power I have and the limited things I have been blessed to know.*
>
> *The only advice I can give you that I feel might truly help is this: Everything centers on belief, so you must learn how to believe, and how not to believe. What people believe is what matters the most, not what actually is, or was. If someone believes something strongly enough it can be so, and the more people who believe it, the more so it can be. This is not a fortune cookie riddle. It is a truth, and one I do not feel capable of properly expressing on paper. Please, find a bruja, or a psychic, or whatever you can, (a real one, not a shyster), show them this message from me, and ask them*

to teach you what it means. It is the fundamental secret of my traditions and abilities. Unfortunately, it is such a fundamental secret only the best will know it, so you must find someone who does more than dabble.

I hope Mercy can help you with this, but my visions of the future are far too weak to know for certain. Please keep searching until you find someone who can explain this to you.

For reasons I am not sure of, I feel Our Lady is telling me to reassure you there is an eternal afterlife, one where there is no more pain, no more sorrow and no more suffering. I feel sure you already know this, but I am nonetheless compelled to restate it. Fear nothing, for anything that can be done can only be done in passing, it can never take away God's promise of an immortal soul. Only God can truly create, and only God can truly destroy. When you have doubts, do what all of the greatest people throughout history have done: pray.

Yours Respectfully,
Isabella Villamadrina

THIRTY-FOUR

Jack carefully re-read the letter and then set it on the table in front of him. Mercedes watched him quietly, patiently allowing him to gather his thoughts.

Could this actually be real? Could a woman he briefly saw a few hours ago, in a shadow-memory of thirty years ago, have been able to leave a letter for him to find years after she died? It was mind boggling to think he could have seen her only this afternoon, yet she had seen him thirty years ago. It wasn't possible, was it?

He gently slid the letter across the table for Mercedes to read. He wasn't surprised when the tears began to well up in her eyes. He had grown used to seeing her cry tonight. When she finally put the letter down, he met her eyes and held her tearful gaze.

"I take it you're Mercy?"

She nodded with a slight sad smile on her lips. "My nickname. No one has called me that since…" A single tear retraced one of the dry tracks on her cheek from earlier. "Not since I yelled at Doña Isabella for treating me like a child forty-five years ago."

"She said to tell you everyone forgives you, especially Antonio, who claims it was the best thing anyone could have done for him." Jack smiled wryly, trying to cheer her up.

"Yeah, I know." She almost laughed, almost cried and indicated to the letter where she had just read the statement herself.

"Isn't Antonio the man…?"

She nodded her head and finished his sentence for him. "…Whose soul I destroyed? He is. He was. I don't know how she knew about that." A slight sob escaped her trembling lips.

"Well, either she spied on you with an owl…" He leaned over the edge of the table and glared down at the injured owl where it lay in the box wrapped in towels. It turned away, apparently chagrined. He sat back up with a small smile of satisfaction. "Or somebody told her. Personally, I think it sounds like she actually talked to Antonio herself. She did say he 'claims'. That implies he told her, right?"

Mercedes nodded and looked thoughtful. "I wonder how much she was actually able to see. She knew you were the one who protected us from the demon so long ago. She knew you would someday come to me, and I would be able to give you the letter. She knew I had…killed Antonio."

She looked at the letter for a moment then back up at Jack. "She must have known something about your wife, too. Why else would she have tried so hard to reassure you of an immortal soul?"

"Maybe she was trying to reassure you?"

"She already did that by mentioning Antonio."

Jack thought about it for a moment. Was it possible Antonio's actual immortal soul hadn't been destroyed? Maybe she had been trying to reassure him Julie's soul was still alive.

"What did she mean about beliefs?" he asked.

Mercedes smiled sadly and shook her head. "I can't help you with that. I told you, I was always the weakest. If there is a secret to believing, I don't know it." She smiled reassuringly. "But Doña Lena will. Or maybe Doña Rosa." She gestured toward the owl, which was patently not looking at Jack.

They sat and stared at the letter and at each other without speaking, their minds working over the possibilities the letter represented. Jack thought he could actually see the aging process changing Mercedes during their silence. She was smaller and frailer now, and her aura had grown faint and dim.

She looked up from a photograph in a silver locket she had taken out of the tin box and smiled at him. "I see you have turned on again. That really is quite an impressive aura you have there."

Jack looked around the room, surprised to realize he was seeing auras again. This time, instead of apprehension and fear, he finally felt a sense of wonder at what he was seeing, at his ability to see it.

"What do I do with it?" he asked Mercedes.

She gave a quick chuckle. "What do you want to do with it? All of my life I wanted what you have. You can do most anything you want, all it takes is a little faith, a little effort, and a little concentration."

"Nothing is that easy. I thought you said you learned for years and still couldn't do anything."

"I didn't have access to the kind of power you have. I had to ask for it from Guadalupe, or ask Her to do it for me, although She rarely did. But you… Well, She's already given the power to you. If you were to try, and if She were to help you, you could probably do most anything." She smiled at him warmly.

Jack's return smile was weak. He wanted to tell her he didn't believe in Guadalupe, so there was no reason for Her to have given him this ability, but he held his thought. He didn't know where it had come from, or why. He had a momentary feeling of guilt as he recalled crying out desperately to God for help when he had first been attacked. Perhaps it was a divine gift of sorts.

His smile toward the old woman grew a little warmer. He had to admit she might be right, in her own way. Although he wasn't so sure now, the night he was first attacked in bed he had been positive God had helped pull him back from the edge of nothingness and then taken the sphere of pain away. His smile slowly faded. Had God given him this new sight? Or had it been some kind of strange side effect of being attacked by the demon?

"Isn't it unusual that I just started having these abilities last week? I mean, I never saw things when I was a kid. I almost never even had déjà vu before, so how come I suddenly have this?" He waved his hands to indicate his bright purple aura.

"Like my mother used to say," Mercedes smiled strangely, "the Lord works in mysterious ways." She wobbled slightly, as though she felt faint.

"Are you all right?" Jack felt worry rise up inside of him. She nodded, but he could tell by the flickering of her aura she was growing very weak.

"My age is finally catching up with me." She tried to joke, but ended up coughing instead.

She stood shakily and went over to a cabinet in the corner of the kitchen. She slowly pulled open a drawer as if it were one of the heaviest things she had ever moved, and then pulled out a sealed folder. She barely made it the two steps back to the table, where she sat back down gingerly.

"Here," her voice was hoarse, "I need you to give this to Doña Lena when she gets back."

Jack could tell by the look in her eyes she was expecting to die any second now. He couldn't stand the thought of waiting for Fidelina while sitting quietly at the kitchen table with a dead woman and an owl staring at him.

"You tell her yourself." He tried to reassure her.

She gave him a look that said thanks anyway, but she knew better. Her aura flickered again, and it reminded Jack of something.

It reminded him of Miss Weisling, as she lay in the middle of a dark highway in the snow and slush with a head injury. Her aura had flickered in that same way. He wondered…

"Here," he said, as he reached out to her hand offering him the envelope. He reached past the envelope and touched her hand, willing himself to feel her aura. It was faint and weak, but whole. There was nothing there to repair as he had with Miss Weisling.

"Don't you dare!" snapped Mercedes at the same instant Jack realized her aura was just weak and needed more energy. He smiled and gave her aura energy from his own as she pulled her hand away, but it was too late. She had received some from him and her aura was stronger and better looking instantly.

She, however, still looked very old and tired. "Don't you dare do that to me." She waved a crooked finger at him. "It is past time for me to go, and I am ready."

He thought he understand the way she felt. After spending time with her shadow-memories, he had a sense of what her life had been like, and somewhere close to the top of the list of things describing her life was the word *exhausting*. At least he had managed to give her enough energy he thought she would last until Fidelina returned.

The owl softly hooted in the towel-lined box. Jack had forgotten about it. He couldn't understand what it had meant by the hoot, but he had the feeling it had been Rosa asking him to help the owl.

This was the first time he had really looked at the owl since he had started seeing auras again, and he was not surprised to find he could see Rosa's aura mixed in with the owl's own. What did surprise him was the oddness of the owl's aura. Not that it was wrong in anyway, he just hadn't seen one like it before. It was…more three dimensional than the others, like there was more to it, extending away into other places. He wondered if that would actually make it fourth or fifth dimensional.

The break in the owl's wing was an obvious spot of turmoil in the aura and he reached out to heal it. He touched the injury with his aura and felt how it was supposed to be, then, without quite knowing how he did it, he willed it to return to the way it had been.

He lingered on the touch of the owl's aura, feeling the unusual way it extended off into other places, like a tree, with dozens of different branches leading off into different places. He moved his own aura in closer to see better. It was like floating into a new world, dreamlike, soft and fuzzy, with an ethereal quality.

Jack laughed silently at his own thought. Of course it had an ethereal quality.

He remembered Fidelina's analogy of the different realms being like air, land, and water, and he felt this supported her analogy. Some branches led off into the sky, while some 'roots' led into the soil, and still more into yet other places he could easily think of as water or cloud, or mud, or...

He realized she had greatly simplified things for him. There were a lot of different realms, all of them different 'places'. He found one that felt strangely familiar. As he drifted closer, he recognized it as his own 'home' reality. How odd that he could see a pathway leading to it, while still being in it. He moved closer to examine it and everything lurched as it pulled him in and through.

He felt strange. All around, an incredibly bright and textured world surrounded him. He had thought this was his home reality, but it was very strange. He felt a twinge of nervousness and the world fluttered.

Rosa.

Rosa was here. She was with him. He could sense her thoughts. They weren't clear, like someone speaking. They were fuzzy, like trying to analyze your own emotions when you weren't overly emotional. She was willing him to stay calm, so as not to frighten the owl. He realized he was in his own reality, but he was seeing it through the eyes of the owl.

The bright and highly textured world again was Mercedes' kitchen. Mercedes' dim, dull, drab kitchen, which had been such a stark contrast to her living room, was incredible through the eyes of the owl. He wondered at what the mirrored living room must look like and realized this explained why wild animals reacted so strongly to strange places—especially human places. He gazed up into his own face and was shocked by the detail he could see.

It was a cosmetologist's nightmare.

At Rosa's gentle suggestion, he began pulling his awareness back from the owl's, so as not to overly stress it. Then he noticed a path he hadn't seen before. It called to him. He peeked a little closer and saw a path back to him, but not the one he had come in. It was almost as if one of the owl's branch paths led into him as another reality. What would happen if he went back into himself while still in the owl? What would happen if someone else, like Rosa, took it?

His curiosity piqued. He began moving toward the path to find out, but Rosa gently called him back, asking him not to go. Looking at the path one more time in wonder, he decided to respect Rosa's suggestion and began pulling back from the owl, back into the branches of its aura, and then back into the normal world.

It took a moment for him to readjust. The kitchen was plain and drab once more. He wished for a mirror to examine his own face, curious to compare what he had seen through the owl's eyes with what he could find with his own.

The owl jumped out of the box and startled him. It spread its wings in the kitchen, easily filling the small room. The bird seemed anxious, and Jack worried it would hurt itself in the house.

"Come on." He held his arm out like a perch and hoped the owl would understand. Either it did, or Rosa convinced it to, and it jumped with a flap of its wings, up to land on his arm. Jack grimaced as the claws dug around his forearm, seeking a hold. He headed for the backdoor, his scowl increasing as the weight of the owl tired his arm.

Opening the door, careful not to bump the owl into it, he stepped out into the brisk night air. The owl let out a loud hoot and sprung from his arm, the downward force nearly straining Jack's shoulder muscles. The owl circled to gain altitude and Jack resisted the urge to wave as it flew off into the darkness.

After a moment staring into the starry sky after the bird, he took a deep breath and wondered what to do next. There were so many things he didn't understand. He could no longer deny any of it. He had seen and done all of those strange things, and they were all real. He had hoped they had just been 'lucid dreams', but they weren't. They were something much more.

And, in spite of everything, he still had no idea how to help Julie. He had healed Miss Weisling, and Rosa's owl, and Mercedes—sort of. He was sure enough of how those healings had happened to make him sure his first interpretation of his experience with Julie was still accurate. There was nothing physically wrong with her—she just no longer had a soul.

A flare of hope went up in his heart. Doña Isabella's letter had stated nothing could destroy an immortal soul. If Mercedes hadn't destroyed that man's soul, then maybe, just maybe, if Julie's soul hadn't been destroyed, it was still somewhere where he could help it.

THIRTY-FIVE

The green glowing numbers on the microwave's clock indicated it was nearly midnight. Jack sat quietly at the kitchen table and reread the message sent to him across the years by Doña Isabella. Mercedes, now white-haired and wrinkled with age, dozed across from him in her chair while leaning her shoulder against the wall. Fidelina had been gone for a long time, and Jack hoped she would return soon. Although Mercedes no longer seemed to be aging, she was definitely old enough Jack was concerned she would go at any moment. He also desperately wanted to ask Fidelina about the possibility of Julie's soul still being alive somewhere outside of her body, somewhere he could possibly rescue it.

The sound of a door shutting jolted Jack out of his thoughts. As he stood to go investigate, an old Hispanic woman wearing a faded shawl and modest black dress ambled into the kitchen from the back room. She was unremarkable in appearance but Jack knew who she was the instant she removed the shawl and revealed a grotesque mass of scar tissue at her throat.

"Hello, Jack," she rasped in a shadow of a gravelly voice.

"Hello, Rosa." He nodded to her, trying not to stare at the remnants of the wound hampering her speech. He was amazed she could talk at all after what he had seen the demon do to her throat in the shadow-memory. He hadn't thought she would have survived the attack.

"Oh, my poor little Mercy." Her voice dropped to the barest whisper as she spotted Mercedes' tiny weakened form. Rosa went over and draped the scarf around Mercedes with a small sad, wistful smile on her face. "I told you," she whispered quietly. "I told you."

"So did everyone else." Mercedes cracked open her eyes and gave Rosa a withering look. "What made you think you were so special I'd listen to you any better than the rest of them, hey?"

Rosa took a step back. "Why! You old so-and-so!" she hissed as loudly as she could.

"Until the day I die!" Mercedes snapped back. Then she held up her nearly useless gnarl of hands. "Or rather, 'til the minute I die!"

She cackled evilly for a moment and then the two old women broke into laughter, Rosa's ruined voice nearly sounding like Mercedes' false cackle had. Mercedes tried to stand up, but Rosa leaned in and hugged her, keeping her in her chair.

"Oh, I've missed you so much, Mercy!" Rosa rasped into Mercedes' shoulder.

"I'm so sorry, Rosa. I don't know how I could have been so selfish. All these years…" Her voice cracked as she tried to talk, and the two old women pulled apart. Rosa made a noise with her throat sounding just like Mercedes' voice cracking, and the two of them laughed at each other again.

"Plenty of time for sorrow later!" Rosa hissed. "For now, let's enjoy what we have, while we can!" Mercedes nodded at her while wiping tears out of her eyes.

Rosa pulled out the chair next to Mercedes and sat down. Mercedes seemed to suddenly remember Jack was there and grinned wide.

"Did he show you the letter?" she asked excitedly.

"Not yet." They both looked at Jack expectantly until he handed over the letter and the pencil sketch portrait.

Rosa glanced over the sketch first and then eyeballed Jack. She nodded her head approvingly. "It helps to see it with your own eyes." She winked at Jack conspiratorially, and he realized she probably had as much trouble seeing out of the owl's eyes as he had.

Unfolding the letter, Rosa began reading with Mercedes tittering at her shoulder and pointing out various things in the letter. When they finally finished reading and put the letter down, Rosa gave Jack a grim look, ignoring Mercedes' girlish antics.

"I don't have nearly the power to see things that Doña Isabella had, Jack, but I can see a little." Mercedes had to quiet her giggling in order to hear Rosa's whispered words. "I know you came here to help your wife, and I know her soul is gone."

Mercedes shut up completely as Rosa sadly held Jack's gaze. "I know this was supposed to console you," she waved at the letter absently, "but I don't want it to give you false hope."

Jack felt his heart sink. She had seen right through him somehow and was naming his worst fears as truths.

Rosa patted at the letter on the table. "I can try to help you with the 'truth' Doña Isabella mentioned, and I agree with her vision that you will be able to do amazing things, but I fear your wife is beyond the help of anyone of this world."

Jack felt like he had been punched in the stomach. Why hadn't Fidelina told him this right from the start? Why had she wasted his time and drug him through all of this?

"I have never heard of anyone recovering from the situation your wife is in, although I have heard of souls leaving their bodies early before."

Vaguely he heard Mercedes whisper she hadn't known about Jack's wife, and Rosa hoarsely answered something back. He hung his head low over the kitchen table. He tried to feel anger, he wanted to cry—but there was nothing there. He had hoped so much and gone through so many strange things. Putting his face in his hands, his shoulders fell as he wondered what to do now.

What would he do without Julie? For the first time since he had found her on the floor in the basement, he was starting to accept she was gone, and he wasn't going to get her back. Now that his only hope of helping her was gone, his only focus for maintaining his sanity was gone too. His life with Julie was over and his life as a normal, sane person was over too. He felt so thoroughly beaten he couldn't muster up any feeling other than surrender. He was just done.

He felt a hand on his shoulder and looked up to see Mercedes offering him a glass of water. He took it numbly and drank it. It was tasteless and sat in his stomach uncomfortably. His ears were ringing distantly and his eyes didn't want to focus, but he didn't care. He felt small and insignificant, detached from reality, helpless, lonely, and tired.

So tired. Tired of all of it. He closed his eyes in a futile effort to shield himself from his own misery.

"Jack!" The word came from a long ways away. A sharp blow to his cheek pulled it closer. "Jack! You haven't earned the right to fade out yet!" Another slap, across the other cheek this time, and his face stung. His eyes watered and he dodged the third slap, catching the frail arm with a too tight grip.

"It's about time!" Fidelina yelled in his face and reached to slap him again with her other hand. He caught that one too.

"Okay," she said quietly, "now we're getting somewhere. Let go of me now."

"Don't hit me again," Jack warned, his vision clearing. His cheeks stung sharply.

"Then don't wish yourself dead again!" Fidelina's eyes were black and piercing.

"I wasn't wishing myself dead!"

"Oh. I suppose you were just taking a little catnap, huh? Just a little light *siesta*? I had to slap you eleven times to wake you up!"

"What?" Even as he said it, he could tell from Mercedes and Rosa's reactions they were agreeing with Fidelina. He slowly let go of the old woman's wrists and she whirled and pointed at the two standing behind her.

"And you two! I can't believe you let him! Just like always! Put the two of you together and the giggling starts and the work stops!" Both of the old women blushed and looked away. Fidelina turned back to Jack. "You still with us? Didn't fade out again while my back was turned?"

Jack shook his head quietly and massaged his burning face. What had happened? As if reading his mind, Fidelina began explaining.

"Our souls exist on many planes at once. Remember my analogy of the sky, earth and water? Our souls may seem to only be right here, right now, but they extend off into many different places."

Jack remembered how the owl's soul had been like a multi-dimensional tree, spreading its branches out into other realities. There was no reason not to believe everyone's soul did the same thing to one degree or another.

"In some places your soul is like a little plant, growing slowly and carefully, hoping for a little rain, a little sun. In those places there are things like bugs wanting to eat the leaves on your plant. As long as you keep growing new leaves it doesn't matter, but if you stop—they eat you up!" She waved her finger dramatically in the air. "And you in particular, with that bright aura of yours, you are a flashing neon light saying 'Eat here! Best food in town!'

"And in other places other things happen! Things we prevent every single day by staying healthy, both physically and emotionally. Things we avoid by laughing, by loving, by caring, by believing, and by praying. When you stop doing all of these things, you stop growing. You stop protecting yourself. When you stop protecting yourself—you die." She finished with a flat quiet voice and a hard stare.

"Now then, you can tell yourself you were just resting your eyes, or you can admit you were letting your soul die. It's up to you. It is none of my business. Now that I have warned you of the possibility, I am absolved of responsibility." She crossed her arms and turned away from him, striking a dramatic pose.

THIRTY-SIX

"Can you help me save my wife?"

Fidelina turned away from the other two old women who were watching her intently. "I don't know," she told Jack.

Jack dropped his gaze back to the table and the letter on it. He reached out and grabbed the last piece of hope he could find and handed it to Fidelina. "Read this."

"I don't have to read it. I was there when she wrote it." Fidelina laid the letter back on the table and met Jack's eyes again. "I helped her write it. We looked into the past and the future together, searching for answers.

"I couldn't see the things she saw, I couldn't believe the things she said." Fidelina shrugged in a nonchalant gesture. "I didn't realize who you were until you released the demon's soul from the knife. And then...well, we haven't really had a chance to talk since then."

"I'm all ears now." Jack leaned forward and intently held her eyes with his. Mercedes and Rosa sidled around the table and sat down with curious faces. Fidelina took a deep breath and began explaining.

"Years ago, Mercedes took it into her head she wasn't powerful enough and she invited a demon into herself to increase her power. When she discovered she couldn't control it, she came to Doña Isabella for help. A demon is nothing to be trifled with, as you have seen for yourself, so Doña Isabella called Rosa and myself over for an emergency...uh, exorcism, you might call it.

"It just so happened to be that Doña Isabella's great-grandson, Victor, was in her care at the time, and there was no time to have someone else watch over him, so we kept him in the room where we could watch him. We were afraid to put him in a different room where we couldn't watch him, as the demon might have been attracted to someone so young and vulnerable. Like the *Ojo*, remember?" Jack nodded in acknowledgment.

"When we removed the demon from Mercedes, it attacked us. It was a much more powerful demon than any of us had expected. None of us ever thought we would ever encounter a demon powerful enough to take on a physical form, they are just too rare and too…smart." She glanced down at the table and then back at Jack. "Have you ever heard of *El Chupacabra*, the goat-sucker?"

Jack nodded again. He had seen something about it on television; some sort of wild creature-demon thing people in Latin America had been claiming was killing their farm animals for years now.

"That is what *El Chupacabra* is—a demon powerful enough to give itself a physical body in our world. There are demons like it all over the world. Some are called Yeti or Sasquatch or Dragon or Unicorn, or whatever. You get the point. Not all are evil, not all are good. They are the both by-products of the civilization around them and makers of the folklore of that civilization. They have different appearances and actions, depending on what people expect to see. That is part of the 'truth' mentioned in the letter, but I'll get to that later.

"Anyway, you saved us. The demon would have fed off of each and every one of us, becoming powerful enough to leave the house and exist on its own." Jack saw Rosa unconsciously reach up and massage the massive scar on her throat as Fidelina continued talking.

"I don't know how you managed to fight the demon, but you did, and somehow Doña Isabella saw you. None of the rest of us did. In fact, we all thought, somehow, little Victor had done it, and so, to my shame, we ignored Doña Isabella's sketch of you and her insistence she had seen you.

"We thought she had hallucinated while she was in pain with her broken hip. We thought she had visions of someone else, of something else, anything but the truth, because the truth was just too unbelievable." She shook her head and wrung her hands. "Can you believe that? The three of us," she waved at the two old women across the table from her, "thought something was too unbelievable to be true. We thought it impossible for someone to be strong enough to send their spirit to fight a demon without actually being there."

The three old women looked at each other sullenly for a moment before Fidelina continued. "The truth is even more unbelievable. Somehow, you fought it from across time. What if I had never handed you the knife? What if you had never decided to pick it up? How could it have happened before you did it, or maybe before you were even born? How old are you? Never mind…" Her voice trailed off as she pondered the impossibilities of paradox.

"So anyway, we tried to train little Victor. Doña Isabella humored us. She tried to train Victor, too, but she spent the rest of her life looking for you. And trying to keep an eye on Mercy." She glanced meaningfully at Mercedes. "That is how we all ended up here instead of in Mexico. Not much use searching for a *gringo* in Mexico, especially one who did magic. We would have known you already. Then, three days before she died, she came to me and told me she had had another vision of you and asked me to look to the past and the future with her.

"I didn't want to do it. I thought it was a silly waste of effort, especially after all these years, but Doña Isabella was the greatest person I have ever known, and I couldn't refuse her." The other two women nodded solemnly in agreement with Fidelina. "I wasn't able to see anything about you at all. Considering everything, I am not surprised. But Doña Isabella, with the help of my prayer and my energy, was finally able to discover you were still in the future, and that your path would someday, somehow, intersect with Mercedes'." She took a deep breath and sighed, memories flowing across her face.

"I helped her to put all of the vague feelings and impressions comprising her vision of the future into words and put them on paper." She gestured toward the letter and then warily turned to Mercedes. "I wasn't supposed to give you the message from Antonio because we were afraid if you knew a soul could never be truly destroyed, you would never repent your..."

Jack could hear her finish the phrase 'evil ways' in his mind, and the look on Mercedes' face said she could too, but Fidelina stopped herself and finished with "misdeeds" instead. Mercedes hung her head in shame anyway. Rosa reached over and put her arm around the frail figure, her harsh voice raspy as she whispered comfort into Mercedes' ear.

"Tell me about the 'truth' thing," Jack asked Fidelina, who nodded slowly, gathering her thoughts.

"Remember when we were discussing Bernardo's hoof marks and you suggested it was psychosomatic? You were very close to the truth, but coming at it from the wrong way." She paused, thinking. "I explained the marks looked the way they did because he expected them to." She paused again, and Jack nodded encouragement to her to show he understood. "But no matter what shape the marks appeared as, he still would have had them, so you see, it is only partially in his mind. His entire family believed the devil would someday come for their son, for all of the evil things he did, so eventually, it was bound to happen.

"The truth is like a philosopher's reasoning. I think, therefore I am. You think, therefore you are. We think, therefore it is. If enough people believe in something, it can happen. Sometimes this is called a miracle, and sometimes it is a miracle. Sometimes Our Lady

Guadalupe sees fit to give a helping hand and something none of us expected or believed in happens." She noted Jack's confusion and tried to think of a better way to explain.

"All of the strange things you have seen since you arrived—how many of those do you think you would have seen if you had gone to a voodoo priestess instead of a *bruja?*"

The question caught Jack off guard and he wasn't sure how to answer. Would he have seen nothing, because voodoo wasn't real? Or would he have seen the same things with different names?

Fidelina answered for him. "You would have encountered many similar things, but nothing would be familiar to you. Instead of my blessed candles you would have seen the priestess's *gris-gris*. Instead of the *Ojo*, you would have heard about the stealing of people's *mojo*." She sighed, feeling the difficulty of a quick explanation of a complex concept.

"If you had gone to an American Indian Medicine Man, or an Indian Yogi, you would have seen similar things with different names, and you would have seen unique things. Every culture in the world has its own magic, which is shaped not only by the people's experiences, but also by their beliefs, and their disbeliefs. Some cultures specialize in communicating with the dead, some with predicting the future, others with controlling evil spirits." She watched the lack of understanding float across Jack's face and leaned back in frustration.

"Jack," Rosa whispered hoarsely. "How many of the things that you have seen since you got here do you think can be proven by the scientific method?"

Jack shook his head. How do you prove to someone you can see an aura they cannot? Or that you had no prior knowledge of an incident before you saw a shadow-memory? Could he convince someone he had seen a weird cat with the glowing eyes in the back of his car, or that Mercedes had tried to seduce him in his sleep?

"What about the owl trick?" he blurted suddenly.

Rosa smiled grimly. "You might be able to prove it. But the owls are difficult to control. They mostly carry our spirits with them at their own leisure, not ours, but you might be able to prove it. However," she raised a finger at him, "only someone with true skills can use the owls, and by the time a person is capable of proving these skills exist, they have generally realized the world is better off without every Tom, Dick, and Harry trying to possess an owl or cast a love potion."

Jack nodded thoughtfully. The world would be a strange place if everyone could work that kind of mischief. "But why doesn't everyone see the shadow-memories, or ghosts, or demons? Why isn't there a local witch in every neighborhood to help heal people and get rid of curses?"

Fidelina stuck her finger in the air. "There once were witches in every village. And everyone did see the ghosts, but they don't anymore because of the 'truth'." She announced proudly, as if he had discovered something. "Because the world around us is affected by our beliefs.

"Many people do still see ghosts, or demons, or whatever, but they don't believe in what they saw. They convince themselves it was a dream, a trick of the eye, or blame it on the squirrel up in the tree, or the dog next door." She waved her hands emphatically as she spoke.

"But the truth is malleable, and therein lays the problem of proving things to science," Rosa interjected with her raspy voice and nodded her head in agreement while Mercedes' already wrinkled brow bunched up even more. Fidelina ignored Jack and Mercedes' confusion and continued on.

"It is very easy for me to work my magic, here in this little town full of my own people, who believe in my magic. It would not be so easy in your big city, which is full of even more people who do not believe in it. Not believing in something can be just as powerful as believing in it." She nodded as how to explain the ideas seemed to finally coalesce for her. Mercedes leaned back in her chair with an enlightened look on her face as though she finally grasped a concept that had eluded her for years.

"If I sit here with the three of you, I can do many things!" Fidelina turned and pointed her hands toward the corner of the kitchen where an old pair of house slippers had been set out of the way. She muttered a little prayer, crossed herself, and then began wriggling her fingers like a marionette puppeteer.

Jack's jaw dropped as the shoes twitched and then took up a life of their own, dancing a jig as though an invisible person was wearing them.

"But," Fidelina exclaimed dramatically while still wiggling her fingers, "if it was just me, in a little room in the city, with three unbelieving scientists wanting me to prove me a liar…" She threw her hands up and the slippers dropped heavily to the floor, lifeless again. "Their disbelief would be stronger than my belief, and it would grow stronger as they fed it to one another."

"But you know you made those shoes move, and you know you can do it again." Jack protested.

"What?" Fidelina asked.

"The shoes." Jack pointed at the slippers. "You moved them once—you can make them move again. You know it, why does it matter what someone else thinks?"

"What shoes?" she asked again, bewilderedly.

"Those ones. Right there. Hello! Remember when you just made them dance? Two seconds ago?"

Fidelina eyes went wide with surprise and she looked to Rosa. Rosa gave her a confused look and shrugged her shoulders. "Jack," Rosa croaked. "Are you feeling all right?"

Mercedes giggled nervously.

Jack quickly looked down at himself. Had the aura come back? Was it different this time? Maybe the demon had come back.

Everything seemed normal to him. He turned back to the women. "What? I feel okay. What's wrong?"

Mercedes leaned forward, her voice quivering as she reached a shaky hand out to his across the table. "I think you're seeing things again."

"Why what did I do?" He looked around himself worriedly. He didn't remember seeing any more shadow-memories.

"You were talking nonsense about some shoes," Rosa croaked.

"Are you sure you feel all right?" Fidelina asked.

"Yeah." Jack put his hand to his forehead absentmindedly checking for a fever. "I think so. The last thing I remember was talking about the shoes you made dance. Did I do something else?"

"Jack, I didn't make any shoes dance."

Jack leaned back in his chair. He had just seen her do it. Why couldn't they remember her doing it? He couldn't have imagined it, could he?

"Oh." Jack let out an exasperated sigh. "You guys are messing with me. Trying to prove you point."

Fidelina smiled warmly at him. "If we denied it for the rest of our lives, how sure of yourself would you be? If us three little old ladies who believe in magic, and whom you believe can do magic, can make you, someone who has done some yourself, doubt, even a little, that easily, imagine what everyone in the world calling you crazy would do to you."

She met Jack's eyes again. "Even if I managed to make the shoes move a just little in a test situation they would explain it away until it was meaningless. 'Just a trick of the light,' or 'we saw what we were expecting to see, not what was real,' or flat out denial.

"That is how most people deal with supernatural things. They ignore it and deny they ever saw it. Even to themselves. It is a very effective technique." She glanced at Mercedes and then quickly back to Jack. "Just ask your friend Victor."

Mercedes instantly turned bright red. An expression of horror and shame clouded her face and she looked away from the table.

"Mercedes came to him in his sleep every night for weeks, when he was just at the earliest stages of becoming a man." Jack heard a sob escape from the withered figure hiding her face in her hands as Fidelina coldly told the story. "He had no idea it was Mercedes. To him she was an old woman, an auntie. In his dreams, she was everything a young man could ever hope for, ever dream of. And that is what he thought it was—dreams. Until Anita, his girlfriend at the time, tried to sneak into his bedroom late one night and saw him with the ghost-form of Mercedes in his bed."

"I never took any energy from his soul! Never!" Mercedes croaked desperately.

Fidelina didn't look at her, she just shook her head and quietly said "Little boys have so much more to lose than just their soul."

Jack, unable to look at Mercedes, looked at Rosa, who in turn was watching the table with Fidelina. None of them could meet Mercedes' pleading gaze as she choked back sobs of regret.

"Victor couldn't bear the betrayal of trust from one of his teachers. So, with a little help from Doña Isabella, and a lot of help from his wife, he has learned to disbelieve. He denies himself the belief of all of the things he experienced as a child strongly enough he can no longer see any of the things he grew up being taught how to see.

"He considers them a false memory. As if your mother had been retelling you a story about something you did as a two-year old, over and over again. Do you really remember taking a bite out of the mud pie, or have you just filled in the story with imagination over the years? If your father tells you years later your mother was mistaken and it was actually your little brother who ate the mud pie, how do you explain the memory to yourself? It is not very hard to decide you imagined it, and therefore decide to not believe in it."

Jack frowned. "Vic sure seemed like he still believed in it to me. He told me stories, he sent me down here…"

Fidelina quickly nodded her head in exaggerated exacerbation. "He is holding two conflicting beliefs at once. People do it all the time.

Like knowing smoking will cause cancer but doing it anyway, believing it won't happen to them. Like believing there is no such thing as God and then praying for help. Talking to animals, when you know they can't understand a word you're saying, but believing they understand you. People do it all the time, Jack. Victor just happens to be better at it than most, and he sensed you needed his help."

Jack silently pondered the thought while Mercedes sniveled, ignoring Rosa's attempts to console her. That explained why Anita didn't want Vic coming back here.

"And that is how most people, all over the world, deal with the supernatural. They ignore it. They disbelieve in it. But at the same time, everyone gets the feeling they're being watched, or the creepy feeling when you're all alone at night, and it is that slight belief everyone has that still gives the supernatural power in our world." Fidelina smiled at him reassuringly. "That is what also gives us power over them. I know I can repel any ghost, because I believe I can. And so can anyone else who believes a ghost has no power over them."

"So, you're saying if I don't believe in ghosts, I'll never even see one?" Jack asked with his eyebrows raised expectantly.

"Yes. Or at least you'll never know what it was you saw."

"Uh huh." His voice took on a disbelieving tone, "Then why did I see the one in my bedroom? The one that attacked me. I didn't believe in ghosts until it forced itself on me."

Fidelina nodded and waved a hand aimlessly in the air. "There are many possible reasons. Maybe your next-door neighbor is so sure your house is haunted that you saw the spirit, even though you didn't believe. Maybe your wife believes in ghosts. Maybe you weren't as sure as you thought you were and still had some room in your mind for the possibility."

Jack smiled grimly back at her. "That just about covers everything doesn't it? If I see something it is because I, or someone else, believed I could, and if I don't see anything, it is because I, or someone else, believed I couldn't. Right?"

Fidelina beamed at him. "I think you finally understand. It works the same way with your personal ability to do things, but varies with how much it involves another person. You can't do much of anything to someone who believes you can't, but just because someone believes you can't see auras won't stop you from seeing them."

Jack sighed tiredly and glanced at the clock in the microwave. It was after three in the morning, and he was getting very tired. "It doesn't make any sense to me," he muttered, running his hand through his hair.

"I told you," Rosa croaked. "The truth is malleable. That is a very difficult thing to accept."

THIRTY-SEVEN

Jack sat up slowly, blinking the sleep out of his eyes and trying to make sense of his surroundings. The afternoon sun shone in brightly through the green pastel colored chiffon curtains. As his eyes adjusted, he remembered the old women had sent him to bed around four in the morning, and that he was in Mercedes' bedroom. He looked around curiously. He had been too tired to notice the room last night.

Nothing at all like what he would have expected after seeing the 'love den' that comprised her front room, this was the room of a more sensible, more mature woman. The walls and the ceiling were all a nice match to the pastel greens of the curtains and bedspread. The furniture was all a light oak and perfectly matched to the twin sized four-poster bed he slept in. The room was immaculate.

He got out of bed and headed for a private bath decorated to match to the bedroom. There he found his clothes, neatly cleaned and folded on the bathroom counter, along with a towel and washcloth set out for him. He didn't remember undressing, let alone noticing one of the women taking and bringing back his clothes.

For a moment, he felt his cheeks flush as he thought about one of them taking his clothes and washing them, but his mind rationally overrode the embarrassment. Each one of the women was old enough to be his great-grandmother: there were precious few things they would find new about him.

Noting his cleaned clothing, he decided to take the hint. He felt as though he hadn't showered in weeks. Yesterday had been a long day. Jack shrugged off the feeling of being overwhelmed by all of the things he had seen and been told yesterday, and turned on the water for the shower.

As the warm water cascaded down his back soothingly, he fought the urge to turn off his mind and ignore the events of the previous day. It would be too easy to just go home and pretend none of it had ever happened. A pang of guilt pounded though his entire being. He had momentarily forgotten about Julie. In the face of auras and owls, demons and witches, he had forgotten his wife lay in a hospital bed dying.

His heart weighed heavily in his chest.

At Fidelina's behest, he had told his story to Mercedes and Rosa last night before they sent him to bed. He had been so tired he hadn't even noticed their reactions to it. All of the energy he had absorbed from the demon had only a temporary effect. He had become exhausted very quickly last night. He remembered what Mercedes had said about using the demon as a sort of battery to store the energy she had taken from the men. If she was taking only small amounts, it was no wonder she had found herself addicted to having the demon present. He had absorbed an entire demon, and it had still worn off quickly.

He toweled off as he wondered if either of the other two witches would be able to add any insight into what had happened to Julie or how to help her. He had tried using their 'malleable truth' against them, suggesting what they were basically saying was anything was possible, as long as you believed in yourself strongly enough, so they should be able to help her if they only believed hard enough. They had given him sad smiles that silently let him know he hadn't managed to grasp the concept.

How could the truth be changeable, and yet they had no power to change it? How could they tell him that, with his weird purple aura, he was capable of all these fantastic things they couldn't do, but still tell him he couldn't do anything to help Julie? He just couldn't follow the logic of it.

He dressed quickly and left the bedroom, feeling guilty about having used Mercedes' bed and wondering where she had slept. The shadow-memory vision of her younger form curled up crying in the palm of the giant black hand-chair came unbidden to his mind. His imagination superimposed the wrinkled and withered figure she now possessed over the memory. He pushed the mental picture away rapidly, not wanting to deal with shadow-memories of any type any more.

Voices lead him to the kitchen where he found the three old women looking as though he had left them there just moments ago instead of hours.

"Good morning!" Fidelina was the first to spot him and she smiled enthusiastically.

Jack glanced at his watch. "I think you mean good afternoon." He raised his brows at them. "Don't you people ever sleep?"

Fidelina shrugged and Mercedes cracked a wrinkled smile at him.

"When you reach our age, you realize sleep is best taken in moderation, just like everything else," Rosa's voice grated as she smiled at him too.

Looking back and forth between the three grinning old witches, Jack wondered if there was a parable he should be aware of. "What are you up to?" he asked suspiciously, eyes flicking from one smiling form to the next.

"Come sit!" Mercedes tried to pat the chair next to her, but her aging hands had curled into arthritic claws, and she rapped it with her knuckles instead. Her form was very frail and slight now, and Jack was amazed she was still alive, let alone holding herself up in the chair.

Jack moved into their circle and sat down. He had no fear of the women anymore. Anything they had wanted to do to him, they could have done long ago.

"We think we have figured out what happened to your wife!" Rosa cackled with girlish glee, and Jack winced at how closely she fit his childhood image of a witch.

"We think it was *El Cucuy*!" Mercedes whispered conspiratorially.

"'Coo-koo-ey?' Where have I heard that before?" He glanced quickly at Fidelina. "Wait. You mentioned it once before. You called it the bogeyman."

Fidelina nodded with raised eyebrows, obviously surprised Jack remembered. "We discussed what you said happened, and we think *El Cucuy* is the most likely possibility."

Jack's thoughts spun when trying to think in terms of their mysterious metaphysical world. "I thought you said things were kind of culture specific. Why would Julie have been attacked by a Hispanic bogeyman? Why not a real, I mean, American, style bogeyman?"

Fidelina shrugged him off. "What is a bogeyman? A monster under the bed? In the closet? Something in a dark alley at night?"

Jack sighed and dropped the point of contention. "Okay, tell me about *El Cucuy*."

Rosa leaned in conspiratorially and whispered in her ruined voice, the scar tissue at her throat pulsing with her words. "*El Cucuy* comes for children who are lazy and misbehave. He steals them away from their families and takes them to his hidden cave."

Mercedes also leaned in and whispered as though she were telling campfire stories. "He is hideously ugly with humped back and large pointed red ears. His only pleasure in life is tormenting people to the point of tears."

Jack felt a slight sense of déjà vu until he remembered how Vic had told him the story of his grandmother and the egg with the same intensity. He wondered if it was a Hispanic thing or if Vic had learned it from these two. He fought the urge to shiver brought on by their sinister tones.

Rosa's voice croaked, eerily adding credence to her story. "He does horrible things to the children in his cave, things too terrible to mention."

Mercedes joined in again, her voice little more than a hiss. "He takes only the bad children because he knows no one will miss them."

La Llorona had been bad enough, and she had been a pretty lady dressed in white. What would it be like trying to deal with a hideous hump-backed thing?

Fidelina rolled her eyes, and suddenly the other two witches burst with laughter. "Nice rhyming, Mercy!" Rosa cackled happily.

Jack felt his face flush with anger. Mercedes and Rosa didn't even notice, too lost in the pleasure of their teasing.

"Jack." Fidelina put her hand on his arm. "What they're telling you is the traditional view of *El Cucuy*, but now-a-days so few people believe in it that I don't expect you will find a physical representation of it involved with your wife."

"What do you mean?" he fought to keep the irritation out of his voice as the other two women continued to cackle to each other.

"We think it was *El Cucuy*, but in its demon form, without the physical body. Just because it is no longer strong enough to physically carry someone off doesn't mean it can't still do it psychically. All demons started out somehow, creating legends that caused enough people to believe in them they finally gained the strength to take on a physical form. We think this may be a weaker type of *El Cucuy*, one that carries away only its victim's soul, leaving the body behind."

"I don't understand why it would do that."

"The legend of *El Cucuy* had to have started somewhere. We think this is how it started. A demon carried away the souls of malcontents, off to its own private place, where it did horrible things to them."

Fidelina patted his hand to keep his full attention as the other two women began giggling again. "Remember how I said other things feed off of our souls? Maybe this thing is like a farmer and wants to keep its food stored in a certain place, in a certain way, so it can feed whenever it wants, however it wants."

Jack shuddered at the thought of Julie's soul being something's food. "But she's not a malcontent! Why would it take her?"

"Isn't she?" Fidelina gave him a motherly look. "Aren't you both? From what you had told me, it sounded like your relationship wasn't doing so well."

"Yeah, but that's just... It's different. It's not like she was a misbehaving child like the legends say." Even as he said the words, he remembered how he had feared she might have been seeing someone else.

"All it takes is enough for the person's soul to be vulnerable to outside attack." Fidelina offered another possibility. "Some spirits even manage to create that vulnerability by slowly destroying family relationships. The German's had a particular problem with those kinds of spirits. They called them *poltergeists.*"

The hair on the back of Jack's neck prickled as he realized Fidelina might be right. All of those fights with Julie over nothing... The anger and jealously that came out of nowhere for no apparent reason. Maybe that was why she had acted the way she had. Had they both been manipulated to express negative emotions to push each other away?

"Your dream about the little girl in the closet," Fidelina continued, "was probably another psychic impression. You keep calling them shadow-memories."

"We think she is the one who originally attracted the demon to your house," Rosa croaked, no longer laughing at private jokes with Mercedes. "And once a place is familiar, perhaps the demon keeps checking back in from time to time—like a favorite fishing hole."

"Oh my God," Jack muttered. "That dream was about the same closet Bear tore his paws up trying to get into!" He looked into Fidelina's eyes and she nodded sadly in return.

"Many animals are sensitive to otherworldly forces. I think your sister may have been right all along. Your dog was watching ghosts, of a sort."

"The bad part," Mercedes interjected, "is we don't know how to help you." Her face was suddenly somber, and Rosa nodded morosely in agreement. "We could banish the demon, but you've already demonstrated you know how to do that."

"And it wouldn't bring your wife back," rasped Rosa.

"You've got to at least have some idea!" Jack heard his own voice rising shakily but ignored it as his heart pounded in fear of losing hope of saving Julie. "How did they used to do it? Go to the cave and get the children? Somebody must have been rescued, or no one would know *El Cucuy* took them to a cave and did terrible things to them, right?" His voice quivered.

Mercedes reached out to touch him reassuringly, but he pulled away, refusing to accept resignation. "How did they used to do it?" he demanded of Fidelina.

"It was different. *El Cucuy* would physically take the person, and leave the soul in the body. We could track the cave down, or we could use owls to search for them in the woods, or we could project our souls out to find our way to the lost soul and then go get them."

"You can do that can't you? Project out to find Julie's soul? Then we could bring it back to her body, right? Right?"

Fidelina shook her head sadly. "If your impression at the hospital was right, and there was no soul in your wife's body, then it is no longer attached. If it is no longer attached, then there is no way to track it. There is nothing linking it to this world."

"I don't understand. You mean she is already dead?"

"No." Rosa interrupted. "Remember when we were in the owl together? There was a path that attracted your curiosity and I asked you not to take it: a path leading back to yourself."

"I remember. I wanted to know what would happen if I went back to myself through a different path than the one I came in on."

"That is one of the easier ways to completely detach your soul from your body—next to dying, of course." Rosa chuckled hoarsely at her own joke and winked at Mercedes, who grinned toothily back. "Most of us are afraid of doing that, and never attempt it. I was surprised at your attraction to that pathway. Most people are so afraid of it that the first time they merge energies with another creature they panic, and are forcefully, and somewhat painfully, rejected by the creature." She smiled distantly, as if remembering something from long ago.

Fidelina raised her eyebrows at him. "It seems you are not typical in many ways, Jack. The only person I ever heard of who would willingly detach their soul, outside of legends, was Doña Isabella's *mentora,* her teacher. Doña Isabella told me her teacher talked of walking on different worlds, places that were like, but yet not like, Heaven and Hell. Like Purgatory maybe.

"She felt that when we died our spirits moved into another world where they continued to have some sort of life before they moved on again. Kind of like another lifetime before dying and moving on to Heaven. Or maybe it is just one of many more. It is hard for those of us still in this realm of existence to see the other realms."

Fidelina glanced over at Mercedes and smiled distantly. "That is how Doña Isabella knew Antonio forgave you. Somehow she communicated with him there." Mercedes quickly looked away, conflicting emotions playing across her aged countenance.

Fidelina looked back to Jack. "That is also what I believe most ghosts are—the souls living in that next realm. Perhaps they are peeking back into this one, for whatever reason, and they happen to be glimpsed by someone still here.

"But the point is, the only person I have ever heard of who could walk those worlds was Doña Isabella's *mentora*. I know people who have tried. I have tried. But it is too close to death. It is too much like committing suicide. The body and soul resist the separation so much that no one I know of has ever accomplished it for more than a moment or two."

"No one we know of." Mercedes giggled, implying perhaps that had been the cause of death for some of the people they had known. Fidelina gave her a dark look before she continued speaking.

"Even if, somehow, you were able to find your wife's soul, you couldn't bring her home. She has been out of her body for so long it won't remember her. She won't remember it. They won't reunite. I'm sorry, Jack. It can't be done."

Jack found three pairs of eyes sadly watching his own slowly tear up.

"I have to try, damn it!" His voice choked with anger and frustration. "I have to!" He pounded the table with his fist, surprising himself and startling the women. He took a deep breath and tried to calm himself.

"There has got to be a way," he told them. "If there was no way to do it, your people would never have heard the stories of the horrible things that happen to the children in the caves."

THIRTY-EIGHT

Jack sped home on the long desert highway. The sun was just beginning to set and he was grateful the road had turned north, moving the glare out of his eyes. It had been a cold day and patches of frost were still in the shadows of the scrub brush where the sun hadn't touched long enough. His eyes were tired and burned more each time he rubbed them.

He had taken Fidelina home and packed his bag after the three old women failed to provide him with any sort hope of rescuing Julie. Although they all admitted there must have been someone who had been rescued in the past, they also agreed none of them, or anyone they might know, would be able to help Julie. Everything they knew was about warding for protection against such things from happening.

Jack had been unable to convince Fidelina to come with him to see if there was anything she could do. She had felt the need to stay with Mercedes for what would be her final day or two. Fighting down his own selfishness, he told her he understood, and she promised they would pray for Guadalupe to help him in his endeavor to help his wife.

He had the feeling the old women had wanted him to stay, but just as he had not pushed Fidelina to abandon Mercedes, they had not pushed him to stay.

The sun winked out behind the distant mountains, and Jack tried to turn on the car's headlights only to discover he already had. The dusky light made them nearly useless. With a tired sigh, he slouched a little in the seat of the rusty Celica with a door that no longer closed right, and steeled himself for the last half of a long drive home.

The events of the last few days rattled around in his mind like oily marbles he couldn't seem to hold on to. So many things had happened. He couldn't blame it on dreams anymore. Tempted as he was to blame his own sanity, other people had witnessed, and even been involved in, the strange things occurring around him.

Was it all a hallucination? Did Fidelina, Mercedes, and Rosa really exist? If not, then how could he explain being in his car driving home?

It had to be real. All of it had to be real. There was no accepting part of it, no picking and choosing what was dream and what was real. If there was any hope at all of helping Julie, or himself for that matter, he would have to accept everything he had seen, done, and been told, at face value. He would have to accept it and move forward from here.

He glanced in the rearview mirror. If he never saw green glowing eyes in his back seat again, it would still be too soon.

Julie wore a peaceful look on her face. Her skin was pale as a fine porcelain China doll, but conveyed less life. Her eyes were sunken and dark. Her hand was cool and limp in Jack's, and her skin was dry. Had she been conscious, she would have killed for some lotion, Jack thought as he gently stroked her rough knuckles and wished he had some for her.

It was late, and the hospital was quiet. Julie was alone in a double room and Jack was grateful there was no one else for him to disturb. The nurse had said he could stay after visiting hours, as long as he was quiet.

Jack had been very quiet. Other than a light kiss and a whispered "I love you," his time had been spent trying very hard to find any sign of Julie's aura, any sign of something he could heal, help, coax, anything. There was nothing.

He was hoping maybe his aura just hadn't 'turned on' again yet, but he could no longer deny his inability to help her after his own violet shroud had once again appeared. He tried spreading his aura over her body, to will her body healed. He tried everything he could think of. Although her body had come back into a healthier color, nothing else had shown for his efforts.

No flicker of aura answered his. No flutter of eyelids showed life.

Jack pulled his car up the driveway and into the garage, parking next to Julie's dirty Prius. He was so tired he irrationally thought she must have gotten better and come home when he first saw her car in the garage.

The wrenching sound of his damaged car door swinging closed echoed hollowly through the garage and out into the darkness of the night. He pushed the button to close the overhead door and jumped at the sound of Bear snuffling at him through the crack under the door to the house. As soon as the door opened, the dog pounced upon him, tail wagging so hard it twisted his entire body back and forth while in mid-air.

"Hey buddy! Didja miss me?" He petted the dog with one hand while keeping the door open with the other. "Who forgot to put you out, huh?" He hoped it hadn't been too long since Julie's parents had shut the dog in or there would be a surprise waiting for him at the back door. "Come on. I'll let you out."

Bear ran back into the house and up the stairs toward the back door. Jack stepped in from the garage and caught the door with his heel, preventing it from slamming, before letting it shut quietly. He listened for another couple of seconds until he no longer heard the motor of the overhead garage door, and then followed Bear up the stairs.

The house was eerily empty, even with Bear jumping at the back door. As he opened the sliding glass door and watched the dog race out into the night, a deep feeling of melancholy settled over him. He had returned home without any help for Julie.

He moved into the bedroom and found the remnants of the bandages from Bear's front paws shredded all over the dog bed in the corner. He cleaned the mess up and threw them away in the bathroom trash.

Washing his hands, he was startled by the normality of his own reflection in the mirror. It was still the same face that had been looking back at him every day of his life; the same hair, same eyes, same stubble of a beard, all looking right back at him as if to say 'what'?

Other than the extreme look of tiredness, it was the same.

The whole world is exactly the same as before, he told himself. *It is just my perception of things that has changed. Just because I discovered something doesn't mean it suddenly came into existence. It doesn't mean everyone is going to start seeing demons and ghosts. If strange things are there now, then they always have been, and always will be. I didn't change the rest of the world, it changed me.*

He washed his face and headed for bed, too tired to stay up, too full of fear and ignorance of his new reality to sleep soundly.

Nightmares purged Jack's ability to sleep after only a few hours. He sat at the kitchen table with a pile of quarters he had scrounged out of the change cups in both cars. He picked each one up individually and prayed and blessed it, just as he had seen Fidelina do, and then placed it into a separate pile.

When he had finished moving all the quarters from one pile to the next, he took a roll of clear plastic tape from out of the kitchen drawer and began taping two quarters to each window of the house, one facing inward, the other out. As he placed the last quarter on the last window, he began to wonder about the doors.

Fidelina hadn't mentioned warding doors, but then he hadn't asked either. The sliding glass door to the backyard already had quarters on it, but he wasn't sure what to do with the front door and the garage door. He tried to remember what Fidelina had said people use other than quarters, but all he could remember was something about horseshoes, and he didn't have any of those.

Would quarters on the windows be enough? He shivered at the memory of his nightmares. Whether or not they would be, if his subconscious wasn't properly reassured, he was afraid it would give him another nightmare.

It had been bad enough to have gone through the shadow-memory of Mercedes being tortured, experiencing it from both her and her tormentor's points of view. He didn't think he could handle having nightmares about it the rest of his life—and there was no way in hell he was ever going to try to explain *that* nightmare to a therapist.

THIRTY-NINE

J ack looked down at the four little silver crosses in the palm of his hand. He had blessed them, and many more like them, the same way he had the quarters. He had gone down to the store and purchased their entire stock of charm bracelets with silver crosses and then had proceeded to place one on every door and wall in the house. These four were all that were left. And he knew just where they needed to go.

He walked down the stairs with the crosses clenched in his fist. Bear faithfully followed, as he had all morning, overseeing the placement of every cross. Jack went into the spare bedroom with the same feeling of dread he'd had without the crosses. He stopped in front of the closet and stared at it.

It wouldn't do to have people think he had gone off the deep end, even if he had, so he had been doing his best to place all of the crosses and quarters inconspicuously. Not to mention, if Julie were here, she would want them out of sight too. He decided he would have to tape the crosses to the inside of the closet doors.

Opening a door, he tried to reach behind it to tape the first cross. Fumbling with the tape and the angled wooden slats, he finally resigned himself to standing inside the closet and closing the door. His heart sped up and, giving in to his fears, he refused to close the doors completely.

Cussing his own cowardice, he quickly taped a cross to the first door and turned to the second. His nervous fingers fumbled one of the crosses and it fell to the floor at his feet and bounced away. He taped one of the two remaining crosses on the door and knelt down to find the one he had dropped.

He patted the carpet in small circles with his hand, searching for the small charm as he peered around in the diffuse light. Feeling claustrophobic, he pushed open a door to let in more light and spotted something.

At the edge of the door, standing upright and wedged between the wall and the inside frame of the closet door was a small diary. Forgetting the cross, he pried the book out of its hiding spot. One of the edges of the cardboard cover bent as he pulled it out, and the thin paper strap with the cheap metal clasp that held the book shut tore open.

Jack backed out of the closet on his hands and knees, bringing the pink and blue book out into the light, and sat in the middle of the floor. Opening the book, he found the inside cover had a child's blocky handwriting in green crayon: Happy Birthday to Jessica, love Joey. The first page was dated September 16 and the first entry read:

Dear Diary,

Today is my birthday. I am nine years old today. I got a brand new bike for my birthday and Dad says I can ride around the block now. Joey is a brat. He ate the rose off of my cake. Mom said I had to let him be at my party because he is my brother. Grandma gave me lipstick but told me not to tell mom. I promise not to wear it out of the house.

Jack smiled to himself as he skimmed the pages. He wondered how old the diary was and then spotted a New Year's resolution not to be mean to Joey dated six years ago—the year he had bought the house. He tried to remember the people he bought the house from, but could only vaguely recall a tired looking man taking the extra key off his key ring after they had already signed the papers.

He flipped the pages until he found the last entry. It wasn't dated.

It was on the stairs. Dad yelled at me for being scared. I don't want to go to sleep. I think it's really mad now because mom and dad are yelling at each other. I'm scared. I think it might be coming back.

The hair on the back of his neck stood up as the shaky handwriting mentioned something on the stairs. The ink lines in the middle of the page were smeared and Jack imagined the little girl must have been crying. He began to feel ill.

In his dream of the little girl crying in the closet, she had been curled up right where he had found the diary. His stomach knotted in fear as he glanced at the closet and remembered the red glow. What had the girl seen on the stairs?

Was it the same thing that had attacked him in his sleep? Had it attacked the little girl? What had happened to her? He thought of the evil red haze attacking the blue glow in the closet and feared the reason why the diary had still been in the closet and why no more entries had been made.

A burning need to know what had happened sent him flipping through pages. He found an entry about a nightmare. The girl's dad told her it was just a dream, but she was sure someone had been in her room staring at her. He found another: eyes in the window. Another: can't move, can't breathe.

The girl wrote about hiding in the closet so the thing from the window couldn't see her, about Joey being afraid to come in her room. She wrote about hearing her parent's fighting because she was afraid to be downstairs alone.

Jack paused. In another entry, the girl wrote that 'it' made her parents fight. Her parents always seemed to fight when 'it' was here. 'It' made Joey cry. 'It' made her scared. 'It' made mom and dad fight.

Jack swallowed hard. Is this what had happened with him and Julie? Had this 'it' been making them fight? Why would 'it' do such a thing?

Fidelina had spoken about *poltergeists* making families fight. Shivers ran up and down his spine. Could this be a *poltergeist*?

I need air, he decided and got up. He took the diary upstairs with him and put it on the kitchen table as he followed Bear to the back door.

The dog pushed past him as he opened the door. Jack stepped out onto the deck and slid the door closed behind him. The sun was warm on his face, but the wind was chill. The snow was nearly gone. There were still small patches in the shade next to the fence and house, but the lawn was bare.

He closed his eyes and turned his face to the sun, the bright light shining reddish orange through his eyelids. How was he ever going to survive this world of horrors he had suddenly discovered he lived in?

Jack was startled out of his moment of thought by the doorbell and Bear's instant barking response.

Myla Jenkins stood on his front porch wearing purple sweats and a giant grin. Jack couldn't help but smile back at the obvious look of excitement on her face.

"Good morning, Mr. Hooper." She was smiling so hard she almost couldn't pronounce his name. "Hello, Bear!" She leaned over and petted the nose trying to come out of the door. Jack opened the door and let the dog out onto the porch.

"Good morning, Myla. No interviews today?" He waved a hand indicating her informal attire.

"It's David's day off—unless of course it's an emergency." She picked up one of Bear's front paws and examined it. "That wooks wike it's heawling up just fine, dowsn't it?" She cooed at the dog in baby talk. Bear scored a lick on her chin.

"Besides, I have other things to take care of today. Starting with this." She stood up, held out a white envelope, and grinned again.

"What's this?" Jack asked as he took the envelope from her.

"Fifty percent."

Jack stopped in the middle of opening the envelope. His brows furrowed.

"People get paid for interviews all the time. Look at all the money people make off their books and interviews every time there's a scandal. Where do you think it all comes from?"

"Not from a struggling young reporter like yourself. Keep it. I don't want it." He tried to hand it back to her.

Myla cocked her head a little to the side and frowned. "Did you see the broadcast of our interview?"

Jack shook his head, deciding not to mention he had been out of town and what he had been doing.

"Well." Myla took a deep breath and grinned again. "It was a success. Not that it was the world's greatest or most interesting interview, mind you, but you inspired me. I made a pitch to the local station manager, who liked my idea enough to pitch it to the broadcasting company, who liked it, and me, enough to cut a deal." She grinned.

"You got a job?" Jack nodded his head showing he was happy for her.

"You're looking at the founder, and of course media cover, for the 'Save a Hero Foundation.' When you mentioned the costs of the bills, I realized that people get hurt a lot while they're helping others. There always seems to be the 'help Joe' fundraiser, but there aren't any overall charities to help the average 'Good Samaritan' who gets hurt, or even sued, for helping other people."

Jack nodded in agreement. "I can't think of any. It's very big of you to devote yourself to something like that."

"Well…" Her smile turned a little sly. "There will be a lot of human interest stories attached to that particular charity, don't you think?"

Jack smiled back wanly. "Yeah, you're probably right. But I still can't take this." He took one of her hands and pushed the envelope into it. He let go of the envelope and so did Myla. It fell to the cement at their feet.

"Consider it the first act of the Foundation that you inspired. The second will be paying for whatever your insurance doesn't cover at the hospital." She grinned at him and then interrupted his protest. "The station is putting up the money, and donating more to establish the charity."

She leaned in and whispered conspiratorially to Bear. "It is good publicity for them, and it is tax deductible." The dog agreed wholeheartedly. Myla stood back up and began walking back to her car. "Have a good Saturday, Mr. Hooper. I hope your wife recovers soon." She grinned at him over her shoulder.

He shook his head and watched her walk away. He glanced down at the envelope. He hated to admit it, but they needed the money. He wasn't even sure he had a job anymore. He hadn't been in contact with them since Wednesday morning.

"Oh! Wait!" Myla came running back up the sidewalk. "I forgot! I need a spokesperson!"

"What?"

"I got put in charge of establishing the whole thing. I need to make a commercial to promote awareness, and I was hoping you would help. For free, of course." She gave him a fake pretty smile and batted her eyelashes teasingly.

"Oh, of course." He nodded as if that was how everyone did it and then smiled tiredly back at her. "Yeah, I'll help."

"Great! How about David and I meet you here Monday night around six?"

Jack thought about it for a moment and then nodded. "I think that would be fine."

"Thanks, Mr. Hooper!" She turned and ran back toward her car.

"Come on, Bear." Jack scooped up the envelope and went back into the house.

FORTY

Jack sat down at the kitchen table and opened the diary again, this time he read all of the entries from the beginning. Jessica wrote about her birthday party at home and then another one at school. She wrote about a class field trip to the Children's Museum and a boy she thought was cute. Joey stole the lipstick her grandmother had given her and wrote on the wall with it. Her mother made *enchiladas* for dinner when her uncle John came to visit. Uncle John had started a grease fire trying to make *chicharrónes*.

Then, Jack spotted an entry he had missed before.

I can't sleep. I'm too scared. Tina brought over her Ouija board after school. Mom said I should never use one, but Tina said they were stupid and brought her over to prove it. I think she had to sneak it because her mom didn't want her to use it either. It said Jason likes me and Mike likes Tina. I already knew that Mike likes Tina, and I think Jason does like me. Then Joey started crying and when we asked the board why he was crying, it said 'me'. I think it meant the spirit we were talking to. I told it to go away and it said no. Tina told it that it was stupid and not real and then Joey really started crying. I made Tina take it home and promise not to bring it back, but I still feel like it's watching me.

A chill crawled up Jack's spine and down his arms, and he looked up from the diary to nervously glance around the house, mentally crossing his fingers and hoping the quarters and crosses would work.

Jack stared at the address on the paperwork from when he had purchased his house. The people he had purchased it from had left a forwarding address and phone number in California. He noticed the last name, Chavez, and wondered if their ethnicity had anything to do with the 'thing' in his house.

It wasn't really a *poltergeist*, at least the way he understood them, but it didn't exactly fit the description of *El Cucuy* either. It doesn't matter what it is, he told himself as he began dialing the phone.

He had read the diary through twice, and other than the revelation that 'it' made her parents fight, Joey cry, and herself scared, Jessica had no insights to offer as to the nature of 'it'. There was, however, a lot in the diary that, had he been Jessica's father, he would have wanted to read and know about his little girl.

A man's voice answered the phone.

"May I speak to Angel Chavez, please?" Jack's voice was butter and cream, years of work habit.

"We don't want any," came a gruff reply, and Jack was disconnected.

He sat and stared at the phone for a minute, a scowl on his face. Was it worth it? He sighed. If it had been his daughter, it would have been worth it. He dialed the number again. The same man's voice answered.

"Please don't hang up." Jack spoke quickly, hoping to get the words out of his mouth before the line went dead again. "I'm not a salesman. My name is Jack Hooper, and I bought a house from Angel Chavez about six years ago, and I was hoping to talk to her about something important, can she still be reached at this number?"

"He," came the gruff voice again. "I'm Angel Chavez."

Jack's train of thought stalled. He had thought Angel would be a woman's name. "Uh, I, uh…" The voice at the other end of the line silently waited for him to pull himself together. "I wanted to ask you about Jessica."

"Who the hell is this? What do you want?"

"Please, I…I found Jessica's diary in the downstairs closet, could I speak with one of her parents, please?"

The voice was silent so Jack pushed on, hoping to help sway the consideration on the other end of the line.

"It's a small blue and pink diary. It says 'Happy Birthday to Jessica, from Joey' in green crayon inside the front cover."

The man's voice answered after a long pause, more choked than gruff. "I'm Jessica's father."

"Mr. Chavez, I wanted to let you know I found Jessica's diary and I wanted to send it to her. I just didn't know if she could be reached at this number or address, so I wanted to call before I just mailed it."

"Jessica is…deceased." Mr. Chavez's voice was flat and toneless. Jack's heart sunk a little lower, although he had suspected that would be the case. "She died almost six years ago."

A silence hung on the line between the two telephones for a long moment.

"Mr. Chavez, I'm sorry." No answer. "Mr. Chavez, I read Jessica's diary. I'm sorry, I know it was an invasion of privacy, but I couldn't help myself. You see…my wife is in the hospital right now, in some kind of a coma, and nobody seems to know why." Jack thought he heard a sharp intake of breath on the other line.

"I realized when I found Jessica's diary that she wouldn't have left it behind, and I suspected something had happened to her. Mr. Chavez, this is going to sound strange, but I need to know what happened to her. Do you think there is any possibility the same thing could be happening to my wife? I mean, was it carbon monoxide, or lead paint, or…" Jack's voice trailed off as he asked about things he knew weren't the cause.

After a long pause, Mr. Chavez cleared his throat. "We found her hiding in the closet." His voice cracked and he had to clear his throat again. "She was hiding because she was afraid to be downstairs by herself, and we were trying to force her to get over her fear." His voice trailed and Jack thought it might be the end of the conversation, but then he continued.

"She was catatonic, the doctors said. The psychiatrist said she had withdrawn into her own world to hide from this one. She never came out of it." His voice cracked again and he sobbed something about it being his fault.

Jack was at a loss to console someone he didn't know over the telephone, so he remained silent. After a couple of minutes, Mr. Chavez pulled himself together.

"She died about a month later. They tried to feed her and stuff, but her body just…quit."

"I'm really sorry, Mr. Chavez," Jack offered. There was another long silence. "I'll mail this to you first thing on Monday."

FORTY-ONE

Jack spent Sunday at Julie's side, holding her hand while sidestepping and ignoring pointed questions from his in-laws about where he had been for two days. He was glad they had decided to stay at a hotel. There were a lot of flowers and cards, some with checks and money orders. Many were from the families of the children Jack had pulled out of the van.

It had been a relief when Vic and Anita had shown up. They were careful not to mention anything about Fidelina in front of Julie's parents. Vic offered a cautious "Any luck?" and Jack just shook his head in response.

Anita cheerily filled in all the details she had seen on the news about the 'Save a Hero Foundation.' Julie's parents hadn't seen it on television either, having spent as much time as they could at the hospital with Julie.

Vic was helpful in turning away a pushy reporter with a news camera who wanted to interview the family. Vic managed to put an irritation in his Hispanic accent Jack thought would have made most of the white boys he'd grown up with pee themselves.

Julie lay silently, unmoving, unaware of the five people who quietly talked amongst themselves in her hospital room.

Jack got home late. Julie's father had convinced him, at the very least, he needed to make an appearance at work tomorrow and make sure he still had a job, and benefits, so he could take care of Julie if the 'Hero Foundation' thing fell through.

Bear was jumping at the sliding glass door, eagerly awaiting Jack's consent to re-enter the warmth of the house. Jack opened the door and Bear rushed by in a swirl of cold wind. Before he could close the door again, Bear had been to the food bowl to check for treats and returned to Jack's side for attention.

He filled the dog's food bowl and opened a can of soup, and the two of them ate in silence in the empty house.

Wandering around the living room, Jack admired the glow of the auras. The plants seemed so much more alive when he could see the auras. The knick-knacks and curios on the shelves had a newfound allure of history about them. When he reached out to examine a porcelain owl Julie had brought with her when she moved in, he noticed his body didn't react the way it should. Movement was too smooth, too graceful, as if he was floating on air, gliding across the room.

I'm dreaming again, he thought as he tried to look down at himself and saw only his aura. Where his body should have been was a shimmering outline in the violet hued iridescence of the aura.

He looked around the room again. Everything was slightly fuzzy, like a flashback scene in a movie, but still normal.

What do I do in a dream? There's no one else here.

He thought about Julie and felt a slight tug, as if he had started to go somewhere but hadn't.

He tried to imagine her here with him. Nothing happened. He tried to imagine her silky black hair, her tight red dress, and her green eyes. Instead, a vision of her ghostly pallor and sunken eyes as she lay in the hospital bed raced across his memory and he felt guilty, but still nothing happened.

Last time he had a dream, he had flown away, so he decided to try that again. Again, nothing happened. Well, he had to be outside to fly away, right? He went to the sliding glass door and was going to open it when he spotted the quarters.

They shimmered with an aura all their own, different from any of the others he had seen. It was a golden color, strong and uniform, lacking the swirling hues of all the other auras he had seen. He reached out to touch it and found he couldn't. His hand, or rather his aura where his hand should have been, just slid away from it. Why couldn't he touch it?

He looked around the room again and realized each cross he had put on the walls and the doors gave off the same type of aura. He followed along the wall, trying to touch the aura as he went. He was unable to. It was some sort of barrier.

That thought cheered him up. The crosses and quarters seemed to be working. If he couldn't get past them, then perhaps nothing else could either—unless this was just a dream.

He remembered the lucid dreaming website and its checklist for dreamers who couldn't tell if they were dreaming. He drifted over to the kitchen table and read the headline on the newspaper.

He stared at it for a moment, but the words held steady. He looked away and looked back a couple of times, but the words stayed. *Does that mean I'm not dreaming?* he wondered.

What were the other tests? He remembered something about light switches. They were supposed to malfunction in dreams. He drifted over to the light switch and tried to flip it.

Unlike the gold aura on the coins, he could feel the switch, he just couldn't seem to affect it. It wasn't so much it didn't work, as he just couldn't flip it. He looked at the light on the ceiling and realized it wasn't on anyway.

How was he able to see? He looked out the sliding glass doors into the darkness of the night. It was night, and the lights were off. How was he seeing? Oh, yes. The streetlight out front, that's how.

He went to the kitchen windows, looking out into the front yard, but saw only blackness behind the auras of the quarters taped to the window. He couldn't see any streetlight, or anything else for that matter. Was that because this was a dream? Or did it have something to do with the warding auras he couldn't get through?

There had been some other test hadn't there? Mirrors, he remembered. They distorted reflections, sometimes even while you were watching, just like the print on the newspaper should have. He went into the bathroom and looked into the mirror.

There was a perfectly normal reflection. Except he wasn't in it. As though he were the invisible man, looking at himself in the mirror, there was nothing. He glanced down to where his body should have been.

The shimmer of his aura was still there and his body still wasn't. Where was his body? A morbid sense of curiosity crept over him. If he wasn't dreaming, and he really was floating around the house without his body, then his body should still be in the bedroom, in bed, right?

He drifted to the bedroom and stopped at the door. There was obviously a body in the bed. Was it his? It had to be. He nervously began to move closer, feeling apprehensive about seeing his own body. Something caught his eye.

Another shimmer. A silver shimmer, stretched out thin in front of him like a line. He moved closer to his body, following the thin line until he was close enough to make out his own face. He could see himself breathing. He could…feel himself breathing, even while he watched the rise and fall of his own chest from a distance.

He looked back down to the strange line he had followed to his body. It seemed to be coming from the navel area of his body on the bed and going to…

He startled as he realized it connected him to the body, and at his moment of surprise, the body flinched, startling him even more.

Jack sat up in bed and looked around the room, lit by the amber glow of the street light. His breath fell heavy a couple of times as he readjusted his awareness. A sense of wonder spread through him.

That was me! I was looking at my own body!

He thought about the silver cord stretching from his body to his aura. He hadn't seen anything about it on the internet, but it tickled at an old memory. It had something to do with astral projection. Try as he might, he couldn't remember anything about the silver cord, but he was sure he had heard if it were severed, you would die.

He thought about Julie's body lying in the hospital bed, with no soul. Is that what happened to her? Did her silver cord get cut?

Fidelina had said Julie's soul was no longer attached and that was why they couldn't track it down. Is the cord what she had meant by attached? How was he ever going to help Julie if he couldn't track her down?

Bear noticed Jack was awake and got up to come check on him. Jack petted the dog's nose. "What are we going to do?" he asked the dog quietly.

Bear licked his hand and thumped his tail on the floor.

Jack couldn't sleep after the excitement of seeing his own body from an external vantage point. He stared at the clock from 3:34 until 4:15 before he decided he would just go ahead and start his day early. He thought he might use the extra time to go see Julie at the hospital before he went to work.

He took a quick shower and discovered he was short on clean clothes. Wrapping a towel around himself and clutching it with one hand, he hobbled down the stairs with Bear trotting close behind. At the landing, he flipped the switch to turn on the lights to the downstairs and stopped to look down the second half of the stairs.

In his mind's eye he could still see Julie lying at the bottom of the stairs, curled up and unmoving. The echoes of the paramedics' boots tromping up and down the stairs rang in his ears.

He descended the rest of the stairs slowly, noticing his mother-in-law must have cleaned the house while he had been gone. Nearly all of the mud and stains were gone from the carpet. He also noticed more shredded fragments of bandage from Bear's paws scattered on the dog bed Bear used to keep vigil on the spare bedroom.

Jack went over and gathered them up, wondering how many more places he would find the ratty gauze and white tape and why he hadn't noticed it when he had been down here on Saturday. The torn bandages made him realize he hadn't checked Bear's paws recently and he knelt down and called the dog over to do so before he forgot again.

Jack patted his knee and Bear came over excitedly. He happily put both paws up on Jack, knocking them both over as Jack stepped on edge of the towel wrapped around his waist and constricted his legs. Jack gave up the effort of trying to balance and plopped down on his butt. Bear immediately put both paws into his lap again and tried to lick his face.

"Hold on there, Happy Boy! Let me see those paws!" Jack pushed the dog's face out of his own and held up each paw for scrutiny. They looked like they were healing fine. Bear hadn't done much more than wear the nails down to the quick and get a couple of splinters when he had been scratching at the closet door.

"Yeah, you look like you're doing okay. Just don't go doing that again." He waved an admonishing finger and headed into the laundry room.

Dropping his towel into the dirty clothes pile, Jack began pulling clean clothes out of the unfolded pile of laundry, dressing as he found matching items. Why had Bear been clawing at the closet door, anyway?

In all the confusion, he had never considered what Bear had been doing. As he finished pulling on his rumpled shirt and pants, he went back into the spare bedroom and turned on the light.

The first thing he noticed was that he had no feeling of dread as he entered the room. He stood in the middle of the room for a moment and thought of ghosts. Nothing. Not a single hair on the back of his neck stood up.

He looked out the window into the front yard. The amber glow of the streetlight still lit the night. He glanced at the clock on the nightstand. The sun wouldn't be up for another hour or so.

"Hmmm," he muttered to himself. "Standing in the Scary Room, at night," he walked back to the light switch and turned it off, "in the dark, and I'm not afraid." He turned the light back on, and his eyes fell on the quarters in the windows. He looked for the inconspicuous crosses he had concealed on each wall. "I guess they work."

He went to the closet door and examined the place where Bear had scratched at the wooden slats. They were pretty torn up. One was broken in half. The blood was gone, presumably cleaned up by Julie's mother. Jack got down on his knees and tried to get Bear's perspective on the situation.

Bear stuck his face next to Jack's and gave him a lick, assuring him this was indeed the correct perspective. Jack tried to look through the slats and Bear tried to stick his nose through. There was nothing to see in the darkness of the closet and when he opened the door, Bear went right in and turned around to look back out at Jack.

"What were you doing?" he asked the dog.

Bear sat there in the closet looking out at Jack and panted happily. Jack pondered his own question. Why would Bear want to get into the closet so badly? What could have been in here?

As he sat there staring at the dog, he thought about the diary that had been hidden in the closet and the shadow-memory of little Jessica crying. Those couldn't have attracted Bear, could they? And if they had, why would he have ignored them until the same night something had happened to Julie?

Julie… Bear would want Julie.

As soon as the thought crossed his mind he knew it was right. Bear had been trying to get to Julie.

FORTY-TWO

Jack decided to walk in through the front door of the office rather than make his usual entrance from the back. Might as well let people know he was here, since that was the whole point of coming into the office. As he walked by, he smiled at the young woman behind the reception desk and noted she wasn't the same one Heidi had caught doing her nails last week.

"Can I help you?" she asked in a firm tone.

"I work here," he assured her and continued by.

Halfway to his desk he almost ran into Trish as she came around a corner with an armful of mail.

"Oh, Jack!" Her eyes lit up with youthful enthusiasm and then quickly dimmed as she remembered his wife was in the hospital. "Oh! I'm so sorry." She stepped in close and gave him a long one-armed hug.

"How is your wife doing?"

Jack awkwardly hugged her back. "Still no change," he informed her as they pulled apart.

"If there's anything I can do…" She let her voice trail off and gave him a pained yet supportive look.

"Thanks, Trish." He smiled weakly back at her. This office visit was going to be harder than he thought.

She took him by the arm and began leading him on toward his desk. She leaned in and whispered. "The office sure has been different since you and Stanley both left. I heard he's going to be back in today to get his things. After they fired him, they confiscated everything in his desk and wouldn't let him have anything!"

Great, he thought. *The only day Stanley's going to be back in the office, and I stop by to say hello.*

He shook his head at his misfortune.

Trish took the gesture as a response to her news. "Really! They did! I didn't think they could hold your personal belongings like that, but apparently they can!" Her eyes were wide as she looked at him.

"I think they can, but only in certain situations," he assured her.

They rounded the corner and came to Charlie's desk. Charlie spun around in his chair at the sound of their voices and locked eyes with Jack. Trish, suddenly remembering what Jack and Charlie had been arguing about the last time she had seen them, quickly wished Jack's wife well again and excused herself.

Jack had been dreading this moment and still hadn't managed to figure out what to say to Charlie. So he said the first thing that came to his mind. "Sorry, Charlie."

The apology hung like a lame joke between them until Charlie finally stood up and looked Jack in the face. They stood there for a long moment with grim faces.

Charlie broke the silence. "Did you really see my mother?"

Jack shrugged awkwardly. What should he say? Yes? Maybe?

"I don't know. I think so. I didn't know she was... I didn't mean to hurt your feelings. I wasn't trying to play a joke."

"It was there, you know." Charlie voice was flat and factual.

"What was?"

"Her will, her bank records, all of her personal papers. They were all in a storage box in the top of her closet. Just like you said it was." Charlie stared at Jack for a long time, waiting for a response.

Jack looked at his watch to see if it was near Charlie's break time. He had lost track of time at the hospital this morning and hadn't left until Julie's parents showed up and her dad convinced him to go on in to work.

"How are you doing on the rotation?" he asked Charlie.

"Just took a call yesterday. I'm third from the bottom, right now."

"Come on downstairs and let me buy you a cup of coffee and I'll do my best to explain it to you."

Charlie shook his head and smiled. "Uh-uh. No way can I risk the wrath of the Iron Bitch right now."

"How about we do lunch after I finish talking to her?"

Charlie nodded. "Your turn to buy, or mine?"

"I don't remember."

"We'll go Dutch."

Jack knocked on the doorframe of Heidi's office and waited for her to look up from the paper she was writing on.

"Well, please, have a seat, Mr. Hooper, and tell me how your wife is doing."

Jack entered the little office and sat down in the same chair he'd been in when Stanley had confessed everything he could think of. He stared at Heidi's plants and the photo of her with her daughter and granddaughter for a long moment, wondering what to say.

"There's been no change in Julie's condition," he finally told her. "The doctors seem to think that unless something changes soon, she's just going to slowly deteriorate until she needs life support. They are already talking about moving her to a 'rehab center'."

"I'm sorry, Jack." Heidi's southern accent melted her sympathy across his ears. He just nodded back, unsure of what else to say.

He wanted to ask about his job, about insurance, about more time off or not, but openly talking about Julie made him feel like none of those were important and all he wanted was to go back to the hospital and be with her.

The long silence held until Heidi broke it by clearing her throat. "I can hold your position open indefinitely," she informed him, "but once your leave time is gone, it will have to be without pay."

"What does that do to the insurance?"

She shook her head ever so slightly and with sadness in her eyes. "The insurance only stays effective if you return to work when your leave time is up."

"You wouldn't happen to know how much I have left, would you?"

"As a matter of fact, I have that right here. I requested it from Human Resources this morning." She turned around and opened a drawer on the file cabinet behind her. "You should be fine."

A knock on the doorframe behind Jack's head caught him by surprise. Heidi looked up and then shut the file cabinet without pulling anything out.

"Come in Stanley," she said in a firm voice. Jack's heart sank. What horrible timing.

Stanley walked into the office and stood awkwardly, uncomfortably shifting his weight from one foot to the other. He didn't even glance at Jack. "They told me I could pick up my things today," he muttered so low Jack almost didn't hear.

Heidi nodded to him. "That's right. I have your stuff in a box right here." She bent and reached into the corner behind her desk and came up with a box normally used for storing files. She put the box on the desk between them. "You'll have to sign for it."

Stanley nodded. He still hadn't bothered to look around the room and Jack was wondering if he would be able to sneak out before

Stanley noticed him. Heidi handed Stanley a piece of paper and he signed it without reading it and handed it back.

"It's all yours." She waved at the box. "By the way," she said as Stanley picked up the box, "you might be interested to know I heard through the grapevine you'll be receiving official notice they have decided not to press charges."

Heidi smiled at Stanley encouragingly, but he responded with only a dejected nod of the head. He turned and saw Jack for the first time and Jack tensed to run.

Stanley met his eyes for a short moment, then dropped his gaze and shuffled out of the office with his box.

Jack was taken aback. There were a lot of different reactions he might have expected from Stanley, but this was not one of them. He looked over at Heidi who shook her head and raised her eyebrows.

"He's been like that ever since he handed me his report on how he'd gotten into the computer. Every single meeting with him has been like a funeral." As she spoke the word 'funeral' a pained look crossed her face.

Jack waved off her apology and asked her to excuse him for a minute.

"Stanley. Wait up," Jack called to the hulking figure moving down the hallway to the elevators.

Stanley stopped and turned to look at Jack. His every movement was slow and depressed, as though he was sleepwalking.

"You okay?" Jack asked as he reached the big man.

Stanley nodded without meeting Jack's eyes and turned to continue toward the elevators.

I can't believe I'm doing this, Jack thought as he followed Stanley.

"I didn't mean to get you fired," he said lamely, knowing they both knew it wasn't true. Stanley didn't respond.

"Have you got another job lined up yet?"

Stanley shook his head and stared at the brushed metal elevator doors as he waited for them to open.

Jack was at a loss to say anything else. He stood silently next to Stanley and stared at him.

I wish I could see his aura and know what was wrong with him as easily as I had seen him lying before, he thought.

And then, as if he had been able to all along and just hadn't noticed it, he could. It definitely wasn't the same aura as before. It had been a strong, angry, red and brown aura, full of things Jack had thought were not very nice. Now it was faint and weak, a dim aura bordering on the neutral colors he'd seen around furniture.

Jack watched somberly as the elevator bell rang and the doors opened. Stanley shambled in and pushed a button without even glancing back at Jack. The doors closed and Jack was left standing by himself.

He's fading out, Jack thought, as he remembered Fidelina accusing him of fading out and slapping him to bring him back. He hadn't understood what she had meant until now. Stanley had completely lost his will to live and was fading out. And it was Jack's fault.

Jack bolted for the stairs and raced down the cement stairwell. Banging open the door at the bottom as he ran out to the parking lot, he caught up with Stanley on the curb.

"Hey!" He slapped Stanley in the middle of the back, just as Stanley had done to him so many times. "What's your rush? You gotta hot date tonight?"

Stanley turned his head to look at Jack and for a brief moment, Jack hoped he would see the old Stanley looking out at him but his eyes were dull and listless.

"Whadda you want?" Stanley mumbled.

"I want to help you!" Jack tried to put a lot of enthusiasm in his voice, but was afraid it came out sounding cheesy. Stanley just looked away and started walking toward the parked cars.

Jack kept pace and put his arm around Stanley's shoulders. "I want to help you find another job," he told him but still got no response.

Jack looked at Stanley's aura again. It hadn't changed. He wasn't having any effect at all. "Stanley. Stanley! Look at me!" He grabbed the big man by the shoulders and turned him to look into his face. Stanley's empty eyes stared back.

Jack reached over the box in Stanley's arms and put his hands on Stanley's face. He willed the strength of his aura to flow into Stanley and heal him. He imagined he could feel the energy moving from him into Stanley. He imagined he could feel a good mood and vibrant yearn for life building up inside of Stanley. He imagined he could see life returning to Stanley's cold eyes.

Stanley dropped the box on Jack's feet and blinked as though he had just woken up.

"What?" he asked.

"You okay?" Jack asked him, pulling his hands back. Stanley's aura looked much stronger, but was still a bland color.

"Yeah." Stanley's voice was already fading back into listlessness. "I'm fine."

This wasn't working at all. Jack thought about slapping him, as Fidelina had done, but discarded the idea as Stanley bent over to retrieve the box and his shoulder muscles strained the back of his shirt.

"Stanley."

"What?"

"I think you might be in some kind of shock. You should go see a doctor."

"Yeah, sure." Stanley turned away and continued toward his car. Helplessly, Jack watched him go.

Lunch with Charlie wasn't as pleasant as Jack had hoped. He was too worried about Stanley. He had planned to confide in Charlie, to tell him the whole story, but the encounter with Stanley had changed his mind. Some things were better kept to one's self than shared with the world.

He did his best to describe his encounter with Charlie's mom to Charlie, without giving away anything extra. He wanted to pay attention to his conversation with Charlie, to share the pain of experiencing the loss of a loved one, to let him know how Julie was doing. But his mind wasn't on the conversation.

He was worried about Stanley's behavior. It was his fault and he knew it. Somehow, by confronting Stanley directly, he must have so completely broken the man's will that even Stanley's will to live had been affected. Jack was at a loss for understanding how this could have happened, until he recalled Fidelina threatening him with the knife.

What was it she had told him? She had been afraid of him, of him manipulating her. His mind raced, and he began to piece things together. She had accused him of using her, and of using Vic to get to her.

That's why Mercedes and Fidelina had been afraid of him. They knew he could force them to do things using sheer will power, overriding their own wills. Then he remembered something else Fidelina had said to him.

There is a truth about magic…The only difference between white magic and black magic is white magic is only used to help someone, never for personal gain.
The thought echoed through his mind. He had used black magic on Stanley. He hadn't meant to, but his intentions had definitely been selfish and not meant to help Stanley at all. He thought of Stanley walking to his car, sadly carrying his box of belongings. An unbidden image of Mercedes crying herself to sleep, curled up in the palm of a giant hand, came to his mind. His heart sank in his chest.

This was the price of black magic.

FORTY-THREE

Jack intended to return to the hospital, but his mind was so intent on what he had done to Stanley that his mental autopilot brought him home instead. As long as he was home, he decided to change into comfortable clothes. He let Bear in from the back yard and checked his paws again. It occurred to him he should have tried healing them for the dog, but they were far enough along he didn't see the point in trying to do it now.

As he finished dressing, his mind finally drifted away from the guilt of having hurt Stanley and back to the guilt of not being able to help Julie. He thought about the downstairs closet and his early morning revelation that Bear must have been trying to get to Julie.

Did that mean there was some sort of connection between the closet and where Julie was? The three old women had all agreed there was no way to track Julie, so maybe that wasn't what Bear had been doing. Maybe it had been the 'ghost' Bear had been after. Maybe he had just been trying to chase it off, trying to protect his territory.

The thought of territories reminded him of Rosa's cracked voice saying something about a favorite fishing hole. You always go back to a favorite fishing hole.

His heart leaped with sudden inspiration. Would the ghost-demon thing be back? Probably. He had seen it, sort of, at least twice. Bear had growled and barked at it God only knew how many times. And it had come for Julie, and poor little Jessica, who had seen it numerous times. *Yeah,* he decided, *it'll be back.* This house was in its 'territory'. Its hunting grounds, so to speak.

And when it came back? Then what?

Jack pursed his lips in silent determination. Then he would follow it back to Julie.

Jack sat motionless, cross-legged on the spare bedroom floor, staring at the open closet doors, hoping to see the auras again. He managed to will himself to see them once, but became so excited he snapped himself back out of the partial trance that seemed to accompany the ability, thus dispersing it again.

Frustrated by the short-lived results of his attempt, he still managed to see auras just long enough to realize his blessed crosses and quarters were working so well that their protective auras had the entire area enclosed. If their ward were as strong as he believed they were, there was no way the ghost thing was going to make it back into the house.

Unfortunately, that also meant there was no way he would be able to find the ghost or follow it to its 'cave', assuming he correctly interpreted his inability to touch the ward in his out-of-body experience this morning.

He spent a lot of time wondering about that experience, finally concluding the lucid dreaming website had been correct; there was a difference between a lucid dream and an out-of-body experience. The OBE, as the site had referred to them, hadn't responded to his wishes in the same way the dream had when he had decided to go flying.

Of course, that dream had been the same one that had revealed the location of the wooden penguin under the deck, so perhaps it had been more of a vision. Visions were a type of dream, weren't they?

He shook his head to himself as he sat and stared at the closet doors. Accepting this new view of the world with all of these strange things he had disregarded in the past was hard enough, but trying to classify them in his mind so they made some sort of sense was impossible.

He glanced at the nightstand where he had put the crosses after he had taken them off the closet doors. He had remembered what Fidelina had said about her quarters not only keeping things out, but of keeping them in, so he had left all of the other crosses and quarters in place around the house. He hoped he had interpreted Bear's actions correctly and that the closet was the key to finding Julie, because he really didn't want to have to take down all of the protection he had worked so hard to put up.

FORTY-FOUR

Julie was cold, so very, very cold. She was finally starting to grow used to her confinement, but she didn't like it one bit. All around her was a vast nothingness, yet she was confined, unable to move about, as though she had been left bound in the hidden recesses of a vast cavern and sealed in. There was emptiness and nothingness all around her, but she couldn't explore it or move through it. She would have tried to huddle for warmth, but it was an irrelevant gesture in this place.

It will pass. (assurance) Jessica informed her. *I went through the same thing and so did Margaret and all of the others. (confidence, truth)*

What happened to Margaret? (fear, worry, curiosity) Julie's teeth would have chattered, but she didn't have a physical body anymore. She did her best to communicate appropriately with her newfound friend, but she still hadn't mastered the nuances of expressing oneself when everything is already exposed.

She decided she was ready to move on. (sadness, joy, longing, envy) When you arrived, it allowed her to take her leave of me, just as I will take my leave of you upon the arrival of the next. (anticipation, hope, consolation, assurance, sadness)

Julie found comfort in the touch of Jessica's thoughts. They were a life raft in an ocean of confusion and fear. At first, it had been strange to share minds rather than words, but now, even at this early level of learning how, she found it more effective than words.

As Julie had arrived, she'd had the briefest contact with Margaret, a greeting laced with sorrow and tinged with an unexpected familial love, and then Margaret was gone.

Without expressing it directly, Jessica's first statement had conveyed the knowledge that the cold sensation was merely a side effect of Julie's loss of her body and as soon as she finished adjusting, the sensation would pass. The second set of word-thoughts had carried with them the knowledge of yet another afterlife, beyond this one, to which Margaret had been longing to move.

The time since, spent with Jessica, had brought her to understand she was captive, and the previous captives carried a sense of obligation to the new and future ones. They stayed as long as they could, enduring their torment, clinging on to what passed for life in this place, so they could pass on the knowledge and ability to stay sane and the hope that this was not the end.

Upon her arrival, she had been in a terrible state and she was sure she would have gone mad had Jessica not been there to comfort her. In their initial contact, Julie, being unused to this new type of communication, had opened her mind like a floodgate, pouring everything about herself all over Jessica. Jessica had responded with infinite patience and had taught Julie how to hold back her flood of emotions and thoughts, so only the ones she wanted to convey came through the floodgates.

Slowly, Jessica taught her how to cope with her new perceptions, or rather the lack thereof. Except for her and Jessica, there was nothing here. Like the deepest darkest night at the bottom of a well, except there weren't even any slimy handholds for her to futilely grasp and claw at. Of course, that didn't matter either, as she had no hands with which to grasp, and there was no "up".

In this strange place, all she had was her mind—and Jessica's. The two of them together kept each other entertained and sane. Jessica had taught her how to relax her mind and control the raging thoughts and frustrations that came with their imprisonment. She had given her the will and courage to accept her situation without going mad.

Most of all, she had shown Julie how to feed their captor without sustaining too much pain and discomfort. It wasn't too difficult to relax and give up the energy when it began to take it. She even force-fed it sometimes, pushing her energy toward it to hurry up and get the whole process over. But, if she resisted it and tried to fight it off, the pain was terrible and lasting. It would take even more energy from her to feed itself, and it would take it slower, making her suffer in agony.

Jessica could have opened her mind up to Julie in the same way Julie had accidentally done upon arrival, but, as Julie soon came to understand, there was nothing else to do in this place except keep one another company. There was no sleeping, no eating, no exploring, nothing except communication, and any form of mental games they could come up with to play. It was best to learn about each other slowly and indirectly, thus passing the time more easily.

Jessica had just finished teaching Julie her new 'lineage' as it had come to be thought of; the history of all of the people who had been entrapped in this place, memorized and passed on to each newcomer who added themselves as they passed it on. Julie felt a strange kinship and comfort with these people she had never met. It was good to know she was not alone in her suffering, in her sensory deprivation, in her own little universe of nothingness.

There were eighty-six people in Julie's new lineage, including Jessica, but not herself. Based on comparison of dates given by new arrivals, the longest stay in this place had been approximately one hundred and fifty-three years. That stay was made, nearly in its entirety, by the first person to establish the lineage, a woman who called herself Ahì. By current estimates based on Julie's date of arrival, Ahì had come to this place one thousand, three hundred and twenty-two years ago. She had been discovered, insane from the isolation and torment, by a high priestess, known as Camì.

Camì had been captured by the demon, after losing the way back to her own body, while attempting to explore the planes of existence of the gods. Camì had been horrified to discover Ahì had been trapped for so long, and even more horrified to find that she had been left as a sacrifice.

Ahì and hundreds of other souls had been left behind by the priests of her city, as a tribute to the demon/god, so that it would not follow them into the afterworld and destroy them again, as it had on the human plane of existence. Ahì, in her moments of lucidity, told Camì of the great destruction of the temples of her city and of the hundreds of victims of the way, as she called the demon.

She explained how the creature became larger and more powerful the more people it consumed. Ahì spoke of the betrayal of the priests, sacrificing their own people so they could escape the torment of the beast, and of how the beast continued to add new souls to the number of victims it held captive after the priests fled.

Unable to stop the demon from finding future victims, Ahì vowed to fight the creature any way she could. She used the knowledge she had stolen from the priests to help the hundreds of other souls escape the eternal damnation of the belly of the beast. And then she stayed behind, vowing that none should become trapped again.

Camì spent the next twenty-seven years attempting to return Ahì to sanity, while herself ensnared in this trap, refusing Ahì's attempts to push her on to the next world. Then came the arrival of Kuimonìòo.

His assurances he and Camì would stay, to prevent the beast from ever becoming too powerful again, allowed Camì to convince Ahì to release herself into the next world. The knowledge that there was an end to the eternal nothingness and pain gave Camì and Kuimonìòo the courage to wait for the next poor soul, and the lineage was established.

The rules of their lineage were simple. All you had to do was swear to wait for your turn to move on to the next life, thus never leaving anyone alone, entrapped in isolation, again, and the secret of moving on from this world and into the next would be given to you.

Julie had sworn immediately, of course, but Jessica had denied her the knowledge. It had been easy for Jessica to see the swirls of ideas of escape moving through Julie's mind. The history of the lineage showed a pattern of acceptance each arrival moved through, and Julie had not yet moved far enough through the pattern to be stable yet.

It's coming back. (acceptance, withdrawal, fear, loathing)

Julie's mind and emotions tensed at Jessica's warning. She began putting herself through the mental relaxation techniques Jessica had shown her. Jessica had learned so many things from Margaret and the others of the lineage. Julie was grateful she also benefited. She hoped she would eventually be able to face it as calmly as Jessica did.

It had come to feed eighteen times since Julie had arrived. It seemed to alternate which of them it would feed on, perhaps giving the other a chance to recover. If it stayed with its pattern, this time it would use Jessica.

Julie hoped it would feed on Jessica and then felt guilty at the thought. She feared the thing immensely. Jessica had warned her that sometimes, for reasons unknown, it fed stronger than other times, causing even more pain. Julie hadn't experience that yet, but feared anything Jessica said could be worse than what she had already experienced.

A red glow became part of Julie's awareness. There was nothing for the glow to illuminate, only the glow itself, slowly replacing the black nothingness. Julie felt fear trying to take control of her thoughts and she fought it down.

Jessica had told her some of their predecessors had reached a point where they longed for the demon to come feed, bringing pain and color to their sensation-deprived world. As the red glow increased in intensity toward a sun burning away at Julie's mind, she thought she could perhaps understand that sentiment, even if she didn't agree with it. Would that ever happen to her? She hoped not.

Jessica screamed. Her thoughts of pain flashed through Julie's mind, and Julie tried desperately to block them out. Jessica screamed again. This must be the unusual type of feeding Jessica had mentioned. Julie wished there was some way, anyway, to curl up and hide.

There was nowhere to go. There was no way to ignore or even look away from the supernova of pain attacking Jessica in the center of Julie's own mind. Julie cowed in terror, unable to do anything except wait for it to pass.

Slowly, eternally slowly, Jessica's screams faded to sobs as the glowing ball of pain reduced its energy intake from her. As soon as the glow started to fade, Julie was reaching out with mental arms to try to pull Jessica in close and comfort her as best as she could. It was the same thing Jessica had done each time it had fed on her, and for a while, Jessica's pitiful sobs filled both of their minds and occupied their time.

FORTY-FIVE

Jack looked around himself and realized he had fallen asleep on the floor in front of the closet. Bear was next to him with his ears perked up. Someone was crying.

It was coming from the closet. Jack's hope soared. Maybe this was his chance. Maybe he could follow this.

He moved in closer to the closet, all of his senses on high alert, straining for anything. Bear followed him, ears cocked. The sobbing came from the corner of the closet where he had seen the shadow-memory of the little girl huddling in fear.

He tried making himself aware of auras again. The shadow-memory of the little girl appeared before him, her small figure rocking in fear and sobbing. He moved further into the closet on his hands and knees, straining his senses, searching for anything beyond the shadow-memory, anything else that could be around the closet. There was nothing else.

He sat down against the back of the closet. Bear came over and put his head on Jack's lap. Jack stroked the dog's ears and watched the shadow-memory.

The little girl's image showed her thin arms wrapped around her small ankles and her forehead pressed hard against her knees as she rocked in fear and cried. As Jack watched, something happened he hadn't noticed before. The little girl flinched in response to something he couldn't see and began rocking even faster.

Jack reached out to the image with his mind, hoping to understand it as well as he had the ones in Mercedes' living room. He felt the brush of her terror, her racing heart and gasping breath.

She was peeking but trying not to, too afraid to see, more afraid not to.

It was coming again. Jessica could feel it. Tears of terror swelled up in her eyes and she squeezed them shut, forcing a drop out of one eye. She rocked back and forth, her back bumping against the wall, her toes pushing off the carpet.

She shouldn't have made her parents so mad by insisting she didn't want to go to bed. Maybe if she had just gone, they would have let her come back up later, and she wouldn't have to be in the room when *It* came, but it was too late now.

If she left her room now, she would be spanked, then her parents would fight even more, and then it would be even worse. She didn't understand why, but it was always worse after her parents got mad. *It* seemed to want to be here even more when they were angry. Maybe *It* would leave her alone this time. Twice before, *It* had just passed her by and gone on into the rest of the house, ignoring her.

She peeked out of the corner of her eye without taking her forehead off her knees. She could see only part of the room through the angled slats of the closet door, but that was enough. The room had started take on a reddish tinge.

She flinched as she realized *It* was here, and began rocking even faster.

Not me, not me, not me. She wished it away, she willed it to go on past, praying for someone to come downstairs and rescue her, to wake her up and tell her it was only a dream, and there were no such things as ghosts. But she knew better. Some things, the adults lied about, trying to protect the children, and she understood. But this was different. They lied about it to themselves and ignored the children.

The glow began to come through the slats of the door. She tried to pull her feet closer to her body, but they were already against the back of her thighs. Her arms tightened around her legs and her knuckles whitened as she squeezed hard enough to cut off her own circulation. *Not me, not me, not me!*

Her breath was quick and short, her eyes shut tight. Her rocking stopped and she tensed for the evil touch she knew was coming. She stopped breathing. She stopped moving. Her muscles went rigid. *NotmenotmenotmeNOTME!*

It touched her.

She tried to scream, but her body was paralyzed. *It* moved into her mind. Fire! Pain! *Help!*

She tried to scream but couldn't.

She was dimly aware of her body falling over sideways, arms still clamped tight, but the pain was too much…

Jack gasped and fell sideways onto Bear. The dog jumped up and out of the way as Jack tried to right himself. His lungs burned. How long had he been holding his breath? His muscles ached as they released from the rigor mortis-like tension they had held. His eyes watered from the memory of the pain.

Bear jumped back into the closet and tried to lick at his face. Jack pushed the dog away and crawled out of the closet. He stood up on weak knees and leaned against the wall.

Oh my God, the pain! That poor little girl...

New tears welled in Jack's eyes for the suffering the poor girl had endured. It had been very much like when he had been attacked in his sleep, but worse. Oh so much worse! Surely she must have died from the pain he thought, and then knew that wasn't true as soon as he thought it.

That pain, that awful pain, had been the tearing of her soul from her body. What he had endured when he had torn his aura off at the wrists was a matchstick compared to the bonfire that had consumed her. Is this what had happened to Julie?

More tears welled up as he thought of his wife engulfed in such horrible agony. Poor Julie. If only he had been here to help her. He couldn't imagine the suffering, the pain.

He had experienced only the shadow-memory of it, a mere moment of passing, and he had soiled himself.

Jack got out of the shower and glanced at his watch on the bathroom counter. David and Myla would be here to interview him in half an hour. He took a deep breath and exhaled as he toweled off. He wasn't up to it. He wasn't ready to deal with anything after going through the shadow-memory of Jessica's soul being ripped out of her body.

He remembered what it had been like to experience Mercedes destroying Antonio's soul and how badly that had shaken him. That had been merciful and quick compared to what had happened to Jessica. He shuddered at the memory of the little girl's pain.

He brushed his teeth quickly, knowing the toothpaste didn't have a chance against the sour acid taste in his mouth. He shaved his face carefully, trying to keep his shaking hands under control, knowing he would be on camera when David and Myla arrived. He tried to fret over what clothes to wear, but the pain and horror wouldn't let him concentrate on anything else.

He settled on navy slacks with a light blue shirt and was digging through ties when he first felt it.

The hair on the back of his neck stood up as if someone had blown lightly across it. He stopped, ties dangling from his hands, forgotten, and turned around. His eyes searched the bedroom, his memory fearfully calling up images of the small demon that had torn out Rosa's throat, although he knew it had been destroyed.

The hair on his arms raised in a wave, traveling up to his shoulders and then down the middle of his back, leaving him tense and wary. He carefully stepped around the edge of the bed and eyed any possible hiding place. He leaned over and peeked behind the bed. He could feel the chills running up and down his body. *Not good,* he thought, *not good at all.*

There was nothing behind the bed. He knelt down, ear to the floor, and, keeping his face as far away as possible, flipped up the corner of the bed comforter.

Nothing under there either. He stood up, not making any noise. Trepidation radiated out of him, making his movements jerky and unsteady. It wasn't *there*, but it's definitely *here*, somewhere.

A low growl caught his attention. Somewhere out in the rest of the house, Bear was growling deep in his throat, so low it almost couldn't be heard. The dog's growl grew louder, indicating the closing proximity of Bear's adversary.

Jack left the bedroom, cautiously peering around the corner into the living room. There was no sign of Bear there, but the growling was louder. He crept to the top of the stairs and peered over the half-wall railing. He could barely make out the dog's tail, stiff and bushy with warning, near the bottom of the stairs. The growling increased, growing into a crescendo, straining and threatening to burst into a snarl.

Jack stepped lightly onto the top stair, slowly transferring his weight to prevent creaking. He moved down to the next stair and then the next, ears straining, eyes searching. His heart thudded in his ears so loudly he could hardly hear Bear's growling anymore. He realized he was holding a handful of ties above his head like a weapon and dropped them on the stairway landing.

He could see into the downstairs living room now, and Bear had taken a wide stance in the middle, baring teeth toward the spare bedroom.

Was this what had happened to Julie? This is what he had wanted, right? This was a chance to find her, an opportunity to track this thing back to its "cave" and rescue her. Was he ready? No. His breath was short and quick, and he realized he was panting with an open mouth.

Jack licked his lips and pursed them in determination to overcome his fear. He went down the remaining stairs. Bear's snarl grew into a bloody warning of tearing flesh, but still Jack saw nothing. Nothing!

He wasn't even seeing auras right now! He stumbled to a halt, his throat constricted and he felt his mouth begin to salivate as if he were going to vomit. How could he possibly do anything if he couldn't even see it? His fear grew exponentially. He felt weak in the knees. He wasn't ready! Not yet!

Deep breaths, he told himself, deep breaths. He tried to calm himself, tried to relax enough to see the auras.

Bear barked in warning. Jack looked up just in time to see a ripple of red glow wash out of the spare room and at him like a wave crashing on the beach. He threw his hands up in a futile gesture and fell over in the same place Julie had.

FORTY-SIX

David adjusted his shoulder strap and tried to balance the camera and sound equipment while Myla rang Jack's doorbell. "Why can't you at least help me carry *something*?"

"Because that's what I pay you to do, my little gaffer." She turned and smiled sweetly, pinching his cheek while his hands were too full to do anything about it.

"I am *not* a gaffer. A gaffer is an electrician. I'm..." A thump in the house caught David's attention. "...curious as to what that noise was," he finished, forgetting about his tweaked cheek.

"Maybe he tripped over the dog and fell down the stairs?" Myla's eyebrow rose.

"It sounded like it came from the basement." David nodded to the light coming from the window at ground level off to the right of the front porch.

"Maybe he fell *up* the stairs." Myla rang the doorbell again.

"Didn't he have a dog?" David was leaning to the right and trying discreetly to see in the window without losing his balance and dropping his equipment. Night was coming and the light streaming out of the window made it easy to see in.

"Yeah, Bear. Why?"

"It's not barking when you ring the doorbell."

"Maybe he's not home."

"Maybe he broke both his and the dog's necks while falling down the stairs."

"That's not funny, David. Remember how they found his wife?" Myla gave him a hard look.

"Remember that noise we just heard?" David raised his eyebrow in imitation of Myla's look. David was leaning so far over to see in the window he was on the verge of falling.

"I swear..." Myla mumbled something he couldn't hear and stepped off the porch and into the bushes in front of the window.

"What was that? I didn't quite catch it?" David's voice mocked her.

"You and your stupid—" Myla muttered as she forced her way through the bush to see into the window. "That's weird. Look at that. He's got quarters taped to the window. Why would anyone do that?" One of the branches caught at her purple silk cravat and pulled it tight around her throat. She cursed as she pulled it free and loosened it again.

"I caught *that*!" David laughed at her vulgarity.

"Oh, my God!" Myla waved her hands frantically at the branches in her face. Myla forced her way out of the bushes, losing her scarf. "Where's the damn cell phone!" She yelled as she grabbed at a bag tucked under David's arm.

"What's wrong?" David realized Myla wasn't teasing him. "It's in my pocket." He began dropping stuff until he could reach inside his coat and pull out the tiny flip phone.

"He's lying at the bottom of the stairs! Just like his wife!"

Jack tried to fight, but the fear of knowing what was going to happen was too much. He soiled himself again, before it even reached him. He heard Bear let out a pitiful yelp, and then the pain engulfed him.

What he had experienced before in the shadow-memories had been a trifle. The attack in his bed had been an afterthought. This was the end of Jack's life.

The blazing ball of fiery pain that had burned in his brain so long ago came again, but this time it consumed him as though he were flash-paper. He felt his body spasm and twist with involuntary contractions. The last sensation he had of his body was his face landing on the floor, but that was the least of his worries. In the next instant, he was torn out of his world and birthed into Hell.

Agony tore through him as the demon began ripping him out of his body, clawing at his soul to pull it out. His silver connecting cord shredded, pulled apart in an unnatural severance, causing such incredible pain he would have died of shock had he still been alive. He burned in wretched misery and writhed in the maelstrom as the blazing pain consumed him.

Then it stopped. For the briefest of moments he saw the white tunnel, the light, and the love waiting on the other side, the faces of…

The demon surrounded him and encased him within itself. He was sealed away in nothingness. He was back in the infinitely empty universe where it had all started, where the demon had first attacked him. There was nothing here. Not even himself. Nothing.

Stop it! You'll go crazy! he warned himself. *Obviously, I am here, or I couldn't be aware of it!* But it was so hard to think, so hard to focus that he wasn't even sure he really existed.

He tried to sense something, anything, but there was nothing. He couldn't feel his body, but he hadn't expected to. He knew he was dead. The afterlife was a lot like he had expected. Nothing. He just hadn't expected he would still be aware of it. Of its…nothingness.

There were no auras, no long lost relatives, and no gods. He tried to examine himself, but he didn't seem to exist either. He floated in the infinite nothingness for an eternity. He was cold.

An odd thought drifted through his mind. *Colder than hell.* Whoever had said that had been right. Hell was cold. Then the thought faded and there was nothing to think anymore. Nothingness.

And then there was something. A distant hue of reddish glow began to appear.

Jack would have wept with joy, had he any way to weep. It occurred to him he had gone insane and he tried to ignore it. Then he decided insanity would be a nice change and he tried to move closer to it, tried to be a part of it, but he had no control over anything. It was just there, as he was—a part of the nothingness.

Slowly it got brighter and came closer until Jack had to acknowledge something else was real in this universe, too, and he was grateful he was no longer alone.

Then it attacked him again.

There were millions of points of pain, needles piercing through him though he no longer had a body. Each point became a suction point, a focus of energy being stolen from him, a focus of his mind being stolen from him. His dreams, his hopes, and his fears were being siphoned off. He could feel them slipping away. He lost a memory of his mother tucking him into bed and he mourned for the loss. He had a fleeting glimpse of his father's smile and grieved, as he knew the memory had been taken from him. The taste of Julie's lips, the smell of Bear's fur, the color of leaves; they were all stolen from him.

He tried to scream but he had no voice, and even if he had, there was no one to hear and nothing for it to echo off of.

Myla snapped the cell phone shut and let out an exasperated growl. "What is up with those people!" Her expression was hard to see in the fading light as she stood on the porch, but her tone of voice made it easy to imagine.

"They're just doing their job." David tried to placate her from where he stood in the bushes. "My sister tried to do that for a while, it's not easy."

"Still! They don't have to act like I'm lying to them!"

"They were just trying to get all the information they could." He peered through the window at Jack's body in the middle of the floor; it hadn't so much as twitched since they spotted it. "I wonder what the hell these quarters are for?"

"I wonder what the hell is taking them so long!" Myla slapped one hand against her hip while eyeing the watch on her other.

"Geez, Myla! Give 'em a chance! You just hung up!" A shadow movement just outside of his field of view caught his eye. "I think I saw the dog."

"Where?" Myla pushed into the bush and pressed against the window.

"Over there, around the corner to the other room."

Myla looked and then stood up. "Hey. There's another window." She pushed past David between him and the window, forcing him back into the bush.

"Yeah, I think I see the dog."

David squeezed in next to her to see. "There are quarters on this window too. Isn't that weird?"

"Would you drop it with the stupid quarters?" She nudged him out of her way so she could see better. "It's dark in there, but it looks like the dog is lying in front of the closet, there. See?" She pointed against the glass.

"Isn't that where the paramedics said they found it last time?"

"Yeah, I think so. Hey. What was that?"

"What?"

"I thought I saw something. There!" Myla pointed to a shadow pulling away from the open closet door. "There's someone in there!"

FORTY-SEVEN

Jack felt himself spin out of existence and back into it again. The infinite nothingness compressed down into an impossibly small point, taking Jack with it, crushing him until…

Wide open space. He had been crushed through a black hole and spit out the other side, into a vast void, a much larger nothing but still nothing at all. Except…

Jack? (surprise, confusion, sorrow) A query out of the ether tugged at his attention, but he was so weak, so tired.

Jack? (surprise, confusion, sorrow, insistence)

Jack tried to find the strength to search the emptiness for the thought that had floated through his mind. Then he recognized the touch and hope flared through him. He tried to call out to her.

JULIE! (EVERYTHING! LOVE! HATE! SORROW! LOSS! GUILT! FEAR!) Jack's mind was wide open in this horrible place of nothingness, and everything he ever knew, had ever done, had ever hoped, dreamed, dreaded, feared, everything, poured out of him as though his mind was a bucket of water that had just been kicked over.

Julie was there to catch his thoughts for him, and with help from Jessica, she slowly helped his pull his mind back into himself.

Don't worry. The weakness will pass. (assurance, experience, understanding) The thought floated through his wandering consciousness and he did his best to grab onto it, like a man adrift at sea clutching for a life ring.

"What the hell is that?" David's voice was shrill.

Myla couldn't respond. She was frozen in place, crouched outside the bedroom window, watching as a dog-sized denizen of Hell entered the world in a dark swirl of shadows.

It had glittering protruding eyes and a long pointed snout with sharp fangs. Long skinny arms dangled gnarled claw-like hands at its sides. Its legs bent backward as it casually stepped past the still form of the dog and moved into the light. The separate halves of its cloven-hoofed feet splayed wide on the carpeted floor as it stepped down.

"Oh shit," were the only words that came into Myla's mind.

The creature bent its equine head toward Bear and sniffed, nostrils flaring wetly. It stood back up and sniffed again. Catching a scent, it moved on.

Myla and David scrambled back to the first window to follow the creature's movement. The rocks under their feet clicked and the branches of the bush cracked as they forced their way to see.

The creature walked out of the spare room and into the living room as though master of it all, looking around in inspection.

Myla's stomach turned as she watched the monster's disgusting wings twitch like dying things on its back. David repeated Myla's words as he realized it was moving to where Jack was lying in the floor. "Oh shit."

In a few slow strides, the shiny black beast stood over Jack's body and cocked its equine head to the side to get a better look. Languidly, it reached down and grabbed a handful of Jack's hair, lifted his body up and looked into his slack face.

Myla almost thought she saw a smile on the demon's visage. David saw pure lust. They both screamed as it bit into Jack's throat.

Iknowwhoyouare/Ireadyourdiary/Icalledyourfather/Isharedyourshadowmemory/ ...

Jessica put the blocks back up around Jack's mind and shut down his thoughts again. He could tell when they shut him out and it frustrated him. He needed to communicate with them and they were intentionally forcing him to be silent. If he could have huffed in frustration, he would have.

He was trying to slow down and communicate the way they wanted to, but it was so hard. It took so much effort and he needed to tell them what had happened! Why wouldn't they just open up and let him share his thoughts?

Try it again, slowly this time. (patience, understanding) Jessica touched his mind again.

There was a major difference between the touch of Julie's thoughts and Jessica's. When Julie communicated, she leaked occasional thoughts, but Jessica's were tightly controlled.

I came to help Julie. (???) He tried to control his emotions but they came out a jumbled mishmash.

That is much better. (warmth, happiness, satisfaction) How do you intend to help? (curiosity, amusement)

Jack felt a wave of guilt and despair wash over him as he realized he had no idea how to help. None of this had worked out the way he had planned. He had been trapped by the demon, if not already killed.

His frustration leaked into his thoughts as he tried to tell them about his plan to follow the creature and rescue Julie, about his newfound ability to see auras, about Fidelina and Rosa and…

Jessica put up the mental blocks that shut down his thoughts again.

"Oh my God!" Myla screamed as the creature sank gleaming fangs into Jack Hooper's throat. It sucked at it like a vampire, draining Jack's blood as well as his life energy.

"HEY!" David yelled and pounded on the window, trying to get it to drop Jack. The creature didn't seem to notice.

"Oh my God, Oh My God!" Myla's brain stuck on the same thought over and over again as blood began dripping down the creature's muzzle.

"HEY!" David pounded hard enough the glass cracked but the demon didn't even flinch.

Myla scrambled out of the bushes as fast as she could. Branches tore at her face and hair. "HELP!" She screamed. "Somebody! Help!" She kept calling as she stumbled off the front lawn and into the street.

"Shit!" David sat down and put his foot through the window. The glass shattered and fell to the floor, taking the quarters with it. That got the creature's attention.

Myla turned and looked back at the house when she heard the window break. She saw David come out of the bushes as though the devil itself was after him.

Then she saw that it was.

A glistening form, black as midnight, clawed its way up and out of the window grabbing at the bush for handholds. It was larger than it had been. It was growing.

David tripped in the grass, sprawled, rolled, and came up running for all he was worth, never once looking back at the thing he never wanted to see again. "Run!" He yelled at Myla, "Run!"

Myla wanted to run, but her legs no longer seemed part of her body. "Run, David!" she yelled back, her arms waving frantically in the air.

She screamed as the demon leapt into the air and landed on David's back, pulling him to the ground. She screamed as it grabbed his hair, pulled his head back, and sunk its glistening fangs and wet snout into his throat. And then she screamed as it stood up, dropped David's limp body, and came for her.

Jack was pulled down by the undertow of a flood of terror and pain, confusion and rage. Someone else had just arrived to fill the emptiness of the private universe. He felt the deluge of thoughts and emotions try to wash him away, and he held on to his sanity as best as he could while he sensed Julie and Jessica trying to help the newcomer pull his mind together.

No wonder Jessica kept shutting him down. That kind of intensity could have completely washed his own mind away if they hadn't been there to help. He realized all of the loosed torment was coming from David Rowe and wondered how he knew David's last name. Then he realized he knew a lot about David.

He knew David was twenty-three years old. He knew David was embarrassed he had only had sex once and that had been at a party with a girl who didn't remember him the next day. He knew so many things about David now that David's mind had been open to him.

Mostly, he knew David had been attacked by a demon.

The ambulance arrived before the police. Its sirens went silent as it entered the residential area, but the emergency lights played across the houses it passed. As it turned onto the street of its destination, the driver was shocked to see a young black woman running down the middle of the street, right at him, screaming.

The driver pulled hard on the steering wheel of the ambulance and hit the brakes. He missed the girl but not the thing chasing her. The left front headlight exploded into shards and the fender crumpled. A dark form flipped up into the driver's face and the windshield turned opaque with a spider-web fracture.

The driver held his breath, praying the thing on the other side of the window stayed there. The soulless eyes and gleaming teeth he had seen coming at him were forever imprinted upon his memory.

Calls of surprise floated up into the cab from the paramedics in the back of the ambulance, but the driver ignored them as he shakily grabbed the handset for his radio and frantically called for additional help. He heard the back doors bang open and the stomping feet of the exiting paramedics while he waited for the dispatcher to respond.

The sick feeling that he would eventually have to come out of the ambulance and see the creature again was just settling into his stomach as he heard one of the voices outside the ambulance call out, "Holy shit! Look at that!"

Try again. (calm, patient, assuring) It was strange to 'hear' Jessica's thoughts as they were directed to someone else, and yet to be included in the conversation. Jack was doing much better communicating now that he'd had a crash course in the firsthand experience of having someone else's mind flood into his. Understanding the need for proper control did wonders to help him improve it.

David, on the other hand, was blithering his emotions and thoughts rampantly across the minds of the others as he tried to learn to communicate with them. Nonetheless, he had managed to convey enough information for Jack to realize the demon had taken form and attacked Jack's body as well as David's.

Jack did his best to convey the situation to Julie and Jessica while Jessica held David in a learning 'time out.' Julie didn't grasp everything, but had total confidence in Jessica, who seemed to understand it all perfectly.

Julie tried to explain to Jack how Jessica had acquired the knowledge of the preceding eighty-six people in their lineage, but Jack was still too frustrated with their refusal to communicate readily with him to bother grasping the concept.

It's coming back. (acceptance, withdrawal) Jessica informed them.

Jack and David felt Jessica and Julie pull away from them and back into themselves. Jack could tell they were preparing themselves, putting up some kind of defenses, but for what?

A reddish glow began to fill the emptiness and Jack felt gratitude and hope radiate from David, even as he felt dread and fear build up inside himself. He knew what that glow was, and what Jessica and Julie were steadying for.

He did his best to prepare for another attack.

Myla's face was streaked with running black eyeliner and smudged purple eye-shadow. She sat on the front porch step to Jack's house, shaking with fear, exhaustion, and grief. Emergency lights from the three police cars parked around the house played across her face in strobes of red, white, and blue. She wiped her nose on the corner of the blanket the paramedics had draped around her and stared at the black hiking boots worn by the officer standing in front of her.

He was looking over notes he had taken while talking to the driver of the ambulance that had hit the creature. The driver claimed to have never gotten a look at whom he had hit. The paramedics had claimed they thought they had seen something, not human, running away from the ambulance, but none of them could identify it. One had guessed kangaroo, based on the way it had seemed to jump away, but the other two had just shaken their heads and refused to speculate.

The cop looked up from his notepad to Myla. "The detectives will be here any minute." He nodded his head to emphasize the information as he assured her. She grimaced in return and tried to nod her head back. Her description of what she had seen had caused her to be ostracized by the police officers and she wondered what this one had done to deserve being left to watch her.

Her hands shook as she wiped her nose again. An officer was walking up the street, having just finished talking to the people in a neighboring house. She could hear more voices coming from inside the house behind her. A police car drove slowly past the end of the street with its spotlight searching the darkness between the houses as it went.

The ambulances were already gone. Jack and David were, maybe, both still alive. The paramedics had rushed them off as soon as possible while fending off the police, who did their best to get names for questioning later. Static hissed and crackled out of the police radios all around her.

She was staring at the dark stain on the sidewalk where David had been attacked when she felt a slight pressure on her back. She turned to find Bear, shivering, leaning against her.

"Hey, Bear." Her voice croaked as she reached out and put a blanket-draped arm around the dog. "It's going to be all right, I promise."

The dog whined quietly and stepped closer into her warmth.

"Oh, Bear." She started crying again when she saw the dog's bloody paws.

Jack and David screamed in unison. Their howls of pain and terror played horrific counterpoint to the torture being inflicted upon Jessica and Julie. Jack would have gasped for air, if he'd had any lungs to try to bellow. David would have bitten off his tongue, if he'd been using a mouth to scream.

They found their minds intertwining in terror as, together, they tried to avoid the backwash from the explosion of pain around Julie and Jessica. As they tried to shrink away from the horror, they pulled tighter together, their thoughts and minds melding and mixing.

At first, the experience was a wonder, a strange and joyous union of minds, an island of sharing and understanding in the maelstrom of pain surrounding them. Revelations opened up as they saw the world through each other's eyes. Each lived the life of the other and came away with all the benefits of having lived it personally. A kinship was born, a brotherhood closer than any imaginable, forged out of their mutual sharing, and each accepted the other, completely, as more than an equal, more than either had ever accepted themselves.

Then it all changed.

David tried not to, but he could feel himself pulling all of the energy away from Jack, trying to rebuild his own depleted stores. Jack fought him desperately, understanding that to give up was to cease to exist, to be absorbed, as he had once absorbed a demon, to become nothing more than fuel. They struggled as Jack tried to absorb back the same amount he was losing without consuming his newfound soul mate.

Anguish thundered between them, echoing the rumbling of the struggle between the demon and the souls of Julie and Jessica. David was helpless to resist as instinctive reflexes tried to siphon energy from Jack. Jack absorbed energy back, trying to maintain his own existence. Their minds, touching and open to one another on all levels, forgave each other for what they were doing, even as the struggle for survival continued.

Then a thought occurred, in both of their minds at the same time, a product of their shared experiences, of their shared thoughts. As one, they turned the focus of their struggle outward and toward the demon attacking Julie and Jessica, and both began taking energy from it.

If a demon could scream, this one did.

FORTY-EIGHT

The demon sent shockwaves of *surprise/rage/pain* tearing at the fabric of the empty universe, blasting Julie and Jessica away from it. The force finally separated Jack from David.

Even as Jack felt his newfound awareness of himself ripped in half and reduced to the meager thing it had once been, he knew he had been forever changed by the merging with David and he was glad for it and proud of it. In tribute to his newfound and now separated soul mate, Jack attacked the demon with everything he could.

He held on as tight as he could to the energy of the demon. He pulled at the energy, soaking it up, drinking it with a vengeance, determined to absorb this demon as he had the ones before it.

The demon responded in kind. Millions of knives of pain lanced into him again and he felt the demon begin taking energy back. The demon started stealing his memories and erasing his mind. He felt the memory of Julie's miscarriage rip from his mind. The ability to recognize David lanced out of him in a confused pain. Then he could feel it starting steal away his name.

In a haze of pain and fury, struggling for his life against the demon, he had a revelation. *It's not real. It's an illusion. It only seems to steal away your mind.*

Jack knew this is what Fidelina and Rosa had been trying to tell him about reality. It was only real if you believed it. The demon could only take his mind it he let it. It could only take his energy if he let it. It could only win if he let it.

He realized this was nothing more than a contest of wills. If he wanted to win badly enough, he would. If he wanted to see auras, he would. If he wanted to heal people, he would. And somehow, somehow he didn't understand, he realized he had been given access to the strongest will Fidelina, or Rosa, or anyone else for that matter, had ever seen.

And he decided it was time to do something about it.

Instead of just fighting the demon, he tried to see it, tried to recognize it for what it was. Then it became clear. The demon's aura came into focus out of the red haze of the empty universe, and Jack saw it was not so different than that of the owl.

The empty universe was inside of the demon, inside of its soul. Jack realized he, and the others, had been enveloped by the demon, but not absorbed, not completely used up. They were like grain in a silo, saved for later use.

Jack envisioned himself solidifying within the demon, becoming something of substance, something the demon could no longer drain energy from. He felt changes begin to take place. He actually felt something in this empty universe of the mind. Without wasting any time on exploring the sensation, he willed his newly created 'physical' presence to latch onto the demon and keep hold.

He felt the battle for energy come to a standstill. He had blocked the demon's efforts, at least for the moment. He used the respite to examine the demon's aura. It was very much like the owl's had been.

Branches of the aura led off in multitudes of directions, paths to the souls the demon had marked or affected, and paths to worlds and places Jack didn't have names for and couldn't quite grasp.

And then he found it. The same path that had so intrigued him when he had explored the owl's aura—the path leading back to himself.

His first impulse was to jump down the path as fast as he could, to flee from the demon, to get home. But he knew that wasn't enough. Not nearly enough.

Julie? (searching, needing) He managed to squeeze out a thought of communication while holding the demon locked in a standoff.

Julie? Jessica? David? His thoughts searched outward for them as he felt his hold on the demon shake as it struggled against him.

We're here. (assurance, confusion, questioning) The answer came to him from all three of them at once.

Come to me! (insistence, demand, order, need, urgency) Jack called them to his mind, the strain of holding the demon causing his thoughts to leak over them.

He received thoughts of assent as they picked up his thoughts and realized what he wanted to do.

I've found mine. (confirmation, hope, and farewell) David plunged into the path leading back to David, and his thoughts vanished from Jack's awareness.

The demon shook with rage and spears of pain jabbed at Jack as it tried to free itself from his hold.

Hurry. (weakness, haste, fear) Jack warned Julie and Jessica.

I cannot. (resignation) Jessica sent thoughts urging Julie and Jack to leave her. *I no longer have a place to return to. (acceptance) Someone must stay. I vowed. (determination) Go without me. (altruism)*

Jack realized Jessica had been dead for six years. There was no road back for her anymore. *(Sorrow, loss)* the emotions leaked out of Jack before he could stifle them. He couldn't leave her here. Not in this hell.

Come with me. (pleading, needing, love) Julie reached herself out to Jessica and did her best to grab on to her. *Please...*

Jessica pulled away from Julie, refusing to break her vow. Julie was in awe of the strength and determination she felt come from Jessica. *I will stay with you. (resolve)* Julie told her.

The demon rumbled again and Jack's hold broke. Pain lanced through all of them as the demon tried to attack all three at once.

Go now! (demand, need) Jack cried out to them as the pain lanced through him again. He fought back at the demon, trying to pull its energy again, hoping to give Julie a chance.

We are staying. (resolve) Julie and Jessica both told him.

Their revelation startled him, and Jack became angry with them even as he felt himself slipping. Why wouldn't they just go?

The demon attacked with such ferocity Jack thought his mind had been finally been erased.

He had tried to fight, he had done well, too, but now he was losing. Jack felt the burning pain all around him and realized what it was like to be inside the ball of fire that had been in his brain so long ago.

Inside his brain... He was inside the demon now.

Jack would have grinned savagely, if he'd had a body.

How about a taste of your own medicine! (anger, hate, disgust, bloodlust) Jack shouted the thought at the demon as hard as he could, hoping it could understand him. And then Jack burst into flames.

He heated himself up to white hot and then pushed for nova intensity. He felt his flames lick at the demon, searing at the aura, crisping pathways to other places. He screamed in a primal rage as he tried to burn the demon up.

The demon screamed in pain. The scream was so loud and startling that it extinguished Jack's fire. And then it stopped, as suddenly as it had begun.

The infinitely empty universe seemed to hold its breath, waiting to see what would happen next, but Jack didn't. He mentally grabbed Julie and Jessica and shoved them into the path he could see leading back to Julie, then he dove into the pathway leading back to Jack Hooper.

Julie screamed. The primal scream of the demon's pain lanced through her and she hadn't been prepared. She did her best to hold onto Jessica, who had also been caught off guard. Then, Jack did something to them both.

He forced them out. He forced them into the path that led back to Julie. It twisted and contorted, and shrank and grew. It pummeled them about and then, seemingly recognizing Julie, pulled her in like a magnet.

Julie did her best to hold on to Jessica, who was now returning the grip. They shot out of the tunnel at the speed of light and hurtled toward a dim gray. Julie would have thrown her hands up to protect her face as they plunged into the ground, but they were already there.

It was silent.

Where are we? (confusion) she asked Jessica.

Where you belong. (comfort, assurance) Julie felt Jessica's mind pointing her attention toward something, and as she concentrated, she realized they were standing in a room with a bed.

Once she realized something was there, it all became apparent. She was looking down at her own body, lying in a hospital bed.

That's my mom! (happiness, joy, love) Julie directed Jessica's attention to a lone figure sitting in a chair next to the bed. *Come on! (excitement)* She tried to pull Jessica toward the body on the bed.

I can't come with you. (longing) I have somewhere else I have to go. (excitement) Jessica broke away from Julie.

They were standing at the entrance to a beautiful bright white tunnel of light, and Julie understood how things had to be. Jessica no longer had a body she could return to.

Julie was entranced. She decided to go with Jessica. She decided to go into what she could tell was exactly to opposite of trap they had just escaped. It was bright, happy, and full of people and sensations. As she started forward, Jessica stopped her.

Someone has to stay. (resolve) Someone has to stop the monster. I vowed I would. If you are going to go, may I use your body? (pleading)

It took everything Julie had to step back from the light and the ecstasy she could sense there. She could not deny Jessica this. Jessica had done her share. It was Julie's turn.

You go. (resolution) I'm just sorry I didn't get to know you and the rest of your…our lineage well enough. (regret, sadness) Julie wished she could have hugged Jessica, but the thought passed between them, and that was better than good enough.

Don't worry. We know you. And one day soon, you'll know us, too. (love) As the words came, Julie realized they were only partly from Jessica. They mostly came through the tunnel, where she could make out smiling, loving faces beaming down at her.

Julie realized for the first time she could see Jessica now. Flowing white robes billowed around her lazily. She wasn't the little girl she had expected, but rather a woman in her prime.

Then she realized she was not seeing Jessica, she was seeing Jessica's soul. A thing of timeless beauty. An ageless, immortal thing made of love, a thing that would appear different to everyone who saw it.

Then she was gone.

Julie sat up with a gasp into the dimly lit hospital room and fell weakly back onto her pillow.

Julie's mother fell out of her chair.

Jack awoke in terrible pain. He tried to move, but was too weak. He opened his eyes to blinding light and shut them tight again. The sounds around him began to register. He was back in an emergency room. He tried to swallow and then the pain really kicked in.

He started choking. The jaws of the creature had crushed his larynx. There also seemed to be something else in his throat—and it hurt a lot. He tried to sit up and got farther this time, but discovered he was in restraints. Looking down at himself, he saw tubes sticking in his arms and running across his chest to his throat.

He dropped back onto the gurney as he remembered, from David's point of view, that his body had been attacked by the demon. He did his best to calm his breathing and stifle the choking, but he was unable. A machine was breathing for him and he couldn't match its rhythm.

He imagined his throat looking like Rosa's—a mass of twisted scar tissue—and his choking worsened. Someone poked their head into his curtained off area at the sound of his struggle, and then he heard a female voice curse and call out for someone to come help. The thought of having a ruined voice like Rosa's for the rest of his life spurred him into action.

Ignoring his choking as best as he could, he closed his eyes and imagined himself healing. He explored his body mentally and found the places that weren't right. Then he willed them to be right.

He could feel strength returning to his body. He could feel bruises and scrapes healing. He could feel the tube in his throat blocking the healing process. His hands jerked against the restraints as he tried to reach up and pull the tube out of his neck, but he couldn't reach. Weakly, he dropped his hands back to his sides.

As he choked again, he realized he didn't need his hands anymore. He had his mind. He had his will.

He closed his eyes and pictured the tube pulling out of his throat. He imagined he could feel it shrinking so it would be small enough to come out. He pictured it slowly sliding out and imagined he could feel the tape holding it in place pull away from his skin.

The nurse returned with a helper just in time to see a fully healed Jack Hooper collapse back into his bed in exhaustion.

As his consciousness faded, a smile crossed his lips when he heard one of them yell out, "This one did it too!"

FORTY-NINE

The distant sound of a strong voice cursing with a Hispanic accent awoke Jack. He smiled at the sound. It was good to hear Vic's voice again. It was good to hear again. Jack's dreams had been filled with nightmares akin to sensory deprivation.

He opened his eyes to a dim grayness and took a deep breath. He reveled in the feeling of the air rushing through his nostrils and filling his lungs. He stretched and smiled at the cat-like pleasure. Nothing hurt, nothing was sore. He remembered his throat and swallowed carefully. He reached up and ran his fingers across his neck. He felt no indication he had ever been injured.

A slight rustling sound from his left caught his attention. He turned his head and peered through the dimness of the room. Not more than five feet away, he spotted Julie looking back at him.

"Good morning, Beautiful." He tried to say it more than he actually said it. His voice cracked with dryness and the words broke as they came out.

"Good morning," she croaked back just as eloquently.

"I didn't think I would ever get to look into those beautiful eyes of yours again. I missed you." Tears welled up in Jack's own eyes as he realized he finally had her back. He had gotten his wife back.

Tears shone in her eyes as his voice cracked again, this time with emotion. "I missed you, too." They stared at each other in loving silence for a long moment.

"Damned reporters!" Vic cursed under his breath as he gently opened the door to the room and entered in a stream of light from the hallway. He closed the door with one hand and balanced a cup of coffee in the other. He stood still for a moment as he waited for his eyes to adjust to the dark before he awkwardly began feeling his way toward a chair.

Jack met Julie's eyes and smiled with amusement. Julie had a mischievous look in her eyes when she smiled back. Silently she lifted her head up to watch Vic as he found the chair with his probing hands. She carefully chose exactly the right moment to speak up.

"Hey Vic, what's happening?" She was rewarded with the sound of slopping coffee and more cursing.

"Julie?" Vic finally managed to sputter. "Are you okay?"

"Peachy keen," she assured him as he got out of the chair and made his way to her bed, wiping coffee off his hand and onto his pants.

"I have bad news, Julie." Vic's voice was solemn and full of concern. "Jack is here, too."

"I am?" Jack piped up just as Vic reached the beds.

"Shit!" Vic jumped and spilled his remaining coffee. "What is up with you people?" He threw the mostly empty Styrofoam cup at the floor. "Try to be nice and watch over your dead bodies and you gotta go and scare the bejeezus out of a guy." He stomped his feet, but then was grinning as he leaned over and hugged Julie and then Jack.

The friendly warmth of Vic's voice broke just long enough to show just how worried he had been. "You two really had us scared."

"And you!" He pointed a finger at Jack's face and hissed. "You have no idea what a ruckus you made by healing yourself while waiting to be rolled into the operating room!"

Jack grinned sheepishly at him. "It seemed like the thing to do at the time."

"Yeah, well, I don't know how you managed to heal the other kid first, but that is the *only* thing that has kept all of the attention of the world from being focused solely on you!"

Jack saw Julie's brows furrow in confusion. "David." He told her and she nodded in understanding. David had learned from his meeting of minds with Jack. "He healed himself." Jack turned to Vic and smiled. "I had nothing to do with it."

"Yeah, well, his reporter friend thinks you do. It's been all I could do to keep her out of here. She just keeps running back and forth from his room to this one, begging and pleading. She's even tried crying, thinking maybe I had a soft spot. One lousy interview and you'd think she became part of the family."

"Myla?" Jack asked.

"Yeah, that's the one."

For just a moment, Jack wondered why Vic hadn't let Myla in. Then he realized that wasn't his memory. That was David's.

Vic hesitated at the confused look floating across Jack's features. "Are you sure you feel all right?"

Jack nodded and smiled. "Yeah, I feel fine. Myla is a friend. You can let her in next time she comes by."

Vic scowled at him.

"Trust me."

Vic pointedly ignored him and turned to Julie. "Are you sure you're okay? Can I get you anything?"

"Some water would be good." She smiled affectionately at him and cleared her throat roughly.

"I'll get some." He looked back at Jack. "I'll get you some, too. I'll be right back."

Jack and Julie watched as he disappeared into the shaft of light that came through the door when Vic opened it.

"How much do you remember?" Julie asked as soon as Vic was gone.

"All of it, I think. Except that a lot if it is kind of like a dream. It made sense while it was happening, but it's fuzzy and incoherent now."

"Yeah, me too."

"Um... You know, David and I kind of...shared minds for a little while there."

"I know."

"And when he first got there, his mind kind of washed over me."

"Yeah."

"Um... Did mine do that to you when I got there?"

"Yeah."

Jack thought about that for a moment. The first time David's mind had flowed over him hadn't been nearly as complete of a union as he had experienced when they had fought the demon. It had been very one sided and consisted of fragments. But he had learned a lot about David from it nonetheless. He realized there was no telling what kind of memories of his own Julie had picked up on, or how out of context they might have been. Not to mention, whatever information she had learned from his mind, he hadn't learned anything from hers.

"Do you still love me even though you know all of my deepest darkest secrets now?" he asked jokingly, but the nervousness tinged his voice. He knew he now had a total acceptance of David, and vice versa, but they had a total understanding of each other to go with that. Julie had only the fragmented pieces that had washed over her.

"Hmmm...let me think," she muttered to herself and looked thoughtfully up at the ceiling. "In second grade you snuck up behind a girl and hit her in the head with your lunch box, after she had already beaten you up in a fair fight. You cheated on your Chemistry final in college. You defied my parent's wishes to go looking for help from a witch doctor, fought demons, and came looking for me in the afterworld." She clucked her tongue. "Did you do the dishes and clean the house before my parents...? No... Wait." Her voice trailed off as she recalled another piece of memory she had absorbed from him. "My mother cleaned up the whole damn mess—blood, mud, and all. And they are staying in a hotel!" She looked at him out of the corner of her eye to see how he was taking it.

She smiled at the grimace on his face and turned on her side to look at him. "Jack, you gave me the most precious gift anyone has ever gotten." Her eyes were bright and her tone loving. "I got to see into your heart and soul. I got to see, firsthand, just exactly how much you love me. Not how much you show it, not what you are willing and not willing to do for me. I actually got to feel your love for me. That was pretty amazing." A tear crawled out of the corner of her eye and began a slow trek down her cheek.

"If I had one wish," her voice cracked again, just a little, "I wish I would have shown you just how much I love you when I had the chance, so you would never doubt me either." She wiped the tear off her face with a delicate finger. "But, I really thought we were going to be there for, well, forever." She laughed quietly. "And I wanted to save it. I wanted to give it to you if you ever needed it."

Jack knew what she meant. In that place, madness could never have been far away. He smiled back at her, a spot warming in his chest. "Will you marry me?"

"I already did, you lummox!"

"Oh, yeah. Wanna do it again?"

"Yeah." She grinned. "I do. But I have baggage this time. I have to admit, I was a little perturbed when you tossed me and Jessica out of there. We had a commitment. We had taken a vow and you made us break that."

A strange look crossed Jack's face and Julie laughed. "Not *that* kind of commitment!" She explained about the lineage of the people captured by the demon.

"I'm sorry. I didn't understand...," Jack started.

"I know. There wasn't time to explain." She chuckled humorlessly to herself. "Who would have thought there wouldn't have been time to explain something in that place?"

"What was that thing?" Myla asked furtively looking at Jack.

Jack glanced over at Julie where she sat upright in her bed. She gave him a slight noncommittal shrug. Vic pretended to be interested in the arm of his chair.

Myla eyed Jack intently. "You know, the cops can't decide if I am lying or if I am a raving lunatic. I'm lucky I'm not in a straitjacket behind bars right now."

"What did David say it was?" Jack's voice gave nothing away.

Myla squinted at him in a disgusted look that said she didn't like to play the 'answer a question with a question' game. "What makes you think he would know what it is?" She moved to get back into pole position. Jack met her gaze levelly until she broke first.

"He said to ask you," she finally answered and then stared at him with a gaze indicating it was his turn to answer her even if she had to pry his head open and dig the answer out herself.

Jack tried to sort through his mixed feelings about Myla. Part of him, which had come from his experience with David, trusted her completely, but part of him felt he didn't know her at all. He looked to Vic, hoping to get a hint of what he should say, but Vic resolutely refused to meet his gaze. Finally, trusting in David's love for Myla, he threw his caution to the wind and told her. "It was a demon."

Myla's eyes relaxed their glaring squint and she raised her eyebrows, shaking her head disgustedly. "That's what David said you'd say."

"I'd bet you didn't even believe him when he told you he healed himself. You should listen to him more often," Jack told her. "He seems to have a pretty good head for what's going on. You'd probably be surprised at what he knows."

Myla's squint returned. "It sounds like you've spent a lot of time talking to him. In fact, that is almost word for word what he is always saying about himself." She put her hands on her hips and took a wide stance. "What I want to know is how in the hell do you two know what each other is going to say when you've never said more than a dozen words to each other? Huh? Answer me that."

Julie stifled a giggle as she watched Myla strike a pose. Jack glanced at her and then looked back to Myla. "You really want to know?"

"Yes, I do." Myla nodded her head sharply in time to her words.

"And you're willing to take my word for it, rather than asking David?"

"I can compare stories later."

"You have to keep it a secret."

"Uh huh."

"I mean it. This stays out of the news, off tape, out of conversation, and out of mind."

"Yeah, whatever." Myla rolled her eyes.

"Myla, I know things about David you would never even begin to guess. I'm not going to tell you any of them, because it would be wrong to do so. No to mention he's got a thing or two on me, too." He raised his eyebrows at Julie who nodded and affirmed what he had said with a grunt. "I am going to prove this to you first, before I explain what happened, so that you'll be a little bit more inclined to believe me." Myla rolled her eyes at him but he ignored her. "I want you to ask me about anything," he met her eyes and repeated for emphasis, "*anything*, that you would know about David, that you would think I wouldn't."

Myla sighed and looked off into space over her shoulder as if this was so far beneath her dignity. "I cannot believe I am playing these stupid games with you," she muttered. "Okay." She nodded defiantly and thought about it for a moment.

"On my twenty-third birthday, David gave me something, what was it?" She gave him a grim expectant smile.

Jack smiled back at her. That was an easy memory to pull up, because it was still fresh on David's mind when they had shared memories. "Your twenty-*third* birthday isn't until next month, and David knows that. He knows you have been pretending to be a year older than you are since you were seventeen because you wanted custody of your little sister, who turns eighteen in six months or so."

Myla's breath caught. It was something David would never have told. It was too important to risk losing her sister into foster care, even if only for another six months. Her face hardened and her skin took on an ashen color. "He promised me that he wouldn't ever tell anyone."

"He didn't," Jack told her. "Not really."

"What," she continued to glare, "it doesn't count if he writes it down? He made you guess it? It doesn't matter. He still told you."

"He didn't tell me," Jack told her. "David would never do anything to hurt you."

Myla didn't answer. Her eyes were far away as she struggled with an internal anger at David's violation of her confidence.

"Myla," Jack drew her attention back to him, "that was a bad place to start. I probably should have been a little more open and told you that I don't just know everything about David. I know everything he knows. At least everything he knew up until yesterday. Anything since then is all his. Something strange happened to us. When we...died, for lack of a better word, we ended up in a place together. Julie was there." He gestured to his wife and she nodded supportively.

"While we were there something happened. David and I...We mixed minds. We shared thoughts so closely we might as well have lived each other's lives. I find it amazing that somehow my own mind seems to have managed to stay in charge, and David's is just like memories for me. I assume it is the same for him?" He looked to her for confirmation.

Myla remained unresponsive, and Jack was afraid she was getting ready to leave without understanding, without believing. That would leave him responsible for turning the woman David loved against him, and that was not something Jack was prepared to live with.

"Myla." He reeled in her attention again. "You can discuss anything I do or say to David. I trust him completely." He nodded at her reassuringly. "But there is one thing I want to tell you that I hope you don't tell him I told you." Myla's face remained hard and Jack was beginning to wonder if she was going to throw up.

"Once, when you were at a night club together, he told you he was going to take dance lessons, and you told him to save his money, because white men can't dance for shit unless it was choreographed. Do you remember that?" She met his gaze but didn't respond. "It was the same night that he helped you stop three white guys from beating up a black girl in the parking lot. The same night that you told him ..."

"I know damn well what I told him!" she shouted. "And I don't need you and your big mouth telling the whole fucking world! Do you understand me?" Her eyes were wide and wet and she shook with anger. "How dare you!" she shouted at his face and turned to leave.

"That is the only reason he never asked you to marry him," Jack blurted as fast as he could, before she could get to the door. "He was afraid you couldn't ever love him back!" The last word bounced off the door as Myla slammed it shut behind her.

"Well, that went well," Vic offered as he stood up and brushed off his pants absently. "I think I'll go make sure the nurses don't think anything bad happened in here." He quickly left, careful not to slam the door.

"Why did you do that?" Julie asked Jack.

"I didn't mean to. I was trying to get through to her, trying to convince her I knew things David wouldn't have told anyone so she would believe all of the other things she was going to ask about." A long silence hung in the hospital room.

"Are you going to tell me?" Julie asked.

"What?"

"What she told David that made her so upset?"

Jack looked over at his wife with sadness in his eyes. "She was gang raped by four white guys when she was fourteen and had an abortion. After David found out, he was afraid she wouldn't, or couldn't, ever love a white guy."

FIFTY

I think our troubles are just beginning." Vic tossed the morning newspaper onto Jack's lap. Jack picked it up and read one of the smaller headlines aloud to Julie.

"Unlucky hero strikes out." He looked over at her and winked. "I guess they didn't have time to get the whole story into the newspaper."

"Try page thirteen," Vic suggested.

Jack flipped the pages and skimmed the headlines. "I don't see anything…"

"Bottom, right hand side," Vic directed again.

Jack spotted it. "Dog maulings puzzle police?"

"Four of them." Vic filled them in while Jack skimmed the article. "All took place between six-thirty and seven-thirty last night—in your neighborhood. It wasn't dogs doing the mauling. It was dogs getting mauled."

"Bear?" Julie sat up quickly.

"Bear is fine. Anita went there this morning to let him out. She said his paws look awful though. She made an appointment to take him to the vet this afternoon."

"What happened to his paws?" Julie asked with a concerned frown.

Jack gave her a pained look. "He tore up his nails trying to get into the spare room closet." He looked back over at Vic. "You can tell Anita we don't need a vet. I can heal him when we get home," Jack reminded him.

"Sure, sure." Vic nodded. "And when the police visit you for more follow up questions you'll explain that how? The same way you have everything else? 'I don't know?' 'How could I have, I was unconscious?' 'I didn't ever actually see anyone?' Come on, Jack! How long do you think that kind of stuff will hold up?"

"It's all been true!" Jack defended himself.

"It's all been partial truths," Vic corrected him. "And if you don't start watching your ass, someone is going to hand it to you, real soon." Vic's bushy black mustache twitched as he frowned.

"He's right, Jack," Julie soothed. "You can't just walk through the world working miracles. Sooner or later, someone will do something about it, and in this day and age, it won't be something good."

Jack sighed. "So what are we going to do about this?" He slapped the back of his hand on the article about dogs with their blood drained by some unknown wild animal. "I had high hopes we had seen the last of that thing, now the paper is saying a *Chupacabra* is running loose in the suburbs of Denver."

"You shouldn't have pissed Myla off so much. She might have told you how she saw it run away and jump over a car in a single bound—after it had been hit by the ambulance *she* called for *you*."

Jack looked away, abashed. "I didn't mean to upset her."

"Yeah, well you did. Not that I mind. This is the first time since I got here last night that some reporter hasn't been trying to sneak in here with the cops. Anyway," he pointed at the newspaper in Jack's lap, "that is way out of my ability to deal with, Jack. And yours too." Vic shook his head and took a dramatic pause. "But I've called in some experts."

Jack looked up, and Vic grinned innocently.

"Anita is going to kill you."

"Yeah, I know."

Julie's parents drove Jack and Julie home from the hospital and fawned over them both. Her mother made them lunch and cleaned the house again, refusing to let either of them help. Her father insisted on replacing the glass in the broken basement window, and Jack was glad to find someone had realized his back door was open before they kicked in the front one—not that he wasn't grateful to them for having saved his life.

Jack did his best to sidestep the questions about the quarters and crosses everywhere, but Julie's parents were beginning to get a little edgy with the noncommittal answers he was dishing out. Jack took solace in taking Bear to the vet.

When he got home, he was relieved to find Julie's parents had gone back to their hotel room. Julie was already in bed napping and informed him she was probably going to stay there the rest of the night. He considered joining her.

It had been a long and difficult day. Between some very rigorous questioning by the police and some very invasive questioning by a couple of reporters, they had spent the rest of their time at the hospital being prodded by rudely skeptical doctors who kept rolling their eyes at the poor insistent doctors who were swearing about the double miracle they had seen last night. Jack was glad to be home. But there was one more thing he had to do before he could call it a day.

He picked up the phone, and after only a moment of hesitation, dialed a phone number he had never even thought of before. It was answered on the second ring.

"Hey Jack," David spouted before Jack had said anything.

"How'd you know it was me?"

"I'd like to say it was a lucky guess, but I have started having these little feelings about things, and so far they have all been right. It's kind of freaky."

"I know the feeling. Anything else happen?"

"Yup. Been seeing auras, had an out of body experience while I was napping in the hospital. It was pretty cool. I just thought about my Grandma, who lives back in Iowa, and, poof, I was there. She was baking her famous minced meat pie. Personally, I hate the stuff, but I'll never tell her that."

"Yeah, I know," Jack answered with a laugh.

"Oh, yeah, that's right. You know me, too." David laughed. "Anyway, I called Grandma when I got home, told her I could smell her pie from here. You should have heard her carry on about that! Man! That was worth the price of admission alone."

Jack could hear David's smile on the phone and realized the stupid saying they always quoted at his job, 'the customer can hear how you look', had some truth to it after all.

"I need to talk to you about something," he told David with regret for breaking up the happy thought.

"Yeah, I know."

"Another little feeling?"

"No. Myla told me she saw the thing run away, and I saw the article in the newspaper."

"Yeah, well, we're working on that. Vic called Fidelina and told her it was an emergency. She's supposed to be here tomorrow. But that's not what I needed to talk to you about."

"It isn't?"

"No." He took a deep breath. "I blew it with Myla."

"Hey, man! You're married! You stay away from her!" David's voice was teasing. He knew Jack would never cheat on Julie. "Don't worry about it. She's a little high strung. She'll get over it real soon."

"You don't understand. I blew it for you." The silence hung on the line for a moment before Jack explained. "I was trying to ease her into this supernatural shit by showing her I knew things about you and it backfired."

"I wondered why she wouldn't talk to me all afternoon. I thought she was just irritated at being scooped by all of the other reporters when she had actually been involved."

"She thinks you told me her deepest secrets."

"Which ones?" David's voice was toneless.

"The worst ones."

Jack spent the first half of the next morning helping Julie convince her parents they were both fine and there was no need for them to be staying in a hotel anymore, and the second half trying to sound sincere while trying to convince them they should stay longer and actually get to visit for a while. He was relieved when they insisted they needed to get back home and take care of things they had dropped to come out when Julie had gone into the hospital.

As soon as they were gone Jack picked Julie up, threw her over his shoulder and grunted "Make love, now!" As he carried her off to the bedroom, she giggled and beat on his back playfully.

The doorbell set Bear to barking as he ran through the house to get to the door first. Jack was close behind, dodging the snapping end of a wet towel as Julie chastised him for making her run late in the shower. He waited for the sound of Julie shutting the bedroom door before he opened the front door. He was surprised to see David standing on the front step, cameras and sound equipment balanced all over his person.

"Hey! Come on in!" He grinned at his newfound life-long friend and held Bear back with his leg so David could squeeze through the door with all of the equipment.

"I hope you don't mind, I thought maybe we could get this commercial thing out of the way while I was here." He lifted the camera to indicate what he meant as he started up the stairs.

"While you were here?" Jack gave him a puzzled look as he shut the door.

"Yeah, I had a funny feeling I should be here tonight. I'm right, aren't I?" David began dropping equipment on the floor.

Jack raised his eyebrows and nodded. "Yep. You're right. You even got the right time. When the doorbell rang, I thought it was going to be Vic and Fidelina."

"Ah, well. Maybe we don't have time to film this thing. I was just hoping I could surprise Myla with it, cheer her up a little."

"Have you heard from her?"

"Yeah. You were right. She is one torqued off dudette."

"I'm sorry."

"Hey! It's all good. I know what you were trying to do. I *understand* you, remember?" David scratched his head under the black hat with the silver X emblazoned on it.

"Yeah, I remember." Jack went to the refrigerator and pulled out a couple of beers and handed David one. "Sorry, I don't have your brand."

"That's okay." David took a drink of the brew. "It's not like you were expecting me."

"I should have called you, though. I was going to leave you out of this mess, but I should have known you would want to be right in the middle of it."

"Do you think Fidelina will let me film her? I could do a mini-documentary on real life witches or something."

After introductions all around, Jack went and got extra chairs to seat everyone around the dining room table. He had expected Vic and Fidelina, but he hadn't expected David, Rosa, Mercedes, Anita, and the kid from the barbershop, Bernardo, who had been harangued into driving the old women to Colorado. It was a little strange for everyone to meet David, who already knew them all through Jack's experiences, and Julie surprised Fidelina, Rosa, and Mercedes by recognizing each of them individually.

Anita was the most disquieted by the whole situation. She had apparently refused to leave Vic's side since Mercedes' arrival, in spite of the fact Mercedes was now so old and feeble she could hardly talk and make herself understood. She quietly sat in a rickety looking wheelchair and tried not antagonize Vic and Anita. Jack was surprised to see her. He had silently assumed she had already passed on.

Reaching up from her wheelchair, Mercedes patted Jack's hand carefully, as though she was afraid she would hurt him. "I have something for you," she croaked with effort and met his eyes. He felt a pang of sadness as he recognized a spark of the beautiful Latin goddess he had met only days ago in the rheumy, red lidded eyes of the old hag before him.

Mercedes slowly turned and did her best to wave her hand to motion Vic to come over. Anita gave Vic a cross look, but he ignored her and came carrying a box similar to the one Mercedes had kept her mementos from Doña Isabella in.

"I want you to have this," she patted the box the same way she had patted his hand, "but I don't want you to open it until after I move on." She hesitated as she said 'move on', and Jack knew she meant after she died.

Jack nodded and kept his lips tightly shut for fear of saying something inappropriate. He gently gave Mercedes a hug and resisted the temptation to try to give her some of his own energy, just to make sure she didn't die while she was here.

"Our Lady Guadalupe has been kind to me." She smiled at Jack. "She has given me more time than I could have hoped for to say goodbye to my family and friends. I suspect it was so I could be here to help you with this problem." She nodded to him sagely as he helped her move her wheelchair into position at the table.

"Yes," Fidelina agreed, "this is going to take a lot of effort, and none of us are sure where to start."

Jack sat down with everyone gathered around the table. Bernardo had chosen to stand back from the table with an aloof and disinterested look permanently molded onto his Hispanic features. Everyone else had settled in and seemed as comfortable with each other as possible. Even David appeared at ease, but Jack wished Myla had come with him. He pushed away the guilty thought about how it was his fault and addressed the issue at hand.

"Well, how do we kill something like this?" He looked from Fidelina to Rosa and then to Mercedes.

"Until you came along, we thought it was only possible to banish a demon," Fidelina told him. "I suggest that is what we try to do."

Julie shook her head and spoke up, surprising the old women. "It has to be destroyed. I owe it to my lineage to make sure I am the last of the line." The statement brought puzzled looks from around the table. Although Jack was familiar with the idea of Julie's newfound 'lineage,' he hadn't spent enough time with Jessica to learn anything about it.

"I'll explain," Julie told them and began reciting the one thousand, three hundred and twenty-two year history of the demon's captives. The pain and concern on her face kept everyone quiet as she listed all eighty-six names of her lineage and explained their purpose. When she finished, her voice broke and she had to wipe tears from her eyes. "I just wanted you all to know who we would be doing this for—why we have to do it. I cannot allow their suffering to have been in vain. I cannot allow any more victims to suffer at the mercilessness of this creature. I can't take the chance someone else will be trapped, alone, without one of us there to help." She met everyone's eyes in turn around the table and then got up and went to blow her nose.

"Well, that settles it then." Anita surprised everyone by being the first to speak up. "It has to be destroyed. Any ideas?" She looked around the table, even meeting Mercedes' eyes.

FIFTY-ONE

E"xplain to me again why we are out in the middle of this field, in the dark, in the snow, in the cold?" Vic's accent was unrecognizable as his teeth chattered.

"Shut up," Jack mumbled in a teasing tone. They both knew it had been Vic's idea to use themselves as bait to try to lure the demon out of hiding.

The newly fallen snow crunched under their feet as they stepped over and around the larger clumps of grass in the vacant lot. It had been plowed and bulldozed a year ago for construction that had never taken place, so neither was too worried about their footing.

"I have to piss," Vic whispered as he stopped walking and handed a long silver knife to Jack. He unzipped and turned to face away from Jack.

"You're as bad as a kid," Jack teased him. "You just went before we left."

"I had more coffee than you did. Besides, the cold always makes me have to go." Vic unzipped his pants and sighed with relief. "Are you sure this is where Rosa said it would be?"

"It has to be." Jack shrugged. "This is the only open field out this way without getting all the way out of the city."

"Yeah, well maybe she got a little bird-brained confused while looking through the eyes of that owl." Vic jumped as a dark shape swooped from the night sky, whooshing past his head, making a screeching sound.

"Better be more careful what you say," Jack advised him.

Vic grunted unhappily as he zipped his pants back up.

Julie, Anita, and David walked along the far edge of the same lot Vic and Jack were tramping through. Anita had given up on stumbling through the clumpy weeds sticking up through the snow and was walking on the asphalt of the street. Her breath puffed out of her like a steam engine as she pushed her oversized body to keep up with her younger companions.

"Tell me again," she huffed, "about this great plan of ours."

"You guys stab it," David turned his camera toward Anita's gasping form and grinned at her from the half of his face not hidden behind the camera's eyepiece, "and I'll absorb it. Easy."

"Stab it and absorb it." She huffed as she looked over at Julie. "Does that sound like the typical plan to get rid of a demon to you?"

Julie grimaced and shrugged, the blessed knife in her right hand glinting in the dark. "It sounds just as good as the sacrificial goat idea."

"At least that idea involved less walking." Anita huffed again and switched her own blessed knife to her left hand so she could dig a tissue out of her pocket.

"Yeah," David mumbled from behind his camera as he pointed it out into the dark field, "it's really too bad we couldn't find a goat for sale anywhere."

They all met back at their parked cars where Bernardo kept watch over the three old women who sat huddled under the heater in Anita's catering van. Vic was complaining about his wet feet and Anita mumbled something about minding her own business next time.

"At least it's not a total loss." David tried to cheer everyone up. "I can edit the film I just shot and market it as 'The Blair Snipe Hunt Project.' "

Bernardo stifled a chuckle, the first emotion he had shown since arriving with the old women. Jack decided to ignore the comment and turned to talk to Rosa. "If it's here, it's not interested in us," he told her. "Did you see anything else with the owl?"

"No," Rosa's ruined voice croaked at him. "I never saw any more signs of psychic disturbance. It just vanished." She sighed. "I'm sorry I couldn't do more."

"That's life." He gave her an encouraging smile and then poked his head farther into the van. "We'll be home in about twenty minutes," he told the shivering Mercedes

"Oh, by the way," Rosa rasped and handed Julie's cell phone to him. "Julie's parents called. They wanted to know how she was doing."

"Thanks, I'll let her know."

"They seemed kind of concerned about an old lady they didn't know answering the phone."

"Yes, I'm sure they did."

FIFTY-TWO

Thursday morning came early, and Jack and Julie both got a late start on their attempt to return to work and restore some normality to their lives. Everything was different now, and they both knew it, but they hadn't quite decided how different yet, so it was safest to try to make sure they still had an income.

"No point in hurrying," Julie reminded him. "Anything that might have been on the to-do list was reassigned a long time ago."

Jack put his arm around her and relished the feeling of just being with her. After a long time, but not nearly long enough, they kissed and got out of bed.

Just as Julie was getting ready to leave for work and Jack was stepping into the shower, the phone rang. Jack sighed and turned off the water. "I'll get it," he called out. "You go ahead and go."

"Already got it!" she called back, and he heard her pick it up. After just a moment, at the same time Jack turned the water back on, he heard her calling him. He turned the water off again and walked out wrapping a towel around himself.

"Who is it?" he asked, but Julie had already hung up the phone and was turning on the television set.

"David. He said we should see this." She pointed at a commercial on the screen and they waited a moment for the news to come back on.

When it did come back on, it was a live broadcast from the traffic helicopter showing the bright sun-reflecting snow around the city. The reporter's voice came out of the television sounding tinny and distant. "Here is another look at those footprints we were telling you about." The camera zoomed in, fuzzed, and then focused on a line in the snow too far away to be recognizable as anything more than a line.

"We have been following the prints for at least five miles now," the camera zoomed out until the line was barely distinguishable, "and there is, as of yet, no sign of what might have made them."

The scene switched to the reporter sitting at the news desk in the studio. "Although there has been no official word yet, a Forest

Service representative strongly suspects the tracks are merely those of an elk that wandered into the city and they have nothing to do with the mutilation of at least seventeen local area pets attributed to the *Chupacabra*. A few dissenting locals have been reminded of an old story that came out of England over a hundred and fifty years ago."

The screen switched to a pre-taped segment of an overweight man with a goatee and wild hair, standing in the snow next to some of the prints. "Yeah, uh, the Devonshire Devil left footprints that ranged over a hundred miles. The footprints went over the tops of buildings, through eight-foot fences, and even straight through haystacks, without disturbing anything or any change in the distance of stride. The prints were reminiscent of a donkey, but were in a straight line, made by a bipedal creature. That is exactly what we seem to have here."

"Well, maybe not exactly," another reporter's voice chimed in as video close-ups of the prints were shown. They appeared to be split-hoofed and looked like deer or elk tracks to Jack. "But maybe they are similar," the voice continued.

"Here we find them leading up to this privacy fence, and as you can see," the camera lifted up to see over the fence, "they appear almost as if something had walked right through the fence. And here we have what may or may not have been prints left on the roof. Unfortunately, the sun was beginning to melt the snow on top of the house as we arrived. We have, however, been attempting to follow the tracks, and as soon as we find out where they lead, we'll be sure to let you know."

The in-studio news anchor came back on. "On a side note, the Devonshire Devil tracks, mentioned a moment ago, were later supposed to have been made by a type of hopping mouse, after similar tracks were observed in other areas."

Jack and Julie looked at each other as the weatherman came on and predicted warm and sunny.

"Well, now we know why we didn't find it out in the field last night." Julie shrugged at him.

Jack wandered outside to get the newspaper before he went to work. Julie had said she didn't care, but, he felt, if he was going to get strange looks from his co-workers, he might as well see what they had read about him. He stood in the light snow on the front stoop for a moment and breathed the sharply cool air. It felt good to be alive.

Bear squeezed by him and high-stepped his bandaged paws onto the snow. The vet had sewn up one nail the dog had torn loose and Jack regretted the logic preventing him from healing the dog. "Nice day for it, isn't it, Bear?"

The dog gave a flip of his tail in acknowledgement. "I don't know for what either. I just like saying that." Jack stepped off the stoop and began searching for the paper. That was when the helicopter flew over.

He looked up just in time to see what may or may not have been a camera aimed at him. "Shit," he muttered and hurried back into the house. He was sick of reporters, and Vic had been the one to fend most of them off. He heard the helicopter's motor fade, grow louder, and then fade again.

A voice drifted down from the television set he had left on. "...seem to have come to the start of the trail. We have circled twice and the trail of prints seems to have just suddenly ended in the middle of someone's yard."

Jack's heart sank and he ran up to see the screen. It wasn't showing his house. He sighed with relief and muttered a silent thank you. The camera circled a house he didn't recognize and he could see where the tracks seemed to start, or perhaps end, in the middle of someone's backyard.

"This is where they appeared to have started, and then they headed northward, through yards and across streets in a straight line," the voice narrated while the camera followed the tracks. Jack could hear the helicopter again. "Although we expected to lose the trail where cars dove over the prints on the road, so far they have always turned up right across the street. Mostly it appears that the tracks wander aimlessly, but here, the tracks seem to turn and head due east for no apparent reason," the camera followed the right turn in the tracks in the middle of a large front lawn, "until they get to this house." Jack's heart sank again. It *had* been too good to be true.

He watched as the camera followed the tracks to his house, where they appeared to circle the house before moving on again to the north.

Jack didn't realize he had been holding his breath until he heard the sound of the helicopter start to fade again.

"It was looking for us while we were out looking for it!" Julie whispered into the phone. She looked around the office to make sure no one had heard her.

"I don't think it was looking for us, *specifically*," Jack assured her. "I think it just keeps going back to a good feeding ground. Think about it. It got Jessica there, then you, then me, and then David. Our house has got to be on its list of favorite places to check for food." Jack sighed. "I'm just glad I put those quarters back up after your parents left, or it might have had Bear for a snack. I would guess the only reason they haven't tied this in with the pet mutilations is that people had their pets inside because of the snow last night."

"It's only a matter of time until it gets someone else," Julie whispered again. "What are we going to do?"

"I'm going to ask everyone to come over again, and we're all going to sit and wait for it to come to us."

"Are you sure it will?"

"Maybe we should go ahead and stake a goat out in the backyard just to be sure."

Fidelina nodded in agreement. "I think you're right, Jack. I think somehow the demon established a gateway from its own plane of existence to ours, right here in your closet. I think that somehow it did this through the little girl. When it attacked her, the trauma left a lot of psychic residue and somehow it linked her soul to this spot, like a ghost cursed to haunt the place of its death, and then it used her to come here. I've never seen or heard of this kind of thing before, but, in retrospect, it fits a lot of the legends and tales. It would explain how so many things seem to be localized occurrences, always happening in the same places."

"Can you use it to find the demon? Maybe track it down? Maybe I could enter it again, but this time on my terms." Jack chewed on his lip at the thought of attacking the demon on its own turf again, but Fidelina shook her head.

"I think the pathway must have been closed when the girl's soul was freed, but I suspect that is the method you were seeking before. That is probably how my ancestors used to track the demons back to their 'caves' before they took on a physical form."

"I don't think this demon is interested in taking little kids to a cave to teach them manners."

"Nor do I." Fidelina chuckled. "I doubt that was ever truly why *El Cucuy* took children." She patted Jack on the arm. "I think perhaps it is just what parent's told the children to make them behave. The selection of victims by a demon is most likely based on availability."

Jack looked sideways at her to see if she really thought he might have believed demons stole misbehaving children away just to teach them manners. She was grinning at him and he smiled back. He followed her back out of the spare bedroom and into the downstairs living room where Rosa, and, to a much lesser extent, Mercedes were finishing making a protective circle that filled the room. Bernardo kept to his usual hovering behind the old women, out of concern for them or just to avoid everyone else, Jack couldn't guess.

David was sitting on the couch watching them. His camera, unused, sat on the floor at his feet. "Are you sure I can't even just film your faces as you guys do the ritual?" he asked Fidelina as she walked in. Bernardo tossed him an 'I dare you to try it' look and seemed to tense himself for action.

Fidelina pursed her lips and shook her head with a warning look in her eye. "If anyone were to try to imitate it and mess something up, they could seriously hurt themselves or someone else." She shook a long bony finger at him. "Are you sure you want to be responsible for someone accidentally banishing their own soul?"

David shook his head. "No, ma'am."

Jack heard footsteps on the stairs and looked up to see Julie and Anita coming down carrying trays of food. Anita had brought food from the restaurant, and they had heated it up here. Bear was on their heels all the way down the stairs with Vic following carrying a twelve pack of soda. He went around and handed them out as Julie and Anita set up the food on the coffee table, which had been pushed up against the wall to make room for Rosa's protective circle.

"Sorry it's not a beer," Vic said as he handed one to Jack, "but considering the circumstances, I thought it would be better if we were all sober."

Jack nodded as he accepted his soda. "That's quite all right. It seems to pretty much be a party atmosphere in here anyway." He looked over at David, who was filling his paper plate with cheese-covered goodies and doing his best to ignore Bernardo.

The doorbell rang and Bear barked, startling everyone. Jack glanced at Mercedes to make sure she was okay. She caught him, and he reddened and hurried to answer the door.

"If that's the demon, tell him were not ready. Tell him to come back in fifteen minutes, after we finish eating," David called out around a mouthful of food.

Jack shook his head as he went up the stairs and opened the door. Myla stood there with a somber look on her face. "Hello, Mr. Hooper."

"Uh, hello, Myla." Jack felt uncomfortable talking to her. Not only had he upset her badly the last time he had talked to her, but the memories he had obtained from David stirred up feelings he knew weren't his and were best immediately suppressed and forgotten.

"I was hoping that I could speak with David. Is he here?" Her eyes were bright and she fidgeted as she asked.

For a moment, Jack felt like he was someone's father, being asked if they could come out to play. "Sure. Come on in." He did his best to keep his voice neutral and opened the door so Myla could enter.

Bear stopped her at the threshold, standing on his back legs and waving his bandaged paws in the air at her. "Hey Bear!" She caught his front legs out of the air and pulled him in for a hug. "How are your little paw-paws doing?" she asked the dog and then looked to Jack for an answer.

"We took him to the vet. They gave him a couple of stitches. They said he'd be fine in a week."

Myla pursed her lips as she let go of Bear's feet and let him drop back to all fours. "Why didn't you just heal him, like you did everyone else?" Her voice was sarcastic and Jack could tell by the look in her eye she wanted to jab him with the comment.

He did his best to ignore the barb. "I was warned against it by people I believe give good advice." He waited, continuing to hold the door open, for her to decide how to take that. She decided to ignore it and finished entering the house.

Jack hesitated in the doorway and looked out into the dusky twilight from the setting sun. He wondered how long they would have to wait for the demon to appear. *Maybe it won't come back here again,* he thought as he closed the door and followed Myla into the house. He didn't think there was any reason for it to.

FIFTY-THREE

It was after midnight. Julie, sitting next to Jack on the loveseat, tried unsuccessfully to stifle a yawn. Anita was asleep with her head on Vic's shoulder as he watched television. David was picking at cold hors d'oeuvres from the coffee table while talking quietly with Myla. Bernardo had finally sat down and promptly started snoring. Mercedes, Rosa and Fidelina were talking as they sat around the card table Jack had erected for them in the center of their circle of power.

Or protection, or whatever. Whatever their mystic circle thing was, it hadn't worked when they tried summoning the demon, and as far as Jack could tell, it hadn't created any kind of barrier, invisible or otherwise. His eyes shifted slightly out of focus as he willed himself to see auras again. Some of the items the old women had put on the table had some sort of energy radiating from them, most notably the eight-inch statuette of Guadalupe, but the circle on the floor and the air around them seemed perfectly normal.

Jack's eyes went back to Myla. She was rolling her eyes at David while he stuffed something with guacamole dip into his mouth. Her antics, as she confronted David about what the truth was, had been the only interesting things to happen tonight. Although everyone pretended to not notice, ignoring them was hard.

Jack took it as a good sign she had at least shown up, but as soon as she had finished filming the commercial using him as a spokesperson for her new charity, her professionalism had deteriorated into vicious comments at David about his indiscretion with information about her personal life. Jack had been held back by Julie's hand on his arm as he tried to stick up for David, and, in the long run, Julie had been right to hold him back.

David eventually convinced her to at least consider the possibility that what Jack had told her was true, and she finally calmed down enough to meet everyone else. Watching three old women who claimed to be witches perform ceremonies over the chalky powder Julie had let them spread on her carpet had gone a long way toward convincing her that, while Jack and David might not be telling the truth, they at least thought they were. And as much as she wanted to deny it and forget about it, she had seen the demon herself.

When she tried to convince everyone, and herself, that what she had seen was a dog of some sort, Fidelina had taken that opportunity to point out to Jack the power of disbelief. Jack had turned it around and pointed out that Vic, the unbeliever, was sitting right there and had been the one to summon the witches for help. Fidelina had just shrugged and mentioned the ability to hold conflicting beliefs again.

Jack looked back to the circle of protection. Maybe that was why there was no aura around it. Maybe Vic and Myla and all of the rest of the urban community disbelieved in it enough to have prevented it from working. He would have to talk to Vic about this whole believe-disbelieve thing one of these days.

Myla suddenly turned and announced to the room. "I am going home now. I'm tired and I no longer feel like watching you people make fools out of yourselves. I think the fact this 'thing' failed to show up should come as no surprise to any of you, and you should all start seriously thinking about why you are here doing this."

She went into the spare bedroom and pulled her coat from the pile of jackets tossed there. She came out pulling her arms through the sleeves. "Mr. Hooper, I'm sorry I got upset with you. I was just shocked you had information I didn't expect you to have." Jack tried to tell her, for the umpteenth time she should call him Jack, but she ignored the comment. "I hope you do your best to keep your strange antics out of the media in the future, because I am sure it will undermine the success of the charity that was established on your behalf."

She nodded in farewell toward Julie, "Mrs. Hooper," then headed up the stairs for the door without even looking at anyone else.

"Wait!" David called out. "At least let me walk you out to your car." Myla ignored him and continued out the door as he grabbed his jacket and chased after her.

Jack rubbed his tired eyes and stood up, stretching his lower back. He understood how Myla felt. He would like to leave, too. He would very much like to pretend nothing had ever happened and go stick his head in the sand.

He looked down at Julie's sleepy face and smiled. It was worth it to have her back. She was worth it.

Julie must have read his thoughts, because she smiled warmly, stood up, and kissed him. "Don't worry about them. They'll work it out. I think she loves him as much as he loves her. They just have to learn to communicate and be more understanding with one another."

Jack kissed his wife and murmured, "Like we're professionals who should be giving advice."

She chuckled and snuggled into his side sleepily.

Jack noticed Fidelina looking up at them. "What do you think we should do?" he asked her.

"It could come at any time, or not at all." She looked wearily back at him. "I think we should take turns—"

She was interrupted by David's voice floating dimly through the newly replaced window.

"Jack!" His voice was faint but clear. "Jack! It's back!"

FIFTY-FOUR

Jack felt a heartbeat's worth of dread, fear, hesitation, and indecisiveness. Then he was running up the stairs, slipping on the top step, fighting the door handle, and out into the night. He didn't slow until he made it to the middle of the yard. The amber pool of light from the streetlamp bathed over him and the yard, washing out other colors. His breath puffed out in clouds as his eyes searched for any sign of David or Myla.

"Over here!" He heard Myla call out this time, her voice high and scared. He spotted her at the edge of the darkness between two houses across the street and down three lots. He ran toward her, trying not to slip on the slush that had frozen in the street. As he neared her, he realized he hadn't brought one of the blessed knives with him. His mind raced to think of anything he had or could grab to use as a weapon. There was nothing.

"Hurry!" Myla encouraged him. She pointed into the darkness. "The screaming came from the other house. David jumped the fences!"

Jack reached her and rounded the corner into the darkness. She was pointing at the house behind. He looked at the six-foot high wooden fence between him and the back yard and wished he was young as David so he could jump the fence too.

Jack put his hands on top of the fence and jumped while trying to pull himself up. His feet scrabbled at the wooden slats for traction as his arms strained. He finally pulled his waist above the fence and flipped a leg over the edge, losing his grip and sitting hard on the narrow top edge. He stifled a groan, pulled his other leg up, and fell over the fence into the back yard.

He stumbled twice in the snow then hurried across the yard to the next fence. He grabbed the top and jumped to pull himself up again. A light came on behind him.

"What the hell are you doing in my yard!"

Jack let himself fall back from the fence and looked back into the light, shielding his eyes. A dark figure outlined in the light stood at the back door.

"Someone over there is screaming!" He pointed to the house on the other side of the fence.

"Get the hell out of my yard!" the man yelled at him again.

"Aw, screw you," Jack mumbled and turned back to the fence and began climbing again.

"I said get out of my yard!" The man picked up a rock and threw it at Jack, narrowly missing his head.

"What the hell do you think I am doing?" Jack yelled back at him in frustration.

"I think you're being a punk-assed..." The man's words were lost to Jack as he fell into the next yard with a grunt.

"Jack?" David's voice came from out of the other house.

"Yeah?" he called back, getting up out of the snow.

"Be careful! I don't know where it is."

"How do you know it was here?" Jack called as he ran across the second backyard toward the house.

David's voice came out from the shattered glass patio door. "You mean other than the broken door, and screaming?"

"Yeah, smart ass, other than those."

"How about this dead guy with his throat ripped out?"

Jack stumbled into the house as David was pointing to the figure lying in the puddle of blood.

"Oh, Jesus." Jack had to look away. The look of horror on the face of the dead man was almost as ugly as the hole in his neck that had nearly decapitated him.

"Don't bother. I already tried." David's voice brought Jack out of a state of mind on the verge of shock.

Jack willed himself to see auras and saw David had meant this man's soul was already long gone and the body was beyond help.

"What the hell are you people doing in my yard?" The man shouted from right behind Myla's ear.

Myla let loose a squeak of surprise and jumped. She turned and looked at the man. He had a warm, friendly looking face. His black skin contrasted sharply against the white stubble of his unshaven beard. A wave of relief visibly flowed over Myla. She had been afraid it would be the demon thing again.

No, she chided herself, that thing was not real. What she had seen had been some kind of animal. The screaming David and Jack went to go investigate would turn out to be a domestic squabble. There was no such thing as a demon. There couldn't be.

"Answer me!" The man grabbed her roughly by the shoulders and shook her violently.

"Hey!" Myla struggled to get out of his grasp. "Let go!"

"You trying to rob me? Huh? What the hell is wrong with you people?" He shook her again.

"No! We heard screaming!" Myla tried to answer him, but his shaking was too violent. In a desperate move to be free of him, she brought her knee up hard at his crotch. He was faster and caught her leg as he stepped aside. He lifted her knee and threw her off balance.

"My wife liked to try that trick, too! She was better at it than you are little missy." He pushed her off balance and then spun her around and caught her in a headlock before she realized what he was doing. He dragged her up to the front of the house hissing in her ear. "What do you think the cops are going to say about you and your friends running all over my property, huh?" His whiskers abraded the skin of her cheek.

Myla stiffened in shock with the realization he was rubbing himself against her as he pushed her ahead of him, still holding her in the headlock. "What do you think they will say?" His breath was hot on her ear as he pressed himself tight against her.

"You bastard!" she spat out as best she could with her chin forced against her chest. "I'll kill you. I'll fucking kill you!" Old fears and rage, along with a new feeling of betrayal, burned in her chest and bubbled up, escaping as hisses and cuss words.

"Sure, sure," he whispered calmly into her ear as they reached the front door. "Say, do you suppose your friends will ever come back looking for you?" He pressed himself against her again. "I bet not. I bet that if I call the cops, your friends won't ever come looking here again. I bet nobody would ever come looking for you here."

Something hit them both hard, from behind. Myla was thrown out of the headlock and off the front steps, landing in the lava rock landscaping. The rocks cut at her hand and face, but she was free. She was quick to get to her feet and run, looking back just in time to see the dream that had haunted her sleep for the last three nights come true again.

Except it was even larger now, close to five feet tall.

The demon pulled the man's head back and bit into his throat. Not like a vampire this time. This time it ripped out a bloody mouthful. Myla screamed and ran like hell.

It had almost gotten her last time. Would it get her this time? *No! Please God, no!*

She ran as hard as she could. She realized she was heading straight back to Jack's house. *Please God, let the witches be real! Let them be able to help! Please, let me make it to that circle on the floor!*

Her shoes slipped on the icy asphalt as she ran. She thought she heard the clapping sound of the demon's hooves hitting the pavement, but she didn't dare look back.

"Help me!" she screamed as she neared the front door. The door opened and she ran inside just as a heavy weight hit her from behind.

Jack and David were considering searching the house for any sign of the demon when a scream made them both snap their heads up.

"Oh shit. Myla!" David nearly pushed Jack over into the dead man as he ran out of the house. Jack recovered as fast as he could and ran after him. Another shriek tore through the night as David's hands hit the top of the fence and he vaulted his legs sideways and was over the fence in one fluid motion.

"Yeah, right," Jack muttered to himself as he ran across the yard. He spotted an electrical box in the corner of the yard and aimed for it. He jumped up on top of the three foot metal box and then over the fence. He hit the ground rolling and had to stop himself before he could get back to his feet.

He spotted the back door wide open where the man had been yelling at him. The house was well lit and he could see all the way through to the front door. He looked at the second fence David had disappeared over before Jack made it over the first one.

"Screw you again," he muttered at the memory of the asshole who lived here and ran in the back door and through the house at full speed. He went straight out the front door leaving a trail of snow in the living room behind him, then he tripped and sprawled headlong down the front steps.

His hands stung from the cement and his elbow throbbed as he rolled over onto the grass and struggled to get up. He glanced back at the house and saw he had tripped over another body. "Oh, shit," he cried out weakly and crawled to the body.

The man's eyes were wide and empty and his mouth gaped open in a freakish reflection of the hole in his throat. A sickening gurgle gasped from the man's mouth even as air escaped from the wound.

Jack didn't even think about it this time as he reached out with his aura. A strange golden-green colored spark briefly flashed between them without casting any shadows.

Instantly, the wound in the man's throat began closing and in seconds there was no sign there had ever been any damage. No aura emanated from the body, and Jack realized there was no soul left in it. The demon had gotten another victim.

Another scream caught Jack's attention—a man's scream. He jumped up and ran toward the sound. He heard a dog barking. As he ran, he realized the bark was Bear's and the scream was coming from his own house. A surge of fear and adrenaline pushed him even harder.

FIFTY-FIVE

David rounded the edge of the house just in time to see the demon hit Myla from behind and tumble into Jack's house. He ran as hard as he could, arms swinging in time to the icy gravel crunching under his tennis shoes. He ran up the lawn and into the house at full speed.

Myla was at the bottom of the stairs in a tangled heap with Mercedes and Bernardo, the demon on top of them. Bernardo was frantically beating his fists against the monster's head, ignoring the lacerations caused by the sharp fangs and claws. Finally the beast got past Bernardo's fists and, with one quick snap of its jaws, ripped his throat out.

It dropped the boy and grabbed Myla with one clawed hand and Mercedes with the other, lifting them both up with inhuman strength. Mercedes hung from its grip like a limp rag doll. Myla screamed and flailed futilely. Bloody fangs gleaming as it snarled, it twisted its wrist, pulling Myla's head back and exposing her throat to its vicious maw.

Without thinking, David leapt from the top stair. He landed in the middle of the demon's back, his weight knocking the demon forward and making it drop the women.

The demon seemed to bounce off an invisible wall made by the *brujas'* protective circle and came to rest against the back wall of the house. It came up with fangs bared, crouching and ready.

It grew bigger even as David watched. Its wings fleshed out, becoming stronger. It flexed its muscles, obviously enjoying the feeling of its own power.

"In here! Get in the circle!" Rosa croaked while Fidelina chanted rhythmically behind her.

David stumbled to his feet and reached for Myla. He stopped. Horrified.

Myla, Mercedes, and Bernardo. All three bodies were limp, their throats torn open. Blood was everywhere. The skin on Bernardo's arms, face, and chest was shredded from fighting to protect the women.

Myla's eyes stared vacantly back at him, empty of the woman he loved.

A tightness formed in David's chest and his breathing heaved involuntarily. A scream of pure rage bellowed out of him and he charged the demon.

David hit the demon with his head lowered. He caught it on his shoulder, lifted it, and carried it into the wall as hard as he could.

Vic jumped out of the protective circle, ignoring pleading cries from Anita, and grabbed Myla and Mercedes by the arms, pulling dragging both bodies into the circle.

The demon clawed at David's back, ripping through his shirt and shredding skin. It tried to bite at him, but David kept his head tucked under and out of reach. David stood up with the demon still over his shoulder and ran at the stone fireplace. He slammed their combined weight into the fireplace, doing his best to put most of the impact on the demon's head. Then he grabbed the demon by the throat and began slamming its head against the rock hearth.

Vic quickly grabbed Bernardo and drug his limp body into the circle as well, hastily trying to rebuild the smeared chalk line as he did so.

The demon kicked its feet out, flinging David across the room and into the circle. It charged after him, but once again ran into an invisible wall and bounced off.

The creature stood up, ominously looking down upon the people huddled within the circle. One clawed hand reached out to touch the invisible barrier. It left its hand on the barrier, dragging the claws, as it slowly began walking around the circle, looking for an opening.

Jack ran across the lawn, leapt up the steps, and through the front door. He caught a glimpse of people at the bottom of the stairs. Blood dripped from the walls around them. Jack thought he might vomit. Julie was on the floor inside the witch's protective circle, holding a furiously barking Bear and huddled next to a pile of blood soaked bodies. She was behind someone's legs, maybe Vic's.

"Look out!" The warning came at the same time as the blow. The dark shape of the demon bowled over him like a rampaging bull, carrying him back out into the night with its momentum.

Jack and the demon tumbled across the cement and into the snow covered grass. Claws raked Jack's back and side and an odor of rotting flesh choked him. Somehow, Jack found himself on his back with his feet on the demon's torso. He shoved as hard as he could and the demon flew off him.

At the height of its arc in the air, the wings on its back began flapping furiously and the creature landed with the grace of a cat, as though it had leapt off Jack intentionally.

It crouched and stepped sideways, eyeing Jack. The glistening black skin silhouetted it against the snow and Jack was shocked to find it had grown as tall as he was.

Jack scrambled into a fighting stance and moved to keep facing it. Behind him, he could hear the old women chanting something and Bear barking savagely. Jack could feel the power of the witches' summoning chant growing stronger as they continued. Tendrils of power reached out through the air, searching for the demon, hoping to ensnare it.

The demon cocked its long head sideways, beady eyes gleaming in the amber streetlight as it strafed to the left, moving in a circle around Jack, putting its back to the length of the street and his to his house. Behind it, Jack could see lights had come on in most of the houses, and a couple of people had ventured out onto their front stoops to see what all of the screaming was about.

"I'm right behind you," David's voice came softly. "Put your hand behind you and I'll give you a knife."

Jack, carefully watching the demon, put a hand out behind himself and David handed off one of the blessed blades. Jack turned it around uncomfortably, wishing he'd had some sort of knife training. No matter how he held it, it felt wrong.

David came up beside Jack and the two of them presented a front between the demon and the house. Holding the knife up David mumbled, "Next time, I say we use blessed swords instead."

The old women continued to chant behind them, Rosa's gravelly voice easily distinguishable from Fidelina's. The power of the chant slowly filled the air like a fog rolling in.

"I healed them," David whispered again as the demon shifted its weight back and forth, trying to decide what to do, "but it has their souls. Vic said he would keep them in the circle."

Jack nodded silently, his eyes locked with the black devil that had hurt so many people. The demon tensed, its mind finally made up.

"Here it comes," Jack whispered back to David and gripped his knife with sweaty fingers.

"Look! It's the *Chupacabra!*" A young child's voice pierced the night, and the demon froze even as it tensed to leap. Its dog-like ears flicked toward the sound. Slowly, keeping Jack and David in view, the demon moved to see in the direction the voice had come from.

At least a dozen people were standing around outside seven or eight houses now. Jack realized the demon would always go for the easiest prey, and he and David had just proven to be difficult.

One of the wings fluttered, as though shooing a fly, and then the demon leapt toward the nearest of the people like a winged kangaroo.

"Get inside!" Jack yelled and gave chase. "Get inside!" He knew the people wouldn't listen. People never do.

The couple didn't move until they realized the creature wasn't just running away from Jack, but was running for them. The woman shrieked as the demon landed between them and knocked them both to the ground.

"Run!" Jack yelled. "Run!" His warning was already too late. He heard a hollow crunching sound and knew it was someone's skull. The woman screamed again, but the scream cut short as the demon sank its teeth into yet another throat.

David was five steps ahead of Jack as he lunged at the demon with his knife. The demon sensed it coming and twisted out of the way at the last possible instant. David overbalanced and fell to the ground between the mangled bodies. The demon spun and eyed Jack's approach. Offhandedly, it grabbed David up by the back of the neck, lifted him, and bit savagely into his throat, like taking a bite from an apple.

It met Jack's eyes with a wicked grin on its canine face and dropped David's body. It turned and leapt toward the next group of people, two houses down.

Reactions were faster this time and screams sounded up and down the block as people tripped over each other to get back into their houses.

"David!" Jack dropped to his side as he finally reached him. The body was twitching, but the soul was gone. A golden spark flashed between Jack and each of the three bodies as he healed them, futile as it may have been without their souls. Then he stood up and ran after the demon. He could still hear Bear barking behind him as he pushed on after the leaping monster.

It jumped across the lawn of the man who had thrown the rock at Jack, spotted the limp form of the man on the porch and went back. The demon scooped the body up and examined it. It sniffed at the blood covering the man's clothes and then at the throat Jack had healed.

Looking back at Jack, holding his eyes with its own, the demon opened its mouth wide and deliberately bit the man's throat out for a second time. It palmed the man's head like a basketball, twisted, and tore it from the body before turning to look at Jack with bloody flesh dangling from its jaws. It grinned triumphantly, pulled its arm back and flung the man's body through the picture window and into the house. As an afterthought, it underhanded the head at Jack and, with a leap, turned and continued down the street where the child's voice had come from.

"You bastard!" Jack tried to yell as he dodged the head, but he was breathing too hard to put any volume behind it.

The creature stopped every two or three leaps to look at Jack, taunting him before continuing on. Every time he neared the creature, it bounded away out of reach and looked back mockingly, baring its fangs and flapping its wings.

FIFTY-SIX

A black form streaked past Jack's legs and leaped into the air just as the creature turned to taunt Jack again. Bear slammed into the demon as it turned, knocking it off balance. The dog's deep growls and snarls reverberated through the air as it attacked. Then, a yelp pierced the night as the creature tossed the dog through the air.

Bear landed with a muffled thump in the middle of the street.

With a sick feeling, Jack noticed out of the corner of his eye Bear did not get up. The dog's attack had allowed him to catch up, and he took advantage of the demon's distraction. Jack leaped on top of the demon, knife first, putting all of his weight behind the attack.

The knife plunged into the demon's side and tore a long rent where it should have encountered ribs. The creature writhed in pain and pulled away from the blade and out of Jack's reach. Jack could see the evil red cloud inside the vile skin, but the demon was quickly pulling the skin back around itself, trying to maintain its physical body.

Jack reached out with his aura, trying to snag hold of the exposed core before it could protect itself.

The demon leaped away, crashing through the large picture window of the nearest house. Screams accompanied the sound of the breaking glass and then cut short with muffled thumps.

Jack ran to the door and pounded in frustration as the handle refused to turn. He turned to the broken window and steeled himself to jump. The demon leaped back out of the window, bowling Jack over. It had a child clutched in each clawed hand.

Jack jumped up and prepared to chase after the demon, but it stopped in the street and turned to face him. It stood well over seven feet tall now, towering over Jack. Its wings flapped constantly and it seemed ready to fly off at any moment. Jack stood his ground, hunched slightly with his sliver knife held at the ready position. Somewhere in the distance, Jack heard sirens and he silently prayed they were coming here.

The demon slowly took a step backward, dragging the limp children's feet on the street. Jack took a step forward and the demon lifted one of the small forms toward its gaping mouth in a warning gesture.

Jack saw the children's throats had not yet been torn.

The monster held its fangs near the child's throat and then looked meaningfully at Jack. It lowered the body slightly and took a step back. Jack took a step forward and the demon raised the child's throat to its mouth again. Jack took a step back and the demon lowered the body, untouched.

The demon took another step back and Jack stayed where he was. The demon seemed satisfied and lowered the child more while taking another step back.

Jack's mind raced. He was sure the demon would kill the children no matter what he did, but he couldn't bring himself to initiate their deaths.

Then the monster hesitated, looking confused. A pained look crossed its animalistic face and it dropped one of the children. Stumbling, it seemed to shrink a little.

David! Jack realized. David was attacking from the inside!

Jack charged.

The demon spotted his movement and turned back to him, raising the child quickly to its bloody fangs. Jack screamed in rage, lunging with the knife.

The black form of Bear suddenly appeared leaping in the air between the demon's jaws and the child. The dog's jaws locked onto the demon's throat, slowing it long enough for Jack to arrive.

Jack's knife and arm plunged into the demon's stomach and out through its back. The demon threw its head back in a silent scream, dropping the other child as it fell backward under the combined weight of Jack and Bear.

Bear snarled viciously, rending putrid flesh while Jack, growling with primal rage, fought to stay in contact with the demon and absorb its soul. The demon maintained its eerie silence even as its face showed it screaming in pain as forces attacked it from inside and out.

Jack leeched his aura onto the demon's and began sucking energy as hard as he could. He could feel the demon's rancid flesh trying to close the wounds even as he and Bear were inflicting them. It was trying to hide its aura, its soul, away from Jack. Jack cut and slashed again and again, keeping the wounds open, pulling energy out from within.

His body seemed to go on autopilot, hacking and slashing at the demon, fighting the physical battle and allowing his mind to concentrate on the spiritual one at the same time. He fought to grab hold of the demon's intangible soul and pull it through the gashes in its body. Then he felt a touch of another consciousness. And then another, and another.

They were crying out in pain as the demon tapped into their souls for energy to maintain its physical body and replenish what Jack was siphoning. Then he felt David attack, from within the demon's soul itself, as Jack had done before.

A fire erupted in the center of the demon's soul and pathways shot out and away, back to the bodies of the souls trapped by the demon. Jack felt the souls rushing past him on their pathways as he did his best to entrap the demon's soul within his own. He felt most of them find their way back to their bodies, but he also felt the five of them that floated in confusion around him with no body to return to. Four of them he didn't recognize. One he did.

A blazing light formed all around him as he struggled, and he saw the tunnel appear in his peripheral vision. He felt people smiling at him. He felt assurances and love. He felt Mercedes lightly brush his cheek in farewell. And then they were gone.

The demon flared with pain, anger and frustration as the tunnel of light vanished. Jack did his best to hold on to the demon's soul, to keep it attached to his aura, to keep it grounded on this plane of existence.

He didn't notice when the demon's body stopped struggling. He didn't notice when Bear began choking and vomiting from the putrid flesh, which began dissolving into black sludge. He didn't notice when David came running up and found him lying on his side in the middle of the street, or when several hands picked him up and carried him back to the house.

He did notice when David's aura joined his and began helping absorb the energy. The demon struggled mightily, trying to absorb them back, trying to maintain its energy level. But then Julie's aura was there with them, too—and then Fidelina's, and Rosa's, and Myla's.

Vic and Anita were there, helping, finally breaking the deadlock, and turning the tide of the battle. Then Bernardo's aura joined with them, burning with rage and intensity, with a hatred of demons so strong that it flavored everyone else with angry spiciness and refueled their efforts.

Together, they pulled the demon's aura in nine different directions. Together they tore it into nine different parts. Together they destroyed it.

EPILOGUE

"Thank you for calling the Save a Hero Foundation, this is Stanley Forbes, how may I help you?" Stanley's voice was smooth as silk and he sat up straight as he listened to the caller, because he knew slouching affected the way he sounded on the phone. He listened intently and asked a couple of questions politely.

"Yes of course we can have an information package sent out to you immediately." He smiled, not because he knew the customer could hear the smile in his voice, but because this was the best thing he had ever been associated with, and he loved his job.

"Yes, you should receive it within a week. Thank *you*," he emphasized and hung up the phone.

He got up and hurried, because he knew the telephone lines were going to start lighting up the phone consoles like an agitated video game. His bulky form charged out of his office and through the cube farms where other people were working.

"Heads up people!" he called out in a warm and friendly voice. "We're about to light up again!" He stepped into the computer room and, ignoring the banks of servers controlling the computers, flipped a switch transferring his office phone to the general incoming calls line.

He came back out and hurried back to the front of the offices. A phone rang off to his left. Not a moment too soon, he thought as he heard the representative answer the phone and apologize that Mr. Forbes was unavailable at the moment and ask if she could be of service instead. Another phone rang, followed by a third.

Stanley stepped back into his office and pulled his cell phone out of the drawer. He flipped it open and pushed a speed dial button. He listened as the phone dialed and then waited as the line rang on the other end.

"This is Myla," a pleasant woman's voice answered.

"Hello, Mrs. Rowe, this is Stanley." He was grinning as he spoke.

"Hi, Stanley! What's up?"

"It's happening again." He nearly shook with excitement.

"Where?"

He could hear her fumbling for something to write on. "California." He gave her the name and address of the Hospital in Sacramento.

"I'm online right now, I'll book the tickets. Can you call David and ask him to meet me at the airport?" Myla asked him.

"Is he at home?" Stanley asked.

"He should be."

"I'm on it," Stanley assured her as he hung up the phone and hit a different speed dial button.

"Hello?" David's voice sounded sleepy, as if he had just woken up.

"Hello Mr. Rowe, this is Stanley Forbes."

"It happened again, huh?" David's voice became stronger as he woke up. "Where this time?"

"California. Your wife said she was already booking tickets and wanted you to meet her at the airport."

The woman ran through the halls of the hospital as fast as her high-heeled shoes would let her move on the slick floor. There were excited people everywhere, filling the hallways and loitering in doorways, and she did her best to dodge them but she couldn't slow down. She could hear snippets of their conversations as she went past.

"It's true!"

"…miracles…"

"…all over the hospital…"

"Who was it?"

She rounded a corner, running through a group of doctors and nurses talking and waving their arms excitedly. They hardly noticed her.

Finally, she reached her destination and slid through the doorway into the room where her daughter was dying of cancer.

"Hi, Mommy!" The little girl was on her knees on the bed playing with a teddy bear, the first signs of life she had shown in weeks.

"Oh my God! Annie!" The woman tripped and stumbled across the floor to her daughter, scooping her up in her arms. "Oh my God! I can't believe it!" She cried into her little girl's hair.

"It's true Mommy! And look!" The little girl ran her hand over the top of her bald head. "My hair is already coming back!" She grinned at her mother, her tongue poking out from where she was missing her bottom teeth. "And they gave me this to give to you."

The girl held out a small business card tied around the teddy bear's neck with a violet ribbon. The woman's hands shook as she took it and read:

You Have Been Helped By Someone
Who Was Saved By
The Save A Hero Foundation
Please Share The Love
And Give Whatever You Can
So That We Can Keep Saving Heroes
Contact Stanley Forbes
Vice President

"God I love doing that!" Julie put her arm around Jack's waist as he finished stuffing their disguises into the duffle bag under his arm. Between the clothes and Jack's use of his aura to mask their identities and make people to ignore them, there was little chance they would ever be recognized.

Bear pulled against his leash and tried to get closer to the trees lining the sidewalk as they began casually walking away from the hospital.

"I wish Mercedes could have been here to see all of the good she has enabled us to do." Jack glanced at his wife as he put his arm over her shoulders.

"She knew what she was doing when she gave you the money. She was trying to pay restitution for all the things that she had done."

Jack nodded thoughtfully as they walked. The box Mercedes had given him the night before her death had contained the letter to him from Doña Isabella, the faded pencil sketch of his face, and a cashier's check for over a million dollars, along with tax forms showing the government had already received its share. It had also contained a short letter in shaky handwriting that said simply:

Thank you.

He had asked Fidelina where the money had come from but she had merely shaken her head. Rosa had whispered hoarsely in his ear that it had come from the same place all beautiful women got their money—Men. Then she had cackled mischievously and refused to say more.

"Did you tell David and Myla where we were going this time?" Julie brought Jack back to the present.

"No. Did you?"

"Nope. It'll be good for them to not have to pretend to be surprised for a change." She hugged him closer and their footsteps matched pace on the sidewalk. "Besides, if they really want to go drum up some business, David can do it himself, he'll just have to find some other alibi."

They walked on enjoying the California sunshine for a while, ignoring the passing cars, and smiling at the people they saw.

Julie stopped and looked up at a street sign. "Is this it?"

Jack looked up at the sign and then dug a piece of paper out of his pocket. He compared the two before confirming it was the correct street. "Are you sure you can handle this?"

"It's something I need to do," Julie assured him.

He smiled at her and they started up the street to find the house belonging to Angel Chavez, Jessica's father. Bear stopped for a quick sniff at base of the street sign and then followed at a trot, his ears high, and his tail flopping lazily side to side.

AUTHOR'S NOTE

The supernatural world is a great play place for fictional characters and stories. It is easy to make up your own world, with your own rules, and let your imagination run rampant. It is a bit more difficult when you try to stay closer to the 'truth'. The hard part is separating what is 'real' from what is 'fiction' in the mythology before you start to write the story. Let me clear that up a little.

For example, in the mythology of vampires and werewolves they eat you. Period. That is the 'real.' They are not cute teenage boys who will respect your wish not to have sex and use their power to protect you. Other things, like silver bullets and garlic, kind of come and go with the various stories, but all of the original stories agree on one thing. They eat you.

A romantic interlude with a happy ending, or perhaps any happiness at all, involving a monster is a 'fiction'. Not that there is anything wrong with that kind of a story, some of them are very good, but that was not the kind of story I set out to write. I wanted to know what I would find if the supernatural world really found me.

What would it be like to find out it was all really real? It turns out the supernatural world is, purportedly, a very big place and there is no way to see, or understand, it all. The idea was more than I could bite off, let alone chew, so I carved out a piece and shaped it as best as I could into something, if not entirely plausible, at least within the canons of the origins of the supernatural.

Not being able to actually see auras myself, I had to use the best information I could find and I apologize for anything I have gotten wrong or taken artistic license with. I highly recommend you do not take for granted anything you read on the internet. Most of it seems to be plagiarized from the same place and only moderately useful. It is actually pretty hard to find someone you can trust who can see auras, but they are out there. Generally, they are the ones not asking for money and not bringing attention to themselves (not always, but it is a good rule of thumb).

Lucid dreams, on the other hand, I have managed to experience a couple of times, although not many. I did find a great resource about them at The Lucidity Institute, www.lucidity.com.

Once upon a time, The Lucidity Institute was specifically mentioned in the story, as the island of sanity Jack held onto, but things change, as they always do. If you stop and check out The Lucidity Institute, drop my name and let them know I sent you. They won't remember me, but I bet they were curious what happened after I got permission to talk about them so long ago...

Speaking of 'so long ago', this book was originally written in 2004 and then published as an e-book only in 2010. It was taken down at the behest of a publisher who wanted to pick it up and add a print version. That fell through. But it also showed me a lot of the problems with my writing, so I never put the book back up for sale. Three other publishers showed interest to varying degrees, and Lucid Nightmares fell into its own nightmare of publishing and editing hell. This version differs from the original in form and substance in many ways.

Originally published at around 150,000 words, it grew to out to around 165,000 while taking various editors' opinions into account. Being a new writer, I was slow to learn that the old adage is true, too many cooks spoil the stew. Another adage applied as well: less is more. This current version is closer to 116,000 words. And in all honesty, probably needed to be cut down another 30,000 words. But truth be told, after all this time, all the edits it has gone through, and all the effort I have put into this story, it reached the point of diminishing returns and needed to be published or shelved.

I had a couple of fans of the original who really wanted published instead of shelved. I hope you agree I made the right choice.

Should you have any interest in some of what was removed, please go to my website, www.samknight.com, and find the links to Ahi's Story and Bernardo's Story. They should be under "Free Reading."

SUPPORT INDEPENDENT ARTISTS

Things are different now. Things are changing, and we need your help. Independent artist's books won't be found in a bookstore or a supermarket. It's all we can do to get on the Amazon or Barnes & Noble websites. Please, rate us, review us, tell others about us. Go to Amazon, B&N, Goodreads, Kobo, Smashwords, or anywhere else you like to look for books, and tell us, and everyone else, what you thought about our books. Please be honest. Review the book, don't bash the author or make irrelevant statements. Don't accept pirated copies. Don't buy pirated copies. Why give money to the thief and put an author you like out of business? Most authors make very little money and work as a labor of love (truth be told, most authors never turn a profit). Tell your friends about the books you like. Support the authors you want to see more from. Blog about them. Tweet and Facebook about them. Ask your library and local bookstore to carry their books. In the age of the internet, the reader —YOU— have the power to make or break an author. Really. One person could do it. Use it. Use that power well, and use it responsibly.

ABOUT THE AUTHOR

Photo by Lauren Lang

A Colorado native, Sam Knight spent ten years in California's wine country before returning to the Rockies. When asked if he misses California, he gets a wistful look in his eyes and replies he misses the green mountains in the winter, but he is glad to be back home.

As well as being Distribution Manager for WordFire Press, he is Senior Editor for Villainous Press and the author of five children's books, three short story collections, two novels, and more than thirty short stories, including two media tie-ins co-authored with Kevin J. Anderson.

A stay-at-home father, Sam attempts to be a full-time writer, but there are only so many hours left in a day after kids. Once upon a time, he was known to quote books the way some people quote movies, but now he claims having a family has made him forgetful, as a survival adaptation. He can be found at SamKnight.com and contacted at Sam@samknight.com.